Forward

There are several people who I wish to dedicate this book to, however, I felt like only a few should be mentioned, the most important ones. The ones who I have chosen have been with me through thick and thin, water and fire, and I am most indebted to them for their friendship and compassion over the years.

First off, I wish to dedicate this book to my very best friend and sister Jerra. You have shown me the most incredible compassion, loyalty, honesty and integrity over the years that you have known me! I wish to convey my absolute gratitude to you and how much of an absolute pleasure being your friend has been over these years!

Secondly, I wish to convey my gratitude and everlasting friendship to my very own Taemeluch, from where A'lari'jah's "Taem'luck" comes from. Taemeluch, you were there to shed light in my darkest days and I cannot tell you what your friendship meant to me during the hours when I felt the darkness would take hold and never let me go. I hope that, if you ever read this, you will feel my warmth and love towards you as one of my dearest friends.

Thirdly, to my granddad who was my greatest supporter. We have had tremendous and sometimes tumultuous days, we have had dark days and we have had joyous days and through it all, we have always had each other. I am eternally grateful for all that you have taught me, for all that we have been through together, for all of the tears and all of the laughter! I love you all fiercely and loyally until the end.

As an obvious but not so obvious last but certainly

not least, I wish to thank everyone who helped make this book become a reality! The editors, the authors, everyone and anyone who ever read bits and pieces and acted as my muse throughout the many, various writing stages! I owe each and everyone of you a great appreciation for everything!

Thank each and everyone of you for being a part of my life, and for being such huge fans and supporters of me in every season! I love you all equally, and with all of my heart!

Introduction

Dear Reader,

Up until very recently, my life's ambition was to survive to see another day, however recent events in my life have reawoken a spark in my heart that I thought was long dead and lost. This spark reawoke dreams, among those dreams dwelt a desire to finish and publish this book which God Almighty guided me in writing.

My life has been far from easy; I grew up in a dysfunctional home. While my family is far from broken, we are also far from perfect. I am only just beginning to understand what a tremendous blessing it has been to have been raised by both of my parents. Imperfect as they were / are, they did their very best to show the love they have for each one of us, and to provide the best home possible. I am waking up and realizing how many people come from broken homes, with only one parent, and it honestly breaks my heart.

Through my many hardships in both childhood and adulthood, I found reading to be an amiable escape from reality, though, later on, I realized how much more amiable writing was as an escape. It started off simple, a bookworm, then moved to writing journals, and then to writing small unfinished stories. I found that I could create characters that told my story, without actually telling my story. I found that I could fashion characters that resembled me in character traits or personality and in these stories I could greatly exaggerate or magnify my story within theirs and express all of my feelings and emotions that I kept bottled up inside without spilling precious secrets. Never in all the years I was writing did I actually think that I would end up here, about to publish a book for the public to read! How blessed am I that the Lord chose me to write such a compelling and beautiful start to a story about a girl who is broken beyond belief and still rises from the ashes and becomes beautiful and strong.

The inspiration for this book came from childhood memories of how I thought about God and the Garden of Eden. I remember thinking that God sounded an awful lot like magic as a child, and in my mind, it was similar, but not the witchcraft like magic that we see today. This was more of a natural magic, a magic that allowed man and plant to communicate together, to be able to compel the earth to grow how it needed to grow, to be able to speak with animals and have them help man with various chores around the garden. I used to think that all of the things in the Bible were magic too, the burning bush, the pillar of fire, the woman who was turned to salt. I romanticized the idea that God wanted us to live in harmony with nature and with himself as it was in the Garden of Eden, and my imagination took hold of me and ran away from there.

It is my deepest desire that, throughout this book and others to come, you would feel much less alone in whatever storm you are weathering in whatever season of your life you read this. It is my prayer that you would find healing and joy in every page you read, and that this book might fill you with the hope of things yet to come. I pray that the Lord touches your heart deeply and comforts you and brings a light into your life.

In Christ's Love and Enduring Promise,
Kristi Hawes.

Chapter One

The day my family perished was no different than any other day. The sun poured down, unfiltered by the trees, into the small clearing. Its warmth evoked a wonderful perfume from the flowers on the bed of the forest floor, the sweetness of honey and the cleanliness of lavender and lilac. Close by I could hear the gentle trickle of the babbling brook. Above me, the birds sang gayly and the forest floor still smelled of damp earth from the morning dew. Not far off I could hear the laughter and chatter of my family (the clearing was no more than four or five meters from my house). A soft, cool breeze tickled my hair and made me shiver slightly. My soft pink dress was much too thin for the colder days of late Summer. There was no hint, not even an inkling, that anything bad would happen in just a few short hours.

Joyous laughter echoed off the forest walls. My A'va'lon'ian friends and I used to come here often to play and share secrets, but I went mostly to escape the chaos of having six older siblings, they (the A'va'lon'ians) went because I was there. I could tell them my secrets, and share with them my deepest fears and my darkest nightmares, and they would whisper back to me knowledge and wisdom. I was safe there with them. Though the A'va'lon'ians are naturally a peaceful nurturing race; they have a fearsome temper when someone threatens their own.

"It is such a lazy day, one of the few days left where the sun will be warmer than the cold wind. The days grew shorter and colder, Winter was quick in approach. Oh! How

I dread the coming of Winter! The days would be short and cold and the sun would hide away behind thick gray clouds for many months; it did feel like I would never see Summer again! I would miss coming to my favorite patch in the woods with my Fairie friends! I wish Summer would never end!" I thought to myself.

I laid down on a soft patch of moss that the A'va'lon'ians made for me, soaking up the last of Summer's warmth, admiring the way their wings sparkled and glistened when the light hit them. Their iridescent, translucent wings cast rainbows on the objects below them as the sun passed through them, it was quite breathtaking. They flew around and danced in the air, rejoicing in my laughter; they would do anything just to make me laugh. You see, the Fae thrive on laughter, it keeps them going, makes them feel as if they are restoring joy and hope into the world again.

I must have fallen asleep at some point, because the next thing I knew was that my mother was calling me inside, the sun was already fast fading in the distance.

"Coming mother!" I called back as I picked up my shoes and ran back to the house.

"Where are yer shoes!? And yer shawl!? One of these days yer gonna catch yer death of cold out there!" My mother fussed, "Go inside and get cleaned up fer dinner!" She said, shaking her head, and slapping my backside as I went by.

I giggled playfully and ran to the wash basin to clean up for supper. It smelled especially good tonight.

"Ma, what's the special occasion?" I asked as she came back inside.

"Whatcha mean?"

"It smells especially good tonight, I figured there was a special reason for such a special meal." I shrugged as I took my place at our large wooden table.

"Donna fash yerself about it just now. I expect you'll ken soon enough." When she smiled, her eyes lit up and sparked like the fae's wings.

I ken she's gonna have another bairn! I thought silently.

I waited as patiently as an eight year old girl could wait, for the rest of my family to take their places at the table. Da' sat at the head of the table on the north wall, Ma' sat at the end of the table on the South wall, each of the bairns sat, from oldest to youngest from North to South along the east and west walls. This was tradition, the head of the house always sat on the North wall, it was a sign of power and good luck.

As everyone was seated, silence fell and Da' began with the evening prayer.

"Our heavenly Creator, we thank thee for the prosperity of the crops this year. We ask thee to protect us and look out for us this winter. Bless this food as we go about yer will here on earth.

Amen."

We all said "Amen" at the same time, and Da' began serving food onto plates and passing them out. Ma' always got the first plate of food, then it was oldest to youngest after that. No one was allowed to eat until everyone had their plate of food and Da' had been served; he always served himself last.

"It is good to be humble and selfless, always serving others before yerself." He would always say.

"Before we begin, I have some good news to share with yeh." Da said, smiling, there was a twinkling in his eyes that sent a flutter of excitement through me.

This is it! I thought to myself, *I am about to not be the youngest anymore!!*

"Ma and I," Da' continued, "have decided that it's time for yeh bairns to begin learning a trade. The girls will each spend rotating weeks at the castle learning from yer auntie and uncle and cousins. And the boys will each spend a week in different places in town. The oldest will begin in the blacksmith's shop, and we will make arrangements from there!!"

I couldn't hide the shoulder slump that happened from

the disappointment of this news, nor the tears that sprang to my eyes as quick as lightning.

"Really, Da!? Are yeh serious!?" Jerome jumped up from the table so quickly in his excitement that he almost knocked his food on the floor.

"Sit down, son!" Ma scolded him.

He blushed, sat down, said a hurried "sorry" and went back to his conversation with Da.

"Yes, I'm serious. It's past time that yeh start learning what yeh might wanna do as ye grow into a man." Da was quite proud that his son was as excited about this news as he was.

"Excuse me?" I injected my meek self into the conversation.

"Yes, lass, go on." Da said, his smile waning a bit.

I blushed, "Sorry, Da, it can wait." I apologized.

"Nonsense. Speak up lassie, don't be shy." He said, his smile was more gentle now.

"I was only wondering, well, does this include me as well? Or only the older girls?" I asked almost as quietly as a whisper.

"Ah, lassie, for another year it will just be the older girls." My face fell and everyone laughed.

"There will be no laughing at this table if it is to poke fun of someone else, or you'll have no supper!" Ma spoke up harshly to my siblings. "There is no need to be cruel, just because she is considerably younger than yeh, is no right to be laughing that she canna join yeh. Think of how yeh'd feel if the situation were reversed!" Ma cursed under her breath and smiled encouragingly at me. "For now, lassie, you'll be here helping me out with things. We will begin lessons for yeh like sewing and crocheting and reading. That way he'll be prepared next year to begin lessons at the castle."

Ma was a kind soul, always trying to find peace between her seven children. Don't get me wrong, being the youngest had its perks. But I would trade those perks to be healthy and older, just to fit in with my siblings. To not be different. This disconnection from the rest of my siblings caused a rift between them and our parents. They thought that I was always getting special treatment and they resented me for it. Ma always told me that they were just jealous of my maj'ickal abilities and that they didn't understand. She and Da always said that as I get older and stronger and healthier that I would fit in better and, in my own time, find my place with them.

The rest of the night went on silently for me. I toned everyone else out because it was too painful to hear their questions about what they would be doing, and if they would be staying at the castle or coming home every night. I sat all alone, wishing for just one single sibling to take mercy on me and be kind, but to them, I was invisible. Too young. Too weak. Too meek. Too naive. Too quiet. Too weird. They never paid me any mind.

Ma's touch on my hand startled me out of my gloomy thoughts, "Would you stay and help me wash up tonight, my love?" She whispered quietly to me.

I smiled as earnestly as I could, trying to hide the pain, and nodded."Thank you." I mouthed back to her as a few silent tears escaped my eyes. Sometimes I felt like my mother was the only person in the world who understood me; she was my best friend.

I finished my dinner methodically, waiting for the others to finish and go to bed so that I could have Ma all to myself. It seemed, however, that time was against me, it seemed to have slowed down, and dinner felt like it took forever to finish that night.

∞∞∞

Finally when everyone was done they excused themselves to go wash up for bed. They did a full circle around the table giving Ma and Da hugs and kisses as they left the dining area. When the older kids had left, Da looked at me curiously.

"Are yeh alright, lass?" He asked kindly.

"I am, in fact, quite sad." I said, tears brimmed my eyelids and threatened to pour over. He got up and scooped me into his strong arms. I drank in his musky, tobacco scent as he held me tightly.

"I ken it's hard, love, and I ken that you feel alone, but as you get older and are able to do more with them; they will be more welcoming of your talents and less put off by you." He smiled his crooked smile and kissed my cheek. "Donna fash yerself about it. I think yer quite extraordinary!" He tickled my ribs before setting me down on my feet at the sink. "Donna ever forget that yer mum and I love yeh very much and we both think that yer very wonderful!!" He tapped the tip of my nose, wiped away a loose tear and went to the fireplace mantle to pick up his pipe and tobacco.

Ma and I washed dishes and cleaned up the kitchen, singing and laughing together, and when we were done, Ma took me to my room and helped me get dressed for bed.

"Lassy, we love you, you ken that, right?" Ma asked as she tucked me into bed. I nodded my head slowly. "Yeh ken that they are just jealous of yeh, right?" My brow creased, and this time I shook my head. "Aye, that's right. They are jealous of the time yeh get to spend off in the forest, not havin' to work and do chores and such. They are jealous of the time I spend with ya, and yer Da spends with ya too. When yer older, and able to do more, they won't see ya as any different than them, because yeh'll be working right alongside them." She smiled kindly and kissed my forehead, "Night, bug, get some sleep. I think tomorrow will be an eventful day!" She laughed softly, blew out my candles and left the room, closing the door behind her.

∞∞∞

I sat straight up in my bed, gasping for air, throat burning, eyes watering."I wonder what Ma burned this morning.."

I shrugged my shoulders, coughing trying to reorient myself.

"Oh no..."

I sat frozen, fear prickled at the back of my mind and neck. My throat began to close, my stomach dropped to the floor and felt sick.

"That is no burnt toast… That is a fire.. And a large one at that… !"

Palms wet with sweat, hands shaking, heart racing, I began to realize what was happening, just as the screaming began somewhere in the near distance.

"My house is on fire! My siblings are burning alive in their rooms!"

And just like that, I couldn't think, I was paralyzed, I couldn't move. My whole body began to quake uncontrollably. I knew that I should be feeling sad right now, but all I could feel was fear and cold.

Lost in my spiraling thoughts, I didn't notice when the fire reached my room until my left ankle was burning. The fire caught my sleeping dress on fire, in no time, the fire had burned up to my thigh and was climbing quickly to my hip. I fell off the bed and onto the floor in a feeble attempt to claw my way out of my room and out of the fires reach. I knew that I wouldn't reach the door in time, that I, too, would be burned alive, but I tried anyway. Suddenly, rough hands were fiercely patting out the fire on my sleeping dress; the floor suddenly gave way and I was flying through the air. I landed, with a huff, against my father's chest, relief washed over me like a breath of fresh air.

"Lassie, listen to me! Listen! There's no time! Yeh'll ken the right time to read these." He said, gruffly shoving a small bundle into my hands. "I love you, lass, more than you know. I will always find you, when the time is right, I will come back and find you!" He opened the front door and the house exploded.

In slow motion, the fire behind us soared up and out of the door; bright, blazing orange and red flames. The blast propelled my father and me forward, and I flew out of his arms. I landed with a sickening crunch, and blackness consumed me instantly.

When I woke again,the sun was high in the sky, blinding me. My mouth was so dry that I had to peel my lips apart.

Where am I?

I thought as I tried to look around me to understand. My head was pounding, my ears were ringing, a hollow ache in my chest and pain riddled my entire body. I couldn't think, my mind was spinning out of control, thoughts sped by in a blurry motion. I took many deep, steadying breaths and, when my mind finally stilled, I opened my eyes and looked around me. I was laying on the ground outside, there was a smoke tinge to the air, no sounds of birds singing their early morning songs, no sounds of kids laughter, no screaming either. I thought back to the night before, trying to understand why I was on the ground and why my body hurt so badly.

The events from the night before came flooding back to me, I remembered the fire and the screams. I remembered how my father carried me out the door and how the house exploded and I got thrown to the ground a ways away from the house. I remembered the sickening sound of bones breaking as I landed on the hard ground. Panic rose up in me like a pot of boiling water, it rose up in my stomach and spread like wildfire in my chest, my throat constricted and my heart raced.

How long have I been here for?

Does anyone know what happened?

Will anyone find me before I die too?

There was no way to tell how long I had been asleep for, or how long ago the fire happened. It had been long enough that I was severely dehydrated and starving, but not long enough that I was dead, so somewhere in the middle. The silence around me was disturbing. No birds singing, no sounds of any kind; it was very unnerving. When I tried to lift my head to look around me, it sent a sickening jolt of pain through my spine, making my empty stomach lurch painfully. I wondered if this was how I was going to die.

I would have been better off dying in the fire, than dying of thirst. I thought bitterly to myself. Anger washed up inside of me, making my heart race and my head pound.

Calm down, Ary. Yer just making things worse for yerself. I attempted to soothe myself, but the pain became too much and darkness consumed me once again.

When I woke up, the sun had gone down and I was shaking from the cold. Every bone, muscle and organ in my body hurt beyond comparison. I knew that I had several severely broken bones, and I knew that I had hours left to live. I would die of dehydration before anything else, except, maybe freezing to death. The temperature was below freezing and I could feel moisture beginning to fall around me. If by some miracle, I was found: I probably would die of pneumonia or some other kind of infection or disease.

My brain was spinning and spinning out of control. Going over every possible way that I would or could die there before anyone found me. By my calculations, two days had already passed, by the end of the next day, if I was not found, I would surely die. If I cut my eyes just right, I could see my former house. I avoided looking in that direction, if at all possible, because it was too painful. Every second of the moments that I laid there awake, I could hear them all screaming over and over again in my head. I had thought that when they were gone, the screaming would stop too. I was unaware of the echoes etched within the memory cells of my brain. I was unaware of the pain they could cause.. Slowly tormenting me until I drew my final breath... It would not be long now, my breaths were numbered; the only question was, what number would be the last one? I counted my breaths and tried to listen to any sound other than my tearless sobbing, but there were no other sounds. I counted to six hundred before the darkness came again. I welcomed it like an old friend.

It seemed like I had slept forever. Good dreams and bad dreams. Didn't seem to matter. I vaguely remember something warm and wet going down my throat multiple times, and I vaguely remember thinking that someone was talking.

If this is what death is like, it sucks. I was expecting to be able to see my family again... oh well...

Death felt an awful lot like a very restless, everlasting sleep ... I was disappointed, to say the least, angry to say the most. I died out there in the yard of my home, and I still could hear them screaming.

I do not know how long the screaming continued on for, it could have been days, months, years even. All I know is that at some point a voice sounded in the midst of my dreams, a voice that brought me confusion and strength all at the same time.

"A'lari'jah, can yeh hear me?" Her voice was oddly airy and sounded far away. "Ary, this is Sr'eya, can yeh hear me, lass?" The voice became more clear, but still sounded far away.

"Aye, I can hear you." I replied weakly.

"Listen, there isnna much time. Do yeh remember what happened?" She asked me.

"You mean the fire?"

"Aye, lassy. The fire."

"Ach... I remember." My voice was thick with sorrow.

"Good, now, Ro'than'iel rescued yeh from the yard and brought ya to the palace. He thought it was the safest place for you to be, however, there has already been an attempt on your life."

"Yah mean, someone has tried to kill me?" I asked, incredulous.

"Aye, lass, someone tried to kill you. Now pay close attention, the King may be back at any minute. I am going to help yeh, yeh've got a lot of physical healing to do, and yeh've got a lot of emotional and mental healing to do. I am going to put yeh into a sleep that will allow yeh to wake up slowly, when yer ready."

"Is it real, then? Are they all dead?"

"Aye, lass, I'm afraid so. I have to go, someone is coming." She was gone as suddenly as she had come.

Time seemed to not exist where I was. Days could have been weeks, or vice versa, there was no way to tell. Everything was just one constant day, no nights, no setting sun, no sunrises, no goodbyes. Just one bright sunny day, where everything was peaceful and happy, I was with my family and everything was right again. Things were as they should have been. The fire didn't happen, I could have forgotten about reality all together in time. However, the universe had other ideas for me. Instead of being allowed to drift off into my peaceful afterlife, I was dragged back into reality. The transition began slowly, I was suddenly aware of conversations happening around me, of people coming and going from my room. I was aware of smells, especially during meal times. The smell of food awakened my previously dormant stomach, I think it might have growled at some point. I was also hyper aware of the atmosphere. I could feel what the people in my room were feeling, their worries and anxieties weighed heavily on my chest.

I was aware of the days passing, I could see the sun make its way across the room and down again, I could tell when my condition changed and when it stayed the same. It felt like I was there sitting on the sofa, waiting anxiously with the rest of whoever was in my room to see if I would wake up or not. I stayed still for days, really because I was unable to move, but also because I was not ready to show signs that I was awake yet. I felt a cold warning in Sr'eya's previous visit, something that she was not telling me, I wanted to feel things out, see what was happening.

Just as I had decided that maybe it was time for me to come awake, the king graced my room with his presence. I had assumed that he was the other person in the room, but I was mistaken. It was shortly after high noon when a loud, sharp rap echoed off the walls of my bed chambers, making everyone gasp and jump.

"Who's there?" I heard an unfamiliar, brusque voice asking through the door.

"King A'lbi'on, I have come to see my niece." He said, his voice was thick with annoyance.

"Enter." The same voice allowed him entrance, the door opened and a pair of heavy footsteps entered the room. His footsteps reminded me of my father's heavy and wary, he sounded tired, when he spoke, his voice thick with many sleepless nights. A'lbi'on came over and sat on the edge of my bed, he held my hand and stroked my hair. I felt something warm and wet touch my face, he was washing my face. His large hands were calloused and strong, reminding me of my father's. I struggled to keep my breath slow and steady, to keep my hand limp when all I wanted to do was squeeze his.

"How does she fair, Sr'eya?" The king asked in a voice thick with emotion.

"The same, my king. No change." Sr'eya said.

"It's been a year, she should have woken up by now. I have to assume that she isn't going to wake up." He said in a dismissing tone of voice. "It's time for us to move on, to accept the reality that this is her reality and it's not gonna change." He said, keeping his voice even and monotone.

"Be patient A'lbi'on! Her emotional wounds were far

deeper and far worse than her physical wounds. Her mind needs time to heal. She will wake up when she is ready to. Your aggravation and endless pacing will get you nowhere but kicked out of here, again. We can do nothing more for her except wait and let her know that we love her, and that we are here when she is ready to come back to us." Sr'eya chastised the king as a mother would scold her misbehaving child.

"You better not be wrong, woman!" Uncle A'lbi'on said crossly, I could almost hear the scowl that was on his face, "I'll be attending matters of the state, I want to be notified the moment she is awake again!" His tone suggested that of a king, full of dominion and authority.

A small chuckle could be heard slipping from Sr'eya, "Are we trying to soothe a guilty conscience there A'lbi'on? You have never taken an interest in this child before, all you have ever cared about was saving face with the public. Making sure that your sister was taken care of and that she had the bare minimum to survive on. So tell me, A'lbi'on, what did you do this time?" Sr'eya's mocking tone and sarcasm shocked and confused A'lari'jah.

"A fate she chose, and you would do well to remember that! Do not cross me, because if you do, it will be the last thing you ever do!" A'lbio'n was angry now.

"Do not forget, sire, I am the full and legal guardian of A'lari'jah. If anything should happen to me, you would never see her again. Furthermore if I feel my life or her life was in danger, you would never find us again! Remember what happened the last time you threatened the life of a loved one? You would do well to remember!" Sr'eya said, all of the rage she had kept inside and had bottled up came pouring out of her. "Sire, I will never give up hope on her, not as long as there is breath in her lungs! If you would like to be relieved of her *burden*," She snarled the last word, "I am always happy to take her home with me, I have the time and the care to give her while she recovers." Sr'eya said, accusingly.

"And if she never recovers?" He asked, a death like

stillness in his voice.

"Well, she will certainly be comfortable until she dies. Whenever that may be. It sure seems like, since *your* physician failed at killing her the first time, she would certainly be better off away from *you*, either way." Sr'eya said, finally cutting to what was really bothering her.

I heard the king take a few steps away from me, I assumed that he was stepping closer to Sr'eya, in my mind I pictured him pointing his finger sternly at her.

"I told you once, and I will tell you a thousand times again, I did NOT order that physician to kill my niece! For now she will remain here. But if she does not wake up soon, I will be forced to accept that she may never wake up again." He growled at Sr'eya and stormed out of the room, slamming the door behind him. I tried not to jump, but was unsuccessful; I just hoped that no one saw. I was not ready for anyone to know that I was awake. Sr'eya's warning came flooding back to me, "There has already been an attempt on your life." She had not told A'lari'jah this to frighten her, but to make her cautious and help her understand that she had come to a dangerous place.

"Sr'eya, how is she really?" I recognized Ro'than'iel's voice, full of worry.

"She's stable, for now. If I had not gotten here when I did, she would have died. The physician that was here was slowly poisoning her, she would have withered up and died, and no one would have known what really happened." There was a sadness to Ithrenniel's voice, a heaviness, a wariness about her that could be felt in the whole room.

"I see. Do you think she will wake up?" He asked, his voice breaking with emotion.

"She already is." Sr'eya said simply.

She must have seen me jump when A'lbi'on closed the door. How else would she know that I am awake? I suppose now I need to show them that I am awake…

Ro'than'iel gave no protest, nor did he question what

she meant. They resumed their silent waiting in front of the fireplace, sitting on the sofa.

The sound of the crackling, popping fire was soothing, it calmed my mind and my soul as I laid there and thought about all that had been said between Uncle A'lbi'on and Sr'eya. I had questions that needed to be answered, but I needed to figure out those questions first. Too many thoughts buzzing through my head to specifically pick one out.

The rest of that day seemed to pass in a haze, thoughts buzzing around like flies, I drifted in and out of dreamless sleeps. I decided that I would wait another night and day to let them know that I was aware of what was happening around me. I wanted to see if the king would come back, or if he had made his expected visit to soothe his "guilty" conscience or not.

But what has he got to be guilty about? It's not like he killed my family, and he said that he didn't tell the physician to kill me, so what could he have that would make him feel guilty?

A'lbi'on came back the next afternoon; he was quite a bit less rude and showed more emotion this time. When he spoke to Sr'eya, it was in a softer regretful tone of voice, "I must apologize for my insensitivity when I was here yesterday. I was rude and unkind to you; I hope you will accept my deepest apologies. You have done much to help her, and without you, she would surely be dead right now. I am grateful to you, both, for the constant care and protection you have bestowed on her." The king told Sr'eya and Ro'than'iel.

I was moved by this, but there was still something off, something lurking just beyond the shadows that I could not understand. Something just out of reach, and it bothered me. Made me not want to trust him at his word.

I felt someone take my hand in theirs, it was a large hand, very warm and slightly callused. I assumed it to be Ro'than'iel's or even Sr'eya's but the voice in my ear was very clearly Uncle A'lbi'on's.

"Ary, little one, come back to us. Fight, little one, fight hard, and come back to us, please! We need you. *I* need you! There has not been a day that has gone by this last year that I have not thought of your mother and father and your brother's and sisters. I miss them dearly! I am so lost without them! Please, find your way back to us soon! You are all that I have left in this world." Something wet dripped onto my face, I guessed that he was crying, he kissed my forehead, long and sweetly, like Father used to before bed or when I was sad. Then he turned and walked, slowly, out of the room.

That night a storm barrelled through the land. It was as if all of mother nature was mourning with Uncle A'lbi'on. Wind beat the rain against the windows. Thunder and lightning exploded in the sky loudly, shaking the foundation of the castle. This storm lasted throughout the night and as dawn broke, so did the storm. As the sun hit late morning, I woke up, slowly at first, blinking my eyes into the bright morning light, blurry and blearily. When my eyes adjusted to the light, I began to take in my surroundings.

I was laying in a large four poster bed, there were sheer sheets draping down from each post, and darker sheets on top of those, the sheets were down on my left side and at the foot of my bed, making my visibility of the room limited. The ceiling was elaborately decorated with fairies, elves, flowers, butterflies, making the most beautiful scenes play out above her, they somehow reminded her of her favorite place to go to on sunny days.

I was underneath a heavy layer of blankets and sheets. I guessed that it got cold during the rain storm last night, and they covered me up with more blankets and closed the curtains on my bed to shield me from the windows. Attempting to move was nearly impossible, I couldn't seem to make my neck muscles make my head move from one side to the other. I could hear and feel Ro'than'iel and Sr'eya in the room, presumably sitting on the sofa waiting patiently. I cleared my throat loudly and they both came darting around the corner. I opened and closed my mouth to indicate that I needed liquid to wet my mouth and my throat.

Sr'eya complied with a warm liquid that hit my mouth and ran down my throat. Choking and spluttering, I had, apparently, forgotten how to swallow. Sr'eya and Ro'than'iel helped to prop me up into a sitting position, leaning my head back onto a pillow because I couldn't hold it up on my own. She gave me a smaller amount of liquid this time, and I timidly tried to swallow it. With each sip of liquid, I got better and better at swallowing.

"Do ye know where you are?" She asked me as I drank.

I blinked once.

"Do yeh remember what happened?"

I blinked once.

"Do ye have questions yeh need answered?"

I blinked once.

"When yer ready, we will answer yer questions as best as we can, honest and true. Take yer time, do not rush. Yeh may find it difficult ter speak at first." Sr'eya said.

It has been a year? I asked so that they both could hear me, projecting my thoughts into their minds. Ro'than'iel was taken aback by this at first, but then relaxed into it.

"Yes, it has been one year, three days. Your eleventh name day is one month away." *Someone tried to kill me.* I stated.

"Aye. We do not know who ordered him to, but he nearly succeeded." Sr'eya answered.

Yeh suspect the king, why?

"Not sure how to explain it really, just a feeling, a sense if ye will." Sr'eya said.

"It's his behavior and actions since you have been here that has made me think that maybe he could be behind this. When I first brought yah into the palace after I found yah, his reaction was cold, dead, almost furious that you were alive. I could be reading too deeply into it, perhaps he was just upset and in shock of what he'd just heard; I donna know for sure.

However, just days after yah got here, a new physician arrived and began feeding yah poison, and I dinna ken it. If it had not been for Sr'eya's timely arrival, he might have succeeded in killing yah. I donna ken where he came from or who hired him." Ro'than'iel said.

There was a long silence, in which I slept again for a while. I was weak and needed as much sleep and rest as I could get. I also needed to get my strength back and get up off the bed and onto my feet again, quickly.

When I awoke again, A'lbi'on was there, holding my hand, face wet with tears. For the moment, all suspicions had been erased from my mind. We spent hours talking and laughing and crying. He told me everything that had happened since I got here, and he caught me up on all the latest gossip, he made my days go by so much quicker and happier. He even helped me sit up and helped me eat my broths. He stayed beside me most of the day, every day. It warmed my heart, and gave me hope and strength to keep fighting and want to get better and stronger. Every day I improved, every day I got more color back into me, more life back into me.

Chapter Two

Nights found me restless and unable to sleep. Tonight, I lay awake remembering what my mother used to tell me before bed every night.

"Remember, little one, you're a real, honest princess. You'll be queen one day." She would always smile.

I used to think that she told all of her daughters this. I used to think that it was just wishful thinking, that all mothers told their daughters that they were princesses so they would have something to dream about.

Goddess, mum was right. I am the true heir to the throne. One day, if I could recover from this malaise that gripped my spirit, I would take my uncle's place on the throne. No wonder he cares so much.

I finally drifted off into a restless sleep sometime in the wee hours of the morning. I had vague dreams of green and violet robes and crowns. The dreams were littered with Faerie folk, and humans alike, strange muddled dreams, as if they were, somehow, future events trying to break through my subconscious mind telling me that I really did have something more to live for.

When I woke up later that morning, feeling more exhausted than when I had fallen asleep, I stared up at the ceiling trying to remember the muddled confusing dreams I had, but I could not recall them at all. Uncle A'lbi'on was just coming in with my breakfast tray, he saw me looking up at the ceiling, admiring its detailed beauty.

"Do you like the ceiling, little one?" He asked me, happy to see that I was admiring it.

"Yes, Uncle, it's beautiful." He had startled me out of my confused thoughts, flashes of two different crowns ran through my mind, but it was all that I could remember.

"I had it specially painted for you back when your father told me that his girls were coming to foster here. I was so excited! I immediately had this room done up for you, and then he told me that it would be a year before he felt you were ready to come stay with us." Grief clouded his eyes when he talked about my family. The pain and anger that lay in his eyes sometimes frightened me, but tonight I was sad for him. I scooted myself closer to him and curled up at his side.

"Thank you, Uncle, it's beautiful and I love it!" I smiled but it was a sad sort of smile. While I was happy to be with him, the mention of my parents brought up a sudden rush of emotions that I was not altogether prepared for.

"I am sorry, princess, is it too soon to speak of them like that?" He asked me, he must have seen me stiffen.

"I do not know, Uncle. On the one hand, I do not want you to feel as though you cannae speak of them, I think it just caught me off guard this morn'." I told him, I shook my head and took a deep breath, "What's for breakfast? It smells delicious!" I said, trying to shake off the darkness that was creeping up in my mind.

"Flat cakes, sausages, ham and eggs!" He announced, "And, how are you doing, Ary?" He asked as he asked as he set up breakfast for us by the bed.

"A little numb and cloudy, to be honest. Had a rough night last night and did not sleep well. I can still hear their screams in my dreams, how I wish the screaming would stop." I said bluntly. He looked stunned at me, and I realized that I had never before discussed this with him.

"I am sorry little one, I am told that, over time, it will get better." He said, sadness clouded his voice.

"Donna fash yerself over it. I should not have blurted that out like that! I apologize. Come, sit! Let's eat! I'm starving!" I said, trying to lighten the mood.

He put on a brave face, and smiled tentatively at me. I tried to be engaging and pleasant in our conversations like I was okay, like nothing was wrong. Yet the truth was, I was not okay. There was a darkness that was lingering around the corners of my mind, a darkness that crept in more every day and I felt like I was drowning in it. True, the conversations with Uncle A'lbi'on brightened my day and helped to ward off that darkness, but now that I was getting stronger and better I saw my Uncle only during meals. He was the king, after all, and he was needed for state affairs. He no longer could put them off and be with me all day long. I understood that, I did, but that did not make me feel any less alone. In that loneliness, there brewed other feelings, painful anger and hatred that welled up inside of me, feelings that I didn't know what to do with, or how to talk about them. Feelings that I thought that everyone else wanted me to pretend weren't there.

One day I heard A'lbi'on and Sr'eya outside of my door talking. I assume that they thought I was sleeping.

"How is she *really* doing, Sr'eya?" A'lbi'on asked her.

"I don't know. Some days she seems to be really good, and others she is so withdrawn inside of herself that I don't think she knows anyone else is in the room with her. I had thought that, with time, she would come out of this, but she seems to be withdrawing more and more everyday." Sadness drenched her voice.

"When I was here all day, she seemed to have more light in her than she does now. When I come to visit her now, she seems to withdraw and become quiet. I fear for her, if she doesn't talk about how she is feeling, she will explode one day, and I do fear for us all when that happens."

"Aye, I fear yer right, but we cannae force her to talk. Be patient, sire, I am sure that she will come back to us soon."

I got so angry that night that I picked up the sharpest object that was closest to me. I pressed the blade heavily into my arm and drew it along my skin.. The pain that came from that cut made me feel alive again, so I repeated it over and over again until I had a dozen cuts on my arm, and my arm ached from the pain so much, I could not continue. I laid back in bed and let my arm bleed, hoping it would be the end of me, hoping that it would take away all my pain and give me rest at long last. I closed my eyes, smiling, knowing that Sr'eya would not check on me again until morning came.

"Good morning, my princess, I came to wake you up, milady, Sr'eya is waiting for you in the courtyard. She said that the fresh air and a walk through the gardens would do you good." She screamed when she drew back the heavy curtains to my bed. I could imagine how I looked to her, pale as my sheets, looking as if I had been through a bloody battle. My right hand still held the knife I had used, bloody and savage looking. She ran from my room sobbing and incoherent.

Several minutes had passed, though it felt like an eternity, when two sets of heavy footsteps came back into the room.

"What have you done!?" Sr'eya demanded, she fled over to me and applied pressure on my self-inflicted wounds at once. She fussed over me, crying all the while, muttering and speaking in languages I had not heard in a long time. As she finished, the king came in, carrying our breakfast.

"What the bloody hell has happened!? I could smell the blood from the hallway." He demanded, angry. A'lari'jah knew that he was scared, his anger was only a mask.

"Ask her yerself!" Sr'eya said, shoving the bandages into a drawer beside my bed. She stormed past him and out the door, muttering all the while.

"A'lari'jah, what's happened?" He asked me, his voice more gentle and kind now.

"Nothing, Uncle, is that breakfast that you've brought? I'm starving!" I said, my voice weak, my head fell to one side, all the strength I had gathered over the last six months was destroyed.

"A'lari'jah Jayd, tell me now and tell me true, what has happened?!?" He said, his voice full of fear. "You were so strong yesterday, and now all your strength has gone! What's happened?!" He demanded.

I knew that I could not deny it, I could not lie to him. I lifted up my left arm and showed him the wounds that Sr'eya had stitched up. I could not bear to look at him, I could not bear to see the grief and shame in his eyes.

"I still don't understand, I don't ... What happened?! Who did this to you?!" He cried, confused and angry.

"I did ..." My small, meek voice came. "Uncle, I did this to myself ..." I said, turning my head to face him.

"But... Why???" He asked trembling, sitting down beside me on the bed, he sat breakfast down on the table beside me. "Why??" He cried, tears streaming down his face, confusion in his eyes.

"Because I wanted to die. That's why, Uncle, is that a good enough reason?" I asked, anger burning in my eyes now.

Uncle A'lbi'on flinched from the fierce fire that was burning in my eyes, "But... Why?!" He asked again like a silly child. He could not say anything else.

"Because it hurts!" I screamed, groping at my chest where my heart was. "It hurts! It hurts and I want it to stop!" I screamed, the anger leaving me now, the pain washing over my eyes, I scratched harshly at my chest. My chest stung and my night dress began to soak up the blood that was now pouring out of the wounds I had opened up again. I began clawing at the stitches that Sr'eya had finished putting in my arms, ripping them out one by one, and he sat there, watching me, dumbfounded.

When I had finished ripping out all the stitches in every wound, blood was pouring out of them again, Uncle A'lbi'on grabbed my arms and held them at my side, his grip was painful, but his hard cold eyes were terrifying.

"You listen to me and you listen well, you hear me?! You are all that remains of my sister! I didn't save her! I failed her! In every way! And I will NOT lose you too! You are too valuable to me, far too precious for me to lose you too! Damn it Ary! Can't you see that!? You are too precious to me to lose! I will NOT let you do this! I will NOT let you die! I will stay here with you all day and all night if I have to! I will sit on you and tie your hands up if that's what it takes! I will NOT let you die!" He shook me harshly, as angry tears swam in his eyes and fell down onto my face with a crashing force. Each tear seemed to hold all his anger. "You are not alone! And you don't have to pretend to be okay! We don't want you to be okay! We need you to NOT be okay! Because the sooner you face this, the sooner healing can come in! This is not healthy! Keeping it all bottled up, and not talking about it, not talking about the pain and anger! Let us in, let us help you!" He was shaking me, my head was swimming, and his face came in and out of focus, I was fading, fast.

"Guards! Go get Sr'eya, and bring her here at once! Hurry! Time is short!" He yelled. He could feel me weakening in his arms, he could feel my life fading fast now, and he knew that he had moments to act before I died right there.

It felt like an eternity before Sr'eya ran into my room. "What's happened??" She asked, her voice frantic with panic and worry.

"She ripped out her stitches!" Uncle A'lbi'on told her. He kissed my head and whispered, "I love you, little one, please don't leave me!" it was the last thing I heard before the darkness took over.

"Ary, little one, wake up." My mother's voice came crashing through the black. I opened my eyes and saw her standing over me, one hand on my face, the other on my arm.

"Mum?" I asked, confused.

"Yes, little one, it's me." She smiled, her eyes sad.

"But, I thought you were dead?"

"I am, little one, and so are you." Tears swam in her eyes.

"I died?" I asked, confused still.

"Yes, little one, you took your own life today." A deep

sadness filled her eyes.

"Mum, if I am dead, why are you so sad? I get to be with you and Da' and everyone else now!" I exclaimed.

"No, little one, you can't. Suicide is an unforgivable sin. It's the one thing our Creator won't allow for. You took your own life to ease your suffering, in this selfish act, you have damned yourself to an eternal fire." Her sadness burned in her eyes.

"But, It Hurt So Much!" I Screamed, "You Left Me Alone! And It Hurts Too Much! I Cannot Bear This Pain Anymore!" My Anger Flooded Out.

"I am so sorry, Ary, we never intended to leave you. We never meant for this to happen!"

"Meant To Or Not, You Did! You Left Me! It Happened! And Now I Am Alone, Suffering, Hurting, And I Cannot Fix It!"

She placed her hand on A'lari'jah shoulder and spoke tenderly, "I know, Ary, I can feel your pain, and I feel your anger. I am still with you, watching over you, guiding you, trying my best to be there for you even now."

My Anger Vanished And A Sudden Hot Fury Took Its Place, "You Promised Me! Said You'd Always Be With Me! That You'd Never Leave Me! You Think That You Being There Where I Cannot Feel You Or See You Or Hug You Makes Me Feel Better?! Is That Supposed To Justify That You Left Me?! Is That Supposed To Make Everything Okay?!" I Screamed At Her, Hitting

Her Anywhere My Hands Could Strike.

"No, of course not, but I hope that in the coming months, it will be a comfort to you. I have to go now, He gave me a few minutes with you. He wants to give you a chance, another opportunity at life. Ary, if you do this again, if you take your own life again, he will not be able to save you a second time. This is your last opportunity to live life to its fullest, and one day we will be reunited. Go, now, and be healed, and remember that I am with you always." She faded into nothing, and I was alone, again.

I blinked my eyes, my head swimming, my stomach lurching, someone abruptly pulled me into a sitting position and bent my head over a bucket, holding my hair back out of my face as I retched into it.

"Oh! Thank the Creator!" I heard Sr'eya exclaim, my ears were ringing and her voice sounded far away.

After I finished retching, I asked, "How long?"

Two days, Ary." Uncle A'lbi'on's voice made me jump. I had not expected him to still be here.

"Dead?" I asked.

"Seven minutes." She told me.

"Unconscious for the rest of the time?"

"Yes. We did not know if yeh'd make it or not. We had some close calls, and at one point we thought you were dead again. I had to give you some blood because you had lost so much." There was a flicker of quiet anger in her voice. A coldness that stilled my heart for a beat.

"Yer angry at me." I stated.

"No." She said.

"Tell me true."

"Yes, Ary, we are angry at you. How could we not be angry at you!?" Uncle A'lbi'on spoke up.

"We spent the better part of a year and a half healing you, helping you, getting you stronger and bringing you back from the dead, and for what?! To have to do it all over again!?"

Ro'than'iel blurted, I was startled at his presence, his anger was striking and it shamed me.

"What the hells were you thinking?! HUH! Did you even consider what you'd put us through!?" A'lbi'on spit, his eyes fire and ice.

Tears brimmed my eyes, I had no right to cry, I had no right to do anything but sit there and listen, and I knew it. "No ... I did not think .... I only wanted the pain to end." I said, emotionless. "I am tired." I said, turning my back to everyone's hurt, angry eyes, I closed my eyes and drifted to sleep. I cannot say how long I'd slept, but when I woke up I was hungry and thirsty. I looked around and saw that there were four maids, and two guards in my room. Each of the four maids stood at each of the four posters of my bed, but not hovering over me. The two guards stood by the door, inside my room, watching me. Sr'eya and Ro'than'i'el and Uncle A'lbi'on were all standing by the fire, wordlessly staring into its flames. The atmosphere was almost electric with all the anger and fear rolling off everyone.

"Excuse me, my Lord, my Lady, my King, but she is awake." A maid close to my head said. The three of them came over to my bed and stood looking at me.

"Well, it looks like she still lives." Sr'eya cold flat voice pierced my heart.

It pained me to hear them all talk like this about me and to me, I was hurting inside to know that I'd hurt them and worse, I had disappointed them. All I wanted to do was make the pain stop, and yet all I did was make it worse. What I had done to myself was nothing compared to the pain I had caused them. All that I had to do was tell them that I was not okay, and yet, somehow I did not feel as if I could.

How do I fix this? How can I change what happened?

A still, small voice in the back of my head said, "You

cannot fix it or change it. What's done cannot be undone, now you move on, and you keep your head up, stay strong and you don't do that again."

"Are yeh thirsty, lass?" Sr'eya asked cordially, her tone of voice icy.

"Aye, a wee bit." I smiled as best as I could, but a chill ran through my heart when she spoke to me.

"Here, drink this." She handed me a cup of steaming liquid that smelled like peppermint tea and honey. The tea was good and soothing, hitting all the right spots and helped energize me and kept me alert. Sr'eya pulled the bandages off of my arms gently. She packed the cuts with honey and put new bandages on them.

"They look better, lass. Honey is helping with the healing process much better than anything else that I have." Sudden tears were streaming down her face, her anger ebbed away. "Lassy, don't do this again. Please?" Her voice was gentle and pleading, "The people left behind need you. The king needs you. He's got a lot happening in his own family, and he cannot bear to lose you." She said, her sadness washed over me.

All I could do was nod. I was crying so hard that I didn't trust myself to be able to speak. I was afraid to say anything, afraid to do anything, the last thing that I wanted to do was cause them more pain. I stayed silent, unless I needed to answer a question that required more than a head nod.

Weeks had fled by and all the while I did not speak to them. Uncle A'lbi'on had fixed me a chair with wheels on it and I found that going outside was refreshing. I hated the physicians who came in and made me do exercises with my legs and arms. They felt silly and filled with pain.

"They will help you regain muscle and strength so that you can walk again, missy." The old English physician had told me when we first started.

At first, he was unnerved that I would not speak and used to drone on for hours about subjects that I did not understand nor care to hear about. He bored me to death with stories of his other patients or histories and stories from the old lands. The History of England and such were so boring. If I didn't hurt so bad when I did my exercises, I would have fallen asleep. Yet, when he would tell his "histories" of the Old Lands, I found that I listened so intently to them that my pain seemed to disappear.

I loved hearing about fairies and elves and dwarves and the battles that ensued and everything he knew about all the maj'ickal creatures that once had the freedom to live freely in Nah'alba. He knew that these stories piqued my interest, and so he continued with them, drawing vivid images in my mind, painting beautiful pictures as he told his stories. Before I knew it, our time was up, and he was leaving for the day. Over time, he became a favorite part of the day for me, apart from my regular visits to the garden after he had gone. I found that breaking my fast in the gardens started my day off in a good way, and supping in them ended my day the same. No matter how bad my day was between breakfast and supper, I could always count on ending my days on good terms.

"Idrenniel, how long do we allow her silence?" I overheard Uncle A'lbi'on speaking in hushed voices, thinking that I was asleep.

"I will let you know when it is time. Right now, she has a lot going through her head, a lot happening inside her heart. She is afraid to do something wrong again, she feels like no matter what she does, it is wrong. The one day that she blurted out to you what she was really feeling, your shock and silence did more damage, I am afraid, than it did good. I know, don't give me that look, I know what yer gonna say, I understand, but all the same, she felt as if she had said all the wrong things at that moment. Now she is punishing herself, she doesn't feel like it's punishing us, she thinks that it's just punishing herself." Sr'eya said. "She will come around soon, don't worry. She is being pulled out of her shell, her physicians are helping with that." Silence fell, and I drifted into an uneasy sleep.

In my dreams at night I relived the day my family died every single night. I could feel the fire burning my skin again, I could feel my bones breaking as my father threw me from the house. None of that carried the amount of horror and feelings as hearing my family screaming again, and the longing for them to stop, and the relief I felt when they did stop. These dreams alone were enough to unhinge a full grown warrior, but the effect they had on such a young mind was horrendous. My mind was reaching its breaking point, I had already tried to end my suffering once, that didn't work out for me, but what if I didn't do it to end the suffering, but to cope with it? What if it was a way for me to deal with the pain, to deal with the nightmares, to keep my mind from breaking? I reasoned that as long as I did not use it for the means of ending my life, then it would be alright. Shallow cuts, nothing too deep, would alleviate my pain and help me to focus and concentrate and keep my mind off the breaking edge.

I sat up just slightly in my bed, trying not to alert anyone to my being awake, "Mistress, did you need something?" a maid spoke up, a candle flickered alive, and there was a rustling of people moving about.

"What is it, Ary? What's wrong?" Uncle A'lbi'on had come to sit on the edge of my bed and hold my hand.

I looked deep into his eyes, searching his very soul, all he wanted was to help, there was only compassion there.

"Uncle, my mind, I feel like it's going to break. I do not think I know how to live with this pain."

"What pain, little one, tell me about it? Perhaps together we can shoulder this burden."

"Everytime I close my eyes, I relive that night. Every time I sleep, I can feel the fire burning me, I can feel the heat of the flames, I can smell the smoke, and my family burning. I can hear them screaming and I canna make it stop ..." There was no fire in my voice, there was no ice either. My voice was flat, monotone, emotionless. I was exhausted, and I just wanted it all to end. "I know that they are gone, I know that they cannae come back, I understand that. But why can I not make the screaming end?"

"By talking about it. By not enduring this alone, by letting us help you with this. This is a burden too big for you to carry alone. This is a burden that each of us can help you with, all you have to do is share it with us." Sr'eya said softly, tears glistening on her face in the candle light.

I nodded my head, closed my eyes and took a deep steadying breath. "Is now a good time, then, or shall I talk in the morning?" I asked, unsure of how to do this.

"Now is always the best time, little one." Uncle A'lbi'on said.

I nodded my head and asked, "Can I, maybe, sit by the fire?" I asked before getting started, I was trembling so hard my teeth were chattering, I hoped the fire would help. Uncle A'lbi'on helped me into my wheeled chair and put a thick fur blanket over my legs and rolled me over to sit in front of the fire. I sat for a while without speaking, just gazing into the flames calmed my mind. I sat thinking about where I wanted to begin, what I was willing to let them know, how deep was I willing to let them in? I decided to tell them everything, because they would see right through a half lie.

I took a deep breath, let it out slowly, and cleared my throat. "I am going to start this off by saying how I am feeling right now, the thoughts and feelings running through my mind and my heart right now. This is not to make you feel sorry for me, this is because it is the best way to begin.

I am feeling the pain of a thousand knives stabbing me in the heart, the pain of the fire, burning my lungs with every breath. The weight of the world feels like it is pressing down on my chest and shoulders right now. I feel empty. I feel like I don't want to keep going, I don't want to keep enduring this pain. Every night I go to sleep, I relive that night with vivid clarity. I can smell the fire, I can taste the smoke in my mouth, feel it burn my throat and my chest again. I can feel the heat of the fire as it gets closer to me, I can feel it burn me again. I can feel my father's arms around me, I can hear his voice echoing in my mind, I can still smell his musky tobacco scent, I can still feel my bones break as he throws me from the front door. Worse of all, I can hear them screaming in my mind, I can hear them screaming and I can remember begging for the screams to stop, begging and sobbing and begging for the screams to end, and I remember the relief when they did end, and I feel ashamed of that relief. I feel guilty for surviving, I feel guilty for being alive, for having a life to live when I should have died in that fire with them!" I broke off, sobbing into my hands, trying to regain control of myself, gasping for breath.

"That's it, let it all out, stop holding it in, just let it go." Ro'than'iel's voice surprised me, I had not expected him to be in the room with them. After several minutes, I lifted my head, still gulping for breath, but more able to control myself.

"I admit that what I did was cowardly, selfish and not okay, but I just didn't think that I could continue underneath the massive weight of this grief and anger. Mum helped me understand that what I did was wrong, and that I would not be able to see them in the afterlife if I did that. The Creator was gracious, he gave me another chance." I said solemnly.

"You saw yer mum??" Sr'eya asked, shocked.

"Aye." I smiled a bit.

Lass, why did ya not tell me this?

I didna think it was important?

This is huge! Yeh have no idea what this means, do ya?

Apparently not.

Did yeh see yer da' too??

No, Da' weren't there with her, just mum.

Interesting.

"I am okay, for right now. My darkness has passed and I am feeling quite sleepy, I would like to go back to bed please." I said, eyes drooping, head lolling as I nodded off to sleep.

When I woke up next, the room was silent, the air felt stale, it was midday or thereabouts. I raised my head, cautiously, no one came running, there was no rustling of bodies moving. I found this odd, hard to believe. Then I took note of my surroundings, my room was in disrepair, moth-eaten curtains hung around my bed, my blankets were falling apart. The fireplace, which usually had a fire in it, had not been used for many years. There was no one in my room, nor was there anyone outside my room. Slowly I sat up, moved my head around, there was no pain, I could move my head, my arms, my legs all with zero pain. Cautiously I swung my legs over the side of the bed and gingerly jumped down onto them. Man! It felt good to do that again! I smiled to myself, lost in the moment of no pain, that I forgot that something was terribly wrong with the castle. There was an eerie silence that had befallen the castle, no birds were chirping, not insects making their noises, no hustle and bustle of servants and guards out in the hallway. I frowned at myself and crept out of my room.

The hallways were deserted, no one was here.

This is odd.. Where is everyone?

Goose Pimples covered my flesh as a voice crept, unbidden, into my mind.

They are all dead.

Dead?! How!? They were just alive! Alive and well! What has happened!?

This is the world 30 years from when you went to sleep, as it would be if you died like you so desperately want to. Everything and everyone that you know and love would be wiped from existence. You see, everything that you stand for, everything that you are, prevents the war that ravishes the kingdom for ten long years, without you, the whole kingdom falls, the mystical creatures devour and ravish the humans, and then turn upon themselves and destroy themselves, there is nothing left on Nah'alba but decay and destruction. You were created for a reason, and without you, this is what becomes of the kingdom.

I felt a chill run through me, I did not understand.

When you say that I was created for a reason, that without me, the kingdom falls into destruction?

Not just destruction, little one, mass genocide. Species against species, then against their own kind. Without someone to keep the peace, to rule both realms, this is what happens. Ary, you alone are the key to keeping the balance. You alone are the key to life in the kingdom!

But, surely, if I die, then someone else will rise up in my stead, someone else will be able to rise up and create peace?

Ary, do you even know who you are? Who you truly are?

My mind went blank, I did not know how to answer this question.

Child, you are heir to the kingdom, heir to the throne of Nah'alba, and heir to the throne of A'va'lon. You are a dual princess, dual heir to two kingdoms. You are the key to keeping peace and balancing out nature and maj'ick.

The scene in front of me swirled and I was suddenly flying high in the sky up above Nah'alba. The kingdom, the island, it was just ruins now, the castle was nothing more than just rubble. Piles of stone and dirt. A deep resonating sadness filled my whole body, my very soul felt the emptiness and the scarring from the destruction of the kingdoms.

Send me back, I want to live, send me back! I screamed to the faceless voice.

I sat straight up in my bed, gasping and gulping for air, every fiber of my body trembling. Sweat ran down my face, my face was white and colorless.

"ACH! Lass! What happened?" Sr'eya rushed to my side, feeling me for fever, "Get her to the fire, she's ice cold!" Sr'eya barked at someone hovering close by.

Two strong arms lifted me up off the bed and carried me over to the fire, someone scooted a heavy chair close to the fire so that whoever was holding me could sit down, a large fur blanket was tucked in around me.

Hours might have passed, days even, and I would not

have known it. I sat gazing into the fire, remembering the castle, Nah'alba, in ruins. The emptiness of the kingdom haunted me.

A'lari'jah, you're in a terrible state, talk to me, tell me what happened?" Sr'eya's voice was like a faint whisper in the very back of my mind, like a distant memory. I sat silent, trembling, unaware of what was happening around me, or who was holding me.

It might have been days later, but the next thing I remember was being doused in freezing cold water.

I gasped and gulped for air and shuddered violently as the cold water hit me. It had done its job and woke me up, I blinked and looked around, a fresh wave of shivering came over me.

"Where am I?" I asked, confused.

"A'lari'jah, you're in the castle, in your rooms, do you know who I am?"

"Yes, but what happened? I remember... " I paused, trying to remember what I remembered. Suddenly the horrid dream came back to me and my face turned pale white again.

"You know, I think she is in shock!" Uncle A'lbi'on said.

"No, I am sorry, I just remembered a dream that I had... That's all, nothing more. Just a dream." I said as airily as I could, it was, after all, just a dream. Or so I kept telling myself.

Spill, whatever woke you up had you pale white, like a ghost, ice cold, unmoving, trembling for well over twelve hours.

I remember going to sleep, and then I woke up and the castle was in ruins, my blankets and sheets and curtains were all moth-eaten and old, falling apart around me at the slightest touch. I got up and walked through the castle, looking for anyone and no one was here, so I said "where is everyone?" and then this voice in my head said, "They are dead." When I asked what happened he said that this is what fate awaits Nah'alba if I die, he said that I am a dual heir to the thrones of Nah'alba and A'va'lon. He said that I am half fae half human. He said that without me there will be a ten year war that ravishes both humans and maj'ickal creatures alike, that it is a genocide, the maj'ickal realm turns against the humans and devours them, then they turn upon themselves and devour each other until no living creature survives. The emptiness that I felt, Sr'eya, *was the worst thing I have ever experienced. I have never felt such sadness, such emptiness, such despair.*

Sr'eya stayed silent, unsure of what to say or how to respond to me. I certainly wouldn't blame her if she didn't believe me. I could hardly believe it myself.

Uncle A'lbi'on put me back in bed and covered me up tightly with my thick fur blanket on top of the other blankets I had on my bed. He bent over and kissed my forehead, "Goodnight little one. Sweet dreams, we will be here when you wake up." He smoothed my hair back and caressed my face and I drifted off into a dreamless sleep.

Chapter Three

Over the next few months leading up to my thirteenth birthday, I worked very hard to get myself back up to being able to walk and get around by myself. I was still very weak, and got tired easily, so I was always being followed by my wheeled chair, but, over all, my strength was coming back and so was my color. As my thirteenth birthday drew closer and closer, the castle was buzzing with servants running to and from the great hall; massive preparations were being made for a huge celebration. Sometimes the thought of it was all a bit overwhelming for me. These days I valued my solitude, the rare times when I was actually allowed to be alone for thirty minutes every day.

Ever since I had attempted to take my own life a year ago (right before my twelfth birthday, the celebrations for which was canceled) I have not had a moment alone, until the beginning of this month when Ro'than'iel prompted that they allow me thirty minutes alone in the gardens three times a day, and from there, if I could prove that I was okay and could be trusted, I could begin to earn more free time away from my constant babysitters. So now, first thing in the morning after breakfast, I was allowed to go to the gardens for thirty minutes before my physician came in to help me learn how to use my hands, feet, legs and arms again.

Uncle A'lbi'on wanted me to begin lessons right away, but I tired too easily after all of my exercises I had to do and I kept falling asleep during my tutoring sessions. In the end, Uncle A'lbi'on agreed that we should wait until I regained maximum strength.

I explored the castle and took naps in my wheeled-chair

when I got too tired to carry on. In my many explorations, I found myself on the total opposite side of the castle, it was colder over here, and there were many dusty, unused rooms. One day I was rummaging through some old dresses that I stumbled across when the door opened with a "BANG!" I jumped and the old dress fell out of my hand and fell to the floor in a messy heap.

"You'll want to take care, miss, those dresses could fall apart if you touch them too much." Said the young boy, no older than myself, who had barged into the room.

"This used to be your mother's room." He said, his eyes observing me in great detail. "Those were her dresses before she left, and never returned." He smiled mischievously.

"So, you were the one followin' me." I stated. He blanched. "Ach," I said with a wave of my hand, "donna look so surprised, I knew you were there from the first time I came over this way." I smiled at him, just as mischievously. We stared at each other in silence for a while before he regained his arrogant manner.

"Here, milady, allow me to pick that up for you." He said mockingly.

"Are yeh here to mock me and make me look like a fool? Or do you actually have a reason for showing yerself now?" I demanded that strange ring of authority in my voice again.

He looked stunned that I was speaking to the crown prince thus, he blanched again for just a second, before responding, "I wanted to meet you, and I thought you would like to hear about your mum." He paused for a second, the most sincere look in his eyes, and then said, "If I am bothering you, I can go." he seemed suddenly unsure.

"No! Please, stay; I would very much like to hear what you have to say about my mother. I miss her so much every day... I come in here because I feel closer to her." I smiled sadly.

"Well, I will tell you what I know, although, everything I have heard is second hand information." He paused, I smiled and he continued. “Are you comfortable? Do you want a fire?” He asked me as I had shivered slightly, trying not to show my discomfort.

“No! I want to hear the story.” I said eagerly. He frowned and rang a loud bell. “Warmth first, then story.” He said kindly. A few seconds later a servant came running into the room, red faced and looking surprised.

“Your highness.” He bowed deeply.

“Ah, Lauraunt, be so kind as to make us a fire and bring us some snacks please? Quickly! Milady is cold.”

“Right away, your royal highness.” Lauraunt said, backing out of the room.

“What are yeh called by, then? Should I just address yeh as ‘yer royal highness’ all the time?” I asked, a slight mocking tone to my voice.

“Eir’im’uhs, milady. Eir’im’uhs will do just fine, leave off the rest of it unless we are in a public setting, and then MiLord will work just fine.” he smiled sweetly . “No need to ask you yours, A’lari’jah. The whole castle is buzzing about you! I began to wonder if you really existed, and, if you did, why you had not shown your face before now! But seeing as how you’re a cripple and all, it makes sense now. When I first heard that Father had taken on a ward, I hardly dared to believe it! Of course, it’s obvious now that it is true.” His laugh was hard, I frowned at that.

“Why so surprised?” I was taken aback by a hard look in his eyes.

“’Tis no secret that my father *hated* your mother. He is the reason that your mother ran away and never came back.” Eir’im’uhs said haughtily. Fear prickled in my stomach.

“Uncle A’lbi’on was the reason she left?” I asked, frowning. I tried to recall what my mother had told me. “Mum told me that she left the castle in the dead of night, she said her life was in danger and she was smuggled away, but she never told me who was threatening her life.” I said. “Is it true?” I asked.

"It is a tale to behold, for sure." He held up a single finger, indicating to stop talking. I fell silent at once and heard the scuffling of feet coming up the hallways. Lauraunt came in the door with his arms full of firewood, a female followed him in, her arms full of trays of food.

"Ah, thank yeh, just set the food trays down on the table under the window, no, don't worry 'bout the dust, just set the trays down, thank you, you may go." Eir'im'uhs said kindly.

Lauraunt finished building us a fire and left with the promise of bringing more firewood.

"Now, I shall start at the beginning of the story, which begins before either of our parents are born.

Our grandparents were from two different parts of the world, two different realms really. Queen Clarissa was from Spain, where maj'ick was practiced openly and no one feared it. When she first came to Nah'alba, it was the same here, but even more so. maj'ick in this realm used to be revered, marveld, worshiped, it was something that was highly coveted and highly respected. King O'ri'on was a great king, he worked very closely with the king and queen of A'va'lon, and there was peace throughout the kingdom's two realms. Fairies and Elves, Dwarves and Nymphs used to roam the castle, we used to employ all kinds of creatures for different kinds of jobs. Myth has it that the gardens looked like those in A'va'lon when the Nymphs were taking care of it.

Anyway, Clarissa and O'ri'on fell in love with each other immediately, she being maj'ickal, him being human. They were married not just for the alliances it would give the kingdoms, but also for the love they held for each other. When your mother was born, it was a glorious day. It is said that her maj'ick spilled out of the womb as she was born and there was a rose bush that grew in our grandparents rooms for many years from it. G'rai'ce was a beautiful child, she was happy and brought much joy to the king and queen. It did not matter that she was not a male, there were no rules inNah'alba preventing the reign of a female leader. G'rai'ce was first in line for the crown, and what an amazing ruler she would have made! She was kind and just and showed mercy where needed, but she was also ruthless and a warrior, she was strong and tough too.

Father was born five years after G'rai'ce, he was a strapping young lad, stocky and hearty from the get go. Walked quicker and had a mean temper about him. He and G'rai'ce got along very well though, their opposite natures balanced each other out. Father knew that your mum had maj'ick in her, Clarissa had brought someone in to help G'rai'ce hone her gifts, so that she was not spending all of her time with G'rai'ce and no time with A'lbi'on. A'lbi'on was five years old when the news that the queen was pregnant again. The pregnancy was a terrible one, Clarissa was terribly ill the whole time, unable to eat, she was weak and then a terrible plague hit the kingdom.

Clarissa was close to birthing time, they had high hopes that she had gained enough strength to make it through the pregnancy alive, though they did not know about the baby. A fever swept through the kingdom in the form of a red rash, later the doctors and physicians named it the Scarlet Fever. It killed twenty-five percent of the population. That included maj'ickal and non maj'ickal peoples. The king fell ill, A'lbi'on fell ill, Clarissa fell ill, every single person fell ill to this except for one."

"G'rai'ce" I interjected.

"Exactly. No one knows why she didn't get sick because even the elves, fairies, nymphs, dwarves were all ill, and she was the only person in all the kingdom to not be affected by the illness.

When Clarissa went into labor, her midwives had G'rai'ce attend the mother and child, since she was the only one who wasn't sick, she was the only who could safely deliver the baby. Sadly the baby was stillborn, and Clarissa was too weak to recover.

O'ri'on never fully recovered from the fever and losing

his wife and child. A'lbi'on turned angry and bitter over the years that followed, he began to blame G'rai'ce for their mother's death." Suddenly Eir'im'uhs stopped talking and motioned for her to be quiet again.

There was a rush of footsteps as Lauraunt came back, as promised, with his arms full of firewood again.

"Begging yer pardon, yer royal highness, milady, I'll just tend the fire and leave the wood here, I won't come back unless you ring."

He tended to the fire and made sure that there was enough wood on it and quietly left the rooms again. Eir'im'uhs followed him out, checked the hallways and came back inside, closing the door behind him.

"He made up wild and ridiculous theories that G'rai'ce could have saved Clarissa, that she wasn't affected by the illness because of her maj'ickal, and therefore she could have saved their mother and unborn sibling. Sadly, these were just not true. G'rai'ce did not have the gift of healing, her gifts were not unlike those of the garden nymphs. From that moment on, G'rai'ce isolated herself from A'lbi'on, who became increasingly more violent toward her, in her rooms and in the gardens.

Finally, O'ri'on was growing weak, and the plan was to have G'rai'ce coronation on her sixteenth birthday, where she would take the throne and rule until her life was over. However, A'lbi'on had other ideas, he had arranged for G'rai'ce to die that night, plotted many different ways to kill her, and set them all into action.

O'ri'on got wind of A'lbi'on's plans and was going to have A'lbi'on arrested, but he was too late, G'rai'ce, by means no one is quite sure of, got smuggled out of the castle. Rumor has it, G'rai'ce herself set up Sr'eya to smuggle her out of the castle the night of her coronation. O'ri'on was furious when he found out, however, he died soon after she fled and the guards were never sent for, ergo A'lbi'on was never arrested.. G'rai'ce went into hiding, and was not seen or heard from for many years. She did not come home for her father's funeral, she did not come to swear fealty to her brother, and she did not come home after maj'ick was banished.

Some said that it had taken a toll on her, and that it broke her heart, losing her family like that. Some said that she had died too, rumors of her death had spread through all of the kingdom.

After two years, A'lbi'on felt increasingly guilty over this and began a search for her all over the kingdom; he exhausted all of his resources to bring her home. He sent riders out who posted flyers in every town, "Have you seen this woman?" with a drawing of how he remembered her to look when she left. He spent a total of five years looking for her.

One day, a rumor had reached the castle walls, G'rai'ce has returned!' A'lbi'on and I raced out of the castle and down into the town, personally searching for her. After being there all day, he began to get frantic when she came up behind him and said, 'I hear you have been looking for me.'

He spun around on his heel, and looked at her square in the face. 'Thank the Creator you're alright!' He cried as he threw his arms around her and embraced her tightly.

G'rai'ce was more than surprised at this show of affection, A'lbi'on had hated her for nearly all of their lives, she was expecting to feel a knife in her back.

A'lbi'on was generous to her. He offered her land on the outskirts of Honey River Cove, Built her a large house, and gave her everything she needed. He offered her husband a post in the castle and a place at his right hand, as advisor.

Though the three grew close and lived in harmony for many years, G'rai'ce never forgave A'lbi'on, and remained suspicious of him for the rest of her life.

A'lbi'on watched as G'rai'ce suffered from the loss of several children, both living and those yet to be born. He watched her many hardships, and saw that she never changed who she was, never turned angry or bitter. A'lbi'on was very proud of his sister, he said so often. He often said how he wished he could change things, go back and fix things. I always found it odd how often he proclaimed his wish to have things differently. He said them so often that we had a hard time believing the genuinity of his sentiments." He finished telling his tale, and waited for me to catch up.

"Wow, that's ... wow!" was all I could say. "So, that explains Uncle A'lbi'on's guilt, and why he is trying so hard with me." I said pointedly.

"What do you mean, his guilt?" Eir'im'uhs asked suddenly.

"It's a look in his eyes, a feeling I get when he's around me, he feels guilty for treating my mum so badly and thinks that if he saves my life and takes care of me the way she would have wanted, that he would have paid back his debt to her, and eased his guilt of driving her away and taking her place on the throne." I explained as if it was plain as day.

"You're like your mother, aren't you? maj'ickal?" He asked me suddenly, an excited glint in his eyes.

"I am sure that I donna know what yer talking about, Eir'im'uhs." I said, a warning in my eyes.

Eir'im'uhs was stubborn, and he didn't give up, until I spilled.

"I don't know what I am exactly." I said.

After that, everything came bubbling out of my mouth before I really knew what I was saying. "I canna figure it out. I have so many questions, and I don't have anyone to fill in the gaps. I had not noticed the maj'ickal when I was younger but only when I was around my A'va'lon'ian friends. That feeling would build whenever I was with them, and I always just let it flow. However, now, this feeling is growing stronger every day and I canna allow that maj'ickal to flow here. I realized that this is what has been causing a great deal of my anxiety as of late. I mean, even Sr'eya doesnna know what I am, only that I am powerful enough to cause her fear. I have to keep all of this withheld, locked up inside me, and sometimes I feel like all of this maj'ick is going to explode out of me!" I said desperately. I looked at him, suddenly fearful.

"Donna fash. My dad willna hear a peep of this from me!" He smiled, a quiet wisdom lay within his eyes.

"I wish I knew of a place that I could go to get the answers that I need, somewhere safe to practice, control and release it. The longer it sits here ... the harder it is to keep it from accidentally coming out." I said, tears running down my eyes at the struggle going on inside of me.

"Ary, I sense great maj'ick in you. Maj'ick that this world has not seen before. I do believe that you are destined for greatness." Eir'im'uhs said, I looked at him stunned. I turned and gazed into the fire, trying to read him, trying to figure him out and understand him.

"You have maj'ick too, don't you?" I asked finally.

"I thought you would never sense it." He sighed in relief. "I thought that maybe I was just crazy." He said.

"It is difficult to sense, like it is masked, like someone has blocked you from it." I said. "I can unlock it for you, if you'd like me to." I said suddenly.

"No, I think it needs to stay locked up, it will be unlocked when the time is right." He said, suddenly guarded.

"Okay, no need to flinch, I won't do anything without yer permission." I laughed.

"I have some of it, but not the full of it, I have enough to know when someone around me has maj'ick I sensed you from day one, your maj'ick is powerful." He smiled. "Your secret is safe with me, not to worry. Give me a week, and I may have a place for you to practice and learn more about your maj'ick and who you are. I would like to do some research though, before we get started." He smiled an excited and mischievous smile. "Come, I had better get you back to your rooms before they come hunting for you, it's nearly your supper time." He said. I looked around and realized the fire had died down to a low burning ember and the sun was sinking quickly on the horizon.

After Eir'im'uhs dropped me off down the corridor of my room, he said, "It is best if they donna yet know that we have met. I leave you here, milady." Then he disappeared into the shadows of the hallway.

I did not see nor hear from Eir'im'uhs for a whole week, and I have to say, it was proving to be the loneliest week of my life. My physicians did their best to keep my spirits up, and Uncle A'lbi'on even surprised me and lifted my sentence of needing constant babysitting, even this did not keep me happy for long.

One night as I was lying awake thinking over the things that Eir'im'uhs had told me a week ago, I heard a door open.

"Pssst."

I sat up in my bed, looking furiously around.

"Pssst" came from the servant's door.

I lit a candle and looked over, Eir'im'uhs was standing there looking rather excited.

"I heard father banished your babysitters! Come with me, I have something to show you!!" He whispered loudly.

"Hang on a minute, let me get out of bed and get my robes and slippers on, will you hand me my walking cane?" I asked and pointed at the main bedroom door. He crossed the floor silently and handed me the walking cane, "Be patient with me, I do not walk well still." I said.

Eir'im'uhs kept pace with me easily, though he was eager to show me what he had found. We didn't speak much as we went, except the occasional, "careful, there's a step here" or "watch your head here". We didn't want to take a chance of waking anyone up.

We walked for what seemed like hours, my legs and back were beginning to hurt so much that it slowed my pace even more.

"Ary, we are nearly there, I promise, do you need to lean on me?" His face showed regret.

"No," I grunted, "I'll be fine." I said.

"I should have made you bring your chair!" he said,

kicking hard at the ground.

"No, I'm fine. This is good for me." I grunted again. He refused to take that as an answer and took my arm to help support my weight. Another hundred steps and we arrived at what appeared to be a dead end. I gave Eir'im'uhs my best scowl, which was actually impressive because of the pain I was in.

"Sit down right here, and watch." He said, leading me to a chair against a wall. He walked over to the wall and touched it, the wall gave way to a secret room. Eir'im'uhs came back and helped me inside, I gasped as we crossed the threshold. The room inside was massive, it was lined with all sorts of books, cushions, dummies and other elaborate things that I couldn't place. I was so tired the world seemed to be spinning, I didn't have the chance to enjoy the full splendor of the room we were in. In fact, I seemed to be falling down, the room swayed and went black.

The next thing I knew, I woke up on a soft cushion in a brightly lit, unfamiliar room. I stirred and groaned in pain.

"Hang on, just a second, I have something here that will help with your pain." *I know that voice, who's voice is that?* I thought to myself as I tried to remember where I was.

Eir'im'uhs came around the corner holding a cup of steaming liquid. "Here, drink this, it will help with your pain and renew your energy." He said.

"Where did you learn how to do this?" I asked after I had finished his concoction.

He threw his hands up and gestured all around him. "These books are filled with everything and anything you might need to know about herbs, maj'ickal healing, how to use your maj'ick, where it all began, so forth and so on." He grinned excitedly.

"Is this what took you so long to find?" I asked

"No, this is what took me so long to find." He said, bringing me a book.

"What's this?" I asked, dumbfounded.

"Look here," he pointed at a family tree. I looked closer and realized that it was my family tree. I gasped, "But, I am on here!" I exclaimed breathlessly.

"And look at this side of the tree." He said, pointing to the left.

"It's my dad and his family!" I said excited for the first time.

"He's the prince of A'va'lon, Ary." He said.

"But, what does that mean?" I asked.

"That means that you are half Fae, Ary, half Fae, half human." He said, eyes sparkling.

"But, what does that mean?!" I said, exasperated.

"Ary, don't you see how rare this is?!"

"No, I guess not." I said, exhausted. "Can we do this tomorrow when I can think straight? Come to my room right after breakfast, and we can do this all day, I don't have my exercises tomorrow." I said, yawning deeply.

"Okay, I'll go get your chair and take you back. I am sorry, I should have waited.." he said, sounding defeated.

"Hey! Come back here!" I said loudly.

"Yeah?" He said glumly.

"It's not that this isn't very impressive, or that I don't appreciate this, or that I am not curious or excited." I told him earnestly "I am just so exhausted right now…" I told him, the deep purple circles under my eyes highlighted and magnified this.

"I know, I just should have waited to come show you until you were feeling better, I knew you'd had a rough day and I thought that this would cheer you up." He said.

"Well, you have succeeded in cheering me up, but bringing me back from the dead? Not so much!" I smiled, he laughed a bit at my joke. "Hurry back here with my chair, questions will be raised if they don't find me in my room in the morning!" I said, shooing him away.

When he came back I had nodded off to sleep, he shook me gently and helped me into my chair. He covered me up with my thick fur blanket and gave me a pillow to cuddle on the way back.

The next morning I woke up and wondered how I got back into my bed. Sr'eya came bustling in with breakfast, smiling and humming.

"You look happy this morning, anything you want to share?" I smiled and teased.

"Well, actually, yes,there is!" She was positively beaming! "We are almost ready to try on your dress for your birthday banquet!!" She said, a huge smile broke out on her face. "Eat your breakfast and we will get started on the last minute fitting so I can hem it and make the adjustments that need to be made." She said.

I rolled my eyes and did as she asked, ate my eggs and porridge silently, sullenly. This banquet was not my idea, and I did not like it. I wanted nothing to do with large crowds of people laughing at how ugly I am now.

After I ate breakfast I saw the servants door to my room open just slightly, two eyes peeked in and then the door closed and he was gone. It wasn't until after lunch that I could finally escape my rooms and go with Eir'im'uhs. This time we didn't forget my chair.

"Sorry about earlier!" I blurted out.

"Well, I guess now we know why you didn't have exercises today!" Eir'im'uhs laughed easily. I laughed with him. He brought me to the door and went and placed his hand over the wall, the wall gave way and opened into our secret room. This time I was able to take it all in.

"Wow, this place is really something!" I exclaimed.

"Yeah, it is. Your mum built it, compelled it into being. The walls of the room have maj'ick deep within them, bits of your mum really. You see, when a compeller compels something, they leave some of their maj'ick behind in the thing that they compelled."

"Fascinating!" I said, "You have really done your research!" I complimented him.

"Well, to be honest my knowledge didn't come from this last week, I have been coming here since I could walk. I accidentally stumbled across it when I was three, I ran away from my nanny and put my hand on the wall in an attempt to catch my breath, I looked down on the floor and the wall gave way, I literally tumbled head first into the room!" He said, I laughed with him at this. "Ever since then I have been coming here to read and escape..." There was a dark look that crossed his eyes as he said that. Something about his face told me not to press the conversation.

"Well, let's have a look at that book you found!" I said, excited to look at the family tree again. "You said something about my father, but I cannae remember what it was that you said." I said.

"Your da' was Fae! He was the crown prince of A'va'lon! You are half Fae, half human!" His eyes blazed like a wildfire as he told me of this bit of news.

"Wait, half Fae? But that's never been heard of before!" I said, confused, and trying to remember something that was tickling the back of my mind. "I had a dream one night, and in that dream I was told that I was the key to the survival of Nah'alba, that without me, the whole kingdom devours itself until there is not a single living creature on it." I said suddenly. I looked at Eir'im'uhs and then went into deeper details of the dream.

"That's amazing, Ary! Not everyone has the ability to see a possible future like that, and then come back from it and still be okay!" He looked at me like I was a goddess.

"Well, I wasn't okay, not for a few days. Uncle A'lbi'on said that I was just staring into space all white and cold as ice for almost two days before they woke me up again." I shivered at the memory.

"Are you cold?" He asked immediately.

"No, just thinking about that memory makes me shiver." I said.

"Well, that's incredible. I wonder what started the war?"

He asked.

"I donna know, but whatever it was, it had to have been pretty big, huh?" I said.

"Ary, what if it was your death that triggered that ten year war?" He wondered.

I sat quietly, outlining the tree and the words absentmindedly for a few minutes thinking about what he had said, "Yes, I suppose that would make sense for what the voice told me. It would all line up and match the time lines." I said thoughtfully.

Eir'im'uhs and I spent nearly every waking moment together after that, we went all over the castle exploring, he'd take me to a new place that I had not been to before and tell me about all the people who used to come here and stay in the rooms. He and I would go into the kitchens and steal food, and get into trouble with the cooks. When I was with him, I got stronger, healthier, and my color started coming back. My stamina became better, and it was not long before I didn't need my physicians every day.

Uncle A'lbi'on came to visit me in the gardens a few days before my birthday.

"Hello little one! Enjoying your time out here?" He asked me, a smile playing on his face.

"Aye, uncle! It is so beautiful and so peaceful out here!" I said, almost laughing.

"Aye, yer mother used to say the same thing. She would spend hours out here, reading and planting and weeding and gossiping with her ladies in waiting." He smiled at the reflected memory.

I smiled sadly, wishing that I could remember more about them, "Did you need something, Uncle?" I asked pleasantly, not wanting to sound rude, but he was interrupting the little alone time I did get.

"Aye, I had something I wish to discuss with you about your cousin, Eir'im'uhs." His face turned serious and I felt the color drain from my face.

How did he know about Eir'im'uhs and I?!

. "First off, I want to say thank you, these last few months have not been easy on him, with everything going on with his mother, and you have really lifted his spirits high."

"Wait, so yer not mad?" I asked, still waiting for the anger.

"No! The second thing I wanted to talk to you about is, how would you feel about Eir'im'uhs being your escort for your birthday banquet?"

"Escort?" I asked, confused.

"It is a tradition that every young lady of court has an escort for a birthday or coronation, and I was hoping that you would accept Eir'im'uhs as your escort?" He asked, eyes cautious, hopeful.

"What does Eir'im'uhs think about this?" I asked.

"He doesn't know yet, I wanted to make sure that you were okay with it before I spoke to him about it." The sound of footsteps made him look up, "Ach, speaking of the devil himself, Eir'im'uhs, my boy!" He said, eyes twinkling.

"I came to ask A'lari'jah a question, but if this is a bad time, I can come back." He said timidly.

"Not at all, my boy, not at all, ask away!" Uncle A'lbi'on said.

"Ary, I was wondering ... well ... That is to say ... " He was wringing his hands in front of him, he came around the front of me and got down on one knee, "It would be my honor if you would accept me as your escort for your birthday ball?" He looked from me to his father who gave him a nod of approval, pride written all over his face, and back to me again.

"I graciously accept." I said, not knowing the formalities of court or accepting something like this. My words had the effect I had hoped they would, Eir'im'uhs ears went bright pink and his chest puffed out, his face beamed with pride and excitement.

"I shall coordinate with yer servants on colors." Eir'im'uhs said, nodding his head and turned to walk away.

"Well, I am feeling rather useless at the moment." He said, trying to sound disappointed, but his face still shone with pride for his son.

"Well, you useless person you, I need a hand getting back inside for my therapy sessions, if you wouldn't mind?" I teased. He smiled and he pushed me back to my room where my physician was waiting for me.

"It's about time! I thought that you were skipping out on me today!" He smiled his jolly smile and we got to work on my exercises.

"I am sorry that I was late today, my Uncle and cousin had a surprise for me about my birthday ball. My cousin came to ask if he could be my escort." I blushed at saying it out loud.

"Did he indeed?" My physician asked slyly.

"Wait, what does that mean?" I asked curious. When he refused to answer, I refused to do my therapy until he told me what he meant.

"Well, to tell yer the truth, mistress, begging yer pardon if things have changed over the time I have been at court, but back in yer mother's day, if a lady was escorted to a ball or a coronation, it meant that the two were betrothed. Yer mother's coronation day she only had her ladies in waiting because yer mum didn't have any suitors come callin'." He told me, looking slightly abashed at his forwardness.

"Wait, are you saying that my Uncle is wanting me to marry Eir'im'uhs??" I asked, shocked.

"Could be. Or it could be that yer still weak and yeh'll be needin' some extra help walking the long aisle through the great hall. Could be both, yeh'd need to be speakin' to summat else about that mistress, I don't know everythin', mind." He said, sounding unsure of why he'd just spilled the truth like that.

"SR'EYA!" I yelled as loud as I could, making my physician jump.

Sr'eya came running in, "Yes, Lass, what is it?" She asked, red in the face huffing and puffing.

"Tell me what you know about my escort and the reason behind it." I demanded.

"Well, the king and I think that you and Eir'im'uhs would make a good match, so we thought it would be good for you to have an escort, extra support to help yeh walk and all, but also some moral support for walking through the crowd." When she got done talking she looked at me suspiciously. "Why did I just tell you all of that?!" She demanded.

"What do you mean?" I asked innocently.

"A'lari'jah Jayd, answer me and answer me true, why did I just tell you all of that?!" She demanded me again.

"I asked a question, and you answered me honest and true, I am confused, where is there something wrong with that?" I asked, a strange kind of authority ringing in my voice.

"Now you listen here young lady, you will not talk to me thus! You will treat me with respect and dignity." She was now red in the face with anger.

"Oh, okay, so I am supposed to treat you with respect when you just flat out admitted to me that you had planned on lying to me about this?" I demanded.

"Well, that does seem a bit unreasonable, doesn't it? Look, just watch yer tone of voice, that's all I am saying." She said, again baffled at why she was spilling her most blunt truths at her. "Well, I have a dress to be gettin' on with, and yer poor physician is frightened." She said, ending the conversation as she turned around and walked out the door.

"Well, I will just have to have a conversation with my uncle about this!" I said in a huff. I crossed my arms across my chest and sat with a sullen look on my face.

"Beggin' yer pardon, mistress?" My physician asked.

I jumped, I had forgotten that he was there. "Yes, what is it?" I asked crossly.

"Er.. Well, permission to speak bluntly?" He asked me.

"You may always speak bluntly to me, good sir." I said, more gently.

"Well … er … Beggin' yer pardon again, miss, but I think

that if you do speak to yer uncle about this, yeh might wanna consider not poutin' when yeh do." He said, a smile tempting the corner of his mouth.

I smiled with him and we laughed loudly, relieving the tension in the room. I was done for the day, and he was massaging me down as he always did when he asked me a curious question. "Mistress?"

"Hmm?" I said, so relaxed that I could drift into sleep.

"Would it be so bad?" He asked me.

"Would what be so bad?" I asked, confused.

"You and Eir'im'uhs?"

"What do you mean by that?" I asked, a little bit of tension in my body.

"Well, it's just, it makes sense ... the things that you have both been through, you can help each other through the dark days. You both have been light for each other, and you would be good together." He said, I rolled over to look at his face, and there was nothing but kindness and wisdom in his eyes.

"Perhaps there is something to that. I am not a child, and I will not be left out of such important information such as this. I don't wanna be kept out of the loop, this is my life, and I have the right to know!" I said fiercely.

"No un's disagreein' there little missy, not at all, they should be tellin' you important stuff like 'at." He said, agreeing with me.

"I will find Uncle A'lbi'on when we are done here and have a conversation about me being kept in the dark." I said decidedly.

When my physician had left I got my walking stick and made my way to my uncle. I found him in the gardens, "Hello, Uncle." I said.

"Oh! Hello Ary! What brings you out here? It's not time for you to be here yet?" He asked.

"No, It's not, I am sorry if I am interrupting, I know that you dona like to be disturbed when you , I came looking for you, just followed the trail of guards and found you easily enough." I laughed.

"What can I do for you little one?" He asked.

"May we sit? I have some things I'd like to discuss with you." I said diplomatically.

"Of course, come, sit." He was polite but confused.

"Uncle, I know that I am not yet thirteen years, but I would appreciate you to be honest with me, straight forward, not hiding things and keeping things from me." I said politely.

"Okay, I understand that. May I ask what things I am keeping from you?" He asked.

"Today I found out that you and Sr'eya have thought that Eir'im'uhs and I would / will make a good match." I said, accusingly. "I found out that the reason a lady of the court would have an escort is if they are betrothed to each other. Is this the truth?" I demanded, that strange ring of authority in my voice now.

Uncle A'lbi'on looked startled at me, "Yes, traditionally, it is correct." He said, anger flashed in his eyes, he closed them and took a breath, when he looked at me again, there was no anger, "Why do you ask this?"

"Because I want to know if that is the reason yer having Eir'im'uhs escort me on my birthday?" I asked, "Traditionally, the people will see this as a statement, one that I am not sure of yet." I said.

"A'lari'jah, first off, I came to you to ask you these things, and I didn't get the chance to explain everything. If I may, I would like to rewind, and start this again?" He asked.

"Okay, I am all ears." I said shrugging, annoyed that he hadn't answered my question.

"A'lari'jah, it is tradition for a young lady of court to have an escort on big events such as birthday banquets or coronation balls. Now, again, traditionally, this escort would be a young male that the king and queen would have arranged to be a suitor for the young princess. Now it is well known, what happened to your family in the fire, and a lot of folks don't believe that you're still alive. The crown pouring in is a large crowd and, while I think that one day you and Eir'im'uhs might make a fine match, I don't want you to face that large crowd alone. And Eir'im'uhs is about the right height to talk with you and help support your weight better than I, I would only make the walk more painful and awkward with your current ability to stand." He said, his words rang true, and I smiled at him, tears brimming my eyes.

"I am sorry, Uncle, I was given wrong information. Please forgive my rudeness?" I said.

"There is nothing to forgive, I would feel the same way. Ary, I know that you are no ordinary girl of twelve, on the eve of her thirteenth birthday, I know that you have strength enough to carry this with you, and strength enough for me to always be honest and open with you about everything. I will not hide anything from you, unless it is to protect your life." He pulled me into a hug and Sr'eya came bursting into the gardens red faced and angry again.

"What do you think yer doin'? Running off without any word as to where yeh'd gone! I've been looking everywhere for yeh! Had me worried sick yeh did!" she huffed and puffed and gulped for air.

"Beggin' yer pardon, yer majesty." She said, realizing who was sitting next to me.

"Sr'eya, I wonder where A'lari'jah would have gotten the impression that we were matching her and Eir'im'uhs together? I wonder why she would have thought that was why he was escorting her to her birthday banquet?" Uncle A'lbi'on asked, eyeing her carefully.

"I ... uh ... well ... I may have gotten the wrong impression, sire. I beg your forgiveness." She stuttered, wringing her hands anxiously.

"Do not let it happen again, if I want A'lari'jah to know something, she will know it, and if you try to *poison* the truth again, I'll have you flogged, you hear me?" Uncle A'lbi'on said fiercely. "You may be her legal guardian, but I am your king, and she is my niece. I will hire my own lawyers and get that fixed right away. Do I make myself clear?" Uncle A'lbi'on barked.

"Aye, yer majesty. Crystal clear." She bowed low and backed out of his presence.

"If she does that again, I want to know. From now on, all information that deals with you in any capacity will be run by you. Is there anything else you wish to discuss?" He asked me.

"Yes, can we just cancel the banquet?" I asked, wrinkling up my face like something smelled bad.

He laughed and tapped his finger on my nose. "You know we cannae do that. The people need to see their princess alive and well, because that is truly what you are, their princess. You know, you are next in line for the throne, right?" He asked me.

"What about Eir'im'uhs?" I asked.

"Eir'im'uhs is a bastard, and either way, your mother was the first born of my father, which makes you next in line." He advised me.

"Actually, doesn't that make me the rightful ruler of the kingdom? By default, I mean." I asked, trying to sound curious about how that all worked.

"Yes, actually, it does. You have been doing some research haven't you?" He asked, his eyes flashed darkly a hint of severe possessiveness behind his look.

"Well, I don't think I am ready for that, hold on to it for me, would ya? Until I am ready?" I said, relief was written all over his face; it was clear that he did not want to give up his throne for me.

"Aye, little lady, I will keep it safe for you." He smiled and ruffled my hair gently.

Chapter Four

At dawn on the day of my thirteenth birthday banquet, the gates were opened and all of the noble ladies and men were admitted into the castle. Although the banquet did not start until that evening, the nobility were always brought in early, fed breakfast and lunch before they admitted the common folk. The common folk were allowed into the ballroom and the great hall to mix and mingle with the nobility during these events, but were always admitted last. Of the common folk, only the ones that were dressed nice enough were allowed inside the castle. Last but not least, those who were of good stock but did not have the appropriate attire, the servants would bring them into the opposite side of the castle and allow them to pick from the "rags" that the nobles always brought with them, it was their way of giving back to the people. When the rags ran out, so did the common folk, for those who were not dressed nice enough were fed and sent on their way with a month's supply of food, hygiene and other essentials that they might need.

I was fascinated at the going on of the castle today. I dressed in a simple day gown and joined my uncle in welcoming the Lords and Ladies into the great hall, where we would soon sit down to break our fast together. About a hundred of the noble Lord's and Lady's passed by, each bowing to the king, and the king nodding his head in return, I curtseyed everytime he would introduce me, as best as I could, and smiled sweetly. Many of them had known my mother and passed their condolences to me, while others told me how much I reminded them of her. Uncle A'lbi'on was kind and pleasant with the families of the great houses that swore fealty to him, but he was stiff and guarded and only as pleasant and polite as customs dictated him to be.

When the last of the noble houses had entered the great hall, Uncle A'lbi'on escorted me through the crowd and up to the large rectangle table at the head of the great hall. The table was lifted up on a platform so that we could be seen by all, and so that we could see all. I was seated at Uncle's right hand, Eir'im'uhs at his left. Silence fell across the hall as Uncle A'lbi'on raised his hands to say a few words before we sat down to eat.

"First off, welcome back to Nah'alba, noble Lords and Lady's! How good it is to see your beautiful faces in the great halls of this empty castle again! For too long, I had closed off our walls to you, but never again will Nah'alba be closed to you! I am opening trade with anyone who would like to begin trading with us again. I open up our borders for anyone who would like to come and visit us. As long as everyone remembers, maj'ick is forbidden here, then we will all get along splendidly.

Today is a celebration for my niece! The lone survivor of her family, today she turns twelve! Please join me in wishing her a long and healthy life!"

He raised his glass and the crowd shouted, "LONG LIVE PRINCESSES A'LARI'JAH!" several times before falling silent again.

"Let the feasts begin!" As Uncle A'lbi'on shouted this, the servants began dishing food out amongst the crowd, starting at the great doors working their way towards the great table we sat at.

"Uncle, why do they call me their princess?" I asked, "Is it common knowledge that Eir'im'uhs isn't yours?" I asked again.

"No, dear child, it is common knowledge that you are the daughter of my eldest sister." He said, eyes twinkling in the candle light.

My brow creased in confusion, "But aren't you worried

about an uprising? A rebellion?" I asked again.

"No, little one, for as long as you are here, by my side, taking part in the negotiations and taking part in the things that happen, they will be happy that you are learning matters of state so that one day, when the time comes, you can take your rightful place. In their eyes, you were robbed of the opportunity to be who you are because your mother and father refused to allow you to come foster with me." He said gently.

I nodded my understanding, but some things just weren't lining up, they didn't make sense. I dropped the matter for now, I would discuss these things with Eir'im'uhs later, and I would have to have a conversation with Sr'eya too, but for now, I tried to enjoy my banquet. The food was exquisite, the best I'd ever had. Of course, until now, I was on a strict diet of proteins and calories to ensure that I got every ounce of strength I could get.

When the breakfast feast was over, Eir'im'uhs escorted me into the crowd to mingle and get to know my subjects. He took me around the room twice before he pulled me out of the great doors and into the main hallway.

"Come with me, I have something I think that you would enjoy." He said, smiling brightly. He led me off towards my mother's rooms, but instead of going into the rooms, he took me into the smaller of the two great halls that the castle had. There the tables were lined with beautiful clothes and dresses and shoes.

"What is all this?" I asked him.

"These are the rags that the nobles bring with them for the commoners that have nothing nice to wear, to change into for the banquet. Every time my father throws a banquet, he requires that the nobles bring all the clothes that they no longer wear, all the clothes their children or grandchildren never wear any more. We have never had so many clothes brought to a feast before. We think it's because it has been many years since the nobles were invited here. They must have been saving their clothes all this time, some of them had entire carriages stuffed full of old clothes they never wear anymore." Eir'im'uhs explained.

"And the nobles are okay with this?" I asked, baffled that they would be so generous.

"They aren't given a choice but to be okay with this. Father always believes that the best way to rule his people is by treating them every now and again. He will throw another big feast at Christmas, and many of the noble families will bring home made dresses and clothes for the common folk. Father's attitude towards his people has become infectious, and the nobles used to really get behind this." He smiled.

"Eir'im'uhs, was it just me or did everyone seem to be a bit on edge in there?" I asked.

"Aye, they did that. It has been many years since many of them have been here, and many of them are the children of the noble families that used to come. Most of them took it as a great personal offense that Father closed the borders and shut himself off in Nah'alba for so long." Eir'im'uhs explained. "Father went a bit mad before he finally found Auntie G'rai'ce, he closed the borders and refused to allow anyone enter or leave Nah'alba, because he didn't want Auntie G'rai'ce to get away from here. And many of the great houses lost a lot of good business and a lot of ships because of it. See, Nah'alba was the halfway point between where they are coming from, to where they are going. Many of the ships that ported here did so to ensure the safety and wellbeing of their crews and passengers. When they were no longer allowed their week-long stay, the crews and passengers got sick and they had to burn their ships and all cargo on them. Many of the great houses lost fortunes in the years that Father closed off the borders to them." Eir'im'uhs said.

"Ach, now I understand." I said, my confusion lifting.

"Come this way, milady, unless you want to be trampled." He said, "The commoners are about to be herded in here for their clothes." He told me, as he ushered me forward to the front of the room.

The great doors opened and lots of doe eyed people came inside, marveling at the sight that met their eyes.

"Right this way! Now, mind yer manners, and don't be stingy! There's plenty of this lot to go 'round! Take yer time, and try things on, our seamstresses are on standby for any adjustments that need to be made! Be patient and take yer time! OI! Listen up!" A maid-servant was screaming at the crowd of people. "Now, anyone found pushing, pulling, spitting, biting, kicking, or otherwise causing disruptions will be escorted out of the castle empty handed! If you all mind yer manners, and be kind ta one another, yeh'll get to go to the banquet tonight!" She said, "Alright, slowly make yer way to the tables, childrens clothes are to my right, adult clothes to my left, mens straight down the middle!" She stood aside and allowed the crowd to come inside.

Excited as they were, the people were very civilized and kind to each other. If someone ooed and awed over a dress or pants suit that someone else was holding, they offered it to that person. I was amazed at how calm they all were, I watched in awe for a long time until I was interrupted.

"Ahem " someone cleared their throat close to me. "Begging your pardon mistress, but, would you be so kind as to help me find me mum?"

I looked down and there before me was a small girl with yellow hair, wearing a beautiful white ball gown, I smiled at her, "Of course, what is her name?" I asked.

"My mum's name's Charlene." She said,

"And what is your name?"

She blushed and shuffled her feet a bit, "Amy" she said quietly.

"Well Amy, my name is Ary." I held out my hand for her, "My friend and I will help you find yer mum, okay? Donna fash yerself, she's here somewhere." I assured her. I turned to Eir'im'uhs who escorted me around the room while I listened to the thoughts of the minds around me. Finally, when we got close to the seamstresses, I heard a frantic mother's thoughts looking for her child. I began to call out, "Charlene? Is there a Charlene here?"

She came running towards the sound of my voice, looking scared and frantic at the same time. Spotting the small child holding my hand, she ran to me and embraced me. "Bless you, chid, bless you!" tears streamed down her face as she scooped up her daughter. "How can I ever repay your kindness, child?" she asked, and then seeing my face for the first time she went straight to one knee.

"Please, don't do that, stand up!" I said to her trying to get her to stand before other people saw, but it was too late, soon every single person was kneeling, heads bowed. I heard a child in the room saying "Mummy, what are we doing?" The mother replied, "It is customary to bow or kneel before royalty." Not knowing what to do, I looked to Eir'im'uhs for support, for help, anything.

"You may rise." He spoke to the whole room, "Please, continue your search, we are here only to mingle and help." He said kindly. The whole room rose and went back to their searching, whispers broke out amongst them all.

"Shall we go and meet your people, milady?" Eir'im'uhs asked me. I nodded and allowed him to lead me around and introduce me to the people. We spoke and visited with all of them, some of them twice.

It was clear that the people thought that she had been cheated, that they believed that she should have been making her way to the throne long before now. It was clear that they thought that my mother had been cheated, many of them still hated my uncle for running her out of the castle.

"He just wanted the throne to himself, his father was dying and his sister was weak, so he took the first opportunity to seize the throne!"

"He didn't even go looking for her, not for years after he was on the throne. Then he went mad and closed us off to the trade that once made us a great kingdom! We who used to be wealthy are now poor and reduced to rags, begging and living in the woods because our homes are unfit to live in."

The complaints went on and on, in great detail, my heart hurt for my people and I longed to soothe them, "Listen, the king and I are going to be in negotiations over the next few months getting the trade opened back up again. He has sent invitations to all the great houses and tradesmen from all over the world, and they will be staying here until we have signed contracts with them. We will make Nah'alba great again, just be patient and give us some time." When I spoke, the whole room went silent, the servants nodded in approval and Eir'im'uhs gave my arm a light encouraging squeeze. "Now, as far as your complaints about my Uncle and my mother, let bygones be bygones, let the past rest in the past where it belongs. A'lbi'on is your king, and no matter his transgressions, he has never been unkind to you. A bit foolish perhaps, but never unkind. Look around you! A'lbi'on is the one who set this up for you, so that everyone would be allowed to join the celebrations today! I have heard your complaints, and I promise to look into each and every one of them!" I told the crowd of faces, they all looked at me like I was their savior. "A'lbi'on is the king, and he will remain your king for many years yet, be kind to him and show him your forgiveness." I pleaded with them.

Later when Eir'im'uhs and I excused ourselves so I could go get ready for the banquet, he turned and looked at me with adoration in his eyes, "When you spoke to them, you sounded like a true leader. You listened to their complaints, you gave them hope and you still pledged loyalty to Father. He would have been so proud of you!" Pride gleamed in his eyes as he left me at my room door, I was blushing crimson.

"Little lady, you have done well today!" Sr'eya beamed at me.

I wrinkled my brow, confused, "What do you mean?" I asked.

"I was in the hall with you and Eir'im'uhs helping the

people find clothes to wear, I heard the words you spoke, and so did your uncle. He left beaming with pride, he said 'she will be a great ruler someday'." She smiled brightly at me as she began lifting my dress off of me. "Come soak in this hot water and salts, it will help ease your aches and make you ready for the banquet later. I will be back in a while to help you out and get you dressed." She said as she helped me into the soaking tub.

The hot water felt good, the steam from the water made my face sweat and cleansed my nose of all the strange smells from the day. I relaxed into the water and soon my eyes closed and I drifted into a peaceful nap. Sometime later Sr'eya barked orders to someone, making me jump.

"Ary, time to get dressed, the banquet starts in two hours and we have lots of work to do before then! Your uncle wants you as early as we can get you there." Sr'eya came over and sat me up, washed my hair with honey and lavender, helped me out of the tub and dried me off.

I spent the better part of the next hour being stuffed into stockings, leggings, girdles and petticoats, until they finally had me so bogged down that I could barely move. Sr'eya took my arm and led me to a mirror, I took one step on my bad leg and cried out in pain.

"It's too heavy for me!" I told her frantically, "GET IT OFF!" I shouted. Frantic hands worked quickly to relieve me of the weight of the hoop.

"The dress will work without the hoop, we will put on her a soft lightweight skirt and leggings to keep her legs from chafing." Sr'eya said as the other girls went to work in taking off the girdle and the stockings, leaving me in a thin silk night dress and leggings that compressed my legs just enough to relieve the pain of standing on them. Next came the dress, a large frilly purple and green dress with no sleeves, it was a modest covering of sheer lace over my chest up to my collar bone, with frilly lace of sheer purple and green flowing off the shoulders down to my elbows. I smiled at it, it was beautiful and flattering to me. My eyes, which were turning a darker shade of violet, popped vividly in the dress.

"Ladies, thank you for your help, I will take over from here." Sr'eya said, shooting the servants out the door and locking the door behind them. "Do you like it, lass?" Sr'eya asked.

"No..." I told her, her face fell for an instant, I smiled big and said, "I love it! It's so beautiful!" I hugged her tightly. "Thank you!" I whispered in her ear.

"Well, there is no point in denying who you are, so you might as well embrace it as best as we can without giving too much away. The purple in yer eyes comes from yer mum, she had the most brilliant violet eyes I ever saw! Even as a child her eyes were shocking!" Sr'eya beamed. "Now, I'll do some coloring on yer face, just to even out the colors, and to make your eyes pop even more, sit still and move when I tell yeh to and I'll be done in a few minutes." She said, beckoning me over to a bench. Sr'eya sat down in front of me and began brushing on different pallets of color onto my face.

When she got done, I looked in the mirror, my face was flawless, my freckles still peeked through, but the blemishes and redness from the fire were no longer on my face. I marveled at her work, I looked as I had before the fire had scared my face. I smiled and tears shone in my eyes.

"No crying now! You'll ruin my artwork!" Sr'eya said with tears of her own in her eyes. "Now, let's do yer hair, and get yeh to the great hall!" She said smiling, beckoning me to sit on the bench once more. "I made yer dress in the colors of yer clan." Sr'eya told me, "Eir'im'uhs came to me and asked me if I would make yer dress in these colors, he said that yer mum's house color was green, and yer da's was purple. He said that yer dress should have a cream backing to it, and the colors should be done of sheer lace in whisps to resemble a willow tree's branches that sweep the ground beneath it." Sr'eya explained the design of the dress. "When I asked him why, he said that you would understand and said nothing more on the subject, except that he would be here one hour before the feast to escort yeh to the great hall." She looked as if she would explode with pride and happiness.

"Eir'im'uhs has proved to be a good friend to me these last months, I am very grateful for his friendship." I said.

"Would it be so bad if he was offering more 'n just friendship, Ary?" She asked me kindly.

"No, I suppose not, but I am not ready to think of those things just yet. I have so much happening right now, I donnae have room in my heart or my head to consider such things." I said truthfully.

"Ary, you cannae dwell on this sadness forever, one day you will wake up and find that the world has moved on and left you behind if yer not careful." She told me, her voice thick with emotion, eyes motherly.

"I know, Sr'eya, I know. I am trying to move past it, but the grief is still so fresh in my heart, it is like a gaping wound that gushes blood everywhere all the time. I fear that I will bleed dry if it doesna stop soon!" I confessed.

"I know it does, little one, but I promise you, it does get easier to carry this burden of grief." She said, a sadness shone in her eyes so brightly that I was taken aback.

"You've lost loved ones, haven't you?" I said suddenly.

"Ach, many of them, I watched my whole tribe being butchered right after A'lbi'on decreed that all maj'ick was outlawed, before we were able to go into hiding. The humans, guards and mercenaries alike, hunted us down deep into the forest and slaughtered my whole tribe. My family died, and what was left of us, children, were taken into captivity as servants, we were sold to the highest bidder and worked until we were allowed freedom. Many of us worked our whole lives for our master's while the rest of us were bought by a fair and kind owner. After we worked for twenty years, educated and learned different trades, we were freed and sent off into the world in our human disguises. My husband, Jhona, lost his tongue because he was accused of lying, the punishment for lying was to lose a tongue." She said sadly. "I have seen many deaths, and I have had my fair share of troubles. I know for a fact that if you just stop, then the world will keep spinning and yuh'll be left behind, begging for whatever scraps yeh can get, until one day you pick yerself up, dust yerself off and move on." She told me, wisdom shining in her eyes.

I nodded my understanding to her and we slipped into a comfortable sort of silence. Her experienced hands braided my hair and left strips of it out here and there to make it look like my dress, with wisps of hair falling like a willow tree down my face on both sides. When she was done there was a deft knock on the door. I suddenly felt very nervous, my hands began to shake. Sr'eya took hold of my hands and smiled kindly at me.

"Take courage, child, you have already met everyone, now you get to go show off for them all." She said.

When she opened the door, there stood Eir'im'uhs, handsome, in a suit with a light green shirt underneath it, and a lilac pocket chief in his breast pocket. He smiled warmly at me and offered his arm. I stood and accepted his arm, grateful for the calm that washed over me when I did.

"You look stunning tonight, milady!" He exclaimed "Do you like your dress?" He asked quietly.

"I love it! Did you see that she did my hair in the same manner?" I asked.

"Yes, that was a nice touch. You know what the willow tree stands for right?" He asked me.

"I have an idea, but I am not quite sure." I admitted.

"There is a myth, if you will, that whenever the descendents of your father come in contact with a willow tree, they will find strength and refuge beneath its sweeping limbs." He said. "Which is why I have brought this for you." He said as he held up a beautifully intricately designed walking staff with a big flat top for her to wrap her hand around comfortably. "I had it fashioned from a willow branch for you."

"Wow, that's incredible; and this, I'm awe struck, it's such a beautiful staff, Eir'im'uhs! Thank you so much! How can I ever repay your kindness?" I told him, giving him a long embrace.

"Do you know that my father and Sr'eya are making plans for you to leave the castle for the next year?" He asked me, a pained look shot through his eyes.

"For the whole year?!" I asked a little louder than I expected. The eyes of the guards and servants in the hallway turned to look at us. We smiled and nodded our heads and waited to resume our conversation until we were out of that hallway.

"Yes, for the whole year." He said, "Apparently Sr'eya believes that you are strong enough to travel, she would like to take you down to her home and introduce you to her family. She has a friend down there that practices alternative medicine and she thinks he might be able to help you with your leg more than the traditional physicians can, she says that you are now beyond their ability to help you." He told me, our pace slowing so that we could discuss this before entering the banquet.

"What sort of 'alternative medicine' does this person practice?" I asked, incredulous.

"I am assuming that it will have some maj'ick involved, but she also said that he can help you heal inside too, the pain and the grief that you carry with you can be helped and that the sooner you get some help with that healing the better. She said for father to think of him as a guide in the darkness, to help guide your path back to the light again." He told me, "Sr'eya is very concerned about this dark cloud that is lingering over you, and quite frankly so is everyone else." He told me, face turning serious.

"Well, I won't go!" I stamped my foot stubbornly.

"But, you must, Ary! You need the help, and if he can heal your wound and help you walk better, then it's a risk you must take!" He pleaded with me, fear and sincerity shone in his eyes. "Ary, go with them and get better and return to us healthy and strong! Please? If not for Father, then for me?" He begged, tears started collecting in his eyes and spilling over.

I reached out and wiped away his tears, "This is no time to be crying! It's my birthday! And if it makes you feel better, I will agree to go with her." I told him, the pain in his eyes eased at once, and he smiled again.

"Come one then, we have a banquet to crash!" He led me forward into the banquet hall.

Just inside the doors we stopped and waited, the announcer banged his large golden staff on the floor three times and the whole room went silent.

"The Crown Prince Eir'im'uhs and Her Royal Highness, Princess A'lari'jah!"

Eir'im'uhs led me forward slowly, A'lari'jah could hear gasps and whispers break out amongst the people as they admired her beautiful dress or commented on her eyes.

"But her eyes! They are exactly like her mothers!" The crowd speculated what that might mean.

"Yes, but her dress is absolutely gorgeous!" others said.

By the time we reached Uncle A'lbi'on, my face was scarlet, Uncle A'lbi'on nodded his head as I attempted a curtsey. He smiled and beckoned me to sit, this time I sat on his left, with Eir'im'uhs on my right.

The night was splendid, many people asked to dance with me, which I refused, explaining that I could not dance with my leg the way it is. I smiled and graciously accepted their birthday wishes and gifts that they brought me. The food was exquisite and the wine was the best in the land. By midnight I was feeling very tipsy and very drowsy. I reached for a fifth goblet of wine but was intercepted by Eir'im'uhs.

"Father, I think I will escort Milady back to her rooms, she needs her rest." He said, face was red with wine himself.

Uncle A'lbi'on stood up and announced that I would be going to bed now, as I still tired easily and needed to get some rest. Eir'im'uhs then stood and offered me his arm again, I stood unsteadily and leaned heavily on Eir'im'uhs. The world spinned out of control and I swayed and nearly fell over. Uncle A'lbi'on still had his hand on my arm and steadied me without anyone else knowing what had happened.

Uncle A'lbilon leaned close and whispered to Eir'im'uhs "Take her out the back way, don't lead her through the people, no need to embarrass her like that." He kissed my forehead and Eir'im'uhs led me behind the table into the servants' halls where my wheelchair was waiting for me. He sat me gently down in it, and arranged my dress so that it wouldn't drag the floor or get caught up in the wheels, laid a heavy blanket over me and returned me to my rooms, where the rest of the night was a blur.

The next morning I woke up late, breakfast was sitting on the table in the middle of the room underneath the big windows. I blinked and pain shot through my head, I groaned, rolled over and vomited on the floor by my bed, rolled back over and buried my head under the blankets.

"Milady, it's time to wake up, it's past lunchtime and the king would like to see you. He's requested that we wake you up and feed you and make you presentable and bring you to see him." A young girl's voice said, making my head pound with every word she said.

"Tell him I'm sick." I groaned. She pulled the blanket off of my head, the light hit my eyes again and I rolled over and vomited again. The girl went running from my room, remarkably light on her feet. Several minutes later Sr'eya came in, pulled back the curtains to keep the light out of my eyes and pulled the blankets back.

"Come one princess, it's time to get up." She said.

I opened my eyes and a pain shot through me again, I rolled over and vomited a third time, but this time I just heaved up nothing. "I won't get up. Leave me alone." I said miserably. I felt a hand on my forehead and a disembodied voice saying, "She's burning with fever!"

The next few days all went by in a haze of throwing up

and passing out and writhing in pain. Sr'eya was at a loss of what to do or what was wrong with me, and I was unable to tell them. In the end they loaded me up into a carriage and I was sent to see Sr'eya friend who practiced alternative meicine.

One look at me and he said, "She's got a bone infection." he tisked and muttered and began feeding me medicine that made me gag. The next several weeks were a blur of being gagged by his bad medicine and terrible pain wracking my whole body. I would scream bloody murder when the pain hit, unable to bite my tongue. Strong arms came and held me down and more nasty medicine was shoved in my mouth and forced down my throat. When the pain fit would subside, I would pass out again for an unknown amount of time and not wake again until the pain began next. Over time, the pain became less frequent and less intense until one day it was no more.

I opened my eyes and blinked around, my head was fuzzy, my vision blurred. I tried to remember where I was, but I did not know the strange place. I looked around for something or someone familiar, but found no one. I closed my eyes again and drifted into a restless sleep. I opened my eyes again and found a woman in white standing over me with her hand on my wrist and a chart in her hands.

"Hullo dearie!" she said cheerily, "Glad tuh see yuh awake! Yeh've been sleeping for nigh on two months now!" she said. I felt an uncomfortable stabbing in my right elbow crease, and I reached over to slap the bug that was biting me, but her hands stopped me, "Donna be messin' wit dat miss, dat is dere to make a-sure dat you dinna die on us. It is what has been keeping you fed and hydrated." She smiled kindly at me.

"Yer accent. Where is that from?" I asked.

"Jamaica, I'll go get de doctor. He'll wanna know dat yer awake." She smiled kindly at me and patted my arm, "Donna mess wit da needles while I'm gone." She reminded me, turned and walked away.

"Hello, A'lari'jah!" A cheery male voice made me jump, I looked around for the face that went with the voice and found an older man with a kind face walking up to me. He lifted me up gently and put pillows underneath me to help me sit up a bit. The simple motion of that made me dizzy and my stomach lurch dangerously.

"I am Sr'eya doctor friend who practices alternative medicines." He said, "You may call me doc." He introduced himself to me. "Miss A'lari'jah, you had a pretty severe bone infection when you got here, that was what was making you very sick." He said, "Do you understand what that means?" He asked, speaking to me in a voice that told me that he believed me to be ill in my head, like my disfigured body rendered my brain incapable of working too.

"Hey, Doc?" I said.

"Mm Hmm?" He responded.

"I may have been sick, but I'm not stupid." I replied.

"Great! You have just passed the first test on comprehension. Now, can you tell me your name?" He asked me, trying to conceal his embarrassing mistake as he quickly moved on.

I frowned, "A'lari'jah Jayd." I replied.

"Perfect. Can you tell me your age?"

"Twelve, I just turned twelve."

"Perfect, and now, tell me what the last thing is that you remember."

"Well, I remember at some point, over several occasions being woken up by some serious pain and getting gagged by medicine that tasted like a donkey's arse…" I responded, my sarcasm was not transferring well, Doc frowned at me. "Sorry Doc, it's my attempt at making a joke.." I said quickly.

"No, that's not it, I am just surprised that you have memories of that." He said, "Usually my patients do not remember anything between the time they get sick and the time they wake up, it's extraordinary that you do!" He explained.

"Well, before that I remember being in my room at my Uncle's the day after my birthday feast waking up and vomiting from the pain that was wracking my body. I remember they tried their best to make me get out of bed but I refused, every time I moved I was wracked with pain which caused me to throw up again." I told him, "I think they thought it was the leftover from my drinking so much wine the night before." Doc was studying me with intent fascination, "Did I say something wrong, Doc?" I asked.

"No, not at all, but you have the most extraordinary memory, young lady!" He said, " You speak with such clarity, it's uncanny." He remarked. "How are you feeling right now?"

"Well, my head is a bit off, kinda like being drunk, and my stomach is rolling with hunger, and I do have a slight headache."

"Yes, the drunk feeling will be gone within the next day, that's just all the pain medicine wearing off right now, we had to give you an unusually high dosage to help counter the pain, otherwise you would convulse and writhe and scream in pain. I had to move you into a private ward so that my other patients could rest." He explained it to me.

"I see, and when you say that it's uncanny, will you tell me what you mean by that?" I asked.

"It's just that, the pain medicine I gave you sometimes, in most cases, causes a person to not remember anything, and if they do remember, it's just blank, there is nothing there. But with you, it seems to have sharpened your mind and memories, that's incredible." He marveled, "Well, I have a few anxious guests who would like nothing more than to come and see you, shall I let them know that you are awake?" He asked me.

"Who all is here?"

"The king, Sr'eya, and the royal prince" He told me.

"I am not feeling well enough to visit, I just want to sleep for a while, will you tell them that I woke up, sat up for a minute and asked not to be bothered until my head stops swimming?" I asked him. He blanched at telling the king that, but nodded his head, helped me lay back down and left me alone again.

The silence of the ward was comforting, soothing, the birds outside chirped happily in the early summer warmth, the sun that filtered in the windows gave me strength and made me feel sleepy. I slept on and off for another two days before I was ready to even try to eat anything. It was three days before I could sit up without my head feeling like I had just gotten out of a dirt devil. When I was able to eat and keep my food down and sit up without feeling like I was going to throw up, I allowed visitors, one at a time.

Doc showed Uncle A'lbi'on in first.

I smiled as he walked toward my bed, "Hey there, you look terrible!" I teased.

"Yer one ta be talkin', little one!" He teased back. "You look as pale as a ghost right now!" He said, "All the color that you had on your birthday is gone now!" He said, sadly.

"Some of that color, especially later in the night, was the fever. I felt it come one after I got into the great hall for the evening banquet. I had hoped that if you thought I was just drunk you wouldn't make a big scene. I thought that I had just over done it, and my body was exhausted. Guess I was wrong." I told him.

He frowned at me and shook his head, "We came close to losing you on the way here." He told me, "I didn't listen to Sr'eya and move you the moment she told me to, I wanted her to make absolutely sure that there was nothing that she could do for you before we came here, and now I realize that in my waiting, I could have killed you." Sadness rolled off of him.

"Donna fash yerself, Uncle. Things happened the way they did for a reason, donna fash yerself over it." I told him, "I am alive and that is all that matters, Uncle." I reached out and squeezed his hand, "Will ya send in the other two please? I wanna see them before I take a nap, and I'm ready to take a nap." I laughed lightly.

"Sure, honey, I'll send them right in. Get some rest, and feel better soon!" He said as he stood and left the ward. A few minutes later Sr'eya and Eir'im'uhs came in and sat down beside me.

"Does he know?" I asked Sr'eya darkly.

Confused, she asked, "Explain."

"Doc, does he know who I am?" I asked again.

"I diddna tell him, and I am the only one who would have told him." she said.

I nodded my head, "Keep him in the dark about who I am, it could be very dangerous for me if he were to know who I am." I told her.

"What do you mean by that?" She asked me.

I explained to her my conversation with Doc and then said, "There was a look in his eyes that said that he would love nothing more than to get inside my mind and figure out how it works." I told them.

"I see, well, I would say that I trust him wholly, but I really don't. I only brought you here because you were dying and I didn't know what to do for yeh." Sr'eya said.

"So, this wasn't the plan all along then?" I asked darkly.

"What do yeh mean by that child?"

"I mean, was this yer doin' to get me to come to your home?" I asked plainly.

"No! Admittedly, Doc was a cover at that time, I had no intention of bringing you to him, I had another friend in mind to take yeh to." she told me.

"Okay, well now that I am here, might as well send Uncle home and tell him that I must stay for awhile until I recover and that while I am here, I may as well do the other things to get better." I told her warily. "You will need to go back with him, let me stay and recover and get better, I'll stay through my next birthday and then come home." I turned to Earmus. "Donna fash about me, I'll be alright." I told him. "I'll be back before yeh know it!" I tried to encourage him.

He smiled half heartedly, "I can't lose ya, Ary." He said earnestly. "I need yeh. You've brought life back into my heart again, light into my darkness, and I am scared to be without ya." He confided in me.

"You are goin' ta be just fine! You're stronger than you realize! And you donna need me there to keep yeh that way. Write to me every day! I'll write to you also! We'll be okay! You'll see! I need to do this, you told me yerself!" I spoke to him earnestly, trying not to cry.

"Yes, but I foolishly thought that I'd get to come with you." He admitted.

"You cannae, A'lbi'on needs yah right now! What would he do without us both? He'll go back to closin' off the borders and keeping Nah'alba off grid again! You canna let that happen! Be there for me in my stead, I trust you to do what is best for our kingdom! I trust you to do what my Mum would have wanted." I said just the right words to instill in him confidence and to give him a reason and something to look forward to.

"Alright, I can do that, I will do that. And I will keep you updated on things as we go!" He said, now excited to go back.

"Send me an owl and I'll get back with you quick as rain!" I smiled encouragingly. "If you don't mind, I'd like to get some rest now?" I asked them both. They left and fell fast asleep almost as soon as they left.

I woke up to someone kissing my forehead lightly. I blinked and looked around, Sr'eya, Eir'im'uhs and Uncle A'lbi'on were all in my ward.

"I am sorry to wake you, little one, but Eir'im'uhs and I are leaving now, we will come back to get you when you are ready to come home, you take your time and get better, really get better okay?" Uncle A'lbi'on wiped tears away from his eyes and he spoke.

I nodded tearfully and hugged him tightly and bid them safe travels. Doc, who had been standing behind Uncle A'lbi'on, came up to me and Sr'eya as they left the ward.

“Well, Sr’eya, despite my attempts, I can find nothing unusual about her, she is now in perfect health and you are free to take her home when she is feeling up to leaving.” He said, there was a definite disappointment about him when he turned and walked out.

“My house is a five minute ride from here, I will send word and have Jhonna meet us here first thing in the morning with a buggy. The sooner we remove you from this ward, the better, I think.” She said, an understanding in her eyes.

I nodded in agreement, “Yes, I think yer right.. There is something not quite right with him.” I said.

Chapter Five

The trip to Sr'eya's home was pleasant, slow paced and beautiful. The weather outside was perfect for traveling, though I was a bit chilled, the warm sun filtering down through the trees felt nice. I leaned back in the buggy and closed my eyes, remembering the last day I had spent in the forest before my family perished. The memory now was bitter-sweet. I hated my innocence, I hated that I was once so carefree and childish, but I also wished that I could be that again. I wanted nothing more than to be carefree and childish once more, but, alas! This was not possible anymore. My mind was restless, thoughts were even more relentless right now.

After everything I have been through, it is no longer possible for me to be innocent. It is my fault, no matter how indirectly, that my family perished in that fire. It is because of my powers and my special abilities that someone sought to kill, and therefore, it is my fault my family died. I know, it is sick and twisted, and, maybe, not even fully true, but I need to blame someone, and I am all I have at the moment. Besides, I have this great, big destiny, or whatever, ahead of me now, no matter how much I didn't want it, and if I was going to be ready for it, I have to begin my journey right here, right now.

I rolled over on my back and closed my eyes, the sun on my face was super soothing, and soon I had drifted off to sleep.

"Ary, we are here." Sr'eya said, gently nudging me awake. I sat up and looked around me.

At first, I mistook her house for a huge tree, but at closer look, it was definitely a house, it had windows in it, and a door. It was beautiful, the front garden had white, pink, yellow and purple flowers, and the greenest grass anyone had ever seen. Thick green ivy, and lush wisteria with purple, white and pink blooms, were growing up the walls of the house, nearly covering the wood underneath it. The wood that was showing was knobbly and knotted and seemed to be twisting and curving, reminding me of a tree trunk. The house appeared to be three stories tall, and rather large around as well. I gasped at its beauty, it felt so harmonious and peaceful.

Sr'eya smiled, "Like it, lass?" She asked.

"I do! It's beautiful! How can you stand to be away from it?" I asked.

"It can be difficult, and I do get homesick for it, and my family, but there are things that are more important than being safe at home." she smiled at me, "Come, meet my family!"

Jhona came and helped me down from the buggy and supported my weight as I walked up to the front door. Halfway up the walk, however, I froze.

I am about to meet Sr'eya's *family! What if they hate me? I did, afterall, steal their mother from them! Oh my gosh! What if they donna like me because I am a princess? What if they think that I am stuck up and rude? What if they think that I think that I am better than they are!?*

Hush, Ary, be calm. Jhona's voice came crashing in around me, silencing my anxious thoughts, *No one here hates you, or has any judgment on you, it is no yer fault that yer family died, it is no yer fault that yah need help and have need of* Sr'eya's *special skills. You are loved here, you are most welcomed here. Come, let's not keep them waiting, they are most anxious to meet you.*

I gathered up my courage once again, took a deep shaky breath, and nodded my head, ready to continue toward the door. Sr'eya opened the door and stepped inside, holding the door open for Jhona and myself.

"Kids! We are home!" Sr'eya called as we got into the kitchen. A sudden thundering of feet could be heard rushing down the stairs, excitement shimmered in the air. Three heads came bobbing toward me, two taller, one shorter, two girls, one boy.

"OH MY GOSH! OH MY GOSH! OH MY GODS! SHE'S HERE! SHE'S REALLY HERE! A REAL LIVE PRINCESS IN OUR HOUSE! OH MY GOSH!" A high, shrill, over-excited voice boomed through the house as, what appeared at first to be a blur, the youngest child zoomed through the house.

Sr'eya laughed loudly and reached out and caught the girl. "Ary, this is my youngest daughter, N'yssa. N'yssa, this is A'lari'jah, she is going to be staying with us to heal and get better. She needs rest and quiet, remember what we talked about?" Sr'eya scolded her youngest child gently and then turned her attention to the other two kids waiting patiently to be introduced.

"These are my oldest two children, J'errian'ah and Dy'llian, they are twins, and each of them share an extraordinary talent and gift of healing that no one has ever seen before." She smiled, proud of her children.

"Welcome to the family, milady." They said together and curtseyed.

"Well, if I *am* one of the family, first thing's first, no curtsying and no 'milady', my name is A'lari'jah, people who are close to me call me Ary. I get that enough at the castle, I donna want to hear it here, nor do I wish you to bow or curtsy to me whilst I am here." I said to them, "It is very nice to meet you both."

"I will show you to yer room, the king's men already brought all of yer things and put them in yer room for yah. " The twins said together again, as they turned to lead me out of the buzzing kitchen and to the stairs. My room was at the very top of the stairs four stories up, not three. It was a solitary room with lots of space and a large bed. There was a large desk sitting underneath a window that took up the entire wall. There was a large fur rug on the floor and a large fireplace in the wall opposite of the bed. I smiled, I loved it, it felt so homey and comfortable. All of my trunks and possessions from the palace were here, all I needed to do was arrange them as I wanted them, and unpack my clothes and put them in… where do my clothes go?

As if they could read my mind, the twins came into the room from behind me, and showed me around. There were hidden doors around the room, a large wardrobe built into a wall of the house, hidden so that the room still felt large and spacious.

"Mum and Da' compelled this room while you were in the sick ward." J'errian'ah said. "The house is made of the tree, the tree is our house, and so it's easy to add or remove a room as needed." J'errian'ah explained.

"Mum knew that you liked space, and that you have a certain fascination with hidden doors, and so she made this room for yer liking, if you donna like somethin', you can just compel it to change, and it will do as you wish." Dy'llian said.

I didn't tell them that I knew nothing of compelling trees to do anything, I didn't want them to think me stupid. I smiled and thanked them.

"We will leave you to unpack and get settled in, Mum will call yah for lunch." J'errian'ah said kindly, leaving the room before I could say another word. It was nice that they did not hover, I had a mix of emotions happening within me at the moment, and not all of them I understood myself.

To distract myself, I began the methodical task of slowly making the room mine. I unpacked all of the trinkets and things that I had been given for my birthday. Before I could move on to unpack my clothes and blankets, S'reya was at the foot of the stairs calling everyone down for lunch. I made my way, stiffly, to my door, as I reached out to open the door, there was a soft knock. I opened my door and there stood Jhona, smiling.

I have come to assist you down the stairs. He said, his voice was less intense in my head this time. I smiled gratefully and accepted his help.

Donna worry, you will be able to walk up and down these stairs by yerself in no time, Ary. He encouraged me.

"Yes, and until then, I have to be escorted down like a rebellious child on housewatch." I said irritably.

No, miss, you get to be escorted down like a princess. He smiled.

"Yes, that does sound much nicer, doesn't it?" I smiled and concentrated on getting down the stairs without falling. When we made it to the bottom of the stairs, Jhona let go of my arm and I followed him into the back yard.

Everyone else was sitting around a large wooden table that was extending out of a medium size oak tree, the table, like the house, was knobly and knotted and wavy like a tree trunk. I walked over and sat down by Sr'eya on the opposite side of the table from Dy'llian, J'errian'ah and N'yssa. Jhona sat down on the left side of me, so that I was in between him and Sr'eya. For a long time we ate in silence, each unsure of what to say to the other.

I began to feel self-conscious and anxious, this was not the comfortable silence that typically fell between me and Sr'eya, this was an awkward, uncomfortable silence, a type of silence that was begging to be broken.

"Yeh have a beautiful house, Sr'eya." I said finally.

She smiled, "I would say, thank Jhona, but he's not much of a compeller, I am the one responsible for the rooms and the way the house looks, so, thank yeh. Do you like yer room?" She asked.

"I do like it, I am trying to get unpacked and settled in." I said. "I appreciate the desk yeh put in there too." I added.

"I figured yeh'll be gettin' a lota letters and papers from Eir'im'uhs that yeh'll need to help him with, and yeh'd need lotsa room to write." She smiled kindly, happy that I approved.

"I expect they will start coming in any time now." I agreed.

"What sorta papers and letters? If yah donna mind me askin'?" Dy'llian asked.

"Well, when I last was there Uncle A'lbi'on had invited the world into Nah'alba again. He is supposed to start negotiations for trade again." I said.

"Oh, okay..." Dy'llian said, not wanting to be rude. I could tell that he didn't really understand what that all meant and what that had to do with me getting letters.

"Let me explain better." I said, laughing internally. "When I was in the sick ward here, it was nearly more'n I could do to talk Eir'im'uhs into going back with Uncle A'lbi'on. The way I talked him into it was by stepping in my stead in the negotiations, see, Uncle promised that he and I would be working together on them and coming to an agreement so that we could open up our borders again. So Eir'im'uhs will be sending me twenty owls a day with a thousand letters and important state documents attached to them. He'll want my advice, he'll want to keep me up to date, and he will want to know what I think of the guidelines and rules and agreements they want to negotiate on." I explained in more detail.

"But, why do you need to be involved in these negotiations? Yer only twelve!" J'errian'ah exclaimed

"Because the people and the great noble families feel like I am supposed to be the one ruling, they are angry at Uncle A'lbi'on for running my mum off at her coronation. They feel as though I have been cheated out of my destiny, so they only agreed to open the negotiations if I had the final say on the agreements." I explained.

"So, the people donna want A'lbi'on to rule anymore?" Dy'llian asked, intrigued.

"It is more like they want to see me have an active role and a good amount of say in the way things are run in the kingdom, they will, inevitably, ask me to allow the return of maj'ick to the kingdom." I shuddered to think of that day.

"You'll agree to it, won't you?" Dy'llian asked.

"It's a bit more complicated than that, Dy'llian. It will depend on a lot of different situations and circumstances." I replied.

"Okay, I'll bite, explain." He replied, his eyes were rapt with attention, curiosity and a passion for learning where part of who he was.

"Well, if I am still princess regent, and not queen, I cannot allow maj'ick to return, I will have to take a stand and show my support and loyalty to my king." I said simply.

"But why?" N'yssa chipped in.

"Because, sweet one, if I betrayed my king, I would lose my head for it, and then there would be no one to restore maj'ick to the kingdom when I do finally take the throne." I replied sweetly. Her eyes got big and round and she stopped asking questions.

"So, if you aren't the princess at the time, if you are the queen, how will that change your decision to allow maj'ick back into the kingdom?" J'errian'ah asked.

"Well, you see, more likely, when I become queen, it will be because A'lbi'on is dead. So there will be no one to chop off my head." I said.

J'errian'ah nodded her head and the conversation ended. After another long period of silence, I had finished eating, I excused myself from the table, eager to go back upstairs where the silence was comfortable and not so awkward.

"Well, if yeh'll excuse me, I'll just head back upstairs to take a nap before I finish unpacking." I smiled and stood to excuse myself. Jhona got up to help me back inside, but I smiled at him and said, "I want to do it alone, thanks though."

I got back into the safety of my new rooms and went back to the task at hand. Lost myself in my thoughts while I unpacked my clothes. I found a place to hang my dresses up in the large walk-in wardrobe that was built into the wall.

This would be even nicer if it had cubby holes for my shoes and a bench to sit on. I thought to myself as I hung up my clothes.

I walked out of the wardrobe and rummaged through another trunk that had blankets in it, I picked up a few of the blankets that were not my favorite, and carried them to the wardrobe. I screamed in surprise and dropped my blankets on the floor, as I saw that the wardrobe had expanded to allow for a wall of cubby holes, large, medium and small, and a bench to sit on with a back on it.

A moment later, Sr'eya knocked on my bedroom door, "Ary, are you alright?" *Knock, knock, knock* "Ary, What's happened?" *Knock, knock, knock.* I opened the door, pale faced, and stood back to the side to allow Sr'eya entrance into my room, she placed her hands on my shoulders and shook me gently, "Ary, what's wrong?" She asked again, all I could do was point to the wardrobe.

Sr'eya walked over to the wardrobe and looked in, seeing the bench and the cubby holes I accidentally created, she came out looking paler than I did.

"How did yeh do that?" She asked.

"I have no idea…"

"Tell me what led up to this happening." She said.

"I was hanging up my dresses, and lining my shoes up against the wall, and I thought to myself 'This would be even nicer if it had cubby holes for my shoes and a bench to sit on.' I came out here to gather up my blankets to put on the floor on the other side of my shoes, and there were those cubby holes and the bench!" I exclaimed.

"But, it takes years to do what you did, even accidental compelling doesn't happen with such precision. Skilled compel ers have a hard time with it, they have to be careful not to make terrible mistakes. She shook her head, "I canna make sense of you, child." She said, "JHONA! COME HERE." She hollered down the staircase. Jhona came bounding up the stairs two at a time.

Yes, dear? He said, confused, *Is everything alright?* He asked, looking worriedly between me and Sr'eya.

"She compelled the closet, Jhona." Sr'eya said, incredulous.

She did what?! Jhona asked, astonished.

"Go look for yerself. Yeh know what it looked like when I did it. Go see what it looks like now!" Sr'eya said.

"I'm sorry... " I said quietly. "I didn't mean to upset you or offend you. I didn't mean to not like what you did for me!" I said, trying to hide the tears that threatened to fall down my cheeks.

"Child, I am not upset... I donna care what yah do to yer room! Make it yers!" Sr'eya said quickly, shocked that I thought she was upset at me.

"I donna understand. Yer clearly upset.." I said quickly.

"I don't understand yer maj'ick, and I don't understand how tah help yeh with it, and the many differen' gifts I have seen our out of yeh, scares me." Sr'eya said, trying to help me understand her state of being in that moment.

"Maybe..." I started to say, but then changed my mind and said, "Sorry.." instead.

"Maybe, what?" She insisted.

"Maybe I should go back to the castle, I can get help there... " I said, trying desperately not to tell her about Eir'im'uhs.

"What do yeh mean by that?" She asked, stunned.

"Well, if yah donna know how to help me, I can go back to Uncle A'lbi'on's and get help there." I said again, plainly.

"Who would yah get to help yeh?" She asked incredulously, "Yer uncle?" She mocked.

Tears really did spill out of my eyes and down my cheeks. "Yah know, I really am tired," I took a shuddering breath, "I would like ta sleep now... You may go." I said simply, walking over to the bed and sitting down dejectedly. Sr'eya stood and looked at me until Jhona came over and pushed her out the door.

Ary, she didn't mean it like that, listen to me for just a minute? He came over and knelt down in front of me. I nodded, showing him that I'd listen.

From what I have been told of you, and yer maj'ickal giftings, no one has ever seen anything like you before. Yeh radiate powers that I donna know what are, or where they come from. Yeh are something very special, and until we know more, we are at a loss on how to help yeh. Sr'eya has always struggled with jealousy issues, especially when it comes to other people and their maj'ickal abilities, even with our own children. It is a power struggle, it is her one sin, her one fault. So forgive her when she reacts this way as we figure things out with you. Donna take her to heart when she gets like this, she'll get over it, she always does. He smiled kindly at me and wiped my tears away. *Get some rest, Ary, I'll come get yah for dinner.* He said, rising and leaving the room.

I sat on my bed, feeling more lonely than I had in a long time. I had cleaned to keep my mind off of the things rolling through my head, that I could not ignore anymore. The thoughts and images that I had pushed away all day came rushing back into my mind in a blur, paralyzing me, I was totally at their mercy now.

Being so close to my home, so close to where my parents had lived, loved, and paid the ultimate price, and for what? Me? A failure? I shook my head and leaned over onto my left side and let the tears wash over me.

Yer not a failure, Ary.

A voice in my head sounded, it was familiar, but strange at the same time, more gentle than Jhona's but still, familiar somehow.

Who's there? I asked, afraid.

J'errian'ah and Dy'llian. Their voices sounded together, and I understood why their voices sounded so strange and yet familiar.

How do you know what I am thinking? I asked.

We do not. We only know how you are feeling. And you are not a failure. Yer parents didn't die for you, they died because someone killed them. Plain and simple. They didn't sacrifice themselves for you, they died because someone decided that they were a threat. J'errian'ah told her

Ary, listen to me. I know these things. And I know that the fire might have been set to try and kill you, but it wasn't only after you. It was after yer parents and the rest of yer family too. See, someone knew that a powerful maj'ickal being lived in yer house, they just didn't know who it was. So their solution was to kill the whole family, only, you survived and thwarted their plans. Dy'llian told her matter of factly.

I don't understand, what do you mean, "I know these things"? Dy'llian, how could you possibly know that? I asked him.

I will come to you and explain in person, it's better that way, I'll be up in a moment. Dy'llian told her.

So will I. We will explain some things to you, and help you find a little bit of peace in all this turmoil. J'errian'ah said; a short five seconds brought a *knock, knock, knock,* to my bedroom door.

"Enter." I said, not bothering to move, J'errian'ah and Dy'llian opened the door and moved silently over to sit on the bed next to me.

"Hey, listen, we have to be careful with inter-mind communication because my mum can listen in anytime she wants to, so when she's in range don't talk to us like that. Give us a nudge and we will arrange a time to talk in private where she can't hear us." Dy'llian told me.

"Why does it matter if your mum listens or not?"

"I just … have a feeling that there will be things that the three of us will want to discuss that we won't want her to know about in the near future." J'errian'ah spoke this time.

"Has anyone ever told you two that you're confusing?" I asked

"No, because we have never had this connection to anyone before. However, M'urlin told us that we would find one with whom we'd be forever connected. He told us that We have been connected since birth, but that none of us knew of the connection, and now the time is here that we have met the one with whom we are connected. Our destinies lie together, wherever you go now, we will follow. No questions asked, no ands, ifs, or buts." They both said, at the same time.

"Okay, so how do you know about my family's death?" I asked them, nervous about what they would say when they answered.

"Because we got burned too, Ary," They both showed me identical scars on their legs that matched the scars on mine, though theirs was less extensive than mine.

"But, how is this possible?" I asked, confused.

"We share each other's pain, we share everything, pain, happiness, sadness, love, etc. we share it between us." J'errian'ah explained, and then she reached over and pinched Dy'llian. I jumped like I'd been the one pinched and rubbed my arm in the same place, then Dy'llian pinched J'errian'ah and I had the same reaction. So, out of curiosity, I slapped my right thigh, just as hard as I could, and they pulled up their pant's leg and showed me the red mark from my hand, as if I had slapped their legs and not mine.

"Whoa, this is insane!" I said, "Do you two know how it works?" I asked.

"No, but we have shown you that so that you'd know…" J'errian'ah said, leaving the sentence hanging in the air for her brother to finish.

"You see, Ary. yer not alone." Dy'llian said.

"Yer not a failure." J'errian'ah insisted.

"Yer the most powerful being this world has ever seen, and no one knows quite what to do with you." Dy'llian said.

"But I don't even know what that means." I said.

"You know more than they do." J'errian'ah said,

pointing downstairs to where Sr'eya and Jhona were.

"What do yeh mean by that?" I asked.

"Well, we know more than they do, so then it stands to reason that you know more than they do, and maybe more than you yerself know that ya know." Dy'llian explained.

"Call me stupid, but I still don't understand." I said.

"Okay, basically, it comes down to this. We can feel what you feel, that includes yer maj'ickal, gifts, feelings, thoughts, emotions, etc..." J'errian'ah began.

"That means that if we are feeling how incredibly powerful you are, then you know that too. Like let's say that yer feeling sad... Well we would know that you feel sad, but if you didn't know what emotion you were feelin' then we wouldn't either." Dy'llian said.

"Also, I can sense others' powers, I can sense other things too. Like I can sense Fae in yer blood." She said.

"You can sense that I have Fae in my blood?" I asked, sitting up looking at J'errian'ah.

"Yes, I can sense the Fae in yer blood, it's stronger than yer human blood. The mixture of the Fae and Human is what makes you so strong. It's like when a vampire is newly 'born' they still have human blood in their veins, so for the first few months of their lives, they are the strongest they will ever be. Only, it's the opposite with you. You'll continue to get stronger, your powers will only grow more. Yer human blood will never leave yer veins, and it will never weaken you, it's what makes you strong. Yer human side is what gives you yer compassion, innocence, love, kindness, mercy, and anything and everything that makes a human human. Yer Fae sides makes you fierce, strong, tough, a warrior, it's what gives you authority and command. It's the ring in yer voice when you demand to know the truth from someone, and the have no choice but to tell you the truth." She went on, "Yer abilities are incredible, and we can help yeh understand them, hash them out, work through them, and control them. See having empaths as yer best friends can be an advantage.” She said.

“What advantage is that?” I asked, listening intently now.

“Well, when you accidentally use yer maj’ick, we can tell you where the trigger comes from, and how you used it, from a different perspective, and in that aspect, we can help ye control it, and not accidentally force someone to tell you a truth they may be sworn not to tell you.” Dy’llian finished.

“So, let me get this straight… “ I said. “You two are here negotiating with me to be my best friends?” I asked, trying to keep a straight face.

“Pretty much.” Said J’errian’ah.

“Basically, yeah.” said Dy’llian.

“And yer being dead serious?” I asked, trying to make sure that I didn’t laugh if they were actually being serious.

“Kinda, yeah.” they both said together.

“Okay.” I said and shrugged my shoulders. I got off of my bed and walked to my window by my desk, which had a small, owl sized opening, to allow for an owl to come in and drop off the letter it was holding in its beak. The owl flew over to the extended branch close to the opening and waited patiently for me to read the letter and send a reply. The owl sat happily hooting and drinking water.

“Sorry, I just need to read this and reply really quickly.” I said to J’errian’ah and Dy’llian.

“Oh, do we need to leave?” They asked.

“No, just give me a minute to read it and send the reply.” I said to them.

“Okay.” They said and went back to laying on my bed.

I opened the letter and read it.

Dear Ary,

I hope that this letter finds you well and at Sr’eya’s

house, I have instructed the owl to try there first, and if you weren't there to go to the sick ward where you were at.

We have been back only a few hours now, just enough time to unpack and eat a good hearty meal.

The negotiations are scheduled to begin the day after tomorrow. Father explained to them that you had fallen very ill and had to be taken to see a special doctor. He told them all that I was an owl away if any of them wanted to write to you and confirm the details of what happened. In fact, he encouraged them to write to you and ask you for the details of what all happened. So expect a bunch of letters today or tomorrow from all of the great houses. They have insisted on doing this before they will open the negotiations with Father, so whatever you do over the next few days, please make sure that you answer their letters promptly so that we don't lose our chance to open up the borders again.

I fear that Father is losing his patience with them, his anger is becoming more explosive every day, and he's isolating himself in the gardens for hours on end. Please write to him and get him to calm down, you're the only one that he listens to, the only one that can break through to him.

Write to me, I am terribly lonely here since you have left. I would love to know how you are doing, and what life is like for you right now.

Awaiting your reply
Your's Truly
Eir'im'uhs.

His letter sent my heart racing, and my face blushing. I sat down and wrote him a reply immediately.

Dear Eir'im'uhs,

I will write Uncle A'lbi'on just as soon as I am done with your letter, I will place them both in the same envelope for the owl to carry back to you.

It is so good to hear from you, your letter has made my day. My day here has been rough, and it's only been one day so far. The day started off pretty good, left the ward at dawn and got to Sr'eya's house about ten minutes later. I met her family and her two oldest children showed me to my new room, which Sr'eya *compelled for me only this morning. I came up to unpack and unload all of my trunks and I accidentally compelled my wardrobe to expand and add a bench and a wall of cubby holes in it, which scared me, and upset* Sr'eya. *Apparently I am too powerful and they don't know what to do with me or how to help me with my maj'ick... I told her to just take me back to the palace and let me go home, but she refused, saying that I needed to be here for the time being, until we could understand more and figure out my maj'ick.*

I will promptly answer all letters written to me and send them back quickly. Write to me regularly, and not just about matters of state, I want to know other things too. And any information you can find about me and my maj'ick and my abilities? I'll take any help I can get right now.

Miss you terribly, it is quite lonely here too, but I think I have a couple of good friends in J'errian'ah and Dy'llian. I will tell you more when I am not so tired, I will write Uncle A'lbi'on tonight and then I will probably go to bed.

Yours truly,
A'lari'jah Jayd.

I folded up the letter into thirds and put it into a medium sized envelope and reached for another piece of paper to write to my Uncle. I could only imagine how he was feeling right now... Lonely and angry and scared of losing me again.

Uncle A'lbi'on,

I am up and about again, regaining strength quickly this time. I am in good spirits, mostly, and doing well. Sr'eya introduced me to her family today, nerve wracking as that was, I think I have found two good friends now.

I am doing okay, Uncle, you don't have to be so worried about me. I am not going anywhere any time soon.

Uncle, please be patient with the Lords and Ladies of the great houses. They have seen someone disappear in the dead of the night from the castle once before, and she never came back. They just need a bit of reassurance that I am coming back, and that I am just an owl away if they would like to ask my opinion on anything specific.

Take a deep breath and relax, what will be, will be, and there is no need for you to get so angry over this. I am okay, and you can stop being scared. Change can be a good thing, remember how happy everyone was when you told them that we are going to open up our borders and start negotiations for trade routes again?

Hold onto that hope and excitement from your people, because they are what will get you through this.

I regret that this happened when it did, I was truly looking forward to sitting in with you and helping with the negotiations! You will do fine! Just remember, I am just an owl away, send me anything you wish for me to look over, and I will send you back my thoughts on it, you just have to promise to keep an open mind and accept what I say, because the noble lords and ladies will only allow this to happen if they think that I have the final say in all of this.

I love you, Uncle, and I miss you. I cannot wait for the day that I get to come home again!

Yours truly,
A'lari'jah Jayd.

I folded this letter up into thirds and put it into the same envelope. I held my arm out for the owl and attached the letter to his leg, he nipped my finger affectionately and flew out the window.

"Sorry about that, that's going to happen a lot over the

next month or so, just letting you know." I said to J'errian'ah and Dy'llian who were still laying on my bed.

"You are more needed than you realize, or than you will ever know. You are the key to the survival of this kingdom, Ary, the people around you would fall apart without you." J'errian'ah said.

"My uncle is falling apart, and if he doesn't get it together so will these negotiations. He needs to put his anger and personal feelings aside and do what's best for the kingdom, if he canna do that, then the whole of this will be for naught." I sighed heavily.

"Ary, it's going to be alright, you will see. You will go see M'urlin and then you will be alright. You must go see him soon, very soon." Dy'llian said suddenly.

"What do you mean?" I asked, "I canna go until these negotiations are over." I said forcefully.

"You could if we go right now, we could be back in time for you to answer all the letters you need to answer and still be here for the negotiations." J'errian'ah said, a sudden spark in her eyes.

"Can we make the trip that quickly?" Dy'llian asked.

"No, but she can." J'errian'ah said, nodding toward me.

"All we'd need to do is get her to the right place at the right time, and they'd do the rest wouldn't they?" Dy'llian asked.

"Exactly. And that spot would be only about a mile into the forest, then we come home and cover for her, and she'll be back by this time tomorrow or just after." J'errian'ah said.

"Okay, let's do it." Dy'llian said, they both looked at me waiting for an answer.

"Strangely, I was actually able to keep up with that and understand it. But who is 'they'?" I asked.

"The fairies, of course!" J'errian'ah exclaimed.

"Oh, right, of course! Should have known that..." I rolled my eyes, my voice thick with sarcasm. "I don't think I can make the journey, I am so tired right now." I said, eyes heavy, head pounding.

"Trust me, when the fairies are done with you, you will be pain free for the rest of yer life!" Dy'llian said.

"Okay, What do I need to take with me?" I asked.

"Nothing, but we will need to find you some pants to wear instead of a dress. Dresses are not practical for traveling through the forest." J'errian'ah got up and said, "Wait here, I'll be back." and she danced out of the room.

A moment later she came back into my room holding a pair of hyde trousers and a shirt.

"They are much softer on the inside, they are fur lined." She said, "Come, I'll help you get into them." She beckoned me into the wardrobe. I sat down on the bench and she helped me out of my stockings, leggins, skirts and dress. Then she helped me into the pants, shirt and boots that she brought in for me. I stood up and was surprised at how comfortable they were. I smiled, ready to go.

"Okay, now what?" I asked. She led me out of the wardrobe to where Dy'llian was waiting for us. He now had three backpacks ready to go.

"Ready?" He asked, smiling big.

"Yep, she's ready, I'm ready, looks like yer ready." J'errian'ah said, they were both smiling as if we were breaking some big rule.

"Alright, mum and da'?" J'errian'ah asked.

"Giving N'yssa her bath and bedtime story, they will be occupied for at least the next hour, gives us time to slip into the forest unseen." Dy'llian said.

"Alright, let's go." J'errian'ah said.

"When we get down stairs, I will get your walking cane, it will help you walk better in the forest, I will also walk behind you and J'errian'ah in front of you, that will help the going be easier. We need to hurry, we are wasting time." Dy'llian explained. I followed them down the stairs and out the back door, across the yard, and into the forest beyond.

Chapter Six

The earth began to quake as the moon rose higher into the sky. My vision shifted and time slowed as the forest around me absorbed the moonlight. Tendrils of light danced around the trunks of the trees and up through the highest boughs, making the leaves explode into brilliant color. It was as if I had stepped out of reality and into a dream. This was what one would imagine a walk on the moon would be like.

The plants took on a new life as the flowers began to open and fairies took flight from them. Dwarves could be heard marching out of their dens to take up defensive patrols along the forests' borders. Hobbits could be seen scurrying about, tending to the exotic plants, making sure that there was plenty of honey and water out for the various creatures. Griffins stretched their magnificent bodies and took flight, unicorns came out of caves and trees to forage. Elves and Wood Nymphs could be heard laughing and singing as they ran and played between the trees. Water Nymphs and Mer-People were splashing in the rivers, humming and singing their strange songs.

Suddenly visions began to swim before my eyes, voices invaded my mind. They all jumbled together and made no sense. I couldn't make out one voice from another, it was just a chorus of buzzing, and then suddenly it was gone, and my vision cleared. Silence suddenly fell and all of the creatures had only one unified thought, "An Earth Communer walks among us this night!"

One by one the creatures of the forest appeared before us,

kneeling on one knee, or bowing deeply. They were a strange gathering of creatures, Centaurs with bodies of humans and legs of horses, Dwarves short and hefty with long, pointed noses and hair down to their knees. Hobbits with their huge feet and large blue/gray eyes. Fairies and Elves with their long slender bodies and pointed ears. Strangest of all were the nymphs, they seemed to sway like the wind, they did not wear clothes like the rest of the creatures, but rather branches and leaves with flowers braided in their hair. Unicorns shone brilliantly in the moonlight, looking almost translucent with long wavy manes and tails, with one knee bent, nose on the ground.

The still, quiet that now filled the once bustling forest was unnerving. Unsure of what to do, or what to say or even what was going on, we all just stayed still, with wide gaping mouths.

“Why are they all bowing?” J’errian’ah whispered tensely.

“I don’t know, I have never seen this before.” Dy’llian whispered back.

I stepped forward to place myself in front of Dy’llian and J’errian’ah.

The elves, hobbits, wood nymphs and gnomes came forward and bowed deeply at my feet and spoke in my mind in one unified voice.

Santiel, Lady of the Garden, we faithfully offer ourselves to follow you from this day, until our last day.

Instinctively I placed my hand out in front of me, palm to the ground, and said to them, “I accept your fealty. You may rise.”

They stood and backed away from me, heads still bowed, taking their place at the back of the crowd.

Next the dwarves, griffins, centaurs and pegasi came forward, drew their swords, and knelt on one knee. Holding their swords above their bowed heads, they, too, spoke in a unified voice;

Taurvantian, Forest Walker, we swear our fealty, our lives, and our swords, to follow and protect you from this day until our last day.

This time, I walked among them, taking each of their swords, in turn, and tapping them on the shoulders, "I, Taurvantian, accept your fealty. You may rise, anointed to protect the forest, and heed my call, should ever I need your swords." When I got to the end of the line, they backed away from me as the others had done, and stood at the back of the crowd.

The Water Nymphs, Unicorns, Fairies and other spiritual creatures, came up to me and sank to both knees, bowing their heads to their chests.

Nimgarthiel, Healer, we offer you our lives, our knowledge, wisdom and guidance. We swear our love, loyalties and lives to you from this day, until our last day. To you, we offer all the wisdom of all those who came before you, do you accept?

I sat down on the ground to complete their circle, reaching out with both hands extended and we closed the circle. Visions swam before my eyes, memories filled my head, new knowledge and wisdom flooded my mind and my soul. I took a stroll through the history of time, and when we were done, I stood and said, "Thank you, most gracious of creatures, for your love, kindness and support. I swear to you, now, to do all within my power to bring peace between the realms, and to restore Avondale and Nah'alba back to its former glory. I swear to be kind and loyal to the creatures of Nah'alba and of A'von'dale, I swear to be just and wise as we make this journey together." I raised my hand and all who were gathered before me bowed deeply again, and the forest went back to its normal activities.

"Okay, care to explain what that was all about?" J'erri'ahn'ah said, breathless and confused.

"Well, it's complicated and we've no time just now, remind me when we get home and I will tell you all about it." I smiled, "Shall we continue? Time is short." I said.

J'erri'ahn'ah nodded and we continued on our way, the journey through the forest had become much easier for me. With the transformation, the forest became much less overgrown, and much easier to travel through. I was so lost in my thoughts that I did not notice that J'erri'ahn'ah had stopped, I ran right into her back and the three of us went toppling to the ground with a grunt.

"What did you stop for, J'erri'ahn'ah?" Dy'llian complained.

"There is a powerful being here in the forest with us, I can feel it, can't you?" She said abrasively. She cut Dy'llian a look that looked close to murder. "Where is your head at Dy'llian?" She spat.

"Lost, I guess, I'm walking behind a storm of emotions here, she's clouding out everything else." He stood up and shook his head, offering me a hand.

Nyssa's brow furrowed deeply, "We are not alone." She said in a hushed voice.

"I can feel it now, whatever Ary was feeling was blocking that out though, sorry." He said gruffly, "But next time give us a warning before you just stop like that, geez." He turned to me, "Are you alright, Ary? Did I hurt you?" He asked me, worry flooded his eyes.

"No, not at all, I'm fine." I said, though in truth I was nursing my right leg more than usual.

"No yer not. Sit down and let me see!" He said his frustration was at a boiling point.

"Please, I'm okay, let's just keep going, I need to get back soon, I'll be fine. " I said, standing and waddling away from them.

"Ary, you're going the wrong way, love, it's this way," J'erri'ahn'ah gently guided me back to the way we were going before we toppled over on the ground.

"Oh, right, I knew that." I laughed a tense laugh.

Princess, welcome to the enchanted forest. I gasped audibly, stopped dead in my tracts and stared around me wide eyed.

"What is it?" Dy'llian asked.

"There is a voice, in my head, a voice that I did not allow, nor do I know." I said, panic rising up inside of me like a pot of boiling acid.

There is nothing to fear, Ary, for I am not here to harm you. The voice said to me.

How is it that you have come to be in my head? I asked, guarded.

I am a very special being, very powerful, and I am here to help you, guide you, keep you safe. My name is Taemeluch.

Taem'luch? I asked, *I know that word, it means guardian, does it not?*

Essentially, yes.

Who sent you? Why are you here? What is your goal or purpose?

That, princess, is a bit of a long story.

Well, do I have a choice at the moment?

I suppose not, come to the clearing and meet me, then I will tell you everything.

"He wants us to go to the clearing to meet him, and says that he will tell me everything." I said.

I will tell you, all three of you. He clarified.

"He says that he will tell all of us, everything." I corrected myself.

"Okay, I guess let's go to the clearing then, I'd like to see this creature and meet him." Dy'llian said.

When we cleared the last row of trees we all stopped. Frozen in place, mouths opened wide in a silent gasp, we saw across the clearing, against the tree line opposite of us, a massive dragon. At full size he stood a thousand times the size of a horse and five times as long as the king's largest ship. Nine long, tooth-like horns extended from his head framing his massive face. A large fin extended down his back and tapered off down his long tail. His eyes shone brightly, though their color I could not discern. They were fierce, yet gentle, and full of answers to life's mysteries.

He held himself with grace and his body showed it. When he walked it was as though he were floating above the ground rather than standing on it. His tail moved like a willow branch, dancing freely in the wind. My eyes were soon drawn to his massive wings. Combined, they were one and a half times the length of his body but only half as wide. When they unfurled we could see the muscles stretch beneath his skin. Although they were large enough to lift him skyward in one powerful motion, they provided me shelter and comfort.

He edged forward; every step he took was slow and calculated, as if to show us that he meant no harm. As he crossed from the shadows into the moonlight he burst into, what appeared to be, bright blue fire.

Starting at the tip of his nose it extended across his face, not unlike flames licking up and dancing in the air, it raced down his back, across his wings, down into his feet, and out his tail. However, where his tail should have stopped, the blue flames revealed three long, hair-like, tentacles extending out of it about a foot. The blue flames made him look so unreal, with the way that he seemed to float on the air rather than walk on the ground, and the gracefulness with which he moved, he didn't seem real to me. I stood in awe, feeling as though I should bow to this magnificent creature that stood in front of me, but I was still frozen.

"Is it just me, or is he actually getting smaller?" Dy'llian asked, voice trembling. It was true, as Taemeluch came closer to us, the smaller he seemed to become.

"Huh, I would have thought that he would look bigger the closer he got.. Not smaller..." I said.

"Yeh'd think so." J'errian'ah added.

By the time Taem'luck reached us, he was the size of a Mountain Wolfe, his head now reached my shoulders so that I had to look down, slightly, to look at his eyes. As he approached me, he stopped and bowed deeply to me.

"My princess." He said out loud. His voice was deep, rich, and soothing. "I am Taem'luck."

"When you said your name was Taem'luck, I never imagined you to be a dragon!" I exclaimed. I stood and looked at him in awe for a moment, and then, remembering myself, I gave a soft command. “Okay, you got us here, now, kindly explain things.”

“I am a guardian, a kindred spirit, if you will. We will be one and the same now and forever. As kindred spirits, our connection will be very intimate. You will feel everything I feel, and I will feel everything you feel. I know when you are happy, I know when you are sad. Did you notice that the connection between us became stronger when you crossed the tree line?” He asked, pausing for me to answer.

“Yes, it was as if my whole body absorbed your presence, as if you became part of me, and I became part of you, as if you entered my very soul.” I told him.

“That’s right, because that is how it is meant to be between a guardian and his familiar. I am here, now, because you have reached a point in your life that you now need me. I have known you since you were born, I have not been allowed to intervene in your life until now, because you did not need me, but the Creator knew that one day, you would need me. He knew that one day, you would be in grave danger, and you would have great need of a great guardian.” He explained to me.

“Is this a temporary kind of guardianship? Are you only here until I am no longer in danger? How does this work?” I asked.

“No, my princess, I am here to serve you from this day until our last day.”

“What do you mean, ‘from this day until our last day’?” Dy’llian asked.

“When a guardian and their familiar become one, they are bonded together for life, their life forces intertwine and they share the same life force. If she dies, I die, and if I die, she dies.” He explained.

I was shocked and my silence was not just verbal. My mind went blank for a few seconds and then began to buzz loudly with overlapping questions and fears.

"One at a time, Princess, and I will answer each question in turn." He said, hearing and feeling my anxiety. I took a deep breath and steadied myself.

"Where do we start? How do we begin?" I asked.

"I will share with you my knowledge and the information that I was created to impart with you, the information that our Creator gave to me to give to you." He said. I nodded to show that I agreed and he said, "Come, sit with me, and I will show you."

I walked forward and sat down, he placed his forehead on my forehead and he began to fill my mind with all the answers to my questions and more. In my mind I saw the beginning of time, the creator of the universe. I saw a vision of perfection of creation, and creation's fall. I saw the world covered in fire, ravaged by war. I saw the world drowned in a vast ocean that covered everything except a single boat. Inside this boat was one family and two of every creature on earth.

"The Creator made all things to be perfect, to follow His perfect will above all others. To glorify His name above all others. He created magical beings who were to wield their powers according to His will, however, some of the magical beings and creatures that He made were tempted to use their gifts perversely, which is against His perfect will, and some succumbed to that temptation. Now the fight is to limit the harm that those fallen do while guiding and protecting the newcomers into the fight."

Taem'luck's rich, deep voice was perfectly suited to narrate the creation story, "our Creator had a back up plan, if you will. An extra helper that not very many know about. He created me and my fellow guardians. We each come in different shapes and sizes. Some are as small as puppies, some are larger than I, each of us have a different skill set and different abilities. We each have strengths and weaknesses and things that we are better at and things that we are not good at. He created us to come and help those whom he directs us to help. Some would be very important, some would be in need of saving from their families until they were old enough to be out of their family's house. Some are like you, very, very special and need extra help to make their way through the life our Creator has chosen for them. Our Creator knew that you would be a very special girl, and that if would take a very special guardian to come and watch over you. He chose me and began to train me long before you were ever born. I remain, to this day, the only one the Creator ever personally trained. I am young and have no field experience, however, I am pure of heart and wise beyond my years. The Creator gifted me with many extra talents and many extra gifts to match yours, he showed me who you would become, and why I am so important to your success or failure. Princess, we are destined for greatness, we are destined for goodness, we are destined to bring peace to this kingdom, to both realms. Together we will accomplish amazing things, and without me, well, the world will be a darker place in it, because without me, there will be no you." I shivered at his last sentence, remembering the dream of the disembodied voice showing me Nah'Alba and Avondale if I was to die.

"Taem'luck, it is an honor to meet you, and to share my life with you." I said, bowing my head deeply in respect.

"Ary, this is where we leave you." J'errian'ah said suddenly, her eyes bouncing back and forth between me and the edge of the forest where Taem'luck stood in the shadows.

Chapter Seven

A thick, pearly, white mist surrounded us. It climbed across our feet and up our legs blanketing us from head to toe. There was a strange, warm, tingling feeling that had spread through my body as the mist began to swirl like a tornado, it was not uncomfortable, but it was not all together pleasant, either. I blinked and suddenly the forest was flashing in front of us. My body seemed to have been transformed, in fact, I felt quite unattached to my body, as we flew through the trees at a high speed. It was the strangest sensation. I could still feel my limbs, my fingers, my toes, but I could not find them. We came to a gentle stop in another clearing where a massive willow tree stood in the exact center. My body slowly materialized underneath me. It was, indeed, another strange sensation, as the warm tingling sensation left and my body returned to its normal state. I nearly toppled over, my legs felt like jelly, all wiggly and weak underneath me. As the mist lifted from my chest and head materialized, I stood (if you could call what I was doing standing), gasping for air. I am sure that I looked quite drunk at that moment. My hands on my knees, half dry heaving, half gasping for air, *If only my head would stop swimming!* The abrupt change in speed and state seemed to make it impossible for me to stand, or breathe, it felt like the forest would never stop spinning.

"It will soon pass, princess. The next time you change form and travel like this, it will be as natural as breathing." An'ti'el explained, her strong hand gripped my biceps, almost painfully tight, to keep me from falling.

When I was finally able to regain my balance again, An'ti'el turned to face me, she took my hands in hers and, locking eyes with me, she said, "Fear not, princess, you are stronger than you know. When you get close to the tree, it will speak to you in a way that only you can hear. You will know what to do, it is instinctual." She smiled encouragingly at me as she gave me a little push in the willow tree's direction. "M'urlin is waiting for you inside and I'll be right here when you come back out." I nodded and swallowed hard, taking the first few steps toward the tree were terrifying.

Twisting and wringing my hands I nervously approached the tree. I kept shooting glances over my shoulder back at A'nti'el, frightened to go in alone. I did not know what I was getting myself into, or who this "M'urlin" was that I was supposed to meet. However, as soon as I was underneath the willow branches, my fears fell away and I felt at home, my wariness lifted and a renewed energy took hold of me. I continued my slow, cautious approach, Taem'luck at my side. I blinked my eyes and stared at the trunk in front of me, it was moving, forming the shape of a door! "Oh!" I gasped out loud.

I approached the door and, to my surprise, it opened automatically. The soft orange glow from the fire that was blazing inside, was blinding to my night accustomed eyes, for a few moments all I could do was stand and blink in it's brightness. The warmth and promise of a soft comfortable seat enticed my curiosity and overrode my caution. The smell of food wafted out of the door making my stomach rumble angrily at me. I placed a trembling hand on my growling stomach and crossed the threshold.

"Hello, princess." An unexpected voice to my right made me jump. I turned toward the voice to see a short elven-dwarfish girl in a red jacket and white pants standing just off the open door. "May I take your cloak? Please leave your shoes at the door. Come in! M'urlin is expecting you." I didn't take my eyes off of her as I took off my cloak and sat down on the bench to unlace my boots.

She was smaller than me with a squashed pug face and a nose that reminded me of a pig's snout. She had two giant, toffee colored, bulging eyes and large bat-like ears with thick auburn hair that fell down to her waist. Her head was largely disproportionate to her small body, I smiled to myself because, at any moment, I expected her to topple over from the weight of it. I smiled kindly at her as she hung up my cloak and set my boots into a cubby hole; she beckoned me to follow her into the tree-house.

The elven-dwarfish girl motioned for me to enter a sitting room that had a massive, roaring fire. To the left was a large squishy chair that faced the fire, its back was to a wooden wall that separated this room from the next. To the right was a tall wooden chair with its back to a large ornate door. The large fire and chairs had originally overshadowed a long table that sat back away from the fire and was no taller than my chest, with a feast of all kinds of food; domestic and exotic fruits, vegetables, milk and honey, cheese, crackers, and meats of all kinds. "Please, come, sit, eat, be comfortable. M'urlin has some things he needs to attend that require his immediate attention at the very last second. He sends his most humble apologies and begs you to make yourself at home until he can make your acquaintance."

When I had my fill of the food, I sat down in the big squishy chair, drinking milk and honey until the sweetness was too much for me. Feeling happy and sleepy, I sat back in the chair, stared into the fire, and watched Taem'luck turn in circles on his great big cushion, which had been positioned to be right against the hearth, directly in front of the fire (dragons love fire and always get as close to the fire as they can). A lazy smile crossed my face as he growled and scratched, trying to shift the cushion exactly right underneath him.

"Ahhhh," he sighed as he got it just right, sinking down heavily onto the cushion, "This is the life right here!" He yawned loudly.

"Don't get used to it, we can't stay long." I told him,

but he was already snoring.

I had just drifted off into a light sleep when the large wooden door to my right opened abruptly, making me jump. In the doorway stood a tall, slender man with a large, blunt nose and bright, gleaming eyes. His silver hair and beard seemed to sparkle in the firelight. His beard was trimmed into a neat goatee and his hair fell to his shoulders. He had a kind face and bright, excited eyes and, as he drew nearer, I saw he had one green eye and one blue eye. He came over and casually sat down in the tall wooden chair next to me, a soft smile played at the corners of his lips. He was an aged man, but not so old that he was bent or broken. He crossed his left leg over his right leg and put a pipe in between his lips. He hummed lightly as he lit his pipe, and puffed on it happily. I sat and watched, realizing that I had seen this man once before.

"I have been waiting a long time to finally meet you, A'lari'jah." Pride swelled his chest like a puffer fish. "We have much to discuss, do we not?" He looked over at me and his eyes twinkled in the firelight.

"I expect we do, but first, I believe you have something for me." It was not a question. My knowledge took him by surprise and, for just a moment, he blanched, not knowing what to say.

"I do, but how on earth do you know that?" He asked.

"The night that you came to my house, the night before my family perished, I had a bad dream and was going to come to my mother about it, but you were in the sitting room so, I watched and listened to the conversation that took place. Father handed you a letter, in the event that things did not turn out the way they had hoped they would. He told you that I should come see you shortly after my thirteenth birthday, but if things didn't go according to plan, I would be here shortly after my twelfth birthday. He gave you a letter, for me to read, should this day happen before he wanted it to." I told M'urlin.

"You've a sharp memory, Princess, yes, I have the letter." He reached into his sleeve and pulled out a piece of parchment with a red wax seal on it, "Here you are. Shall I give you some time to read it, alone?" He asked me. I nodded my head and began to break the seal on the letter.

My dearest A'lari'jah,

Oh, how the years have changed the hearts and minds of the people around us. Past grievances have created wounds that cannot be healed and fear has festered in the hearts of so many people from the many lies that have been told about those of us who were born with extra gifts. The world has become jaded and cruel for us. So many people look at the population of those of us with maj'ick and feel only fear and cruelty, believing that we are evil and mean to harm and hurt everyone and everything.

The world was not so cruel once, but... I suppose that is like a fairy tale to you now. I cannot even imagine the world you are living in now. It must be so confusing and so frightening. I only wish that I could be there to soothe your confusion and quell your fears. I only wish that I could be there to tell you this in person. I only wish that things were not as they are, but alas! They are.

If you are reading this, then it means that something terrible has happened and your father and I are dead. Do not be angry or bitter about this, for our time has only come to an end so that you can have your time to shine. And you will shine ever so brightly! You will bring hope and love and joy to the realms, along with peace.

Remember, little one, people all around us do terrible things in the name of love. Most often, it is really fear that really drives them to do terrible things. There will come a time in your life when you will be faced with a lot of big decisions. Know thyself in order to know the people you are surrounded by. Know thyself, so that you will be able to distinguish those who truly do things out of love, and those who do things out of fear. Your father and I love you very deeply. Ary, always remember, no matter what happened, no matter how it happened, you must carry on in life without us now. You must not let anything keep you down, or hold you back.

Love, Always,
G'rai'ce

My dearest beloved Ary,

My love, I cannot imagine the pain you are going through at this moment of your life. I imagine a terrible tragedy has occurred, I cannot begin to guess what might have happened, or what will happen henceforth. I can only tell you this; you were NOT an accident! Surviving this terrible tragedy, there is no shame in that! There is never any shame or guilt in surviving! You survived for a reason! The Creator has a purpose for you, His perfect will is not yet done for you yet. Rejoice in the time we had together! Never forget us! And, little one, do not pretend that you are okay, do not try to be strong and tough, because if you do, a deep seeded darkness will enter your heart and mind. This deep seeded darkness can only be driven out by powerful maj'ick, a maj'ick that very few ever live through. If you have held back, and you do have that darkness in your heart, forgive yourself of anything you hold against yourself, and you will be set free. This was, in no way shape or form, your fault. Surviving this terrible tragedy is okay! You must live! You must learn to thrive! The Creator has BIG plans for you, little one! So, remember that we love you, and we will always be with you, because we live in you, in your heart, in your memories. We will never leave you, so long as you never forget us. Keep living, it's okay to be happy! It's okay to be relieved, it's okay to feel joy at surviving! It's okay! Just let go and let God.

A'lari'jah, time is short, but there are things about me and about yourself that you *have to know. This is going to be difficult for you to accept, but please try to keep an open mind and an open heart, this information was kept from you solely to protect you.*

My mother is the queen of the Fae, Queen Verisiel, my father was King Ar'ron'hil and you are their granddaughter. When you were conceived, your mother fell ill one month into her pregnancy with you. I took your mother to A'va'lon to see the healers and seekers and to see why she was dying. I went, under pain of death, to essentially beg my parents to allow her into A'va'lon, you see, when I married your mother, they took away my Fae rights, my Fae body, my Fae maj'ick. They banished me from A'va'lon and stripped me of my title, my life, my immortality, and my maj'ick, they told me that only under pain of death was I to return to A'va'lon.

When I returned to beg for your mother's life, and your life as I found out later, my father was much changed, and desperate to make things right, so in his last days, he made all arrangements for your mother and you to have the very best care the Fae could offer. They took you out of your mother's womb so that both you and your mother would survive.

By now you must know your origins, that you are more Fae than you are human. Not only that, but you are the rightful heir to both thrones, human and Fae. When A'lbi'on dies, he dies childless. Yes, I know about Eir'im'uhs, but he is but a bastard in the eyes of the church. This leaves you, G'rai'ce's daughter, the one true heir to Nah'alba to take the throne. The laws have changed and women no longer are required to marry to be considered an heiress. You have come into a very dangerous time in your life. You must be vigilant! Don't ever let your guard down! Your maj'ick is so different from anything I have ever encountered before, A'lari'jah, you are truly one of a kind. Your human maj'ick and your Fae maj'ick have melded together, giving you powers beyond imagination. You must not allow darkness into your heart, you must not allow yourself to become corrupt. There is too much at stake.

I must go now. I love you so very, very much, I so wish I could have been there to tell you this in person. Good luck! Ary, and be safe, my love!

Love, Always,

Your Father,

M'kary'ano.

I sat for a long time, staring into the fire thinking of my parents and all that had happened since the last time I saw

them. A soft clearing of throat stirred
me out of my thoughts.

"Did you find any comfort in the letter at all, child? Or just pain and misery?" He asked me gently.

"There is some small comfort, I suppose, in knowing the great lengths they went through to make sure that I was taken care of when they were gone." I smiled sadly. "But they are gone, and I am not, and now I have some understanding of why, though it raises more questions than it answers, it truly is a complicated and confusing time." I sighed heavily. "Knowing what I am, helps me to understand who I am supposed to be, and also why someone wanted to have me killed."

"What you are may define you to a point, but who you are, it can never shape. Who you are was instilled in you by the teachings of your parents, by the heart you were bestowed with. If you have a kind and gentle heart, then you will be a kind and gentle person. If you have a hard and cruel heart, then you will be hard and cruel, not unlike your uncle." He said, I opened my mouth to say something, but then changed my mind, "Make no mistake, Ary, your uncle is a cruel, vicious man who will stop at nothing to ensure that his illegitimate son rests on the throne after he is gone. He will do all within his power to make sure that the true and rightful heir will never sit on the throne. What he does not know, and will never know, is who Eir'im'uhs truly is, and what he is destined to do, for if he did, Eir'im'uhs would surely be dead." M'urlin said, an air of mystery hung over us.

"What do you mean? Who is Eir'im'uhs?" I asked.

"Ah, wouldn't it be nice if I could tell you everything tonight? Alas! That is something that will have to be revealed to you at a much later time, for tonight is about you, not anyone else." He said. "I see that you have finally met your guardian. I suppose now that your parents are dead and you are living within the enemies walls, you need to be protected more than you did before." He eyed Taem'luck with curious eyes. "Though, I would have thought him to be much more impressive."

"M'urlin, he is a shapeshifter, he can change his height and appearance at will, to suit my needs." I said to him, "When I first met him, he was a thousand times the height of a horse." I explained.

"Ah, yes, well, that makes more sense then, doesn't it?" He said, amused.

"Shall we get on with it?" I asked with anxiety edging in my voice, "My time is very limited." I explained.

"Ah, yes, time, you see, works very differently here, Ary, when you step in, time speeds up inside and time, outside, slows down. So out there, you haven't been gone but for a couple of minutes, whereas here, you 've been here for an hour. You have time, time to relax, to take a load off, to escape it all for a while." He smiled, and I relaxed, breathing deeply and for the first time in a long time enjoying the peace and quiet. M'urlin was easy company, the silence that fell between us was easy and comfortable.

After a long while I said, "M'urlin, someone close to me is lying to me, aren't they?"

"Yes, I am afraid that there is one claiming to be someone they are not. I cannot tell you who, for there are some things that the Creator does not reveal even to me." He said, a sadness filled the air around us now.

"I have no idea who it is, I am surrounded by such emotions that I cannot filter it all out, and my gifting in this area is weak, diluted, it's not natural for me to use this gift." I said.

"Yes, well that is because it is not *your* gift, you are simply siphoning it from the twins, their empathic abilities rub off on you and you can feel a bit of what they feel. Does that make sense?"

"Yes, I think so." I said.

"I could give you something to help you in this area, if you would ." He said suddenly.

"What do you mean?" I asked

"I have the ability to bestow upon you two gifts, gifts that would help you on your journey, gifts that also come with a great price." He explained, eyes still fixed on the fire.

"What kind of price? Are we talking about having to give a life for these gifts?" I asked.

"That is a very good question, but no. The price that you would pay would be your burden, and your burden alone. The gifts will give you great strength, but they can also be your weakness. They will assist you, but they bear a heavy weight for you to carry with you all the days of your life. Once accepted, you cannot return them. They can cause you great grief, and the burden of them can often leave you feeling alone, it is a heavy burden, princess, and requires much consideration." He said.

"May I know the gifts you wish to give me and the burden they carry before I accept or deny them?" I asked.

"The first gift would be to read the minds and hearts of those around you. This goes far beyond the twins empathic ability to feel what another is feeling. This is, by far, more intimate. This would allow you to know their deepest, darkest thoughts. Should you wish it, no one would be able to keep a secret from you. Should you find yourself in a threatening situation, you would be able to know who your friends and enemies are. It will take a lot of practice, and it will be quite overwhelming at times. This will be something that you will have to learn to turn on when you need it, at first it might come up when you are in need of it, unaware of the 'switch' so to speak. The mind reading part of this may not ever turn off, this may always be on." He said. "This is the heavy price you would pay with this gift."

"And the second gift?" I asked.

"It works hand in hand with the first one, without the first gift, you cannot receive the second.The second gift is that you would always know exactly who is standing in front of you. That you will always see someone exactly for who they are, beyond their maj'ick disguises and see the person for the maj'ickal creature they hide underneath." He said.

I sat and thought, for I don't know how long, when I finally said, "I accept."

"Then so shall it be." He reached over and placed his hand on my head, "there may be some pain, but stay as still as you can, and it will all be over very quickly." He said.

I gasped as his hand turned ice cold. It was as though I had gone for a swim in a lake in the middle of December. My breath puffed out in front of me in white clouds. I shivered and breathed raggedly making it almost impossible to sit still. When it was over, he took his hand off my head and the warmth from the fire washed over me again.

After I sat there for a while and defrosted, I asked him, "My parents, they knew they were going to die, didn't they?"

"Your parents always knew it was a high possibility. Returning to Honey River Cove was very dangerous, especially with you. There was still a bounty on your mother's head, a bounty the king failed to remove. Later he justified that he did give the decree, removing that bounty and exonerating your mother. All that failed to remove the bounty, or who continued to seek out the bounty, would be executed in the town square. I suppose that as our king, he should be believed. I do know that he already tried to kill G'rai'ce when they were children, and that he would have done anything to keep her and her children off of his throne. However, the king appears to be a changed man, and if that is, truly, the case, then perhaps what he said was true. Otherwise, why would he take the true heir to Nah'alba under his own wing when he could have had her murdered in her sleep?" M'urlin surmised.

"Well, someone did try to kill me, while I was dying. There was a physician that had poisoned me, the king denied that he had paid the man to do it and was very adamant about that. Uncle A'lbi'on has been kind to me, I do not suspect him at all. I choose to believe that the king had absolutely nothing to do with it, the king ordered the physician executed in the town square and his head to be spiked at the main gates. He sent a message to the whole kingdom that 'this is what happens when the king's ward is threatened' and for no one to ever cross him, in this regard, again." I told M'urlin.

He stroked his beard, eyes thoughtful. "I suppose that it's possible that he had nothing to do with it. I am suspicious of several people at the moment, but I have nothing to go on, just feelings and possible motives, but none of them line up, none of it makes sense." M'urlin speculated. "Anyways, enough with all this, child, is there anything else that you'd like to ask me?" He asked.

"No, I am full up on knowledge and information, I feel as though my head might explode." I laughed. "I do feel ready to go home, now, though." I said.

M'urlin nodded his head and reached out and touched my arm, his eyes turned dark and serious. "Beware, Ary, there is one in your midst who is not who they claim to be, whether they are friend or foe, I do not know. Even with your new powers, it will take you by surprise.

There is one in your midst who is not who they claim to be, who will betray and hurt you deeply. There is one in your midst who was a traitor, but is making amends for past transgressions.

Keep your eyes open, your mind sharp, and never go anywhere without your guardian. Keep your guard up and stay alert, but never close your heart off. Never allow darkness to enter, for if you do, it will be the end of us all." M'urlin eyes had slid side to side with a white film that covered them, when his eyes shifted back into focus he smiled and said, "Now, you may go. May our Creator bless your path, and open wide the doors you need to embark on your journey. Stay safe! Stay alert!" He got up and went back into his study, leaving me shocked in the chair.

I stood up and walked to the door, Taem'luck at my side. The door opened at my approach, I pulled my shoes back on and my cloak over my shoulders, and walked back out into the dark forest. An'ti'el was waiting for us where she left us

"Come, time is short, and I have one more thing to give you before I take you home." She said to me, she placed her hand on my head and said, "This might hurt, princess." A hot burn started at my head underneath her hand and coursed through my body. Like a high fever burning through my body, I cried out in pain and fell to the ground, An'ti'el's hand never left my head, writhing on the ground the heat burned through me, hitting my back and my hip and then my legs. It felt as though I was right back in the fire that had hurt me so badly, the fire that had consumed my family. It was unbearable, intolerable, and it seemed to last an eternity. I laid on the mossy ground trembling, a cold sweat had soaked my clothes. I couldn't move, I couldn't see anything, the pain that seared through my body made me wish that I had died in the fire with my family.

As suddenly as it had hit, it was gone, and I was pain free. My vision had come back and I could hear what was going on around me. An'ti'el's hands were still on me, in fact, her whole body seemed to be on me. When my eyes focused again, I realized that An'ti'el was, indeed, sitting on me, her strong arms holding me down.

"A'nti'el?" I asked.

"Oh, thank goodness, I began to think I had done something wrong!" She exclaimed, "I did not want to go back to the queen having failed in this." She got up off of me and helped me to my feet.

"What was that?? I feel so different!" I said, my body no longer ached, I stood straighter than I had ever done before, and my bones were loose and limber again.

"I have restored you to your true self. I have unlocked your Fae DNA and I have healed your body, mind and soul." A'nti'el said, "This is your birthday gift from your grandmother. Shall we go? We need to get you back before the sun rises, and the sun will be rising in a few hours." She told me.

I nodded my head and accepted her hand, the pearly white mist enveloped us again, and we flew through the forest at lighting speed. She stopped right at the tree line that bordered the forest behind Sr'eys's house.

"This is where I leave you, princess. If ever you have need of me, hang this charm on the willow tree in the back, and I will be here very quickly. There will be a surprise coming to you very soon, be on the lookout! Be safe, guard yourself, and stay vigilant!" And with that, she was gone. I stood looking at the charm for a moment, it was an iridescent butterfly wind chime. When the sun hit it at the right angles, it sparkled and cast rainbows everywhere. I smiled, remembering the rainbows that the fairy's wings used to cast in the sunlight.

Chapter Eight

I stood at the edge of the trees for a while, thinking over everything that had happened, marveling at the amount of knowledge I had learned in a short amount of time. I looked into the sky at the position of the moon, I had only been gone for two hours, maybe two and a half at the most. My mind buzzed with questions, I was overwhelmed and quite exhausted.

A sudden commotion brought me out of my thoughts. Sr'eya's angry voice could be heard from the top floor of her house.

"Gone!? What do you mean gone?! Gone where?!" She screeched.

"Mum, she'll be back soon, donna fash. I promise, she is safe." J'errian'ah was trying to soothe Sr'eya, who's anger was so fierce I could feel it where I was standing.

"You tell me now, and you tell me true! Where has she gone?!" Her voice was a deadly whisper now.

"I cannae tell yeh, yeh'll have to wait until she comes back to ask her." Dy'llian said, adamantly.

"Don't be angry at them, love, if she made them swear not to tell, then they have to stand by that promise." Jhona said.

"I will be angry at whomever I please until that girl is safely back in the confines of my home!" Sr'eya spat viciously.

By this time, I was standing outside the back door, waiting for the right moment to go inside.

"I'm back!" I hollered, hoping to make her stop yelling at everyone.

They all came to the back door, and gasped out loud, mouths gaped wide.

"Er... Sorry, I dinna mean to cause such a fuss. I thought I had a bit more time to get home before you discovered I was gone...." I said, their stares made me self conscious, "Er.. Why are you all staring at me?" I asked, confused.

J'errian'ah took off running up the stairs, her heavy feet could be heard all the way up and back down again. When she reemerged, she brought with her a full body looking glass. Unable to speak, she placed the glass in front of me and beckoned, urgently, for me to take a look.

I stood quite as still as a stone statue. Not daring to move, barely willing to breathe, for fear that the magnificent creature in front of me would disappear.

As I studied the creature the first thing I noticed was that she stood quite tall, at least two feet taller than myself. Her back was straight, her leg was not twisted and distorted. The creature had a very dainty and feminine appearance, she seemed to dance while standing still. Her long slender face had a pert, upturned nose. Her mouth was sweet and lush, light lavender in color, that held a sad sort of brooding that turned her lips down at the corners.

What troubles lurk in her thoughts? What longings would part those sweet, delicate lips into a wide smile? I thought.

Her small dainty face was home to two wide, almond shaped eyes that blazed with curiosity, intelligence, and wisdom, but, somehow, still held their innocence. One eye was deep emerald while the other eye was deep violet. Both eyes had a golden circle around the pupils that glowed like low embers, not unlike flames, flickering like fingers, beckoning one in. Her eyebrows sat lightly against the skin. While her skin appeared satin smooth, her brows were like molded iron gates, stretching over her forehead; protecting the secrets hidden behind those bars. A show of quiet, elegant strength on this beautiful creature.

Below her eyebrows sat three sparkling gems, emerald,

gold and purple. The small wispy lines that might have started out as laugh lines, stretched across her eyes, from corner to corner, had now morphed into strong, bold cords that created a pattern of a butterfly across her cheeks. Each wing spread out above and below each eye, meeting each other across the bridge of her nose, highlighting her eyes and the freckles that now painted her face. In the middle of her forehead, between her eyebrows, was a spiral with two dots at the top of it. An'ti'el's imparted knowledge told me that this genetic marker symbolized her place in the Woodland Fae's tribe.

Her long wavy hair cascaded down her back and over her left shoulder like a multi-colored waterfall. The roots were a deep violet lightening ever so slightly all the way down to their white tips. There were twists of hair wrapped in golden ribbon and a few braids littered the underside of her hair. Green and golden highlights scattered amongst her purple hair.

I gasped as I realized the creature had two sets of wings attached to her back. Her wings were magnificent when extended in their fullness and reminded me of a majestic butterfly. Neither set of her wings were straight along the edges, they flowed like a jagged cliff side. Full of strength for flight, but also gorgeous in their glittering paleness. They curved behind her like an archangel and the bottom of her wings swept into the elegant swirl of a long, forgotten heritage - one thought to have been lost in modern times.

That swirl... catches my attention and I want to investigate more. The stories I've heard about wing swirls like that!!! Could they be true??

There were two long slender antennas that reached away from the wings and curved over her head, they came to a narrow swirl at the tips, hanging over her head like an angel's halo. The creature had four beautiful rings on her forearms, two rings per arm. Glowing brilliant neon blue, the rings reminded me of blue veins, as windy as a river and as luminescent as the moon. They seemed to dance and move around both arms, midway between her wrist and elbows. I also noticed that the creature had white markings all over her pale arms, they looked like twisting vines with flowers that seemed to never stop moving. The vines moved like a snake winding its way up her arms, where they collided with a much bolder marking, another genetic marker that, at first glance, looked like a swirl of lines, but when I looked closer I saw the outlines of a butterfly wing, each shoulder was identical.

"It would seem that Fae ladies come into their own much earlier than any other species." I jumped as Sr'eya finally said something to break the silence that hung in the air. Sr'eya was trying not to sound too shaken by my changes.

"I suppose yeh'll be hungry, then?" Sr'eya asked me, I nodded absentmindedly and she stalked off to the kitchen muttering under her breath.

I hung back for a few moments and studied myself more closely. I was surprised to find that I was a young woman, with full breasts and a slender hourglass body, my shoulders and hips were a bit wider, but my face still held its youth and innocence.

I only peeled my eyes away from the looking glass when I smelled food wafting out of the kitchen making my stomach growl at me. I walked to the kitchen and sat down at the table with J'erri'ahn'ah and Dy'llian.

"I am sorry that I got you into trouble." I said to them quietly.

"Donna be sorry, love. We did it to help yeh. I would do it again, even knowing that I'd get yelled at for it." Dy'llian said.

"She was just worried about you, she needs to learn to let yeh grow and to stop holdin' on so tight to yeh." J'erri'ahn'ah said, rolling her eyes. "Yer not a little girl anymore." She added.

"Aye, while that may be true, I've been quite helpless after the fire, wheelchair bound and unable to do much by myself for myself. Over time, she will come to learn that I am now healed and much more capable than I was before." I smiled and patted Tayem'luck who had taken the form of a mountain wolf. The glorious thing about mountain wolves was that they were the size of a small horse.

As silence fell in the room, my internal debate was turning into a full fledged war inside of my head. I was concerned about M'urlin's warning.

'Beware, Ary, there is one in your midst who is not who they claim to be, whether they are friend or foe, I do not know. Even with your new powers, it will take you by surprise.

There is one in your midst who is not who they claim to be, who will betray and hurt you deeply. There is one in your midst who was a traitor, but is making amends for past transgressions.

Keep your eyes open, your mind sharp, and never go anywhere without your guardian. Keep your guard up and stay alert, but never close your heart off. Never allow darkness to enter, for if you do, it will be the end of us all." M'urliln's eyes had slid side to side with a white film that covered them, when his eyes shifted back into focus he smiled and said, "Now, you may go. May our Creator bless your path, and open wide the doors you need to embark on your journey. Stay safe! Stay alert!'

Is it wise to reveal all that M'urlin and I talked about? The gifts that he gave me? The warnings and the conversations? Or should I keep it all to myself and not reveal any of it? Such a heavy secret to hold within, to keep to myself.. What should I do? I don't know what to do... I thought to myself as Sr'eya was making breakfast.

If I may, princess? He paused for a moment, testing to see if his advice would be accepted, and then continued, *you may not know who you can trust and who you cannot trust until it is too late.*

Then what would you have me do, Tae?

I, humbly, advise that you do not reveal all that M'urlin gave you, only reveal a small piece of the truth. Those who are to be your strongest allies will seek you out and seek the whole truth. Those who are not to be your strongest allies will accept the truth that you offer now as the whole truth.

Yes, I do think that is wise, Tay. Thank you, yeh've saved me from internal damage, I think.

I felt Taem'luck chuckle and there was peace in my mind again.

The air was tense as Sr'eya placed breakfast on the table in front of us. Eggs, bacon, ham, porridge, fruit. It was practically a feast. Sr'eya kept cutting her eyes at me, with a hard pained look on her face.

"If you want to know, Sr'eya, just ask." I said impatiently.

She let out a long hard sigh and asked, "Fine, what happened when you went to see M'urlin?"

"We talked." I said, offering no more explanation.

"Well," She barked at me, rudely, "What did you talk about?" Her mind was screaming in my mind, asking the questions she really wanted to know.

"Oh, the usual I suppose, my parents, my heritage, my lineage, that sort of thing." I said dismissively, shrugging my shoulders. J'erri'ahn'ah and Dy'llian were shaking with silent laughter at my side, I cut them a sharp look to tell them to behave.

"Fine, will you please just tell me what happened? I'd like to know where you went, because it's obvious that you didn't just see M'urlin, and it's obvious that something else happened. And why on earth have you brought that flea infested mountain wolf into my house?! Wolves do NOT make good pets!" Her face was flushed with anger.

"I will tell you all what happened, if you wish, but only after breakfast is eaten, the table is cleared and the dishes done." I told her kindly.

"Why wait?!" She barked.

"Because you need to calm down before I begin talking,

and because I am very much hungry right now." I explained calmly.

"How dare you speak to me as such!" Sr'eya spat, she was getting geared up for a long winded yelling spree, but I cut her off.

I stood up, tall and proud, every bit the princess I was supposed to be, "Do not speak to me as such, madam! You are my guardian, you are NOT my parent. I am the princess, heir to two kingdoms! I am your superior, and you will begin to treat me as such!" I commanded, the ring of authority in my voice was much thicker and heavier now.

"Yes, your highness. I forgot my place, your highness, please, I beg your forgiveness." She said, head bowed, her mind had stopped screaming at me. She submitted to my authority, knowing full well that I could, at any point, tell her that she was no longer my guardian, but I did not wish to do that. She was only trying to take care of me and guide me along the path that she thought was best for me.

The silence in the room was heavy, and awkward as we all sat down to eat the breakfast that was served, the echo of what had just happened still hung in the air.

"Ary, I am curious about the dog?" J'erri'ahn'ah probed.

"Yes, the dog, he's actually a dragon." I said smiling. "Tae, show them." I said.

He morphed into his dragon self, staying the same size as he was in dog form. Sr'eya gasped and choked on a bit of egg, Jhona smiled in awe and J'erri'ahn'ah shrieked.

"This is Taem'luck, my guardian." I explained. "Taem'luck, this is my adopted family." I made the introductions.

"It is very nice to meet you all." He bowed his head in respect to the rest of my new family, and they bowed in respect as well.He turned himself back into my long haired wolf and laid back down at my feet, eating crumbs off the floor.

"But, how!?" was all that Sr'eya could manage.

"Well, I guess he's been with me all the while, he said that he's been watching out for me my whole life, that he was there when I was born. He said that the creator told him not to reveal himself until it was time, and I guess it was time." I said.

"But… Why?" She asked, baffled.

"Because I need his protection, his guidance, his help and wisdom." I explained. "When I visited with M'urlin, we didn't just talk, either. He imparted with me quite a bit of wisdom and knowledge, and he also bestowed to me two gifts." I told everyone sitting at the table, in between bites of my breakfast.

At that moment I felt a great surge of what felt like rage hit me hard. I was confused..

Tae? Why is there anger here?

Not anger, princess, jealousy. The emotion you are feeling is jealousy.

This made me angry. *Who, in their right mind, would be jealous of me?! Do they not know!? Do they not understand!? The massive weight and sacrifices that this burden weighs on me? How huge is this burden for me to carry? And it is me who must carry it, and me alone.*

No, my princess, they do not know, nor could they ever understand this. The only thing they are thinking about is the fact that M'urlin himself chose to give you a great gift, not all who go see him are granted such things. It is rare that M'urlin gives a gift, and rarer still that one should accept his gift. It's only happened once before, and that person proved that he could not handle the gift he was given, and since then, M'urlin has been very greedy with handing out any gifts of any capacity to anyone.

Why? What happened?

The last time he gave out a gift was four hundred years ago, and the man nearly brought about the end of the world before he was stopped.

Oh! Was all I was able to say to that.

I sat quietly while I processed what Taem'luck had told

me. I was vaguely aware that my once pale markings and wings were now glowing brilliant red. I listened to the thoughts of everyone at the table, trying to pinpoint who the jealousy belonged to, but it was impossible to tell with everyone here and my gifts underdeveloped.

I will find out soon enough. I seethed, *it's only a matter of time that jealousy should rear its ugly head again. The intensity of that emotion will not go away easily.*

"A'lari'jah, do you realize ... Hang on, why are you glowing red?" Sr'eya stopped in the middle of her sentence, astonished that my pale markings, so easily missed before, were now glowing like low burning embers.

"Er...I'm not really sure." I replied, now examining myself. "What were you asking?" I asked, distracted.

"I was just going to ask if you realize what this means?"

"Yes, of course I do!" I snapped, my wings flashing an even darker shade of red. "I probably understand that better than you do!" Everyone tensed at my sudden abrasiveness. It was clear, in that moment, that Sr'eya was the cause for the jealousy I felt earlier, the question was, why? "I'm sorry, it has been a long night, I am just tired and disturbed by why I'm now glowing red... Maybe we can discuss this another time?" I stood to excuse myself from the kitchen, wanting to seek solitude from the buzzing in my head that drowned out my own thoughts.

Chapter Nine

Uncle Al'bi'on argued with me over this for a few days, but in the end agreed to these terms and conditions I had revised. I argued that, as they are not forbidden in their own country to use maj'ickal they should not be put to death if they slip up and use maj'ickal, they should be allowed to return to their ship for the remainder of their time here and be allowed to return to their home. No banishing, no keeping people from coming back, just arrest them and let them come back. There was no need to overreact, or we would lose our chance of having trade with these people. The rules will be gone over by an officer of our guard before they leave the ship, they will all gather on deck, they will remind everyone of the rules, and anyone caught breaking them, would spend the remainder of their time under boat arrest.

In the end, he agreed, and thought it best to try and keep our bridges from burning this time. He also knew that if he didn't change these and adhere to them, I would not sign off on them, and we would lose trade with everyone.

Negotiations for opening up our borders and making trade possible again between all nations took the better part of a year. There were six nations in total who completed negotiations with us, nine others who refused because of the maj'ick ban, and six who did not like any of the attempted negotiations, and left Nah'alba in the middle of the night.

It was a difficult time, because the trade negotiations were tedious, they needed to know fair prices for the items that would be traded, the quantity in which they would trade, how the slaves were to be brought through, where they would stay, how long each ship was allowed to stay in port before having to leave again.

Current standing we had successfully negotiated and signed contracts with:

Hesperia would bring in their spicy cultural influences with their spicy foods, seasonings, herbs, they would hire out chefs and bring in pre-qualified people, (that is to say, non maj'ickal people), to come and stay on a long term basis. They would bring over a lot of their clothing influences at cheap prices so that we could begin to give our people a sense of self-worth and help them to feel good about their appearances. Hesperia was on board with the maj'ickal ban and went as far as to say that any one of their country men who were found practicing maj'ick would be imprisoned and sent back to Hesperia for a trial and execution in their home land. - Personally, I was not totally okay with this, but I could not argue as I had to take up my Uncle's laws of the land as my own for the time being.

Shiwei would bring in some of the same things as Hesperia, cultural influences, but with them came gurus, and spiritual guides, they would bring over their religious beliefs and practices. They would bring clothing, materials such as burlap, hydes and skins for clothes, and other things, and they would bring livestock to trade for fair market prices. Shiwei would also bring with them exotic animals to trade for pets, circus animals and more.

Largalon would bring with them cotton, wheat, beans, rice, leather and shoes, materials to build with and weapons of all sorts. They would also be participating in the buying of slaves and servants to take to their home lands and sell. Largalon would be sending people over such as doctors, midwives, philosophers, priests, pastors, ministers, teachers and other such influential people to stay on a long term basis.

Alekbula refused to do much of anything except trading small items such as sandals, slaves and food type items including coffee.

Chapter Ten

On the morning before my fourteenth birthday, J'erri'ahn'ah, Dy'llian and I sat underneath the willow tree, thick as thieves enjoying the freshness, being lazy, laughing and talking.

"I gotta say, it is very nice not to be stuck behind my desk! It feels good to not have mountains of paperwork, negotiations and letters to deal with now. I still get the odd letter every now and again, but for the most part I am pretty much done. I'd say that I have, nearly single handedly, brokered peace and trade for the whole kingdom between some of the most notorious nations in the world! I'm excited for Nah'alba's future, I do believe it will be fantastic!"

"I think you have done an amazing job, Ary! You have worked so hard, and stayed on top of everything so well, I am super proud of the way you've handled things!" Dy'llian said.

"Although, we have missed you, quite a lot! I say we should plan a day to go out together, just the three of us, take a trip and go see the village or something." J'erri'ahn'ah said.

"Maybe we could go for a picnic and spend some time in the village, that would be nice, maybe we can go to my home, I could show you where I grew up, and show you the sunflower patch I used to play in, it used to be beautiful this time of year!" I said, excited at the prospect of adventure.

"Are you sure that's a good idea? Going back to the place your family perished?" J'erri'ahn'ah asked.

"It's time that I put the past behind me and moved on, and what better way to do that than to go back to where it all began?" I said, sounding more confident than I felt about it.

"Okay," J'erri'ahn'ah shrugged, "If that's what you want to do, then let's do it! Shall we make a day to go soon?"

"I was thinking we could go tomorrow?" I half hoped she'd protest, I wasn't at all sure that I wanted to do this.

"Oh, Ary... We can't do it tomorrow, Mum would be devastated if you weren't here for your birthday!" Dy'llian said, sympathy etched his voice.

"Why? It's *my* birthday, and saying goodbye to my family once and for all is, after all, more important than a party." I said, defiant.

"Well, if that's what you want then we are behind you. But... You have to be the one to tell Mum." J'erri'ahn'ah said.

"Okay, I'll go tell her now. In fact, why don't we make this an overnight trip and leave tonight? I know the innkeeper, we could have a good room tonight to sleep in... if yer up for it?" I said, hopefully.

"Okay, sure, Ary, whatever you want to do..." J'erri'ahn'ah said, worry etched her voice, though she did not profess it.

I walked inside alone (J'erri'ahn'ah and Dy'llian wanted to be out of the firing range, so to speak), and found Sr'eya in the sitting room working on a needle point.

"I am going to my home tonight, I will spend the night and return on the morrow before the sun sets, and J'erri'ahn'ah and Ranul will escort me. When I return we may celebrate my birthday however you would like us to." I said, there was no question, no room for refusal.

"Ary, are you sure?" Sr'eya asked, nothing but concern in her voice.

I nodded my head slowly, "I need to do this. My family perished the eve of my tenth birthday, it's only right that I go back tonight to say goodbye." I said, sadness filled my heart so great and so heavily that it was almost more than I could do to stand underneath it. "Birthdays do not hold the kind of joy that they used to, they are, instead, filled with sadness and darkness. It's time to change that."

"Okay, if yer sure, I'll pack you a back of food, you three go and get ready, I'll be done here in about an hour. Do you want Jhona to walk with you?" She asked.

"No, thank you," I shook my head and turned to leave, but turned back to her and said, "I am sorry, Sr'eya, for mucking up your plans for tomorrow."

"No, donna fash, love, this is more important than a celebration. I just wanted to cheer yeh up, yeh've been stuck in yer room all year with no relief and I just wanted to give yeh a good day, new memories and all that." She smiled sweetly. "You go on and do what yeh need to do, we will be here waitin' fer yeh when yeh come back." She smiled and went about gathering up food and putting it in three knapsacks.

While I headed up the stairs, I telepathically talked to J'erri'ahn'ah and Dy'llian.

Yer mum's okay with it, come and get ready to go.

A few seconds later they came barreling through the back door and up the stairs. An hour later we were all dressed and ready to go, knapsacks over our shoulders, backpacks on our backs, we had all changed into traveling clothes, soft pants and hide shirts. We said goodbye to Sr'eya, Jhona and little N'ysssa (who cried because she couldn't go with us).

The journey into the village lasted about an hour and a half , and from the edge of town to the inn took us ten minutes. It was a quiet, uneventful trip, we laughed and talked and watched the birds, deer, rabbits and other wildlife. When we were hungry we stopped on the side of the road to eat. We took our time, and enjoyed being away from home and together out in nature.

When we reached the inn, I took a deep steadying breath

and opened the door to allowing J'erri'ahn'ah and Dy'llian to go in first. I stood just inside the door, looking around, recoiling at the slew of memories that hit me like a ship. Stealing myself, I went to the bar to ask after the owner.

"Excuse me, sir, I am looking for..."

Before I could finish the great big barkeep had turned around, looked me in the face for a couple of seconds and bellowed, "BLESS MY BEARD! A'LARI'JAH BACK!"

I blushed and tried my best to hide my face, "Jaymes! My gods yer still here?!"

"Where else would I be, little lady?" He laughed a jolly laugh, "How in M'urlin's beard have you been?! Where have you been for that matter!?" He asked, picking me up over the bar and hugging me tight.

Jaymes was a large man who seemed to be wearing the same shirt and vest as he wore when I was little. He smelled of ale, stale beer, old food, sweat and a bit of tobacco. His face was large and round, eyes were sunken in, small and beady, but they twinkled with excitement. He had a gruff beard that was in desperate need of a trim, his hair was shaggy and unkempt, but his smile was kind and friendly.

"Well, I've been at Uncle A'lbi'on's, recovering from some serious injuries." I told him, he sat me down on the bar, just as he had done when I was smaller and.

"Tell me about it?" He begged.

"Well, Jaymes, it's a long story, and we are all very road weary, hungry and thirsty. It was a long walk here." I said, the twinkle in his eye came back.

"Come wiff me, I got just the thing fer ya!" He said, opening up the bar for J'erri'ahn'ah and Dy'llian to walk through, he helped me down off the counter and led us to the back. There was a smaller dining room in here, a cozy fireplace for the winter months, and a small table with six chairs around it.

"Sit down, I'll get ya a drink and some food and then yuh can tell me all about it!"

We sat down and I began talking; I filled him in on everything that had happened from the day the fire started to the day I walked through his door. I talked in between bites of food and swigs of drink. He sat at the table, chin on his hand, listening intently as if I was telling him the most invigorating story he'd ever heard. When he was all caught up, he took a great big handkerchief from his vest and blew his nose loudly on it, wiped his eyes and shook his head.

"That's the saddest story I ever heard, little miss." He said, "Though, I suppose it had its good points too, eh?"

"Yes, Jaymes, it's had its good points, and it's had its bad points. I'm still alive and kicking, and so that's a good point." I told him.

"What brought you here today?" He asked.

"It's the third anniversary of their death, I came to say goodbye." I told him stiffly.

"I see. You know, someone went up there and buried all of them two years ago. No one in the village dared to touch them, we all had hoped that someone would want to bury their loved ones, but no one ever came. Then one morn' I wen' up there to pay my respects, as I did regularly, and they was gone, they was. They had been buried, I found them under a willow tree by the creek." He said, "Still dunno how it happened or who did it, but someone did." He was confused, but shook his head and moved on, "So, what can we do fer ya?" He asked.

"I was actually hoping Maude was here today..."

"Nah, she's out for a while, little one's sick and all, might not make it." He said sadly.

"Ach, that's no good, I'll have to run by and see her, how about this, can you spare us a room for the night?" I asked.

"Aye! Done! Anything I can do fer yeh, little lady?" He asked, he looked me dead in the eyes, "I owed my life to yer pa, and I mean to repay him by doing whatever I can do for yeh, Ary. My sword, my life, it's yers, if ever yeh should need it." He bowed his head deeply. "Right, follwer me, I'll show yeh yer room." He said gruffly.

He reached into his vest and pulled out and single golden key, "I have been holding ontuh this for three years now, can't wait tuh show yuh." He said.

He led us through the main dining hall and up the stairs. When we reached the top most landing, he reached up and opened a hidden hatch on what appeared to be the ceiling of the inn. He pushed it up and continued the climb up the stairs. We followed him through the hatch door, which he quickly closed behind us, and stood aside to let us take in what we were seeing.

"We added an extra floor that cannae be seen from outside, when looking at the building it looks like it has three stories, but it's got four. We closed it off, and put in a secret door for it. Yer da' helped us with this, and yer mum too. There are five rooms here to use as you will. This place is secret, no one will ever know yer here, and if yeh ever need to keep it that way there is a secret stairwell in the back, it leads down into the private dining room we were in earlier, that room also has a secret door to the back alley way, for private access, if yeh ever need it." He said to me, "Come, take a look, pick a room, I am most anxious to know what yeh think about it all!!" He said, his smile was as large as his large face would allow it to be.

We took a look around, it seemed that my room was already designated, with my name on the outside, I decided I would wait until last to see my room, I wanted to see all the others first. We started with the room closest to the hatch door, on the right side, it was a natural wooden door with the place for a name on it, if someone claimed this room. Inside the room were brilliant greens and yellows. The bed was a huge feather bed with soft feather and fur blankets, and large fluffy feather pillows.

There was a chess set at the window, overlooking the town, with two chairs sitting opposite each other. There was another table and a few chairs placed in front of a fireplace, they were upholstered with fancy embroidery designs on them, one a bright green, one a bright yellow, the other was bright yellow and green mixed together in odd patterns.

There was a large rug that stretched across the floor underneath the chairs that sat at the fireplace, the tables sat next to each chair, on top of the rug. The room was the perfect place for a guy to stay. There were pictures and paintings of deer and elk and hunting pictures, and mounted heads on the wall too.

"This is nice, but too green for my taste." Dy'llian said, "But I do like that chess set!" He said, walking over to take a closer look. It was a pure marble chess set, the pieces strongly resembled dwarves. "But I like animals on my chess set, not dwarves, dwarves don't play nice." he said, setting the piece down. We walked out of that room and closed the door behind us, the name plate stayed empty.

The door to the left of the hatch was the same sort of door, but when we opened it, it was decorated in bright pink and yellow. The room had the same layout, the only difference was, there was no chess set, and quite a larger wardrobe. This room seemed a tad bit bigger, as it had a place for sewing, needle point, knitting, crocheting, and other such hobbies and tasks that ladies usually did to pass the time. The bed had more pillows on it, and they had furry pillow cases over them, the comforters were softer in material and the bed seemed to be more feathery than the other room we had been in.

"I think I like this room, my favorite colors, and tons of space, and soft fluffy pillows! I think this room was made for me! But I want to look at the other rooms just in case." J'erri'ahn'ah's eyes were twinkling with excitement.

We left this door and J'erri'ahn'ah's name appeared on the nameplate, as if the room knew that she liked this room, but was still unsure.

The next room we visited was on the right again (we went in a zigzag pattern), it was also another boys room. The room had the same layout, but was very different from the other, it was dark in its colors, dark midnight blue and black. It had constellations and stars printed on the ceiling that glowed as brilliantly as the sun though, the window was smaller to give the space less natural light. On the walls there was a moon, and a sun, currently the sun was lit up, telling us that it was day time.

There was no chess set in this room, instead there was a desk with paper, fountain pens, ink and book shelves full of books that lined two full walls. Dy'llian wrinkled his nose at this one, "I liked the yellow and green room better." He said, we all laughed.

The bed on this one was very different, it was made of what seemed to be synthetic materials. It had stars and constellations on it that also glowed brilliantly, the pillows had other types of stars and nebulas on them, it was a very interesting room, to say the least.

"Look, there is a telescope at the window!" J'erri'ahn'ah pointed out.

"Huh, I missed that the first time!" I said, looking closer now, my eyes adjusting to the dimmer light of the room, I saw more details about the books sitting on the shelves. They were all astronomy books, myths and legends and how to read the stars.

The next room we went into, on the right side of the hall, was another girls' room. It was baby blue and pink, very calm and relaxing, and it had the biggest window of all the other rooms so far. There was a large being with a soft squishy cushion on it, with a bookshelf underneath it. The bench had pillows on it, to put behind your back as you leaned against the wall to read. It was very pretty, striped with both colors.

The layout was much the same as the other rooms had been, fireplace and chairs, rug on the floor, the large feather bed, the only difference was that this one had a pink and blue sheer canopy showering down from the large four posters of the bed all the way to the floor. The blankets were all fur, lined with feathers, and there were TONS of pillows on the bed. It looked so inviting and comfortable, but J'erri'ahn'ah didn't like it, she was not a reader.

"I like the first one best, I think I'll keep it, since the next room is your's." J'erri'ahn'ah said, "I really do like that room." She smiled brightly. I nodded and continued on to the last boys room across the hall.

This room was simpler than the other two, neutral earth tones, some soft, but dark, greens, browns and beiges. There was another chess set in front of a window that was larger than the first room, but not as big as the last room we were in just now. The bed was more firm and there were only a few pillows on it.

The chess set was a set of Fairies, and Dy'llian was in love. "This one is mine." He said, eyes shining. There were some books scattered here and there, the pictures on the wall were of nature, not hunting, and it suited him perfectly.

We moved onto the very last room in the hall, the room with my name on it. I was almost nervous to open my door, unsure of what we would find behind it. I stopped, looking and admiring the door in front of me. It had a willow tree carved into it, with sunflowers, lavender, lilacs and other such flowers that could once be found in my favorite clearing of the woods where I once played with the fairies. At the top, all around my name, were butterflies and Fairies.

I opened the door and found the room to be dark emerald green and violet in color, elaborately decorated with strips of sheer materials streaming down from the top of my bed, to the floor. The chairs in my room were extra squashy and the embroidery work that matched the markings on my arms perfectly, they were in all different colors. The bed was even softer and more squashy than J'erri'ahn'ah's, but my sheets were satin and silk, my comforters were silky smooth on the bottom side and fur on the top side, and extra thick.

There were not as many pillows, but the pillows that were there were absolutely astoundingly large and fluffy.

In one corner there was a large desk with all kinds of spots and spaces and cubby holes for organization. There was a large stack of parchment and several fountain pens (different colors and sizes) and a few quills, with several bottles of ink (again, in different colors). Behind this massive desk was a full wall window, with a few smaller windows that revolved to allow owl mail to come in, sheer curtains of emerald green and violet hung from the ceiling, flowing to the ground like a strange colored waterfall. There were books on shelves against one of the walls, the shelves lined the wall from left to right and from as high to the ceiling as they could go and still hold books to the floor. The books on these shelves varied in subjects, from all things Fae, to how to rule a kingdom, and table etiquettes.

This room was definitely the largest room of all, and I felt self conscious about it, because it was also, in my personal opinion, much nicer than the other rooms too. I had a full sized table and six chairs, with several other chairs in front of a much larger fireplace.

“Wow,” I said, “Da’ really outdid himself here…” I said, feeling embarrassed.

“I do not envy you this big room, Ary, it’s too purple for my taste.” J’erri’ahn’ah said.

“Yeah, purple isn't really my style either.” Dy’llian added, we all laughed.

“It’s so big, it’s much bigger than all the other rooms.. I feel bad..” I admitted.

“Look, your room is bigger because this is where we are gonna be more often than not, you have a room capable of entertaining people, where as ours are just for one or two people, not all of us. One day, you might be surprised how many people might be here.” J’erri’ahn’ah said. She smiled, “Hey, enjoy this! Cause you deserve it!” She said. “Look, there’s a note for you on the desk.” J’erri’ahn’ah said.

“I’ll read it later, right now, I need to go see Maude.” I said “We have spent a lot of time here, and we may already be too late to help her.” Worry etched across my face.

“Okay, well, let’s go see Maude then.” Dy’llian said.

“In yer wardrobes yeh’ll find that there is a cloak for each of yeh, in the color of yer rooms, these cloaks were specially made by G’rai’ce, and enchanted by yer grandma, they will cloak your presence from people passing by you in the streets, if you choose to stay invisible, these will do it for yeh.” I had forgotten that Jaymes was still there.

“Jaymes, what do we owe you to stay here?” I asked, looking for my coin purse.

“Little lady, yer dad would come back from the dead to haunt me if I charged yeh to stay in a place that he built special fer yeh.” he laughed, “Come now, Maude’s babe don’t have much time.” He said, “I’ll show yeh to the secret stairwell, yeh’ll be able tuh find yer way from there easy ‘nuff.” He said, hurrying off towards the wall at the back part of the inn. He placed his whole palm against the wall, as if to lean on it, and it gave way to a stairwell.

“This’ll lead yeh right inter the dining room we was in earlier, put yer hand on the wall just like I did and ye’ll find the doorway to the alley no trouble. Jus’ knock three times on the wall if yeh can’t find it, and I’ll come show yeh.” He said, “Bes’ be gettin’ back to the bar, I expect people’ll be missin’ me soon.” He turned and walked away from us, through the secret hatch and down the stairwell that led to the dining hall.

We walked down the stairs and into the small cozy dining room that we had been in before when we talked to Jaymes. I put my hand against the wall where the alley way was at, and the wall gave way to outside. I draped my cloak over my shoulders, pulled up the hood and stepped out onto the busy alleyway. Not a single person seemed to notice me, nor the door that I had just stepped out of. J’erri’ahn’ah and Dy’llian followed suit, and I led us off towards the woods.

We reached the edge of town and I led us even farther out, there was a lonely little hut with a fire burning in the hearth. I knocked on the door, and waited.

The door opened and the young girl said, "Yeh canna be here! The little one's got the sickness, yeh have to leave, now!"

"I cannae do that, young lady. Yeh need to bring me yer mum, right away." I said, "Show her this, she will understand." I handed her my mother's butterfly pendant that Maude had given my mother a long time ago. She closed the door on us and we waited for a few moments.

A few moments later an older woman, more worn than I remembered, answered the door, her face angry and accusatory. "Where did ya get this from!?" She demanded, shoving the pendant in my face as she pushed herself out of her door to stand on the porch forcing me to take a few steps back.

"You gave it to my mum, who, in turn, gave it to me the night she was killed. She said that it would bring me good fortune and I would always know that she was close by." I said. "Maude, let me help you." I pleaded. "I can help you."

Maude was momentarily shocked into silence as she studied me closely, and then, after several tense moments, awareness shone in her eyes, "A'lari'jah! My how you've changed! Come in, quickly!" She said, tears in her eyes.

"He's through here, been sick for weeks, it's all I can do to keep him hydrated, at this point. All I can do is pray for a miracle." She said.

I bent over the little boy of about three years, sweating with fever, pale and thin from lack of food and water, the boy was barely holding onto life. His breathing was labored, shallow and came in short quick gurgling gasps.

"Okay, I can help him, you need to leave the room." I told Maude.

"I don't care what you do, I don't care how you do it, and I don't care who asks questions, I've kept more secrets in my lifetime than you could ever know, I am not leaving his side."

She said, stubbornly planting her feet to show that we would have to forcibly remove her. Of course, she knew that I didn't have that kind of time, so I nodded my head.

"Okay then. He's got fluid buildup on his lungs, I need to remove the fluid and get his lungs clear before I can do anything about the infection that caused this." I said, "stand back, and whatever you do, do not touch him." I lifted my hands over his face, closing my eyes. I concentrated hard on the sound of the liquid in his lungs, "I'll need a bowl or something to put this into when I get it out of him." I told Maude who ordered her daughter to bring a bedpan.

Concentrating on the sound of the fluid on his lungs, again, I willed it out of him. His chin lifted up, tilting his head up, opening his throat, his lips parted wide and a nasty brownish liquid came out of his mouth and nose. He made a nasty gurgling, choking noise that seemed to last forever. Dy'llian had to restrain Maude from rushing to his side. She was sobbing and begging for me to stop.

When I had finally pulled all the liquid from his lungs, he took a great, jagged breath, his back that was previously arched, sank back down on his bed, his breathing long and even now instead of shallow and weak.

"Maude, please trust me?" I said, "My mother taught me well, but my grandmother taught me better." I told her, transferring the liquid I was holding between my hands into the bedpan that her daughter had brought in.

"J'erri'ahn'ah, that'll need to be properly disposed of, that can cause more people to become ill if it's not properly cleansed." I told her. She took the bedpan and performed a purifying spell on it, cleansing it of all putrefaction, leaving only pure water.

Meanwhile, I was bent over the little boy looking for the root of his infection, and I found it in his brain. I laid my hands on his head and my whole body glowed golden. Everyone in the room gasped to see my markings glowing as I healed the boy. He groaned and turned his head. It took me a while to cleanse his little brain of the infection, but when I was done, his fever was gone and he fell into a peaceful sleep.

"He's okay, Maude. He will live. If anyone asks, tell them I punctured his chest and relieved the fluid on his lungs, and that the infection drained out with the fluid, essentially healing him." I told her. She hugged me tightly and let go. Dy'llian caught her as she fell into a dead faint. I laid my hands over her and helped her find peace, I turned to her daughter.

"That water is pure water now, sweet and perfect for drinking. Give it to your brother in small amounts, it will help him strengthen him . Give him honey and tea and broths at first, no solid foods for at least a week. Your mother will sleep for a while, you will need to take care of him until she is rested. Give her my love when she wakes up, and call for me with an owl if you need me, the owl will know where to find me." I hugged her and wiped away her tears, "Be brave now, little one, everything's alright. The sun will shine, once again, on your sorrows, and all will be well." I hugged her tightly again until she took a deep steady breath, then we threw our cloaks around our shoulders and pulled up the hoods, and left feeling considerably better about ourselves.

"Now where?" J'erri'ahn'ah asked.

"We go back to the inn, and eat." I told them, "I'm famished now."

We walked back to the inn, through the secret door and up the secret stairs back into our rooms. Once we had freshened up and changed clothes (our wardrobes were full of all kinds of clothes), we went downstairs to the little dining room, where Jaymes was waiting for us.

"Hello, miladie's and mi'lord, I have yer first course ready fer yah if yer of a mind to eat now?"

The table was beautifully set with three plates, bowls and glasses with elaborate silverware (which was actually solid gold). In the middle of the table were several candles lit, to give off a golden orange glow to the room. It was quiet here, where we could converse without other people eavesdropping.

"This is beautiful, Jaymes! This must be Maude's finest china!" I exclaimed.

"No, actually, these were sent just after you arrived by a young Fairie named An'ti'el. She said that it was a gift from yer grandma, oh and she left yeh a note on the desk upstairs." He told me, a twinkle in his eye as he winked at me.

I smiled bashfully, "Also, how is Maude's son?" He asked

"I believe he will be alright now." I said, a twinkle shone in my own eye. It felt good to help others for once, to be a productive part of the community instead of a burden now.

"Sit down, yer first course'll be out in a moment." He said, pulling out my chair and then rushing over to pull out J'erri'ahn'ah's chair.

"Jaymes, why are you doing this for me?" I asked suddenly.

"For starters, I made yer parents a promise to help look out fer yah if anythin' ever happened to 'em.

Secondly, yer my princess, and the true heir to the throne of Nah'alba.

Here, read this, yer da's last request to me is in it." He said.

"Oh! I don't want to read that, Jaymes! That's your letter, not mine!" I told him.

"I know it, milady, but I thought yeh'd like ter read it, yeh know? Understand the way they was thinking befer everythin' happened the way it did." He left me holding the letter in my hand. I felt dirty as I opened it, like I was reading his private diary.

The letter did explain a lot, but it left many more questions in my mind that I had before. Questions I would never have answers to. I folded the letter back up and laid it down on the table. J'erri'ahn'ah and Dy'llian had been staring at me the whole time. I sighed heavily and rolled my eyes, "Fine, I'll read it to you." I picked the letter up and unfolded it again, this time reading out loud.

"Dear Jaymes,

Keep her safe.

Protect her.

Stand by her side when the time comes. She'll need every supporter she can get.

You're dearest friend
M'Kary'ano."

"I have but one question about all this. If they knew what was coming, why didn't they pack you all up and leave?" J'erri'ahn'ah asked, not realizing that Jaymes had come back in the room.

"Because they knew that it had to be. It had to come to pass the way that it did. Yer parents were not going to leave, sadly they knew what was coming for 'em, and they knew that, no matter where they went, they would always be found, as long as you were alive. So, they chose the risky choice of staying and letting it happen, o'course one of 'em was supposed ter survive the whole thing, and be here to guide you and take care of you, or make sure that you went where you were supposed ter go, but things didn't happen that way, so they instilled a guardian. Being G'rai'ce and M'Kary'ano, they didn't fully trust any one person to the well being and safety of their daughter, so they made sure that more than one person was watchin' out fer ya, making sure that there were people strategically placed to keep an eye on ya. Me own daughter is a maid in the king's household as we speak, to keep a close eye on ya, and report back to me if anything happens. An' she's not the only one either." He explained as he carefully ladled hot soup into our bowls.

"This here is lamb broth, enjoy. The lamb chops will be coming soon." He said as he left the room once again.

"Wow, Ary, your parents sure went through a lot of trouble to keep you safe for when they were gone."

J'erri'ahn'ah remarked. "It's just sad that they knew that this was all going to happen before it did. I don't think I would like to know if I'm going to die, or how or when." She finished, shoveling steaming spoonfuls of soup into her mouth. There was silence for a few seconds before Dy'llian said, "This is truly wonderful soup! "Why did we bring food from home again?" He asked playfully. We finished our three course meal in silence, and then dawned our travel cloaks, and took off to my old home.

Chapter Eleven

An awkward silence fell between us as we made our way out of the village to my old home. The tension and anxiety was almost unbearable and, in an attempt to break that tension, we made comments about the wildlife that we saw, or the trees that were bent at awkward angles, or that had been struck by lightning. We tried to make conversation about the flowers, small ponds, and other such vegetation, all to no avail. The tension was far too thick to be broken, so we rested in the silence, allowing our minds to wander wherever they may. Taem'luck followed silently behind us, giving me space and allowing me to think and prepare myself for the devastation that was in store for me.

When we came upon a fork in the road that stopped me dead in my tracks, it felt like we had been on the road for hours when, in truth, it had only been half an hour. My chest rose and fell rapidly beneath my panicked breathing. My heart felt as if it was trying to run straight out of my chest and as far down the road as it could get. My palms felt sticky with sweat, my face prickled with perspiration, tears swam in my eyes and my head raced with memories of the past.

"Ary? Is this it?" J'erri'ahn'ah placed her hand on my forearm softly, but the look on my eyes answered her question.

"Take yer time. We're in no hurry." She said, backing up to stand behind me.

It took me some time before I was capable of taking the next step; my mind was being flooded with incalculable childhood memories, my last one was of this road as it disappeared into the distant horizon when Ro'than'iel carried me away.

I took a deep steadying breath, trying to get my emotions and panic under control. I reached back for a hand, or a wing, or anything, something to hold onto as I took that next step, and was answered, not by one hand but by two hands and a wing. I looked around and there stood J'erri'ahn'ah and Dy'llian on each side of me, and Taem'luck behind me, with his wing on my back. I nodded and, one slow, grueling step at a time, I led them to my house.

It was more devastating than I could have ever described it to be. I knew that the house was destroyed, but somehow, in my mind, I never could picture it as anything but whole; so, the image of it burnt to ashes was overwhelming. I fell to my knees, my breathing came in gasps of sobs, I clung to the hands holding mine for my life. I couldn't do this. I wouldn't do this. Why was I torturing myself for coming back here?

Ary, yer no' alone in thus. We are here wi' you, lean on us, and we will help you through it.

Their echoing voices crashed in around me, a welcome distraction from the pain, their touch eased my sobs and calmed my breathing, my head stopped spinning and I found the strength that I needed to continue on.

As I approached, great trepidation entered my heart, my hands trembled and my whole body shook with grief. I could not make myself walk over the threshold of the house, I could not endure the memory of them all screaming, it was too real just now. I turned, instead, and walked through the yard, to the little clearing that I used to play in, the clearing that my Fae friends and I visited every day. I was not surprised to find it empty, bare, and quite a lot less impressive than I remembered it to be. Though the clearing itself was still here, the ma'jick that used to be here was now gone. I smiled sadly, tears running down my cheeks. It looked and felt so empty and sad now, all the life seemed to be gone from the whole place. I expected it to be empty, but I didn't expect it to feel dead. I heard J'erri'ahn'ah and Dy'llian approach from behind.

"I used to come here, every afternoon, right after lunch, to play with my Fae friends. This place used to be beautiful, sunflowers taller than I was, Lilacs, Lavender and Mint grew here also. The Fae used to have little houses and waterfalls, there used to be a little pond I would splash in during the mid to late Summer months. It was so maj'ickal! I could come here and get lost for hours, playing, laughing and splashing in the pond.

Water Nymphs, Woodland Nymphs, Fairies, Elves, Dwarves, Deer, Rabbits, Hedgehogs, and so many more, all used to come here to play with me. I do miss those carefree days. Though I hate myself for having been here more than I was with them. I always did hate being inside, I always did hate being cooped up and made to cook and clean and learn, I chomped at the bit until my mother released me to come outside. Now I wish that I had spent more time with them, all of them, because now they are gone, and I have more memories of being here than I do of being with my family." I sank to the ground, bitterness and hatred rose up inside of me, I found myself unable to cry. I just sat there, miserable and feeling utterly alone in the world now.

We had been sitting there for an immeasurable amount of time when Taem'luck suddenly started growling, a low deep, rumbling growl from deep within his chest, his markings lit up, he was on high alert; there was danger nearby.

"There is someone just beyond the tree line, someone who feels both familiar and unfamiliar, it's a strange feeling." I whispered to J'erri'ahn'ah and Dy'llian, Taem'luck had been on guard the moment he sensed him. In wolf form, he was quite impressive in his defensive position between us and the stranger who had stopped his approach. His giant paws planted in the ground quite as immovable as a mountain, his reddish brown hackles stood straight up, his teeth bared and a low rumbling growl emanated from deep within his throat.

He stood and looked warily at my guardian, pale faced, hands in the air, "Forgive me, I was not expecting anyone to be here, no one ever comes here, and no one knows about this place." He said, a nervous tension in his voice.

I know that voice, I have heard it before, but where did I hear it?

I tried to piece together what he was saying, piece together what his words meant, but my mind was still reeling from the pain of being back here again. I shook my head and tried to clear my thoughts.

"I don't understand..." I said, "I don't understand, sir, explain, please?" My broken sentences said too much about my state of mind than I wished they had.

"My family died here three years ago today. I come here every year on this day, to wish my youngest daughter a happy birthday and to talk to my wife again." His voice was thick with emotion.

"I don't understand, I can't... I don't... I don't understand..." I said, still trying to shake my thoughts free, trying to clear my head so that I could piece together what this stranger was saying.

"Madam, are you well? Do I need to fetch some help??" He asked, his voice was thick with worry and concern, he thought that I was mad.

"Your family..." I said, still trying to put it all together. "*Your family....*" and then it hit me, and my mind clicked. When the rage hit, it was as if the whole world turned red, "That, sir, is quite impossible!" I stood up, shaking. *Finally, I have someone to lash out at.*

"I suggest you leave, sir, before I have my guardian make you leave." I told him, I did not want to fight, not really, and this stranger did not deserve to have my angry grief thrown at him.

"I am sorry, Madam, to have disturbed you, I would quite like to continue on about my business and leave you be. I assure you, I mean you no harm, I just mean to visit my family on this day." He told me, adamantly reminding me that he was not leaving any time soon.

"Sir, you will leave me with no choice but to have my guardian force you to leave, if you do not leave of your own accord." I told him, my voice still quivering with anger.

"No, madam, I will not leave until I have visited my family, as I have done for the past three years. I assure you, I will not be going anywhere but to their grave site, that's all I wish for." He said, his own anger was showing through his carefully masked emotions.

"I ASSURE YOU, SIR, THAT YOUR FAMILY DID NOT LIVE HERE." I screamed at him.

"No, miss, I assure you, this is where my family lived. I have been here many times. I buried what remained of the bodies of my wife and children, minus one, but I put a grave marker for her anyway." He told me, confusion saturated his voice.

"Is this a sick joke!? Who's idea was this? Did Eir'im'uhs or A'lbi'on put you up to this? Who would be so cruel?!" I spat at him, my voice was venomous.

"I could ask you the very same question, madam!" He spat back, his voice icy. "Three long years I have mourned the loss of my family! For three long years I have come here to be closer to them! And not once, NOT ONCE has anyone ever bothered to come here! And now, all of a sudden, out of the blue, here you sit, in my youngest daughter's favorite spot, claiming that it was *your* family that died here! I should be asking you who you are! And what you're doing at *MY* home!" His rage was impressive, but so was mine.

"YOUR DAUGHTER'S FAVORITE SPOT?! I ASSURE YOU, SIR, THAT NO ONE BUT ME CAME HERE!"

"You? Wait..." He said, now confused by my words. "What is your name, madam?" He asked, his anger ebbed away.

"A'lari'jah Jayd McM'Kary'ano." My chest swelled up with

pride as I said my full name.

"A'lari'jah Jayd McM'Kary'ano??" He said, puzzled by this. "But that canna be right..." He said. He fell to his knees, hands on either side of his face like he was trying to hold his head from splitting in half.

"But, that was my daughter's name, that is, that was... " He was overwhelmed and muttering not unlike I had been a few minutes ago.

"Prove that this was your home. Tell me what hung over the hearth in the sitting room" I said.

He was silent for a long time, and just when I was ready to give up hope, he spoke up.

"A portrait of my family hung up over our hearth." He said, "The painting was a bit odd, the artist seemed to have been drunk when he painted us and we all ended up looking like idiots. Everyone of us had larger than normal heads, and specific features that were exaggerated. My wife's long hair was exaggerated to be like Rapunzel's." He seemed to be lost in the memory, it was difficult not to listen, "My youngest daughter, though, that was the funniest one, she was so tiny that no one could make her out, he drew her with wings and violet hair, one eye green, one eye purple, and very large bug eyes." He said, "Is that proof enough?" He asked.

It was I who was taken aback by this, no one who had visited our house had known that I was in the picture, everyone always assumed that it was painted before I arrived in the family. "No, it's not, tell me something that only my da' would know, something that no one else knew, not even my mum." I said, my father and I shared a secret, and if he knew this secret, then maybe, just maybe, he really was my da'.

"A'lari'jah was afraid of the dark." He said.

"Mum knew that. She would always leave a light on for me." I told him.

"Ach, but G'rai'ce didn't know that she slept with a specific blanket that I made for yeh, it was a dark emerald green and violet velvet blanket that was six inches no matter which way yeh measured it. It was embroidered with a willow tree, butterflies, sunflowers, and fairies." He said.

I gasped and sank to my knees, shaking and sobbing.

"No, that is quite impossible. M'Kary'ano is dead! MY DA' IS DEAD! I saw him die!" I screamed as loudly as I could.

"You... You watched him die? How?! On'y way I see that happening is if yer a psychic?" He was bewildered, enraged at *my* preposterous claim

"No, *sir*! I was there!" I screamed at him. "If you are who you say you are then you carried me out of the house! The explosion threw me out of your arms, and you were gone!" I said, still screaming, trembling from head to toe now.

"YOU WERE GONE! YOU LEFT ME! AND YOU'VE BEEN ALIVE THIS WHOLE TIME?! NO, SIR, MY FATHER IS A BETTER MAN THAN THAT. HE WOULD HAVE STOPPED AT NOTHING TO FIND ME!" This time my voice echoed off the trees, my rage shook the leaves and the ground quaked beneath me.

He stood up and walked towards me, he sank down to the ground to look at me, I looked up at him and gasped. His face was a face that I had only seen one time, in memories that An'ti'el showed me, the image of a sad young Fae man, once heir to the throne of A'lbi'on, blue hair, tall and muscular with a long pointed face, and lanky arms and legs. A man who was striking in his beauty, and power. A man who looked exactly like the one sitting just out of the shadows of my favorite clearing.

"Did you really come searching for me?" I asked him, barely able to control my own emotions.

"Yes, I searched far and wide, for days and days, weeks, and months. I couldn't find anything to tell me that you had survived." he said sadly. "If I had known that you had survived, I never would have stopped searching for you." He told me, a fierce grief raged in his eyes not unlike the fire on that tragic night, three years ago.

"I was thrown forward, out of your arms. I laid there for three days and two nights. Ro'than'iel found me near the end of the third day and took me to Uncle A'lbi'on, where I was bedridden for a year."

"You are with A'lbi'on!?" Horror struck his brilliant eyes, and I sat back away from him.

"Yes, I am with Uncle A'lb'ion and have been since Ro'than'iel found me. Why?" I asked, a bit annoyed with having to repeat myself. *Didn't I just say that?*

"It's just not where your mother and I had planned for you to live.." He looked at me for the first time and gasped. "A'lari'jah, look at you!" He exclaimed.

"What? Oh, I suppose I have grown a bit since you last saw me." I smiled, suddenly feeling shy.

"Grown? My gods! You've evolved!" He said, awestruck at the sight of my Fae features.

I blushed, realizing that he could see through my human facade, "Queen Verisiel gifted me with healing from my deformity from the fire. You see, when I was thrown from your arms, my back and hip and leg all broke in several places. When they mended, they mended crooked, leaving me no more than a crippled girl who couldn't do anything for herself. An'ti'el healed me, and when she did, she also unlocked my full powers, and this was a direct result of that." I told him.

"Have you met An'ti'el?" He asked me, "I suppose, then, that you have met with M'urlin, as well?" He asked.

"Aye, I huve. He did tell me that there would be an unexpected surprise waiting fer me right around the corner, of course that *was* a year ago." I found it interesting how that came about.

"A'lari'jah," He started to ask something but then hesitated and seemed to change his mind.

"Aye?" I encouraged him to continue.

"Well... I was just wonderin' if yeh'd like tuh see them?" He asked.

"Yes, I think I would." I told him, he helped me to my feet and offered me his arm. I beckoned to J'erri'ahn'ah and Dy'llian to follow, Taem'luck already at my side.

"That's a gorgeous dragon you have there, Ary, I suppose that since everyone you once had to protect you was gone, you needed a guardian." He smiled, "I am grateful to you, Taem'luck, for looking out for her."

"Oh, I'm not going anywhere, just because you're back." Taem'luck said, "Our bond is for life, my oath is until we die, there is no separating us now."

"Oh! I am very well aware of that, I didn't mean to imply that you would be leavin' now." Da's answer seemed to satisfy Taem'luck, and nothing more was said on the subject.

He led me down to the river, where a little cemetery rested beneath a willow tree. Eight crosses, each one a name burned into them, stood erect over the dirt inside of a gated area.

"You went through a lot of trouble with this, it cannae have been easy." I said.

"No, I had to scoop up each one of their ashes and put them inside of a jar, which I had to make first, and then bury them. To bury a soul in a garden with no gate prevents the souls from going home." He told me.

"I saw mum." I said suddenly.

"What? Where? Is she alive too?" He asked.

"No, Da' I saw her when I died one day." I told him.

"Wait, you died?" He asked, shocked.

"Yes, Da', I did." I told him, "But that's a story for a later time." I tried to redirect him back to the cemetery.

"No, it's not, it's a conversation for right now, I need to know." He said.

"Da', trust me, you don't want to know this." I said, but he grabbed my arms and twisted them up.

"Ary, what did you do!?" He said, the deep scars in my arms had not faded when I got my new fairy body, they sat there reminding me of the most terrible thing I had done.

"The day before my twelfth birthday, I broke a glass and took a shard of it and sliced open my arm in an effort to make my pain go away, and to relieve everyone of the burden that I thought I was." I told him.

He reached out and pulled me close and held me tight. "Ary, I am so sorry! So sorry!" We sank to the ground and there we stayed for an immeasurable amount of time.

"We need to get back to the inn before Jaymes sends out a search party for us!" I said suddenly.

"I'll go back wi' yah. Wanna catch up wi' my daughter." He said, "If that's alright wi' yah. Lass?" He asked.

"Brilliant!" I exclaimed. And we left the cemetery just as the sun began to set.

"Here, M'Kary'ano, probably best if no one sees yeh walking wi' us." Dy'llian said, handing him the invisibility cloak. Da' looked at him like he was crazy, but donned the cloak anyways, but understanding registered on his face as he pulled the cloak around his shoulders. He smiled, "I had forgotten about these!"

"Look, there's a fire up ahead!" Dy'llian said, pointing at the smoke in the air just ahead of us.

"Aye, friends or foe do you reckon?" I asked quietly.

"Dunno, only one way to find out, J'erri'ahn'ah and I will walk ahead of you two, if the coast is clear we will signal you, you take off your cloak and come on up, if it's not, just follow with us with your cloak on." Dy'llian directed me, then turned to M'Kary'ano, "I probably donna need to tell you this, but you should keep yer cloak on the whole time."

We nodded and they went off, I followed about ten paces behind them, wanting to know first hand what was going to happen.

"Evenin' folks! Y'all headin' back to the village?" The older man at the campfire asked.

"Yes sir, my sisters and I are traveling into the village." Dy'llian said. At that I walked up and stood beside them, without my cloak on, Da standing right beside me with his on.

"Well, yeh'll be needin' this." He said, handing us a torch each, "Be safe tonight, it's a good clear night, means robbers will be on the roads." He cautioned us.

"Much obliged, sir, have a good evening." Dy'llian replied, leading us all off to the road again. The torches made our trip easier and faster. We were able to get back to the inn just in time for supper.

I had special instructions that dinner was to be served before we went down, and that no one was to come into the room with us while we were eating. Da came down and ate with us, he kept the cloak close by so that if anyone came in he could cover up, hopefully, before they saw him.

After supper, we all went back up stairs to our hidden floor. Da' chose the starry room to stay in as it was the closest one to my door that wasn't a girls room. After we'd freshened up and changed into more comfortable clothing, we gathered in my room in front of my large fireplace and caught Da' up to current events.

Da wanted me to start right from the moment the fire exploded behind him and I was thrown from his arms. I went into storyteller mode, I was a natural born storyteller afterall, and in great detail I told him everything that had happened from that day until today. When I had finished he was quiet for a long time, we just sat looking at the fire, waiting for his mind to stop reeling from three years of information crammed into a few hours.

Finally, he was ready to begin his bombardment of questions.

"First thing's first, the scars on your arms, tell me about them." He said, it was not a question, in no way was it a request, it was a command, and I obeyed.

"They happened a few nights before my twelfth birthday, I heard Uncle A'lbi'on and Sr'eya talking in hushed tones about me, and it made me angry at myself." I said, my gaze into the fire was so intent that it seemed like I was actually making the fire brighter and hotter.

"What did they say that would make you feel the need to do this to yourself?" He asked, trying to keep his emotions in check.

"It was simple. I closed myself off to them, I pretended that I was okay, I was not being vulnerable and showing them that I was not okay. They were discussing my health as if I was not there, as if I was all alone. It was how I felt. I felt as though I was expected to be okay, to not be upset or in turmoil from it. Whenever I did bring up the subject it was always met with deflection and a change in subject. No one wanted to hear that I wasn't okay, no one was listening to my pain, no one could hear it. So, I marked myself so that people would know that I was hurting. I never intended to actually leave this world, I just wanted people to see that I was not okay, that I was hurting because it felt as though they couldn't hear me." I kept my eyes locked on the fire, I did not want to see the pain and disappointment in their eyes.

"Mo melda..." He said, voice breaking tears streaming down his face, still I refused to look at him. "Dè a rinn mi? What have I done?"

Chapter Twelve

As the days passed us by, I noticed a shadow lingering over us all. Time was closing quickly and soon we would all go our separate ways, saying goodbye to our loved ones again. My fifteenth birthday would find Taem'luck, J'errian'ah, Dy'llian, Sr'eya and myself back at court with my uncle, leaving behind Jhoana and J'erri'ahn'ah. My father would go back to A'va'lon.We had all agreed that it would be far too deadly for M'Kary'ano to show himself in court again. I was heartbroken. What was I going to do now? I had just found him and now I would have to say goodbye again. I felt like leaving him would destroy me.Our departure day was still a few days out, and they seemed to drag on by in slow motion. The days felt longer and the nights sleepless and restless. We were all underneath a heavy cloud of sadness. With only three nights to go before we would embark on our journey back to court, we were all sitting in front of the fire, laughing and enjoying each other's company, telling stories and remembering good times. After the laughter died out, and the fire was but embers, I sipped the last of my hot chocolate and laid my head on M'kary'ano's shoulder. I must have dozed off because the next thing I remembered was being carried up to my bed.I sat straight up in bed, knocking Taem'luck to the floor in a startled state; I had this horrible, sinking feeling that something was very, very wrong.

Taem'luck stood up and shook himself off and growled softly at me for knocking him on the floor.

"Sorry, Tae. I have this weird feeling in the pit of my stomach. I can't shake the feeling that something's wrong." I said, trying to rub the butterflies out of my stomach.

"That's alright, it just took me by surprise. What do you mean "feeling"?" he asked.

"I don't know, it woke me up, something doesn't feel right, can't you feel it?" He frowned and concentrated, "I feel it now. It's getting stronger ... A'va'lon ... she is crying out in pain, she's suffering, something's wrong. She's dying." He spoke in chopped up sentences, wincing at the pain he felt from A'va'lon.

Shivering, I got out of bed, donned my robe, and went to the fireplace to stoke the fire and add wood to it. The moon was high in the sky, telling me that it was still really late in the night. I held my stomach with both arms folded over my middle.

"I don't like this feeling, I feel like I'm going to be sick." I groaned. Looking out my window, seeking any sign that something was wrong.A sudden, quick rap at my door startled me, "I wonder who that is." thought to Taem'luck.I crossed the room and opened the door; M'kary'ano was standing in the hall.

"Aye, thought I'd find yeh up. Best be getting dressed, I 'spect we will be leaving soon." he said as he disappeared down the hallway.

I did as he bid, dressed as quickly as I could and stole down the stairs, Taem'luck at my side. I could hear An'ti'el as I neared the bottom. I stole through the living room and stopped dead in the doorway of the kitchen.

An'ti'el was barely standing, her usually bright face was ashen and fear was written in her eyes. She curtsied to me, "Highness" she said, her voice was cold and raspy, her eyes looked half crazed.

I nodded my head, "An'ti'el" I replied dryly.

"We must go! We have to go! Might be too late, but we have to try! We must try! It's too late. But we have to try! Can't just give up! Should have been here sooner, but she said no! Oh! We need to go!" She was saying, rocking back onto her heels and bouncing up onto her toes.

"Where?"

"A'va'lon!" When her eyes met mine I felt like I was staring into an abyss.

"Why?" She blinked and the look she gave me made my heart stop dead in my chest, my body went cold like it had been doused in ice water. "A'va'lon is dying, you foolish girl! And you're standing here asking questions! How dare you! We must go! Now!" She hissed at me.I closed my eyes and reached out to her mind, it was frantic, panicky, crazed and there was a darkness that was trying to take hold of her.

"An'ti'el" I commanded, a shadow filled the room, my voice sounded like it was booming, echoing off the walls, ringing with authority, my body grew to the full height of the kitchen, "An'ti'el, I command you to come out of the darkness back into the light!" There was a blank look on her face for a few moments, her eyes rolled back to expose the whites; the darkness in her mind was warring with her, and then she fell forward, leaning heavily on the counter top and blinked.

"Forgive me, majesty. I don't know what came over me." her voice was laced with exhaustion, breathless and quiet as a whisper."Not to worry, An'ti'el, time to be off, yes?" I tried to be as light and nonchalant as I could.

"Yes, take my hands!" J'erri'ahn'ah and Dy'llian had just joined us. We took hold of a hand each; I blinked and we were in A'va'lon.I knew that we were standing on solid ground, but my body felt like I was still flying through the woods. I saw everything by the triples, my mind was blank and spinning and my stomach lurched. I leaned over and vomited all over my feet. As if through water, I could hear An'ti'el droning on about something, but when I threw up, she stopped talking and began tapping her toes on the floor. I heard her mumble something that my ringing ears couldn't understand, but whatever it was, it made my father angry."Then you will make time! You could have come to us before now, when mother was sick, you didn't have to wait until it was almost too late to come for us! You had time, you had a warning, and you chose to ignore it, now you will make the time to wait until she can recover from your lightning fast transport!"An'ti'el mumbled something else that I couldn't understand, my vision was growing dark and I remember weakly saying, "Da?" He caught me before I fell into my vomit. He carried me somewhere and laid me down on something soft, it felt like he was holding my right hand. "Sleep now, my love, all will be right again when you wake." And I was gone."Ary?" An unfamiliar voice sounded in my head. "Ary, can you hear me?" She asked again."Who's there?" I whispered weakly."It is I, Verisiel." I could hear it now, the sound of a queen in her voice."Grandmother?" I asked, a bit confused."Yes, dear, it is so nice to hear your voice, to get to meet you!" She said.

"What's going on?" I asked. "The last thing I remember was being sick and passing out.""Yes, it did take a while for you to be conscious enough for me to get through to you. I don't have much time now, my life force is fading quickly now." She said, " I have already transferred my title to you, I've been waiting to speak with you, wanting to meet the woman who would take my place." I could hear the smile in her voice. "I want you to know, I've watched you your whole life, kept tabs on you, and I am so proud of who you are! The obstacles you've overcome and the pain you've struggled through! You always come out on top! Maybe dragging yourself through the battlefield, broken, bruised and battered, but never destroyed! Always victorious! I am sorry that you have endured so much, and that there is so much riding on you! I wish that I could stick around and be there when you are crowned, but alas! if that were the case, I'd be queen and you wouldn't." Her smile was weak now, she was sad.

"Grandmother, I ..." words failed me at this moment. Of all the times I wished I could speak to her, all the things I used to say that I would tell her, my mind went blank. "I love you." Is all I could think to say. "I love you, and even though I did not know you, I will miss you." I said.

"No, dear child, you will miss the idea of me. I promise that I would not have made a very good grandmother. I was a queen, and for far too long that was all I was, so I am afraid that I would have made a poor grandmother." She said sadly. "One of my many regrets." She sighed.

"What will A'va'lon do without you?" She smiled again, "She will be brought up out of her ashes, like a phoenix, she will rise and shine as bright as the moon. You will bring her to a new age, a new era, and show her a whole new world of possibilities and opportunities and equalities. You will bring her so much joy, and so much growth and so much light. She will be just fine without me, I have chosen my successor well." I could feel her pride radiating off of her. "Grandmother?" I asked."Hmm?" "Thank you." I said.

"For what?""For making my life possible." I felt her frown.

"What do you mean?""Do you not know?" I paused, thinking about it all. "I suppose it would be alright to tell you, one last good deed before you die. It was you who made me possible. Aranhil hated my father, he despised that my father chose my mother over him and A'va'lon. He never would have restored his immortality if it had not been for your tender love for your son. He watched you, followed you when you would visit him, followed you to the wedding. He knew that you visited M'kary'ano and G'rai'ce, and in doing so, he saw a life fulfilled. A life well lived, and a successful love and a pure sweet joy. It was in following you and seeing them together that restored his fatherly heart and softened him toward restoring his immortality. Before he passed away, he had planned on restoring his title too, but he never got the chance." She was quiet for a while, I could feel her thinking, reflecting, "It's odd that he never said anything about it. He could have had me executed for disobeying him."

"No, he would never have done that. His love for you ran deeper than his love for A'va'lon, and your deep love for M'kary'ano made him love my father too. It was you who saved us all, your love was what made me a possibility. It's why I think that you would have made a good grandmother, even if you don't think so."

"Thank you, child. You have made me happy in my last moments. Be blessed, and stay safe!!" Her last words faded as her life force did.I woke up to my father whispering in my ear, "Ary, it's time to wake up." I blinked my eyes in the bright light. "What time is it?" I asked." Around mid-morning, before lunch, but after breakfast." Dy'llian said, nursing a growling stomach.I looked around me, I was laying on an elaborately decorated bed, Taem'luck was laying at my side, and Veri'si'el was gone.

"She spoke to me, you know? She waited for me to come round before she left. Said she wanted to meet me before she died." I smiled.

"That's wonderful! You would have really liked her!" He said. "Time to get up, we have witnesses who need to sign the scroll and then brunch and dress fitting to take place today then coronation tomorrow!" M'kary'ano was excited, and tired.

I sat up and Taem'luck came over and attacked my face, licking me all over.

"EUGH! TAY! GROSS!" I laughed and he jumped off the bed.

An'ti'el bowed as I got off the bed, she handed me the scroll, "Majesty, we will go to the throne room where those who witnessed the transfer of title will sign the scroll with their maj'ickal seal and then we will all go to brunch together. You will just read the inscription on the back of the scroll and then they will come up and read the inscription on their side of the scroll. They will hold their hand over the parchment and, when they are done speaking the inscription, their hand will leave a maj'ickal seal underneath it." An'ti'el explained as we walked along the corridors to the throne room.I nodded my head and tried to keep up with her, she walked very quickly and I was still half asleep."Here we are." She said, apparently she brought us in the back way. Looking me up and down she frowned, "Well, I suppose you'll do for now." She opened the door and bowed me in.

Once we got inside the massive throne room, I saw that there were twenty Fae folk standing in a line, waiting to make their mark and move about their day. They were not grumbling or talking amongst themselves, they were all standing patiently and dignified while I made my way to the top of the dais.

"Come one! Come all! Come make your mark and sign your seal and bear witness to the events that have transpired." I stopped reading and looked behind me, An'ti'el was sniggering but urged me to continue.

"Come one! Come all! Come say your lines and witness history in the making! Come declare your allegiance and swear your fealty, come give your life, your sword, your word to the new queen of A'va'lon!" I finished reading it, and even the noble Fae Folk at the bottom of the dais were having a difficult time keeping a straight face.

They came one at a time, knelt down in front of me and placed their hand over the scroll and read the inscription;

"I have borne witness to the transfer of title between V'eri'si'el and A'lari'jah.

> We bear witness that A'lari'jah is the rightful heir to the throne of A'va'lon.
>
> Me and Mine declare our allegiance and swear our fealty to the rightful heir of A'va'lon, A'lari'jah. From this day, until our last day, we swear to come to her defense, to cross oceans and move mountains, to lay down our lives if the need ever arises, to defend A'lari'jah in her absence as well as in her presence.``

When they were done, the scroll had twenty seals on it, none of them protested, none of them challenged the claim. When it was all said and done, they conversed freely and with a friendly attitude with me and mine, walking with us to the great hall to sit and feast together. They were all a bit interesting and strange folk. Dwarves, Gnomes, Elves, Pixies, Nymphs of the water, Nymphs of the air, Nymphs of the woods, and Nymphs of fire, Centaurs and Fawns, Pucks, Pegasi,

Merlyn, all sorts of creatures I had yet to learn their species or nature. It was quite wonderful to converse with them.

The Dwarves were creatures of the mines, protecting the forest and all within, they served for centuries as the first line of defense of the enchanted forest. Marching her borders and keeping out those would do her harm.

The Gnomes were the gardeners, tending to and caring for the whole forest. Making sure that all is growing well, they were responsible for the health and well being of the forest, both mortal and immortal. They tended to wounds, healing them and making sure that no darkness could come in through them. They were the second line of defense, though small, these creatures could pack a mighty punch, and could do some serious damage to those who would harm their forest. The Elves were warriors, third line of defense, they were gatherers, they gathered and harvested the foods in the forest and took them to A'va'lon for all creatures to partake of. In A'va'lon, all food was freely given, not sold at the highest cost, but freely given to all who needed, so that none within her gates went hungry. The Elves supervised the distribution of food, cared for her homeless, helped her lonely and healed her sick. The Elves did amazing things, their maj'ick was unrivaled. Next to the Fairies themselves, they were the most powerful creatures in the forest.

The Nymphs cared for the waters, the woods, the air and fires. Where there was need, the fire nymphs scorched the ground so that the old could be burned away and new could take its place. The pucks were servants, if you will, they did house work, cooking, fine needle work and other such things for people in exchange for small gifts such as milk, or small trinkets of appreciation. They were the best at what they did, and made the most exquisite needlework, but beware, if you upset a puck they became hobgoblins. Hobgoblins were horrid,mischievous things, ugly and grim and made a wreck of everything, but if you don't make them upset, they are quite friendly creatures. Centaurs and Fawns had a whole other "world" ; they were set apart and lived amongst themselves, seldom to come out and take part in the community of things. They lived in the forest, going about their days, making predictions and keeping to themselves. Every now and then a Centaur would come out with a warning, a sign or a prophecy, and the whole world would stop what they were doing and listen. The Fawns followed the Centaurs, taking care of them and the ground they walked on, clearing sicks, stones and other such obstacles out of their way, fetching them food, firewood and cooking and cleaning up for them. The Pegasi lived in the sky, noble and majestic creatures, kept to the heavens except for special occasions. They watched over us all from above, fighting wars that we could not see between the Creator and his greatest enemy. The Pegasi did what the Creator bid, they protected him and watched over the world. On a rare occasion a Pegasi would come down and bond with a particular human until that human either became unworthy of them, or died. Most often the human the Pegasi would bond with were pure of heart, mighty and courageous, a hero of sorts. And more often than not, they would lose themselves in the crowds and the people and become villains, their Pegasi would be their last hope, if they still had a Pegasi their deeds were only skin deep, they had not yet penetrated the heart or corrupted the soul, but when the Pegasi would leave all hope was lost for them. The Pixies were the most benevolent creatures that were there to swear fealty. They could be your best friend or your enemy and you would never know the difference. One positive thing was that once they swore something, they would never break that trust. Tricky as they might be, if you earned their loyalty, they could be really good assets. They would do your bidding and make the most wonderful spies. if they did not swear loyalty to you, beware, they will trick the socks off of you.Breakfast passed quickly, conversations were plentiful, and the food was good. After we ate, we all went our separate ways and An'ti'el led me back to my room. "Majesty, let me introduce you to your new lady's maids. Ke'yahn'ah, Ki'ri'ah, and Ky'wahn'ah. They are sisters. Triplets, and good hard workers. Their family fell on some hard times a while back and I've been grooming them to work with you ever since." The girls curtsied as their names were called. They were nearly identical in physical features. All three of them were short, slight and pale with dark brown freckles sprinkled across their noses and cheeks. Their ears were not as pointy as other Fae's and their noses were small and button-like. They each had different colored hair, soft pastel blue, pink and yellow. "Milady, I am Ke'yahn'ah." Said the girl with the pastel pink hair. She was clearly older than the other two, or at least had stepped into the older sister role.

"Milady, I am Ki'ri'ah." Said the girl with the pastel yellow hair, she was clearly the middle child, sweet and shy.

"Milady, I am Ky'wahn'ah." Said the girl with the pastel blue hair, the youngest, the wild and artsy girl. She was the most outwardly excited one of them all. I was sure that they were all excited, but Ke'yahn'ah was too polite and courteous to show it and Ki'ri'ah was too shy and modest to be outwardly excited."Let's get you fitted for your big day tomorrow!!" Ky'wahn'ah said, jumping up and down. "Just you wait till you see the dress! You're gonna love it!" Ke'yahn'ah shot her sister a look and she immediately stopped bouncing and stood with her hands clasped in front of her.

"Remember, she's our queen, not our friend." Ke'yahn'ah snapped. "Forgive my sister, majesty, she's just excited and forgets herself."

"No need to apologize, you're not my slaves, bound to stand still and not have a mind or a personality of your own. You're just my maids who get paid handsomely for your services, in private, behind closed doors, you may be yourselves, and if it's too much I will let you know." I smiled. I never wanted them to feel uncomfortable around me, "I am your queen, but I am also more than just a queen, my status does not define everything about me." "Nevertheless, you three best not forget your places. I don't care what she says, you are not her friends, you are her servants, nothing more, just servants." An'ti'el said firmly.

"Wait a second, you just said, 'I don't care what she says' as if I'm no one. I'm the queen, An'ti'el, whatever I say goes. And I say that they may be my maids, but they do not have to act like they don't not have minds or personalities. Not behind closed doors, if you don't like that, well you know where the door is." I told her curtly."Well, tradition dictates that they act professionally and cordially." She snapped at me sarcastically.

"Well, isn't it my job to dictate tradition to be broken? Isn't that the whole point of appointing me as queen? Isn't that why I was born? Or is that something that you believe only skin deeply? Because if I am to break tradition, I cannot have someone who only believes in breaking them when we are in the public eye." I told her firmly. "Furthermore, ma'am, if you want to be sarcastic, again, you know where the door is, I will not tolerate your benevolent behavior. Not today, not any day."

"You're not queen yet, A'lari'jah." She told me, I could see tears welling up in her eyes.

"You're right, I'm heir apparent, tomorrow I will be queen, but I will not accept this attitude from you; you're either with me, or against me. Which is it?"She paused for a long hard moment, tears running down her eyes, unable to speak, unable to look at me.

"I know this is hard for you, she's not even cold yet and here we are planning on taking her place. Well, let me tell you, I can never take her place. I may sit where she sat, sleep where she slept and eat the food at the place she would have eaten it, but I can never take her place. I never want to. I am my own person, I am my own queen. And if you don't like that, if you can't get behind me in this, if you don't REALLY want to break tradition with me then you know where the door is. You know where I stand, you know what I aim to do, what will it be, An'ti'el?" I was hoping, praying beyond all that she would stay, I didn't know how I was going to do this without her. She was crying harder now. "I'm sorry, majesty. It's just hard to accept that this is really happening. Just a few days ago she was healthy and happy and just fine and suddenly she was sick and then dead. We didn't have much warning. We had enough to have gone for you when it happened, but we didn't think it was so serious until it was and by then it was too late." She sobbed. Clearly she needed this time to grieve for her late queen and close friend."An'ti'el, I'm so sorry." I said, unsure of what to say in this instance. I wanted to be sensitive but I also had a bunch of other questions that I wanted to ask her.

"It's okay, you can ask, I know you want to." An'ti'el said through her sobs.

"No, An'ti'el, all that can wait. Right now you're hurting, and relationships come above everything else." I told her, though she was right, my mind was buzzing with questions, but I did my best to push them aside. I refused to become a cold heartless ruler who didn't care for other's emotions and feelings. We sat with An'ti'el on the floor for a long while, letting her cry out her pain and grief of losing her queen.

"We weren't just queen and adviser, you know?" She said when she could talk again.

"Yes, of course we know, you two were close friends." I said.

"Close, yes, we were lovers, after Aranhil died. She turned to me for comfort, and things just led to another and we became lovers." She said.

"Oh!" I said, shocked. It all made sense now, it all clicked into place. "I understand An'ti'el." Again, my mind was buzzing with questions that I couldn't help but blurt out. "How did that work?"She busted out laughing, "Oh, dear child, you have much to learn." And that was all she ever said about it. We sat for a while, me thinking about how two female lovers would work, her catching her breath and calming down.

"Now, your dress, majesty." She said.

"Yes! Show me this dress!"

"So, you know that Pucks do the most astonishing needlework right? Have you ever seen a Puck's handy work?"

An'ti'el asked, a light shone in her eyes again, a gleam of excitement.

"No, I can't say that I have." I admitted."You're in for a treat, then." She said, pulling me forward.

She covered my eyes with her hands so that I didn't see the dress before she was ready for me to. I could hear my maids rustling with fabric and closing the door to the wardrobe."Okay, now, look!" She let her hands drop from my eyes. Laying on the bed was the most intricately embroidered dress I had ever seen. They had done an astonishing job on it. The willow tree stretched from the bottom of the dress all the way up to the bosom, it looked so real, the detail was exquisite. The willow branches almost looked alive when the dress was moved around. I sucked in a breath of awe and stood admiring the dress, not daring to move, in case it wasn't real.

"Come touch it! Feel the fabric!" Ke'yahn'ah said, showing more excitement now. I went to the bed and touched the fabric and jerked my hand away.

"It feels like water!" I exclaimed, surprised.

"Aye! It does! It feels amazing when you wear it, though you won't really notice it through all the other layers today, but the rest of your gowns will go on your body without the extra layers, you'll be able to feel it more then." She explained.

"I see, Ke'yahn'ah, I don't want to wear any of the clothes here in A'va'lon while I am here. I will wear this one, but nothing else." I told her.

"But, why not?" She asked, looking quite disappointed.

"Because I canna take them with me, and when I go back it will make it very difficult to wear my uncomfortable cotton clothes that my uncle has made just for me." I explained, feeling disappointed as well.

"Oh! Miss! Your clothes will be going with you! My sisters and I will pack them all ourselves!" She said happily.

"I canna be bringing this back with me! How will I ever explain it to my uncle!?" I exclaimed, baffled."Donna fash about that! Yer Uncle won't know the difference between our dresses and the ones that he provides yeh with! Not as long as ye have us as yer maids!" I thought about what she was saying and decided that it made sense. They were, after all, Fae folk with powerful maj'ick.

"Wow, though, this is gorgeous!" I said.

"When you're crowned queen in Nah'alba, you'll be wearing this dress then too!" An'ti'el said. "In the meantime we will take good care of it, protect it and make sure that nothing happens to it." She said.

"Okay, well, now what?" I asked.

"Well, now you come stand on this podium and let them fix the dress to your size, and you listen to me drone on for hours about laws and customs and such." She said, yawning.

"Look girls! She's so bored with it, she's already yawning!" I teased An'ti'el and we all laughed a bit."Oh, hush!" An'ti'el teased back, "I just can't sleep very well right now." She said, more seriously.

"You really should see a healer, they can help you sleep, you know?" I said.

"Yeah, but I'm just so busy all day and by the time it's time to sleep I am just too tired to go all the way over there to see the healers. They are a good two or three miles away from where I sleep." She explained. I made a mental note to have a healer meet her at her room that night. They stood me on the podium and measured and pulled and twisted and pinned and gabbed and laughed and talked and didn't talk for hours. I felt like my stomach was going to fall out of my bottom by the time lunch arrived. When we had finished eating lunch, everyone was super sleepy from the food, An'ti'el droned on some more about the coronation and where I would kneel and what I would say, and by the time supper arrived I was exhausted. I knew everything by heart though, thanks to An'ti'el.

"Now we are finished with all the serious heavy stuff, do you have any questions?"

"How would a coronation have been done traditionally?"

"The heir would walk in, through the crowd of high class

citizens, the throne room would not be opened, up to the dais. She or he would lock eyes with the High Priest or Priestess as they reached 100 steps into the room, from there they would bow at the bottom of the dais and say a prayer, where they would be escorted from the bottom of the steps to the top by the high priest or priestess, and then they would bow on a cushion at the altar and repeat after the priest or priestess their vows, and then stand and be done with it.""Sounds quite unimpressive." I said.

"Oh, remarkably so." She replied.

"Tell me why the change? Why now?"

"Changing this up shows them that we are serious about changing traditions. This is the most revered, sacred tradition of them all, and by changing this one up begins your reign in a new light, under a new moon, under a new tradition. The altar has been made specifically to fit you, who you are, and it's maj'ick will last until you die, and when you die, the alter will die as well. You will take it with you to Nah'alba, and it is where you and the Creator will have your communions, your prayers, heart breaks, healings, it is where you will live the most important part of your life spent in prayer and meditation with Him." she explained.``I see.`` I said, trying to picture what it would look like.

"Don't bother trying, you'll never guess what it will be, you'll never picture it in your mind's eye." She said, teasing me back. "I helped design it." She said smugly. "I wish I could stay here forever. I wish that I didn't have to go back to Nah'alba. I will miss this companionship I have found here." I said sadly.

"I understand. At least you will be able to take some of us home with you." An'ti'el said. "I will stay here, though, retired and living life."

"What will you do?"

"I don't know, you know? I never really thought I'd have a life outside of the palace. I never really wanted anything else besides this. I always envisioned that I'd be here, working alongside the royals until I was old or dead." An'ti'el said sadly.

"Then why leave?"

"It was Verisiel's wish, that I would retire and find someone else to love, to have a good life with children." She smiled."But, if it's not your wish, then why do it?" I asked.She shrugged her shoulders, "Just seems like there is no more room for me here anymore." she said."What do you mean?"

"Well, with Dy'llian and J'erri'ahn'ah who won't leave your side, your father and Taem'luck, there just doesn't seem to be room for me, just don't seem like I'm needed anymore." She said sadly. "Oh." Was all I said, I feel like she was looking for more than that, but I wanted to give it time to see if this was really what would make her happy, to see if she would get more excited over it the longer time went on. I wanted to gauge her and see what she needed, and feel her out over the next twenty four hours. And then I would say something.

"It's getting late, and I would, very much, like to see my family before I hit the hay. Would anyone feel up to the journey to find them and bring them here?" I asked. An'ti'el jumped to her feet and bowed herself out the door.

"Now, Ke'yahn'ah, fetch me a healer, and do it quickly." I said.

"Are you feeling bad, majesty?" She asked, I shook my head and said, "Quickly." She ran off.

"Majesty, I have the healer here." Ke'yahn'ah said a few minutes later.

"Bring them in, please?" I said.

the healer came in and bowed, "I need you to prepare something for An'ti'el, something to help her sleep, she's exhausted and I need her clear minded tomorrow." I said.

"Right away, majesty." She said, "Shall I bring it to you or where shall I take it when it's done?"

"Take it straight to An'ti'el room." I said, "That is all." I dismissed her quickly, not wanting An'ti'el to come in and find her there.

The healer left and Ke'yahn'ah asked, "Why do it in secret, majesty?"

"Because I don't want her to have a chance to reject it." She looked confused so I explained more, "An'ti'el is in pain, she's suffering the loss of a lover and beloved queen, she thinks that her nightmares and sleep deprivation is her punishment, a punishment she will carry until she dies, if needs be. If she knew that I had planned this, she could refuse it, telling the healer not to make the potion.

"Can't she still refuse it when the healer brings it to her room later?" Ki'ri'ah asked quietly.

"Yes, but I don't think she will. you heard her, by the time it's bedtime, she's too exhausted to do much but fall into bed."

"Oh! but of course! How clever you are!" Ky'wahn'ah said.

"Well, it's only clever if it works." I winked. "Now, a woman in my station must ask these things." I said, looking at my maids, "Forgive me for this. Tell me true, tell me now, can I trust your discretion, not just in this, but in all things?" I asked, compelling them each to tell nothing but the truth.

"Yes, milady, we will carry your secrets to our grave, we will die before we betray your confidence." They said in unison.

"Thank you." I said.

"Milady? Why did you ask us to forgive you?" Ky'wahn'ah asked.

"Because I have a way of making people tell me the truth whether they want to or not. They have to tell me their whole truth about the subject at hand before the compelling wears off." I said.

"Oh." They said, "You're forgiven." Ke'yahn'ah said, shrugging her shoulders.

"Yeah, you're forgiven, one can never be too careful, especially not the queen." Ky'wahn'ah said.

Ki'ri'ah stayed quiet.

"Ki'ri'ah..." Ke'yahn'ah beckoned, "She asked you to forgive her. do you?" She nodded her head, but refused to speak.

"What's wrong?" I asked. The other two shrugged their shoulders and said "She sometimes gets like this with some people. She will warm up to you eventually."

"She was okay until I asked you to tell me the truth of the question I asked." I said, "Are you scared of me?" I asked.

"No, milady." She said, but it was a lie.

"Why are you frightened of me?"

"Because I have things that I don't want to tell anyone and you could make me tell you." She said.

"I see. Come sit with me for a moment." I said, patting the seat next to me at the table. She came over slowly trembling from head to toe. I placed my hands on either side of her face, one finger on her temple, thumb on her cheek and my other two fingers behind her ears. Her eyes went blank as I opened up my heart and my mind to her. Several minutes later, her eyes came back and she sat up on her own again. "I understand now, milady. I am sorry I ever doubted you." she said, tears ran down her face.

"What did she show you?" Ky’wahn’ah asked.

“Everything." she said."What do you mean everything?"

“Come, I'll show you, if you really want to know." I said to Ky’wahn’ah.

She looked at her sister who nodded her head. Ky’wahn’ah came over and sat down in front of me, leaning back against the chair's back. I did the same thing with her, showed her the same things I showed Ki’ri’ah. Her eyes went blank and her body sagged back.After several moments she came to and Ke’yahn’ah took her place. When we were done all three girls sat with tears in their eyes, shocked and unable to speak. A knock at my door told me that An’ti’el found my family and brought them to me.

"Enter." I said.

They all came in and sat down around the fire in various chairs.

"What a day!" I sighed sipping hot chocolate like we had done all the nights before this one.

"What a day." Everyone else agreed, there was a collective sighing that took place and then naught but the fire crackling.

"Miss," Ke’yahn’ah said, "Would you like more chocolate?"

She asked quietly, clearly still upset.

"Yes, thank you." I said kindly.

"What's with them?" An'ti'el asked."I showed them my life, and the future and the things that I was shown, the things that I see, and how my mind and my heart work. They were unsure that they could trust me. So I showed them that they can."

"Then why are they so ... upset?"

"Because my life has not been easy, and to young, innocent girls who have kind, loving hearts, it's heartbreaking to feel years of pain and anguish in a span of just a few minutes." I said. "They will be alright soon, and they will know me more than most." I explained.

"But, is that wise?" An'ti'el asked.

"I wonder, did Verisiel not do the same for you?" I countered."That was different." She said, her face flushed bright red.

"That was something that Fae only did to those with whom they are intimate." She said.

"Not this Fae." I said. "This Fae does it to gauge the reactions of those who intend to be close to me. Those who intend to be in my rooms every day, who will see me dress, undress, bathe, eat, sleep, and care for me when I'm sick. I'd say that's a pretty intimate relationship, wouldn't you?" My father had become very interested in what I was saying.

"Ary?" He asked.

"Yes?"

"Would you show me?" I looked him in his eyes and almost refused, what would it do to him? To see how I suffered without them? Would it break him? Would he be able to handle it? I did not know, the only thing I knew was that I could not refuse his request. I nodded, "If I do this, I will show you everything, I won't numb it, or skirt around the things that might hurt you." I warned him.

"I don't want you to. I want to know everything." He said.

We sat on the floor and I placed my hands on his face. He

didn't go limp nor did his eyes go blank, he sat looking me in the eyes as everything flashed in his mind, every little thing that had happened over the years, all the way through today. When it was over, he scooped me up in his arms and wept.

"I am so sorry." Was all he could say to me. The others sat quietly observing, keeping their eyes averted, looking into the fire, everyone but Taem'luck that is. He came over and sat down in my lap and started licking us both in the face, he bounced and jumped and went in circles until he knocked us both backwards and we were laughing hard from it all.

"Well, he sure knows how to ruin a moment." I said, standing up, laughing. "Anyone else? While I'm handing out my life's story?" I asked.

Dy'llian and J'erri'ahn'ah both lined up. "The good thing about us, we have a telepathic link, so you need only show one, and the other will see it." J'erri'ahn'ah said.

Dy'llian sat down in front of me, "I'm the strongest when it comes to this sort of thing, J'erri'ahn'ah likes to faint." He teased. She sat down beside him holding his hand. I showed them the same thing I showed everyone else. When we were done they were both crying, "We knew some of it, but we never imagined it was like that." They said.

We all went back to watching the fire until it died."Well, off to bed then." M'kary'ano said.

"Yep, right behind ya." Dy'llian and An'ti'el both said.

"Thank you, for this." An'ti'el said.

"For what?" I frowned.

"Sitting in front of the fire and relaxing." She said, "I have not done that in a very long time. I believe I was a child the last time I did that."

"Well, with me, it's a must. Every night this is what we do. We unwind and relax with a good cup of hot chocolate." I smiled and gave her a hug, she held on for a while before finally letting go and going to bed.

J'erri'ahn'ah was still there after everyone else went to bed. I frowned and looked at her.

"I thought we could spend the night together. I figure you'd need some pillow talk tonight." she smiled.

"I'd love that." I told her, "Is my bath ready?" I asked.

"Yes, miss, we made you two, one for each of you." Ke'yahn'ah said, she led us into an adjacent room with two large tubs in it in front of a fire. "Enjoy, ladies." She said, leaving us to bathe.

"So, you'll be queen tomorrow!" J'erri'ahn'ah said."Yeah! I know! It seems impossible, doesn't it?" "Nah, I always knew you'd be queen one day, just never expected it to happen before you were sixteen." she laughed"Me either!"

"I suppose this changes things, doesn't it?"

"Changes things how?"

"Well, you'll be queen now, it means I'll have to treat you differently."

"You'd better not. I'll fire you if you do." I told her.

"Fire me?! What now you're paying me?"

"If I must." I laughed heartily.

"Well, I think we can come to an agreement." We laughed."Just in public, and only in A'va'lon." I said.

"Agreed. Boy, I can see your uncle's face now..." she said, "Having to bow to you!" She giggled.

"He'd be so furious! He'd probably kill me himself." I said, half joking, half serious.

"Creepy, if you think about it though, cause he probably would!" J'erri'ahn'ah said.

"Wow, way to ruin the joking mood." I said, "But you're right. Can I tell you something?"

"Of course." She said.

"I won't be queen of Nah'alba on my sixteenth birthday."

"What?! Why would you say that?"

"Because my uncle, while alive and able, will never allow that to happen." I told her simply, yawning with exhaustion.

We drifted into a thoughtful silence and enjoyed our baths, afterwards we headed to bed where we giggled and talked for an hour or two more before exhaustion took us into a deep sleep.

Chapter Thirteen

I was too anxious to sleep long, I woke up about an hour or so before Ke'yahn'ah came to wake us up. J'erri'ahn'ah was sound asleep with no anxiety or worries in the world. Ke'yahn'ah came in quietly scuttling from the room into the bathing room, preparing us a bath and putting more wood on my fire. I heard her adding herbs and salts to the tub, and then more water, then I heard her leave again. I had decided to try and cat nap while she was away, but she came back far too soon.

"My lady, I thought that you would be in your bath already!" She said with surprise.

"You knew I was awake?" I asked.

"Aye. Come enjoy your bath, you'll need it today." She said. "Breakfast is on its way here, you'll have to eat while we get you dressed and ready to go."

"J'erri'ahn'ah? Time to get up, love. Ke'yahn'ah made us baths!" I said excitedly.

J'erri'ahn'ah and I stumbled, half asleep, into the baths room, stripped our clothes and got in the baths Ke'yahn'ah had prepared.

"YOW!" I hollered as my foot touched the water.

"Oh! I'm sorry! I made it a wee bit hotter than normal! It was necessary to melt the honey and the herbs." She explained.

I forced my way into the water and after the initial shock of the heat, the hot water soothed my anxiety and calmed me down. She bustled about the room as quiet as a mouse. She was in and out and all around, made my head dizzy to watch her, so I laid back and closed my eyes.

"Miss? I'm sorry, but it's time to get you dressed." Ke'yahn'ah woke me up, my bath water was almost cold, J'erri'ahn'ah was already out of hers. I climbed out of the tub into the warm towel that Ke'yahn'ah was holding out for me.

The warm towel helped stop my nervous shivering, my teeth quit knocking together anyways, though the room was warm and steamy, there was a chill in my heart.

"Come, miss, yeh'll be alright! Yeh'll feel much better when you put on your dress." Ke'yahn'ah encouraged. "Wait till you see what we picked for J'erri'ahn'ah to wear!" she said, her excitement was contagious and soon enough it spread to me.

"Look, Ary!" J'erri'ahn'ah spun round and round in circles showing off her flashy new dress. It was pretty, baby pink and baby blue, she was stunning in it. It was flattering to her form, and it made her deep blue eyes pop. Her hair was shaded in an ombre style down to her back in cascades of pink and blue matching her dress. She smiled and giggled as she marveled at her new dress.

"Wow! J'erri'ahn'ah! You look ravishing! Everyone will be staring at you tonight!" I told her.

She shook her head, "Nuh-uh, I've seen your dress. You will definitely be the talk of the century in that dress!" She said.

"Why?" I asked.

"Because it's not the traditional coronation dress that all the queens have worn for centuries before you."

"What do they normally wear?"

"White. Like a wedding."

"Oh, really??"

Ke'yahn'ah laughed, "Yes, really. The reason behind this was because it was said that when the princess became the queen, she married her kingdom, and divorced all others." Ke'yahn'ah said, "But we aim to change that view, because you'll have two kingdoms to rule, not just one, and you canna marry one without divorcing the other." She said.

"Hmm, makes sense, but how will my dress portray that?"

"Because you'll not be wearing the traditional dress, you'll be wearing a dress we created just for this day." She said, "You will, when the time comes, wear it when you are crowned in Nah'alba as well. But that will not be for many years yet." She said.

"What do you mean? I'm supposed to be crowned when I turn sixteen. That's just next year." I exclaimed.

"I'm sorry, miss, I opened my mouth when I was not supposed to." She said, her face colored and she turned her back on me to face the bed where my dress was.

"Ke'yahn'ah, turn around here and tell me what you mean!" I commanded.

"And if I refuse, will you make me!?" She cried. "Because I have sworn not to say anything about it to you!" She said, fear in her eyes when she spun back around to face me.

"You swore to whom?" I asked.

"An'ti'el." She admitted.

"I see. Then we'd better not break that oath." I said more gently. "Now, about this dress." I said. She smiled, "Thank you, miss." She said, turning to begin getting me dressed.

A knock sounded at the door, I had not gotten undressed yet, "Who's there?" Ke'yahn'ah asked.

"Ki'ri'ah and Ky'wahn'ah." Came a small voice.

"Come in, quickly! We need to get her dressed!"

"Apologies for running late! We were needed in the kitchen for a few minutes."

"Well, hurry up now! We've been waiting for you two!"

I complied with her wishes, got out of bed and into the bathing tub, it was hotter than normal and the herbs were much stronger. The hot water and herbs soothed my raw nerves. She bustled around the room, cleaning it up, and laying out the particulars of my clothing and when she had finished she came over and began bathing me, washing my hair and brushing it until it shined.

"The other day, you had other ladies in here with you to help you with all of this, why is it only you today?" I asked.

"Oh, my lady, they will be along shortly, I... well..." She

stopped, embarrassed to say what was on her mind.

"Tell me, what is it?" I prodded gently.

"Well, I wanted to bring in people I trusted completely, for when we are to go with you back to Nah'alba, and it's taken them a few days to be vetted by the appropriate channels, they are changing into their work clothes and will be along promptly." Ke'yahn'ah said. "I employed my sisters." She added shyly.

"But you trust them?"

"With my life, princess."

"And mine?"

"I do, princess, they are good women, like myself, who just need someone to believe in them. I would not have brought them on if I thought otherwise. I couldna bring on anyone else because of that." Her passion was shining through now. "We grew up almost destitute, and if my mother had not had the opportunity to work closely with the royal family before she passed away, she made a small income and pulled us up out of the mire, but after she passed away we were forced to seek employment. An'ti'el put in a good recommendation for me, and until you came here, I was her personal servant. She said later that she was grooming me to take care of you when came the time." I enjoyed listening to Ke'yahn'ah talk about her family and her life, it was a nice reprieve from the monotony of courtly things. She prattled on talking about her family and her home for a good long while, and I relaxed into the easiness of the conversation, until a knock at the door pulled us out of the past.

Ke'yahn'ah went to the door and cracked it, then opened it wide and admitted two small girls. She was smiling brightly, they were hesitant, fearful.

"Princess, these are my sisters, Ki'ri'ah and Ky'wahn'ah." They curtsied as she said their names.

"At your service, your royal highness." They said in unison.

The two girls were smaller than their elder sister, with

the same blue hair and slanted eyes. Ky'wahn'ah was slight, almost sickly in her thinness, very pale, with large fearful eyes. Ki'ri'ah was hefty, but not overweight with smaller curious eyes.

"Come in ladies, do not be afraid, the rules are simple. When we are in my rooms you may address me as my lady or princess, outside of the rooms you may address me as your royal highness or my lady." I said to them, "If you prove yourself to be hard workers who are honest and trustworthy, you will follow me to Nah'alba and keep doing the same thing you are doing here. Follow Ke'yahn'ah's instructions, and try to stay unnoticed." I smiled encouragingly. They smiled back, but there was great trepidation in their smiles.

"Princess, your water's getting cold and it's time to get you dressed. Lots to do, ah, that'll be your breakfast." She said as there came another knock on the door. "Ki'ri'ah, go fetch the tray, careful not to let anyone in as she's not dressed." Ke'yahn'ah said, Reyna nodded and scuttled to the door. A commotion ensued and Reyna was adamant that the person not enter, Ke'yahn'ah barely got me covered before a stranger stepped into my room. I fled behind my changing curtain and threw on my shift and my robe and covered myself up, and came out careful not to show fear to this man.

Ki'ri'ah was sobbing, Ke'yahn'ah was frozen, and Ky'wahn'ah was torn between running to get her sister and hiding beneath the bed skirts. I took a step towards the man and two hands grabbed mine.

"Princess, you mustn't!" Ke'yahn'ah said urgently, but one look from me and she dropped her hands and back away from me, suddenly more afraid of me than the stranger.

"Who are you, and why have you broken into my room, sir?" I demanded, right at that moment, Taem'luck came into the room, growling and advancing on the man.

He dropped to his knees with his head bowed, "Forgive me, majesty, I come with news, news that you need to hear." He said, visibly trembling from head to toe. "Please, I beg you, hear me out, and then you may behead me." He said.

"Speak to me, and speak to me the truth, or I will have you executed for trespassing." I barked at him, the authority that rang in my voice resonated around the room and filled up every bit of the empty space between him and I.

"Majesty, I am a rogue fae... For that alone I deserve a mortal life. When I joined, I did not know what they were going to do, I swear it, they had me bound and gagged so that I would not tell anyone." He was rambling, panicked, unsure of where to start and how to say whatever it was that was so urgent.

"Man, spit out what you wish to say, or I will call the guards!"

"Majesty, I know who killed the queen, and I know what they plan to do next." He told me, never daring to look at my face.

I turned to Taem'luck, "Go get my father." He leapt from the room.

"Ky'wahn'ah, close the door. Ki'riah'ah, drink some water and calm yourself. Ke'yahn'ah go to your sisters, calm them down." I barked orders as was my right to do so.

"What is your name, sir?" I asked, trying to be kind and compassionate.

"I wish to not give my name for the sake of my family, majesty." He said to me, "I do not wish to see them punished for my actions."

"So be it, I shall not press it, tell me what information you possess, and do so now man."

He went into great detail about the rogues and where to find them, he told me everything there was to know, including the name of a spy. A person who he knew to be very close to myself and my mortal king.

“Majesty, she is a rogue fae named I'dhrenn'i'el Bree Liondrand. She was a mercenary for many years until one day about thirty years ago when she dropped off the face of the earth. Some believe that her conscience caught up with her and she couldn't stand to kill anymore, but I know better."

"How so." I asked pulling up chairs for us to sit in while he talked.

"Because I knew her, a long time ago she and I were intimately involved. She had no soul. Whatever soul she had she sold it to become what she was. Heartless and ruthless and flat out cruel. She was the best in her profession because she would do whatever was necessary to get the job done. She didn't care about anything or anyone, including me. We were involved but there was no love lost between us when she disappeared. I was merely a means to an end. She had built an empire, the dark fae were at her beck and call. She owned them. She had some sort of weird control factor going on, she could control everyone and everything somehow. There were very few people that she couldn't control."

"So, if I'dhrenn'i'el really was that good at what she did and she had an empire beneath her, why would she just disappear." I asked, intrigued.

"To know that, we have to go back to the beginning." He said, looking at me for the first time.

"Okay, better get started because I have places to be tonight that are very important." I said, but my hostility was gone; I felt like I was talking to a friend.

He nodded and continued with his story. "I'dhrenn'el'l was born in a now extinct tribe of woodland fairies. These weren't your typical wood nymphs. They lived in tree houses at the tops of the tallest trees. They were, primarily, gardeners and wood carvers. One day when S'reya was young, still a faeling, teenager years in human years, she was sold into slavery by her parents. She always thought that she'd been abducted, because her parents arranged it that way with her captors. S'reya spent fifty years in slavery to a family who were less than kind to her. In many ways they broke her spirit and she began welling up anger inside of her heart.

When she was freed, she went back home, looking for her family, expecting a warm, welcoming reunion, but instead she was met with guilt and shame from, not only her parents, but the whole tribe. When she finally worked out what happened, she murdered them all and thus becoming a dark fae. She was no longer a woodland fae because the darkness that consumed her as she murdered every man, woman and child from the village had now rewritten her very DNA.

She was approached by the rogues a few years later, recruiting her into their corps. She accepted and within a matter of five years had rooted out all of the high leaders and elders of the rogue fae corps and had now begun to build her empire. She became a bounty hunter and created a rich full life for herself.

About thirty-five years ago I'dhrenn'i'el was approached by a psychic and was told a prophecy. The psychic said that one day a king would rise, a human king, who would hunt down and kill all races of fae kind. He would hunt down and kill humans too, humans with maj'ickal abilities. However, from him would come a hybrid girl who would become the most powerful being of all time. She would reunite and heal the rift between the realms and bring peace to the realms for hundreds of years to come. From her will come many generations of descendants that will also bring peace to the land and then later one of her descendants will bring the end of the world. A few years later I'dhrenn'i'el disappeared, never to be heard from again … until a few days ago when she contacted the rogue fae corps again."

"What is she after?"

"No one knows for sure really. There is speculation that she may be after you, some say that she wants to test you to see how powerful you really are. Others say that she wants to kill you and keep the end of the world from coming. All I know for sure is that the people you love are in danger. She will stop at nothing to kill those that you love. Eir'im'uhs and A'lbi'on are her first targets because they are the most visible and easiest to access. However, exposing you is her primary goal. She wants you out of the way for now, but we don't know if she intends on removing you for good or just for now."

"I believe that you speak the truth, and the truth is all I ask of anyone. You will tell my father exactly everything you have told me, save the name of the spy that you told me, and you will return to your station in the midst of the rogues. Play your part well, and you will be rewarded. Fail me, and I will make you wish you had never been born."

I looked up as the door opened and M'Kary'ano and Taem'luck walked in, "Father, take this man to your study, protect him with your life, write down everything he tells you and keep that information safe. When he is finished, see to it that he has food and water, and then he is free to leave, no further questions asked. You are not to inquire into his work or where he will be going. That is all, thank you." I turned around and walked towards my bed waiting for them to leave to start getting ready for my coronation.

"Ary, are you alright?" Taem'luck asked, concerned.

"Yes, quite, though I fear I may have frightened my servants to hell." I said, feeling very sad about that.

"They will recover, Ary, but you must be more careful! A strange man, you don't know what he could have done to you! You could have been hurt!" He chastised me.

My anger had not fully subsided and I turned it on him, "Do not tell me what I do and do not know. Do not question my judgment, Tay. I am your princess, soon to be your queen. I know what is right and I know what is wrong and I am more powerful than most." I declared. "You have no right to come in here tonight and chastise me for protecting my own when you were not where you were supposed to be! It is your responsibility to watch over and protect me, it is your responsibility to be attached to my hip, to never leave my side, and tonight you did not honor your bond with me. You know who I am, Tay, better than most. You know what I am capable of and He bowed under the weight of my scorn like a dog bowing to his alpha.

"Forgive me, majesty, I was angry at myself for not being

here, and scared for you."

"It is forgiven, of course, Tae. You know that I can't not forgive you. But you cannot go around treating me like a child, or like a weakling. I was before, but I am not now." I told him, my voice softened, my anger dissolving.

"Princess, are you ready to dress now?" Ke'yahn'ah's voice made me jump. I turned around and the three girls were standing by my bed.

"Yes, thank you. Are you three alright?"

"Yes, we will be fine." She replied, her voice was guarded.

"You need not fear me." I told them, but they flinched as I drew near.

"I am sorry, majesty, but I have never seen power like yours before." Ke'yahn'ah said. "No in nobody, not ever." she shook her head, fear in her eyes.

"Look at me, Ke'yahn'ah." She obliged hesitantly. I am the same girl you were talking to an hour ago. I am still me, but when someone threatens those I care about, I am fierce in my protection. That's not something to fear." I tried to console them, to explain, but only time would show them that I would not turn against them. "Come, let us get dressed and ready for my coronation."

They dressed me in an elegant, jeweled dress that was made of deep violet velvet with thick emerald satin hems, the embroidered stitches were in the same type of design as the markings on my arms and legs. They were symbolic to my tribe, symbolic to my heritage, and my right to be ruler. They draped a heavy velvet cape over my shoulders and fastened it around my neck. The whole thing took two hours to get into, what with the corset and the hoop and the other such items that needed to be put in place to make the dress look just right.

It was a floor length ball gown, heavy and thick, but it was fit for a queen. When they had finished dressing me, it was time to do my hair and my face, and then I would be ready. They didn't add much to my face, they mostly put glitter on my face to highlight it and make it sparkle, they added jewels to my forehead where my swirl was over my nose, and they highlighted the butterfly wings that stretched across my cheeks. When they had finished, they did my hair in an intricate braided bun, and placed a tiara on top of my head. They stood back to admire their work. Pleased with my appearance, they announced that we were, indeed, ready and ten minutes later I was walking to the throne room.

As I passed through the hallway that led to the throne room, J'erri'ahn'ah stopped the procession and said, "She'd want to see this first." She brought with her a full length looking glass and put it in front of me.

The creature in the looking glass took my breath away, the markings on her body and her wings, which were stretched out behind her, were glowing brilliantly, her eyes sparkled with pride and excitement, she looked every bit the queen she was about to become. She truly was the most beautiful creature I had ever laid eyes on.

I took a few steadying breaths and looked for my father, who was not within this procession. Disappointed, I nodded my head, and we continued. J'erri'ahn'ah and Dy'llian took their places directly behind me, as my advisers and closest friends, where my father should have been walking.

We stopped in front of the doors and waited for what seemed like an eternity, and then, just as they were about to open the doors someone's hand reached out and grabbed my left elbow. I turned to face the person who needed my attention and nearly cried.

"Da! You made it!" I said, tears threatened my eyes. "I am so scared right now!" I confided.

"Little one, look at you!" Tears streamed down his face, "I am so proud of you right now! Gods, you are the most magnificent image I have ever beheld. Your mother is cursing this day, because she is not here to see you right now." He smiled, "Do not be afraid, love, we are all here with you, and here we will stay, for all eternity."

I bowed my head in respect and shook the tears away,

then smiled and nodded to the doorman, I was ready.

Chapter Fourteen

Standing in front of me, ancient and proud, were the massive oak doors that normally led into the antechamber of the throne room. Today, however, they decided to remove the antechamber for this one day; it allowed for more guests to fit into the throne room.

Beyond these doors stood all of A'va'lon. Not just all the nobles, or high counsels or the high class of A'va'lon, I mean, all of A'va'lon, young and old. It was an intimidating thought. Thousands of people gathered behind these doors, whispering and gossiping excitedly. I could hear them, feel what they were feeling, I knew what they were all saying, the questions they were asking about me.

"Is she really as young as they say she is?"

"Don't know, they say that she's barely older than twelve moons!"

"Twelve moons!? She's younger than me! Maybe I should be queen!"

The group of children laughed, "Shut up! Yer so daft yeh can barely tie yer own shoes! Like they'd let you be queen!"

I smiled as they teased each other. The thoughts of the children were so innocent, they were easier to concentrate on than the minds and thoughts of the adults. Their minds were uneasy, concerned, stubborn and set in their ways. They knew what my being queen meant, and a lot of them had already guessed at what happened to the queen.

"Wonder what kind of queen she will be?"

"Well, better than a dead one, right?"

"Don' know. Suppose so, but who knows? I mean, she's an outsider, she's not even a full Fae, she's half human! We are going to be led by a hybrid!"

"Aye, but who better to forge peace with the human world than a half human?"

"Who wants peace with them? I say we give them the war they are begging for!"

"Nay, war isn't what Ver'i'si'el would have wanted!"

"Aye, but she's dead!"

I shook my head, trying to shut out their voices, their excited, nervous chattering. My mind was racing with all the anxieties of the kingdom, I shared in their fears, their worries, their concerns and their excitement. I found it difficult to distinguish my feelings from theirs. My heart was pounding, my palms were wet with sweat, I couldn't breathe, I began to feel dizzy.

Breathe, Ary, just breathe. I told myself, I tried to focus on something closer to me, something that was right in front of me. The only thing that I had to focus on were the doors. I began tracing their patterns absently at first, but with each passing breath, I began to take in the intricate details that told stories from a long-forgotten past.

The main doors in A'va'lon, the doors that were massive and oaken, all told stories. Stories from her history, stories of the great Fae who changed history, altered the course of the Fae forever. One day, I would be up there, on these doors, a great queen who would become a legend. I would become the one queen people would never forget, I would forge a new empire and I knew it.

The thought of that brought me back to reality and panic set in again.

"Hey, Tae?"

"Yeah?"

"Hold down the fort for me, okay?" I said, breathlessly.

"Why?"

"I am ... going to the privy ... yeah ... the privy." I closed my eyes and turned to run, but large, hot hands clasped my shoulders and firmly held me in place. I struggled a bit, well, more than a bit, I struggled so hard my hair fell.

"An' just where do yeh think yer goin'? Eh, Lass?" My father's voice came crashing through all the other voices, through all the fears and anxieties.

"Away! Far, far away! I can't think, I canna even hear my own voice or thoughts!" I cried.

"Ach, I understand, but running away never did anyone any good, love."

"It'll do me some good!" I sobbed, I felt like I was going crazy.

"Aye, I reckon it would feel that way, but yer wrong, lass. If yeh start runnin' now, yeh'll never stop. Once you go down that path, love, it's very difficult to come back from." He knelt down to look up into my face, his hands caressed my face gently wiping away my tears, "Ary, yer braver than yeh believe, stronger than yeh seem, smarter than yeh think, and more loved than yeh know. Yer a kind, wise soul with so many wonderful people behind yeh. Yer not alone in this! No, go shine bright, my star!!" He spun me back around to face the doors, a calm spread over me, blocking out the crowd's voices, blocking out their feelings. Taem'luck and my father were projecting a protective barrier between my mind and theirs. J'erri'ahn'ah and An'ti'el came around and fixed my hair and my trane. Moments later, the trumpets sounded signaling that it was time.

The massive oak doors swung open, the trumpets silenced, a beautiful flute music picked up where the trumpets left off. The music was a whimsical, woodsy sound. I counted to ten, waited another five seconds, and then I began my long, slow walk through the crowd up to the dais.

As I entered, it looked like a massive wave had hit the

crowd as they all knelt on one knee, fists over their heart, heads bowed. As I passed by each row, they stood and watched me walk down the aisle.

"Take a step ... 1 ... 2 ... 3 ... 4 ... Take a step ... 1 ... 2 ... 3 ... 4 ..." I chanted to myself, trying very hard not to run up to the dais. I was two hundred, fifty steps away from the top of the dais. Two hundred and twenty-five steps from the bottom of the dais. All I had to do was keep my eyes straight, my head up, and not faint in the middle of all my people.

You must not show weakness, not today, not on your walk to the dais. This is basically like a walk of shame, if you misstep, if you falter, if you look like you're about to faint, or fall over, it's game over. Right now you have the element of surprise, they don't know you, they don't know anything about you. Right now, we can take them all by surprise, storm the castle and show them a confident fourteen year old who knows what she's doing. But if you falter, if you show weakness, they may reject you as queen. Keep your eyes pointed forward, as hard as it will be, do not look at the crowd. If you must, look at the High Priest or Priestess, they can entrance you, hold your vision so that you can't look anywhere else, but you'll have to get one hundred and fifty steps in before they can do that for you.

I remembered what she told me the day before, and it gave me the courage and the strength to keep walking. I kept my eyes fixed ahead of me, on the two people standing on the Dais in front of the throne.

The High Priest and Priestess looked like stone statues, and not just because of how still they were standing. They both had ashy skin, pale blue eyes that almost looked white, white hair and they were super thin. I supposed that this was what an albino Fae looked like. I imagined that they were stiff, uncomfortable people with little to no sense of humor, with nasally voices. I smiled as I imagined what they would sound like as they spoke during the oath.

As I was staring at them, lost in my imagination, I noticed

a movement to the left of the High Priest and Priestess. I shifted my eyes and saw the altar for the first time. It had been conjured from a young willow sapling, when this was all said and done, the sapling would be potted and sent with me back to Nah'alba. It was currently bent over like a bench, with its willow vines flowing to the grown like a skirt. It shifted and moved giving it an eerie feel.

When I finally reached one hundred fifty steps, I could lock eyes with the High Priest and Priestess. I met their eyes and I felt weightless again. Like they had removed all my stress, all my worries, all my anxieties and fears. They gave me a sense of peace and relaxation. I walked with grace, effortless and worry free all the way to the bottom of the dais. They let go of my eyes as I knelt on the cobbled-stone floor and said a silent prayer.

"Creator help me. Guide me, bring me through this to the other side." It was all that I could find the words to say. As an afterthought, a much later after thought, I found different, more elaborate words to say, but I'm getting ahead of myself now.

I rose and walked up the twenty-five steps, counting slowly to four after every step. When I reached the top, I bowed my head and the High Priest and Priestess placed their hands on my head and said a private prayer over me.

"Creator we ask that your blessings flow from our new queen, we ask that you work your light and your maj'ick through her guiding her into this new chapter in her life. Be with her and guide this shining star as she walks into a new role and begins to guide the kingdoms into a new era. Instill your wisdom, kindness and compassion on her and open the hearts and minds of all Fae to what she will have to say to us all." They prayed in one united voice for all Fae-kind. Their voices were pleasant and soft, almost like a soft trickle of water, smooth and fluid. Their voices reminded me of flowers blooming in the early spring.

I stood up and walked over to the altar, which bloomed

vibrant butterfly blossoms all over the vines as soon as it felt my presence near it.

The High Priest stood opposite of me, he said a few words in Faeish that I didn't quite understand, when he spoke again, his voice had been maj'ickally amplified.

"Please state your full, true name."

As he finished the skies above us clouded up with dark dangerous looking clouds. Thunder rumbled across the sky like a hungry dragon, lightning flashed across the sky bright and blue like the dragon was spitting fire at us all. An ear splitter, earth shaking clap of thunder sounded after an exceptionally close and bright flash of lighting sent everyone diving for cover.

A white-hot stabbing sensation hit my left leg at the same time as this flash of lightning, I heard a blood curdling and saw a terrified look on the High Priest's face and then my vision darkened and went out.

"Ary! Ary!" My mother's voice pierced the dark veil that had clouded my eyes moments before. I looked around, I was disoriented and confused, I was in the woods, somewhere, I heard a voice in the distance, but whose? What was happening? Where was I? Why did I feel like I was missing something or forgetting something?

"Ary! Ary!" My mother's voice came again, she was behind me somewhere. I took a few moments and allowed my eyes to adjust to the brightness of the sun's light. I realized that I was standing on the path part way between my house and my sunflower patch. I turned around and walked a few feet and emerged from the woods. The light that had been dimmer and green in color was now blinding and pure white.

Mum was standing in the back door looking out over the lawn for any sign of me coming home.

"Well! Look who finally decided to come home!" She said, smiling, relief in her eyes.

"Sorry, mum, I fell asleep, I guess. I didna hear you calling me."

She smiled, "Ach, lass, donna fash yerself, we never could keep you out of that sunflower patch. Come on, saved yeh a plate." She opened her arm inviting me in for a hug.

I joined her in the doorway, she placed her arm around my shoulder and squeezed tightly for a moment, and then let me go eat my food.

"Where is everyone?" I asked, with six siblings and my da', there was never a quiet moment in our house.

"Ach, don't yeh remember? They went to town to fetch last minute supplies for the trip North." She reminded and gently chided me.

"Ah, that's right, slipped my mind for a moment." I lied, the truth of it was, I had no memory of anything up until the moment I heard her calling to me in the trees. It was a strange feeling, an empty sort of sad feeling. But there was still this nagging feeling that I was missing something, forgetting something, and not just my memories, like a whole other life that I was meant to be living. I shrugged my shoulders and finished my food.

"Well, lass, what'll it be tonight? Game of chess? Some knitting? Trivia? Book reading?" Mum asked me, an excited gleam in her eyes.

"What do yeh mean?" I asked.

"Well, it's just you and I here tonight, the others willna be back 'till tomorrow noon time, so I figured we could hang out, spend some time together." I could tell from her smile that she and I rarely got any time together at all, I wanted to say yes, I really did.

Something's no' right here, lass. I donna know what it is, but somethin's no' right. A voice in my head told me. The voice sounded familiar, like I should have known the name of the person speaking to me, but I couldn't place it.

"Maybe we could sit by the fire and read some books?" I said, hopefully, something to take my mind off of things, to clear my already empty head.

She nodded, no look of disappointment crossed her eyes,

reading books by the fire made her just as happy as playing chess.

"Ma'?" I asked.

She looked up and smiled in answer, "Yeh havena called me that in a vera long time, I forgot how it feels."

"Would you be up for a game of chess? Or are we both rubbish at it?" I asked.

"Who you calling rubbish!? We are the master's at chess!" She was teasing. I smiled and we decided on having a game of chess.

"Look at the time, would yeh!" Mum exclaimed after four intense games.

"Uh-huh, yer only sayin' that cause yer tired of losing." I laughed.

"Well, maybe!" She got up and gathered our tea mugs, "How about a good cup of hot chocolate and a good story before we call it a night?" She asked, I nodded, "Stoke the fire and pick out a book, I'll be back with the hot chocolate."

She walked out of the room and I went to stoke the fire. I felt elated, happier than I had felt in a long time. For some reason I had the feeling that it had been a long time since I had seen my mum. I walked over to the desk and picked up my favorite book. It was not really a story telling book, it was more like a history of myths and legends, but it was my favorite. Mum came back into the sitting room and we pulled up our chairs close to the fire and mum opened the book.

"Never could understand why yeh liked this particular book so much. Let's see, shall we read the story of the lost princess?" She asked.

I shook my head, "Nah, I would like to read the one about The Fae Queen who saves the world." I said.

She looked up at me over her nose and flipped through the pages, "Here it is. Are you ready?" She asked. Mum never could resist a good story, her eyes always lit up when she read stories out loud, she did all the voices for all the characters.

"There is a legend of a young queen who was half-fae,

half-human who was born in Nah'alba when maj'ick was forbidden by the mortal king. This king was an evil man, he hunted and executed all maj'ickal creatures. Those who managed to escape went into hiding, fleeing back to A'va'lon, or into dark shadows and holes in the ground, too scared to surface again. Other's created human-like disguises and were able to build lives in Nah'alba as humans, have families and carry on much as they used to.

This young queen didn't know that she was a queen, but the Fairies created a special place for her to play, in a small clearing just inside the woods that bordered the back of her house. They planted all sorts of maj'ickal flowers and when she would play with them, they loved to cast rainbows as their iridescent wings caught the sunlight. She would spend hours in her maj'ickal flower patch with her A'va'lon'ian friends, playing and laughing and having fun.

One night, she had fallen asleep in her flower patch and she woke up to the sound of her house burning, her family screaming. The Fairies came and took her away to A'va'lon.

When she turned sixteen, she was crowned the queen of the Fae, and a few days later she inherited the throne of Nah'alba because her uncle had passed away. She fell in love with a boy who stood by her side and gave her great courage, and strength and who loved her faithfully for her whole life."

She closed the book and smiled. "She kind of reminds me of you sometimes, you and your sunflower patch." She said thoughtfully.

I frowned, thinking about it, "What was her name?" I asked.

"You know, that's the oddest thing, it doesn't name her." She said.

I shrugged and finished my hot chocolate, kissed my mom on the cheek and went to bed.

I slept fitfully that night, tossed and turned and had dark circles under my eyes. Mum came in with breakfast, said that I looked like a ghost and sent me back to bed.

I slept a bit better, but my sleep was still haunted by strange dreams of fires and fairies. I chalked it up to the story mum and I read the night before and shrugged it off. Mum knocked on the door just a few minutes after I woke up again, bringing in lunch.

"Yer Da' is back! And he brought in the doctor from town to check in on you. I told him that you've been better in the last two days than I have seen you look in years." She beamed; such hope shone out of her eyes. "I'll send him in, better get dressed." She closed the door behind her.

I got up and threw my robe over me, I was much too lazy to dress more appropriately. A soft knock at my door told me that the doctor was just as eager to see me as I was to get some answers.

"Come in." I called, sitting down at the table to eat my lunch.

The door opened and in came a small mousy man with a balding head. His nose reminded me of Pinocchio, his eyes were small and beady and when he spoke, he had a strange British accent and an uncomfortable sort of raspy voice.

"Ah! And how is my favorite patient today!!" He asked, his smile was enthusiastic and warm.

"I'm tired, but I'm good."

"Why tired?" He inquired.

"Didn't sleep well, had odd dreams." I shrugged, "I don't know, ever since yesterday something has felt off."

"What do you mean, off? Off how?"

"I don't know. Just have this feeling that I am missing something or forgetting something, but not like I'm forgetting something from this life ... Like I have a whole other life out there that I am supposed to be living, and I'm not living it. Everything just feels weird. Like I have this feeling that my mum and I have not seen each other in a very long time, and yet, I know that I see her every day."

"I see, so you have feelings that you can't place, dreams that you find off, and everything just feels weird?" He asked.

"You don't believe me, do you?" I asked.

"I do believe you, Ary. I've come to find that you are a very curious being, with a very curious mind. I told you from the beginning, I will always be in your corner, I will always believe you."

"Why do I feel like I've lost something, or like I've lost a life. I feel empty. I have no memories beyond yesterday, I emerged from the woods out of a black veil and heard my mu calling out to me. I have no recollection of why I was in the woods, or anything that happened before that. No plans, nothing, it's just empty." I frowned, I felt crazy, sounded even crazier. I went into details about the dreams I was having and the feelings I had, and when I was done he looked at me and said the most simple thing I'd ever heard him say.

"Ary, go home."

"But, Doctor, I am home."

"Ary, you need to go home. Go home, Ary."

"Doctor you're scaring me, I am home, Doctor this is my home."

"Go home, Ary." He walked out of my door and never looked back.

I called after him, "Doctor! Doctor! I am home Doctor!" I ran after him through my room door, but when I opened the door, there was nothing there. No light, no house, no woods, nothing. A hot pain spread across my forehead and began to blind my eyes, burn my nose and I fell backwards. There was no end to the falling, I just fell through the darkness with nothing above, below or beside me. After what felt like an eternity, I heard someone, distantly calling my name.

"A'lari'jah." They called. "A'lari'jah!" Their voice was more urgent every time they said my name.

I opened my eyes, I was still falling, but I could see, as if through a looking glass, the people standing around me in the throne room, shaking me, trying to wake me, but I just blinked and stared absently into space, still falling through my black hole.

"Lads, on three, 1 ... 2 ... 3... Now!"

Another hot pain spread across my head, it blinded my eyes and I was now falling through a white pit of nothing, it was bright, too bright, I wanted to close my eyes, to pull away from the blinding white, but I couldn't move. I was stuck. Falling through time and space, falling inside of my head.

I began to feel the floor beneath me, someone's hand under my head, a strange texture on my legs. I felt the pain in my head fade away, and I heard voices around me. "A'lari'jah, can you hear me?" A voice asked me, he sounded muffled, like I was listening to him with my head under water.

I blinked. I tried to look around, but I was still falling, still falling through my never-ending white tunnel of nothing.

"What's happening? Why isn't she responding?" Someone's voice demanded.

"We don't know, sir, we have cleansed her as much as we can, the rest is up to her. She has to want to come back to us, sir, and right now, she doesn't want to come back to us."

He was right, I didn't want to come back to them. I didn't want to lose my family all over again, I didn't want to have to say goodbye to them a second time. I couldn't bear it. I wouldn't bear it. I didn't care that there were people who needed me, I didn't care that there were two whole kingdoms that hung in the balance of life or death.

"Ary, Little one, can you hear me?" My father's face appeared next to me; we were falling together. "Where are we falling?"

"I donna know... Da' Just fallin' I suppose."

"What are you running away from, lass?"

"Reality."

"Ah, reality can be a real bitch sometimes, can't she?"

"Aye, she can be."

"What is this all about?"

I projected to him the memories of being back home, with him and mum, spending the time I did with her playing chess, reading books, drinking hot chocolate by the fire, and he understood my grief.

"Time to come home, child." He said, and he reached out for my hand and I took it.

"A'lari'jah? Can you hear me?" The voice said again. He was a handsome Fae with a chiseled face and bright lime green eyes and black hair. "Majesty?" He asked, seeing the recognition in my eyes.

"Aye, I can hear yeh." I said.

"Welcome back, majesty, are yeh alright?" He asked.

"I've been better, to be perfectly honest. Yeh'll be chief sentry then, right?" I asked him.

"Aye, that's me."

"We will meet later to discuss this. Are there measures to prevent this from happening again?" I asked, he nodded, and I said, "Then let's waste no more time! We've a schedule to adhere to."

Slowly, I edged my way back up to my knees and looked at the High Priest, "Now, where were we, before we were so rudely interrupted?" I asked, the crowd erupted in giggles and snickers.

"Please state your full and true name." Even with his voice maj'ickally amplified, it still reminded me of soft water trickling and flowers blooming in early spring.

"A'lari'jah Jayd Riversong MacM'kary'ano." I said loud and clear, realizing that my voice had been amplified too.

"Do you swear to uphold the laws of A'va'lon to the best of your ability?"

"I do swear to uphold the laws of A'va'lon to the best of my abilities."

"Do you swear to keep with her traditions, passing them down the lines to the new generations?"

"I do so swear to change these traditions, to put an end to the old, and bring about the new. I swear to bring A'va'lon into the light, to hold her up and let her shine as bright as the star she was meant to shine as. I swear to bring A'va'lon and all her peoples there into a new age, an age of moving forward and forging a new empire."

"Do you so swear to protect A'va'lon from threats both without and within her borders? To rule with a swift hand, a pure heart, and a clear mind?"

"I do swear to protect A'va'lon from threats both within and without her borders. I swear to rule with a just, merciful hand, a pure heart, a clear mind, and a wise soul, I swear to rule with mercy, love and compassion to all her peoples."

"Do you swear to rule A'va'lon until you cannot rule anymore?"

"I do swear to rule A'va'lon until I can rule no longer."

"Do you swear to appoint a new heir before your time is up?"

"I do swear to appoint a new heir before my time comes to an end. I swear to be wise and cautious in my choosing, and to make sure that the one I chose is worthy to carry my mantle, to continue to move A'va'lon forward, never falling backwards."

The High Priest turned to pick up the crown, the High Priestess came over and handed me the staff and the crystal ball that had rested upon the altar, the staff in my right hand, the crystal ball in my left. The High Priest came back and placed the crown on my head, "Rise, Queen A'lari'jah." He held out his hand and as he walked around the altar, he turned me around to face the crowd, "A'VA'LON, I PRESENT YOUR QUEEN!" The crowd erupted into loud cheers, screams and whistles.

"LONG LIVE THE QUEEN!" the crowd shouted. The High Priest moved me towards the throne. "LONG LIVE THE QUEEN!" I placed the staff in the hole on the right arm, the crystal ball on the left, "LONG LIVE THE QUEEN!" I sat down and the throne quivered and shook but stayed stone.

"Donna fash, majesty, it will change, sometimes it just takes a bit longer than other times." The High Priest whispered in my ear. I bowed my head in thanks.

The whole place seemed to be holding its breath, waiting for the throne to change. When it did begin to quiver, everyone watched closely, blink and you miss the transformation. The chair quivered and shook and vibrated and then turned into a willow tree, young, tall and proud. Its weeping vines swept down just above my head producing the same vivid butterfly blossoms. The trunk scooped in and made a cozy chair padded thickly with soft, squishy moss. The arms still held the staff and the crystal ball, but the tree brought them closer to me, so that I could reach them with my back still against the chair.

We waited for a few minutes, I began to get antsy, wondering if I was supposed to do something.

"We are waiting for the first pledge of fealty, majesty. Whoever comes forward first shows great courage and encourages the rest of them to come forward as well. Mind you, most people like to wait a few minutes before coming up, they enjoy admiring the chair." The High Priestess whispered in my right ear, she smiled as she added, "This is quite spectacular!" I smiled but did not reply, I waited patiently for the first pledge of fealty.

Two movements happened at the same time, my father made a move towards me, and so did J'erri'ahn'ah and Dy'llian. They stopped, looked at each other, did a sort of dance, and then laughed.

"Go ahead, sir, we will be right behind yeh." J'erri'ahn'ah said.

M'kary'ano bowed his head in thanks and walked up the twenty-five steps to kneel at my feet.

"My queen, I pledge my loyalty to you, you have had my heart since the day you were born, and now you have my sword, my life and my soul if ever you should have need of them, from this day, until my last." He placed his closed right fist over his heart and bowed his head deeply.

"Come, M'kary'ano, stand by my side, from this day, until your last." I invited him to rise and stand at my left side beside me.

J'erri'ahn'ah and Dy'llian came up, knelt in front of me, and in one unified voice, they said,

"My queen, my sister, my best friend, we pledge to you our loyalty. We give you our undying, unconditional love and friendship, we pledge to you our hearts, minds, souls and lives if ever you should have need of them, from this day, until my last day." They saluted the same way my father did and waited for my invitation.

"Come, J'erri'ahn'ah, stand at my right side, from this day until your last. Come, Dy'llian, stand at my left side, from this day until your last." I said, Dy'llian came over and stood on the other side of my dad, but the High Priest rearranged Dy'llian and placed him in between my dad and me, putting Dy'llian at my left side.

"It's best this way, because they will be in Nah'alba with you, your father will be here, ruling in your place." He told me.

I was taken by surprise at the next pledger, Jhona and N'yssa came forward and knelt at my feet.

"My queen, we pledge to you our loyalty, our unconditional, undying love and friendship. I swear to always be with you, to protect you as best as I can and keep you from harm. I swear to be by your side from this day, until my last day, you have my sword, my heart, my body, and my life if ever you should need them."

"Rise, Jhona and N'yssa, I accept your pledge of loyalty. I wonder though, where is your wife, sir?" I asked, fear had struck my heart.

"Majesty, when we left, she was not feeling well, I hope that my pledge can stand in the gap for her until she is feeling up to pledging to you herself." There was something there that shouldn't be there, I stopped everything, put Jhonna and I into a bubble where no one could hear what was happening but me and him and Taem'luck.

"Jhona, speak to me the truth of the matter." I said, there was anger behind my eyes that made him blanch. "Jhona, I mean it, I've already had my life threatened once today, I need to know the absolute truth of the matter!" I demanded, the ring of authority in my voice sent him back to his knees, he had no choice but to answer truthfully, my compelling was too strong for him to resist.

"Majesty, please forgive my cover up, I do not know where Sr'eya is. She has been gone since you left, she left without a word and hasn't been back." He bowed his head and a silent tear ran down his face.

"You are forgiven, this time. But Jhona, do not ever lie to me again. You may go." I told him. I was angry, worried, confused, fearful, but for now I had to shake those feelings off and continue with my coronation.

An'ti'el came up next, she knelt at my feet and said her words to me,

"My queen, it has been my absolute honor to serve with you, you have my loyalty for the rest of my life, but I beg of you to release me from your service and allow me to move on and have a life of my own."

"Are you sure this is what you want, An'ti'el? Or is it what my grandmother wanted?"

She paused, and that was all the answer I needed, "Then no, I will not release you from my service, you will continue to work for me until it is your desire to leave, not anyone else's. Come, take your place beside me." I motioned for her to join J'erri'ahn'ah on my right side. She complied, not sure of what had just happened.

Taem'luck came up and bowed deeply to me for a long time, and then came over and stretched out and walked in circles and finally laid down on my feet. The crowd giggled as they watched his very dramatic show of protection, and the gasped as he "coughed" out a stream of fire, finally he yawned and laid his head lazily on my lap.

Really, Tay? Was that really necessary?

Well, perhaps not, but it was fun. Besides everyone here needs to know who is protecting you, you've already had one attempt on your life today, and if I show off a bit, hopefully that will make

them less inclined to try again.

Fair is fair, but your head, on my lap?

Oh, this? This is just for your attention and affection. I thought about climbing up on your lap and curling up into a ball …

Before I could stop him, he leapt onto my lap, large at first, and heavy, but as he circled around and around his size shrunk to that of a small dog, or a rather large house cat, and he laid down coughing out a puff of smoke.

Yes, this is much better, I have a better view, and you can pet me easier.

I laughed and shook my head. *You really are a character, aren't you?*

I am sure that I have no idea what you mean! He chuckled.

The next pledger came up and knelt at my feet, it was the chief sentry.

"Dru'cyl, majesty, at your service. I pledge to you my undying loyalty and protection. Madam, I swear to protect you always, to always stay vigilant, alert and on guard, to never let anything or anyone slip through my careful watch again. Madam, I failed you, and I now offer you my head."

"I shall not accept it!" I said aghast. The crowd gasped and their hands flew to their mouths. Any other king or queen would have had their executioner take off this man's head for the incident that happened earlier today. "Do you or do you not pledge me your loyalty?" I asked him.

"My queen, I pledge to you my loyalty. I swear to protect you from this day until my last day. I pledge to you my life, my body, my sword and my armor from this day until my last day." He did the same salute as my father.

"Rise, Dru'cyl and take your place beside M'kary'ano." I said. Again, the High Priest rearranged them, placing my father in front of the Chief Sentry and moved Dru'cyl between my father and Dy'llian.

I got up and walked over and stood in front of the men standing at my left side. I pulled my father forward and stood him in front of the throne, and then pulled Dru'cyl out and stood him directly behind Dy'llian and then put my father back in his original place. I stood back and nodded my head in satisfaction and sat back down, Taem'luck jumped back into my lap and curled up.

Not only did that imply that I was changing how things are done, but I also told the High Priest that I was the one in power, not him.

The rest of everyone else in the kingdom lined up and began making their way down to the dais. The remaining pledges of loyalty took the rest of the morning and part of the afternoon, it was just after midday when the last person had come and pledged their loyalty.

"Was that everyone, then?" I asked, speaking directly to the person who had been checking people out of the book as they came up.

"Not quite, ma'am." He said. "While we had a better turnout than when Queen Verisiel took over the throne when Ah'ran'hil passed away. But we did have a bigger turn out when Aranhil took the throne." He said.

"What percentage of the population showed up?" I asked.

"Eighty percent, majesty."

"Send out a survey group, a group of about ten people to go to the different people's houses to do a survey on what they think of their new queen. Send ten people who are young, innocent and not intimidating, this is simply information for me to know what I can improve on. I want to show the people that I noticed their absences and want to improve. Create a questionnaire and let me see if before you send it out, and then I want the results sent directly to me, no one else is to see them until I do."

"Yes, your majesty." He said to me, bowed and left the throne room.

"Now, to my rooms for a nap and food." I said, Taem'luck looked up at me and pouted.

"I just got comfortable." He said out loud, everyone laughed.

"Before we go, what are your names?" I turned and looked at the High Priest and Priestess.

"Vi'k'tur and Vi'o'lah, majesty, twins." They said together.

"And your pledges of fealty ... or are you exempt from taking them?" I asked.

"It is not tradition for the High Priest and Priestess to swear fealty to the queen as we already have an immortal fealty to the Creator." They said.

"I see, so if I am appointed by the Creator to forge a new empire in the Fae nation, does it then not stand that you would have pledged your loyalty to me publicly to instill even more confidence in the people?"

"Yes, majesty, but it has never been done before. To pledge to you our loyalty is to turn our back on the Creator." They said.

M'kary'ano opened his mouth to interject but I held up my hand to silence him.

"So, then I assume that you do not believe in me, that you do not believe me to be who I claim to be, or who everyone says I am? That my grandmother was mistaken in appointing you as my High Priest and Priestess, then?"

They were silent, searching for the right political answer, "Majesty, it is just not done."

"I see, so do you want to keep this position?"

"Yes, majesty, it is our honor to serve you."

"But you don't want to show that you are loyal to me?"

"It is not that we do not want to give you our loyalty, majesty."

"Then, what is it? Because we can stand here and argue back and forth all day long, but at the end of the day, if I am not satisfied with your loyalties and where they stand, then I will not have you in my confidence."

They were silent. "But Majesty, you have our loyalty already."

"Do I?" I asked, "And, pray tell, how am I to know to whom you're loyal? After today's incident, do you think that I am going to take any chances? Do you think that I am going to have anyone in my immediate confidence, or within the palace walls for that matter, that I cannot trust? Do you intend on standing here and arguing with me on what you seem to think is intelligent, when really, all this is telling me is where your loyalties do not lie? What am I to think about this? Your unwillingness to bend the knee makes me question if you should be allowed to be a Priest or Priestess. Look at my guardian. Is he not appointed by the creator? And yet, he showed his loyalty to me. I am not asking for your life, or your soul, I am asking that you swear to me that you are my subjects, and no one else's. There is a band of rogue Fae's running around here, on the loose who killed your previous queen, and have already tried to harm me. I want to make sure that you are with me, because if you're not with me, then you are against me, correct? So, you see the dilemma here, don't you? I am faced with an impossible decision, but make no mistake, I will make it if I need to." I said. I am pretty sure that I took them all by surprise, after all, I am no ordinary girl of fourteen.

Their eyes got wide as I threatened to take away their status in the priesthood. They immediately fell to their knees, "Majesty, we beg, forgive our lack of understanding and insubordination. We should have been the first in line to swear our loyalties." They bowed their heads dramatically, "Majesty, our loyalty, as representatives of the priest-hood, lie with the crown, with you. Our loyalties as Fae citizens are solely with you, and our creator. We believe that you have been appointed by our Creator to be the greatest queen this kingdom will ever see. We pledge you our loyalties, our knowledge and wisdom from this day, until our last day." They stood and saluted with their right hand over their hearts.

"Will you get with Dru'cyl and bring him to my rooms before the banquet? I believe that he and I have much to discuss."

"Yes, Majesty, I shall make arrangements." Vi'k'tur said.

Chapter Fifteen

"An'ti'el, I would like to talk with you, if you do not mind?" I asked, trying to make it sound like a request, the last thing I wanted to do was command and demand people around.

"Of course, majesty, right away, majesty." She said, she was distant and quiet.

"Walk with me." I said, we took off walking to my rooms, "The rest of you may join us, momentarily, go and change if you wish, and then meet us in my rooms."

"Now, I am sorry, perhaps I should have handled the situation earlier in private. I didn't mean to make you feel uncomfortable..."

"It's... It's alright, majesty. You are my queen, from this day until my last." She replied.

"Do you know what my gifts are?" I asked her. She frowned and looked at me with an odd expression.

"No, majesty, I have no clue." She said, "I know only that you are the most powerful Fae I've ever known. I can feel your power, but I have no clue what they are."

"I have the ability to ... read minds ... for a lack of a better way to put it." I told her.

"I see." She was uncomfortable now.

I laughed, "You miss my meaning. I am not threatening you. I am telling you the reason I made the choice I made. I was fully prepared to release you, but at the last second I heard your mind scream out to me not to." I told her.

"I understand, majesty." She sighed in relief.

"I want you to make the decision YOU want, not what you think I want or what tradition dictates for you to do. I want this to be something that you decide, not something my grandmother had predestined to happen. She's not here anymore, but we are."

"Well, honestly, I am not sure what I want." She said, I could feel her searching her heart and mind for the answer, but she was confused.

"An'ti'el, you do not have to decide right now, or within the next day or week. You can take as long as you need to make this decision. I want you to do what makes you happy. This is something that you have done for most of your life now, and when you are in your element you glow with joy. That's all I want for you, no matter what chapter of life you're in." I told her.

"Thank you, my queen. It is an honor to serve with you." I looked at her and she looked at me.

"Now, cut the formalities and tell me what you really think."

"I am honored, Ary, that you want me alongside you with everyone else. I am moved beyond what I know how to express. It means more than I have words to give." She smiled, tears in her eyes, "It is going to be an amazing and exciting journey to share with you."

I walked into my rooms and Ke'yahn'ah and Ky'wahn'ah were waiting for me. As soon as I walked into the doors, they began stripping off my clothes one layer at a time. When I was finally free of the hot heavy materials of my coronation dress, they dressed me in a simple gown that I could nap in and not destroy the beautiful gown they had set aside for the banquet. When I was dressed, I had just sat down at the table when a knock came at the door.

"Who is there?" Ke'yahn'ah asked through the door.

"M'Kary'ano, J'erri'ahn'ah, Dy'llian and Taem'luck." Ke'yahn'ah spoke an enchantment and the doors unlocked and opened.

They all bowed as they entered, sat down at the table and began filling their plates with food.

"So, what do you plan on doing with those who did not show up today?" M'Kary'ano asked me.

"I am not sure yet. Basically, I am hoping to weed out the bad apples in this. Those who refuse to answer the questionnaire I will deem as having something to hide. Those who answer the questionnaire, well, let's just say that I will know who's lying and who's not lying."

"Dare I ask you what you mean?"

“Well, the questionnaires will be enchanted, of course. The papers that turn pink are the ones that are lying and those who are hiding something will turn red.

Those who are telling the truth will stay white, but they will sparkle.” I said.

“And what do you plan on having done to those who are lying or hiding something?” J’erri’ahn’ah asked.

“I will have them closely watched, if they prove to have no connection to the rogues then they will be left alone. Those that have connections to the rogues will continue to be followed and we will learn all there is to know about the rogues, if we can find them out.”

“Ah.” Everyone said, they all sighed a sigh of relief.

“What did you think I was going to do?” I asked, confused.

“Well, let’s just say that where we thought this was heading, we weren’t sure that was the direction you were wanting to go with leading A’va’lon into a new era.” M’Kary’ano said.

I smiled, “I may have pledged to rule kindly, and mercifully, but I also pledged to protect them all, and we are on the brink of war. I cannot overlook this act that has been done, I cannot allow this to go unpunished, I have to think, I have to act, even if it’s in the shadows for now.” I said to them.

“We understand, majesty. We just made the wrong assumptions.”

“May I butt in and ask a question?” J’erri’ahn’ah asked.

A knock came at the door again; a clearing of the throat and Vi’k’tur’s voice came through the enchanted doors.

“My queen, will you permit me to enter?” He asked.

I nodded to M’kary’ano and Taem’luck to go and open the door.

Vi’k’tur stepped inside and flung himself into an over-dramatic bow that flipped his long hair over his head and hung down, almost touching the floor. “Majesty.” He said, swinging himself into an up-right position again, his hair falling over his shoulder “Forgive the intrusion, madam.” He paused, waiting for me to answer.

I had just stuffed my mouth full of food so I waved my hands for him to continue.

“I made arrangements, as you requested, with Dru’cyl, and I do apologize, ma’am, but he insisted on meeting with you now.

I tried to keep my irritations under wraps, "Bring him in." I said and stuffed my mouth full of food again. Everyone else kept on eating like there was nothing going on.

Dru'cyl walked in, clicked his heels together, stood up straight and put his right hand over his heart, "Majesty, forgive my intrusion, but I thought it best to discuss this now, rather than later." He said.

"So I've been informed." I drawled.

"Majesty, I stand here ready for my punishment for allowing you to be harmed earlier today." He said, he stood taller and puffed out his chest, helmet under his right arm.

"Oh, I see, so I take it, then, that this is a confession of guilt?"

"What?" He blanched. "Pardon me, my queen, but I do not understand."

"Well, you're here begging for punishment over something that I assumed was the fault of someone else in the crowd, so I take it then, that you are confessing your guilt in this?"

"No, ma'am, no. Not at all, majesty." He said, pale faced.

"So you are not the one who brought physical, mental and emotional turmoil upon me, then?"

"No, ma'am, no. Not at all, majesty." He repeated himself.

"Glad we got that settled! Now, come! Sit! Talk! Eat!" I turned back to my plate of food but Dru'cyl didn't move an inch.

"Begging your pardon, majesty, but I don't understand. I failed you. I failed to protect you! I should have been able to prevent it!" He was torturing himself.

"I see, so you are admitting to guilt, after all then?"

"I am to blame, majesty."

"I see, so then you are the one who harmed me? Or what exactly is it that you are to be punished for? Just so that I am clear on what to tell your family."

"I am to blame for not stopping it from happening, majesty."

"Oh, okay! I understand now!" My sarcasm was coming out loud and clear now, "You knew this was going to happen! Therefore this is a confession of guilt, you are here to explain to me how it is that this plan came to be in your knowledge and why you failed to stop it?"

"No, majesty. We did not know. We could not have known." He said.

"Well, sir, forgive my ignorance, but I am confused. First you are admitting guilt, and now you are saying that it would have been impossible to have known that this would have happened." I paused, weighing my words more carefully. "So, which is it, sir, are you guilty of failing to prevent something that no one knew might happen? Or are you guilty of failing to prevent something that you knew was going to happen?" I asked. I held up my hand when he started to speak. "Because, sir, if it is the first, then you are no more guilty than my father or my guardian. However, if it is the latter, then that, sir, is treason, and I will have your head for it. Think very carefully before you speak next sir, because I will do what needs to be done for my kingdom." I told him, danger lurked in my voice, a shadow behind my eyes.

He thought for a few moments, and said, "Majesty, my humblest apologies, you are quite right. I was just as ignorant as anyone else. There was no possible way for me to have known that something like this might have happened. Nothing like this has ever happened before. I could not have prevented it even if I had tried to." He bowed his head in defeat.

"Good! Now that we have that cleared up ... Unless there was anything else you care to confess to ... ?" I left the question hanging for a moment, there was no reply, "Good, now! Come! Sit! Eat! Talk! Stuff your face and take your fill of the wine! It will be many hours before we eat again!" I told him.

Dru'cyl came and awkwardly took the empty seat immediately opposite of me, hesitantly reached for a plate and filled it up with food.

"Now, where were we?" I asked. "Ah! Yes! J'erri'ahn'ah, your question?" I inquired.

"I was wondering where my mother was today. I was shocked that she did not show up." She said, fear in her eyes.

"I do not know, J'erri'ahn'ah. Jhona said that she left just after we did, and he has not seen her. He had hoped to see her here, hoped that she had followed us, but she's not been here. He asked around, went to all the places she was most likely to be, but she wasn't there." I told her.

"What will you do?" Dy'llian asked.

"I am sure that there is a perfectly logical explanation for all of this." I told them. "Donna fash, all will be revealed with time. When we get back, we will ask her." I told him.

"And if her answer is not 'perfectly logical'?"

"We will cross that bridge when we get there, okay?" I smiled warmly. Trust me, please? I begged them silently. They both nodded their heads and put it out of their minds.

After we had sat stuffing our faces for a while, Dru'cyl looked up and said, "Majesty, if I may?"

"When you are sitting at my table, eating my food, you are family, Dru'cyl, formalities are annoying at this point." I said, "But go ahead."

"I have some grave news, majesty." He said, the air in the room got a bit less relaxed than it had been.

I waved my hand above my head; I was stuffing my face with food again.

"We were unable to catch the person who did this to you." He paused and waited, when I made no move or reply he continued. "Majesty, she got away." He said again, emphasizing his point a second time as if I hadn't heard him the first.

"I am well aware that 'we were unable to catch the person who did this to you' means that she got away, Dru'cyl, please, continue."

"Of course, your majesty, apologies. We were able to trace her maj'ick into the crowd, but at a certain point she dispersed her maj'ick and tied it onto about three other people. We know that these three people did not do this." He said.

"And you know this ... how, exactly?" I asked.

"Because we tested their maj'ick against the maj'ick that we captured from her. None of their maj'ick matched the sample we have."

"Ah, okay,please, continue."

"Well, it might be possible to apprehend her ... after you leave for Nah'alba."

"I'm sorry," My father spoke up, "Are you suggesting a trap?"

"Not at all, sir, my apologies, what I am saying is that we can embed the maj'ick we captured from the criminal into A'lari'jah and when that person uses their maj'ick around her, she will know it."

"How?"

"Well, majesty, you would ... inhale her maj'ick, through your nose and make an imprint in your memory."

"And how would I know when she uses her maj'ick around me?"

"Because your markings would glow blue, majesty."

"Markings?" I blanched.

"Yes, majesty, the markings on your winds ... and your body ... would glow ... blue."

"Why blue, though?"

"Because that's what color her maj'ick was when we captured it."

"Ah, okay... and I would ... ingest it?" I asked.

"Aye, majesty."

"I would be infecting myself with her dark maj'ick?"

"No, majesty, merely creating an imprint of it in your mind." He said.

"Okay, when do we start?"

"I will prepare everything and have it ready for you first thing in the morning, majesty." He said.

"Alright, well that's that."

"Not quite... majesty..." Dru'cyl said.

"Oh?" I asked.

"Well, there is still the matter of your security to discuss." He said. "I recommend doubling your sentry guard and having at least three with you at all times." He proposed.

"I think not, Dru'cyl. I have my guardian, and he is worth one hundred of your sentries."

"I understand, majesty, but even he was not enough to prevent this attack on you."

He had come close to angering me, but Taem'luck spoke up, "Pardon me, sir, but I think that you are mistaken in this."

"Oh? Well, do enlighten me." He was being very sarcastic towards Taem'luck.

"Majesty, permission to speak openly?" He asked.

"You have my permission to divulge the information to him." I told him.

"I kept my distance, Dr'ucyl, because I was told to." Dru'cyl frowned.

"I made him promise me that he would back off a bit today, I wanted to be free to move about the room in my head to comb and vet and see into their minds. When Tae hovers too closely, he veils what I can see, because of his telepathic shield that he places over me, it dampens my powers, and helps me to focus." I said calmly. "Now, sir, kindly remove the hooks that you have placed in my guardian and let us focus on the issue at hand."

"My apologies majesty, of course. We believe that whomever did this had close, intimate knowledge of you. We believe that whomever it was knew too much of your life. The details in your vision, Ary, that was incredible. No one who didn't know you could have created such a perfect vision of your life."

"Well, then you are mistaken, again." I told him, "I know the people who are close to me more intimately than you know. I know only three people who have known me my whole life. One of them is sitting in this room with us. One of them sits on the throne in Nah'alba. The third person is at home with her husband and her youngest daughter, waiting for us to meet them in Honey River Cove so that we can get to my uncle before my fifteenth birthday."

"Well, let's weigh this out carefully, majesty, if you will indulge an old man?" I nodded, already knowing where this was going, but I would indulge him. "Your uncle might have hired someone to do this to you." He said.

"No. He would have hired someone to hurt me, maybe, but not with maj'ick. Never with maj'ick. My uncle despises maj'ick, and if he was to hire someone to hurt me, it would not be with maj'ick." I paused. "Continue."

"Your father went missing from your life for three years, Ary, you do not know where he went, you thought he was dead, the whole world thought he was dead, and then he mysteriously turns up out of nowhere, just before his mother dies, and you become queen."

"Ah, the old, "Missing in Action, maybe he isn't really who he says he is" drag. First off, my father didn't disappear. My father was here, in A'va'lon the whole time after the fire. But that's not my story to tell, if you need to hear it from him, he is sitting right here, now is the time to hash this out, I do not need any distrust between anyone in this group, because if anyone distrusts anyone sitting at this table, then I will make arrangements and adjustments to who works where."

I turned and looked at my father. He hesitated, but

nodded.

"M'Kary'ano, tell us your story, and tell us true." I commanded, my voice rang with authority, and he had no choice but to tell us all the whole truth and nothing but the truth.

"Three nights before the fire happened, M'urlin stepped into our world and came to our house. He came to warn us, to beg us to move, to flee and to leave. He sat with us for several hours, hashing it out, debating, arguing, and in the end, he became angry and left."

"If I may, sir?" M'Kary'ano nodded, "Why did you not heed his warning?"

"My wife and I discussed it, and we decided that if we messed with fate, then fate would catch up to us no matter where we go. You see, Years before, when A'lari'jah was just an infant M'urlin came to us with a vision. The vision was of a horrible fire that killed all that were in it. Everyone of us. His vision was that A'lari'jah would die, and the savior of both kingdoms would not live to save everyone.

We heeded his warning, we didn't do nothing, we prepared, we moved A'lari'jah to the smallest room in the house, right off our bedroom. We made arrangements with certain people, appointed guardianships, and plans and wrote our letters. We had time, his vision said that she was older, but no older than thirteen. So, from the time that she was an infant, we knew that this was a possible future.

M'urlin came to us three nights before, his warning was that it would happen before the next full moon rose, which was only five days away. He begged us to reconsider leaving, and begged us to send A'lari'jah with him so that he could hide her away from the world and keep her safe. He begged us to allow my mother to take her, to raise her in A'va'lon, to become the heir of A'va'lon, and be raised as a princess, ready to assume the throne when it was time.

But we told him no. That if this was fate's design, if this is what the Creator had deemed would happen, then it would happen, and there was nothing that we could do to prevent it.

He was angry when he left, and we didn't see him again after that. G'rai'ce and I prayed day and night that we would, at least, be able to save A'lari'jah. And we did.

G'rai'ce and I took turns sleeping outside of A'lari'jah

door all night, we would get her out first, and then everyone else, if we could. We almost missed it, almost messed it up. G'rai'ce went to investigate a strange noise in the back of the house, and she never made I back to the front of the house, by the time I was able to realize that something was wrong, that the plan had been thwarted, it was nearly too late, Ary was on fire, and screaming in her bed, and I barely got her out of the house in time.``

"What happened to you?" Dru'cyl said, annoyed at hearing the whole story all over again.

"Patience, Dru'cyl, give him time, and he will tell you, he has no choice right now." He nodded, confused, but he was silent again. M'kary'ano continued.

"I reached the front door, opened it, stuffed letters under her arms and the house exploded. The force of the blast forced me into Fae form, six inches tall. I had lost my memory and wandered aimlessly miles from my home for weeks. My mother found me, and took me to A'va'lon. By the time I recovered my memories, it was too late ... A'lari'jah had died, and I couldn't save her. I was so distraught that I couldn't come out of my six-inch Fae form for a year, and then for the next year I couldn't stay in humanoid form for more than a few hours at a time. By the time I was able to stay in humanoid form, it had been three years, and my mother had started grooming me to take over for her.

On the third anniversary of my family's death, I went to the house, like I had done every year, to lay flowers on their graves and to talk to them. Except, this time, there were people there. People I didn't recognize. People that I had never seen before. So, we confronted each other in the clearing, where Ary used to play with the Fairies as a child, and it turned out that she was my daughter and I was her father. And a few weeks later we found ourselves here." He finished his story and blinked, my compilation was over, he was free.

"Dru'cyl, tell me why you think that my father was the one who would harm me. Tell me now and tell me true." I commanded.

"Because I am looking for someone to blame, in my old age I am paranoid and suspect anyone and everyone if I cannot find a logical, reasonable explanation." He said, he blinked and looked at me with fear in his eyes.

"I have the ability to make people tell me the truth, no matter if they want to or not." I told him. "Do you believe his story?" I asked.

"Yes, majesty, my apologies, majesty." He said, fear still in his eyes.

"Continue."

"Yes, majesty, well now we must logically weigh out Sr'eya." He said, waiting cautiously. When I had no response, he continued, "I find it suspicious that she has suddenly come up missing. Her husband does not even know where she is." He said.

"Yes, I find that suspicious and odd as well, but I do not think that Sr'eya would do such a thing. She's not that powerful, and that kind of power, well I just don't think it's her."

Dru'cyl nodded his head and continued, "Well, the only other person I can think of is A'lbi'on. He tried to have your mother killed twice. And succeeded the second time. Why not now?"

A dark and dangerous look crossed my face, anger flashed in my eyes like flames in a fire, "You don't know what you're talking about." The room darkened a little and everyone, except Dru'cyl, shrank back away from me.

"Forgive me, majesty, but I have it under good authority that your uncle was the one who hired the man who started the fire that murdered your family. My source says that you were his real target, not them." He said, a dark look had crossed his face. He was testing me, he was testing my powers.

What is it that you expect me to do? I asked his mind without him knowing what I was doing.

To lash out like a child, to explode emotionally.

"Sir, you are mistaken. My uncle may have tried to have my mother killed when she was younger, but he's a changed man. My mother's death nearly destroyed him. Again, you donna know what yer talkin' about." I said, I allowed the anger to stay in my eyes but I pulled the darkness back again.

A smile crossed his face ever so slightly. "Of course, majesty. My apologies, majesty. The reason still stands, someone close to you did this. I beg of you, in these dark hours, stay together, stay alert, stay vigilant!"

"Dark hours?" I asked.

He blinked, shook his head and looked at me, "Well, I might have been a tad over dramatic, I've just always wanted to say that. However, I do advise you all to stay in groups, stay alert, and stay vigilant. Whoever did this, they got away once, they might come back and try it again." He said.

"Understood, sir. Thank you for your concern." I said.

A small clearing of the throat announced Ki'ri'ah presence. "Pardon me, ma'am, forgive my intrusion..." She said meekly.

"What is it Ki'ri'ah?" I asked kindly.

"It's just... I couldn't help but overhear your conversation about the person who did this to you..." She said, "It's just... well, I know who she is..."

"You do?" I asked.

"Yes, milady, I recognized her maj'ick."

"Can you explain what you are talking about?" I asked.

Ke'yahn'ah stepped forward and hugged her sister tightly. "It's alright, Ki'ri'ah, you can tell her." She said kindly, stroking the girl's hair.

"Well, my queen, what it is... you see... a few years back, my da' got into a bit of trouble. It was a huge misunderstanding, but before he could prove that he was innocent, the bounty hunters found him, and well ... I'd recognize that maj'ick anywhere." She said.

I looked at Ke'yahn'ah, "I'm so sorry, but to an outsider, she's not really making any sense."

"Yes, milady, I'm sorry, it's just her nerves. See, she is scared she will be in trouble for speaking this out loud ..."

"Maybe your sister can tell me?" I asked Ki'ri'ah, "That way it's not so stressful for you?" I said kindly, she smiled and looked up at Ke'yahn'ah.

"Well, our father was a good man, he worked at the smithy's every day to earn a coin for us to put food on the table. His coin was good, but it was hard work and it wore him out, he was exhausted all the time.

Anyway, he made friends with the wrong sort of people, and when he found out who they were, he got out as fast as he could, but it was too late, he'd become their scapegoat. The sentries were called, and my father ran. He went into hiding, and then a reward was placed on his head, wanted alive.

The bounty hunters came in the middle of the night, she

was the best of the best, she had a powerful gift for tracking and capturing these 'criminals', with her on the trail, my da' stood no chance.

She was ruthless, and cruel, she burnt down our house to flush him out, my mum and baby sister perished days after from smoke in the lungs. Da' didn't make it out of the house, he had been under the house in a small cut out that we put our vegetables in to keep them cool.

Ki'ri'ah here has a very special gift, she can sense the powers that other Fae have, and she can always find her way back home, no matter where she goes, by following the maj'ick.

When that happened in the throne room, Ki'ri'ah followed the maj'ick, and it was, in fact, I'dhrenn'i'el.

I'dhrenn'i'el went dark when she was Faeling. Her family were all captured and taken into slavery, she's not originally from Nah'alba, she hid herself on the ship that brought her family over from Hesperia. Her family, along with half the other slaves, got sick and died on the way over, they were tossed into the sea and forgotten. When the ship landed in Nah'alba, I'dhrenn'i'el got out and found herself in a free land, a land where all creatures lived in harmony with each other. Where she had a home again. However, the darkness had settled in her soul, and there was no going back from it… when a Faeling turns dark and then turns sixteen with that darkness still in her heart, she will forever be dark. The only person who might have been able to help her was M'urlin, but she refused. She got in with the worst of the worst, and she went into hunting and trapping her own kind and selling them for profit. It was said that she once ripped the tongue out of a young boy for fun, just for a laugh. He got sold to a nice family who paid him well for his work and said that he was free to go whenever he wanted to. He stayed with them until they got old and died, and then he came home and married a young Fae girl named Sr'eya."

"What happened to I'dhrenn'i'el?" I asked.

"No one really knows, I lost track of her after she ripped that poor boy's tongue out, it was like she just vanished off the face of the earth, that boy he turned out okay though, from what I hear. The healers here, when he first came home, offered to regrow his tongue for him, but he refused. Said that it would always stand as a reminder of where he came from and the things that happened to him. Anyways, there are rumors that she got wind of a prophecy that would change the world, and she wanted to be a part of that, to help shape the one whom the prophecy was about. It is said that she changed her biological properties and became someone else, but no one knows who, and no one has seen or heard from her since."

"What was this prophecy?"

"Again, no one knows. It's all just guessing games, hearsay, and rumors. There are a lot of them, and I was inclined to believe that one of her 'criminals' got the better of her and killed her. At least until today. She's alive and she was back here in A'va'lon today, but there was something wrong with her maj'ick."

"What do you mean, wrong?" Dru'cyl asked.

"It was off, mixed with a different kind of maj'ick. It's like... Elfish maj'ick almost, mixed with Dark Fae maj'ick." Ki'ri'ah's face was all scrunched up as she thought about it.

I got down on my knees in front of her, "May I try something? It willna hurt a bit, I just would like to see what you saw, and extract her maj'ick from you." She frowned. "I promise it willna hurt." I said. She nodded.

I placed my hands on her head, like An'ti'el had done with me to share the memories that Verisiel had sent her to share with me.

"Think about today, and what happened, walk me through what you saw, and what you did."

I was standing close to the front of the crowd, watching me kneel on the cushion. The clouds began to gather above, and thunder rolled like an angry, hungry dragon. The throne room darkened, and the crowd began to get nervous.

"Please state your full, true name." Vi'k'tur, the High Priest, said.

A blinding bolt of lightning shot out of the sky, I screamed at the platform but seconds later an ear splitting, earth shaking clap of thunder drowned out my screaming. I had fallen over and passed out.

Ki'ri'ah had just sensed the maj'ick, it was close. We turned and there was a hooded figure in a dark midnight blue cape staring up at me. She was blue in skin tone with black hair and pitch-black eyes. She was very beautiful, thin and appealing to the eye, but she was emanating a purplish black maj'ick out of her and a feeling of evil rolled off of her. I concentrated on her maj'ick, picking it apart, putting it into my memory, felt it, and picked through it as it flowed out of her.

I let my hands fall from Ki'ri'ah's face, "She was right behind you!" I gasped. She nodded, fear was in her eyes.

"She had locked eyes with me at one point, I thought for sure that I was about to die, but then you came to and sat back up and she took off." Ki'ri'ah said.

"Well, you stay close to my rooms, or with me and Taem'luck when we are out and about, I don't want anything happening to you. Dru'cyl, assign guards to her and her sisters, they are not to leave the palace until they come with me to Nah'alba." I commanded.

"Did you get a good sense of her maj'ick?" M'Kary'ano asked.

"I did. And it's familiar, Ki'ri'ah was right, there is a different species of maj'ick underneath the Dark Fae maj'ick, I just can't place it. It's familiar though. Very familiar. Dru'cyl was right, whomever she was, she knew me, but not well enough. She knew my weakness, but she didn't count on my strength. She won't underestimate me again."

We all sat in silence for a while, and then I decided that it was time for a hot bath and a bit of a nap, so everyone left and I sunk into a hot peaceful bath and took a long nap.

Chapter Sixteen

I wonder what time it is. I thought as I yawned and stretched and looked out my window. I thought it was odd that no one had woken me up yet. *Maybe it's not as late as it feels like it is.* I shrugged and got out of bed. I picked up a book from the small library in my room and sat on the window seat to read until a soft knock sounded at my door.

"Majesty, it's time to wake up now. It's almost time to go to the banquet ma'am." Ky'wahn'ah whispered through the door.

"You may enter, Ky'wahn'ah." I said lazily, not looking up from my book. I smiled as she walked over to my wardrobe and pulled out my gown for the night.

"My apologies, majesty, my sisters are helping out in the kitchen as they are a bit short staffed at the moment." She said to me.

"Why are they short staffed?" I asked, something felt off to me.

"A lot of the staff that was here prior to your coronation received specific instructions from Verisiel before she died to retire to a quiet home life. Most of the staff, majesty, had been here nigh on a century now. They really do deserve a new chapter." She explained. "It's tradition that the new monarch brings on his or her own staff." She added.

"I am sensing that 'tradition' is going to be tough to break around here." I chuckled. "Seems to be the only thing I have heard since I was inaugurated."

She laughed, "The traditions will be easier to break than you think, majesty, the people are open to the future, we have been waiting a long time for this day. I believe that you will find people lining up to support your decisions."

"Thank you, Ky'wan'ah, I really needed to hear that."

"Shall we get you dressed, madam?" She asked politely.

I stood up from the window where the sun had warmed my back, put a bookmark in my book and laid it down on the desk, and allowed her to change my clothes; she was so short that I had to sit down for her to help me get dressed.

"My apologies, majesty, in future I will remember to bring me a stool to stand on, that way you do not bow to an inferior." She said, her face colored.

"Donna fash, dear, I donna mind at all."

She dressed me in a satin floor length dress that stayed true to my tribal colors.

"Hope you like purple, green and gold, ma'am." She teased.

"Why is that?" I asked, a bit confused.

"Because the royals wear nothing but the colors of their tribe."

"Why?" I asked, "Oh, wait, let me guess… It's tradition." We both laughed.

"No, majesty, it's a protection thing for you. It's so that wherever you go the people and the sentries know who you are."

"Wouldn't that make me more of a target?" I asked.

"No, majesty, it keeps you safe. When you walk amongst the people over the next several days, you will understand." She said.

"Can you no' just tell me?" I asked.

"Aye, I could, majesty, but… to experience it for yerself will squash any and all doubts that you might have. Explaining it to you is one thing, but living it, walking amongst your people, majesty, well… words fall quite short."

"I think I understand. If someone had tried to explain to me the feelings that would run through me today, and the feelings that I experienced as I was crowned, I wouldna have understood it as well as I did when it happened. Say no more of it. Tell me, what is your favorite thing to do in A'va'lon?"

Her eyes lit up and sparkled, "Visit the wishing tree, my lady." Her smile reminded me of mum's. A smile that illuminated her very core and made her seem like she was glowing.

"Your smile could light up a room, you know. Just like my mum's." I told her, she colored again and ducked her head. "What does one do at the wishing tree?" I asked.

"Well, some make wishes to it, they write down their wishes on special paper with special ink, and they fold them up and hang them on the tree. Other's go to pick a wish from the tree and grant it, if possible. If it's impossible we get a bit creative and come up with some way to try and make the wish come true in a different way. For example, if someone is wishing for their parent to be released from the hospital, we canna usually do that, because they arena going to make it, and there's nothing that we can do to change that, so we take them and their relative out for the day, with special permission from the nurses." She said.

"And which do you do?" I asked, already knowing the answer.

"My sisters and I go at night and pick a wish and come up with our own creative ways to help grant it. We pick one wish between the three of us." She glowed as she talked about this.

"Take me with you, when you go again?" I asked, "I'd love to help grant someone's wish." I said, a light lit up in my eyes for the first time in weeks.

She smiled and nodded, "Majesty, we are done here, may I escort you to the great hall for the banquet?" she asked.

"I was rather hoping to get that honor myself, if you donna mind. It's not every day that one's daughter becomes queen, after all." My father's tender voice sounded from the door.

"How long had you been there?" I asked.

"A while, but I didn't want to interrupt your conversation. I think it's wonderful that you want to grant wishes, Ary!" He smiled, still glowing with pride.

"Da' you look positively dashing!" I said, he was wearing a tuxedo of purple and gold, his hair was gelled up and with his glow, he looked happier than he'd been in years.

"Ach, I'm not the one everyone will be staring at tonight, my love. All eyes will be on you. You sure are a vision in your gown." He said admiring me was always his favorite thing to do.

"Thanks, Da'. Why does your suit not have emerald in it?" I asked.

"Emerald was yer mum's color." He smiled, there was a tiny bit of sadness in his eyes, but it quickly vanished. "It looks ravishing on you." He added.

"Well, come on then, our guests are waiting." I said, accepting my Da's arm. I felt Ky'wan'ah's mood change to sad. I offered her my other arm, and her face lit up. "Why don't you both escort me? Ky'wan'ah you can show me the best place to sit with the people! And after you can introduce me to the Fae people so I can mingle." I said, "Mingling is good, right?" I asked my father.

"Yes, mingling is excellent!!"

When we arrived at the great hall, everyone else had already been seated and were waiting on me.

"You're late, majesty." A'nti'el whispered.

"The queen is never late. Everyone else is simply early."

"Yes ma'am. Open the doors!" She announced.

The trumpets played and the doors opened. The sentry inside the doors announced my arrival.

"Queen A'lari'jah Jayd Riversong MacM'kary'ano escorted by M'kary'ano and Ky'wan'ah."

Everyone rose and bowed as I entered.

"Thank you kindly, let's eat!" I said. Everyone cheered and Ky'wan'ah led me to sit with her and her sisters, my father followed and Taem'luck, who never left my side now, laid under my chair.

"Will you sit with us?" She asked me.

"Of course I will!!" I said, excited that she wanted me to sit with them, Ky'ri'yah shied away from me.

"Don't worry about her, milady, she's just nervous." Ke'yhan'ah said.

"But it's more than that, isn't it? She's afraid of me." I told them. "She fears my power, I am the most powerful being she's ever met, and that's saying something. Because compared to that Fae today, if I went dark, I could destroy the world." I smiled kindly.

"Yes, milady, you're right, you could. How do we know that you won't?" Ky'ri'yah asked from behind Ke'yahn'ah.

"Guess you'll just have to stick around long enough to find out, won't ya?" I teased. "Listen, I almost went dark. I was in a sad place for a while, just before I met my da' again. I went to see M'urlin about it all, to find my head and my path again. To do some soul searching and to try and come out of my sadness. Here, hold my hand, let me show you something." I invited the three of them to join hands with me.

When they took my hands, I opened myself up to them, I allowed them to see my heart. They saw the struggles I went through and the pain I dealt with following the death of my family. They walked through the years with me, the dark places in my mind when, the time that I opened my arms and let most of my blood flow out one night. They saw it all, and they saw me go to M'urling, and say goodbye to my family. They saw the visions that I was projected into when I collapsed on the floor earlier that day, and how my dad was able to bring me back.

"So, you see, I have good people to keep me on the right path, and I'm better off for all the people who are in my life and who are close to me. I'd be honored if you three would be a part of that group." I told them.

Ky'ri'yah opened her eyes but they were all white, her hand and my hand were still connected. "I see a light, a bright light like a star, illuminating your path and your future. You are going to be A'va'lon's shining star, to bring peace to Nah'alba and A'va'lon once again. But beware, there are traitors amongst your inner circle. There are people who claim to be one thing but are another. You will find a great ally and a great enemy amongst them. Your dark days are not over yet. There will come a time soon that will test you more than you've ever been tested before. One final test. If you fail, the world will fall into chaos and doom and Nah'alba will become a black void. If you pass, you will be the greatest queen this world has ever known." She blinked and shook her head, pulled back her hand shyly.

"I'm sorry, I can't help it. It doesn't have an on or off switch, it happens rarely but when it does happen it's usually very serious." Ky'ri'yah explained. "I will be with you from this day until my last day, to never walk through that dark place alone." She pledged and smiled. "I like you, Ary." She said at last.

"Ky'wan'ah and I both are of the same mind, milady." Ke'yahn'ah said.

"Why did you no' pledge in front of everyone?" I asked, curious.

"When you collapsed, we were sent to fetch a stretcher and a mask for you in case you needed immediate intensive care. When that was over, we were sent to ready your rooms with food, fresh clothes, linens and a bath. When we came back, no one was here but you and your family, and you were in a heated conversation with the High Priest and Priestess." She explained. I nodded and no more was said on that.

After everyone had finished eating and the tables had been cleared, Vi'k'tur called for everyone's attention.

"Here, here!" He announced, the room fell silent. "If I may have your attention for just a few minutes, there is something that has never been done before, that needs to be done now." He paused and then looked at me, "My Queen, will you come sit up here for a moment?" He asked.

I stood up and walked over to the chair and sat down.

He knelt on one knee and bowed his head, with his hand over his heart he began in a loud clear voice;

"My queen, I pledge to you my loyalty, my honor, my wisdom, my guidance and my knowledge. I recognize you as the appointed one that the Creator has sent to guide us all into a new era, into a new realm. Into an era of peace and prosperity, that we may all thrive together as one, united kingdom, and no longer have two separate kingdoms. I pledge to you these things from this day, until my last day." He stood up and his sister took his place.

She knelt and said the same words that he said, stood and saluted me and took her place at my right arm. Suddenly there were people who had not pledged earlier in line to pledge to me now. I smiled and welcomed them forward.

The last three to come forward were my maids, "Majesty, forgive our late pledges." They knelt on their knees,

"We pledge to serve you honorably, loyally, faithfully and with the utmost discretion. We swear to keep your secrets, or you may take our tongues. We swear our services, and if we break it before you release us, may our lives be forfeit. We swear to share with you all our knowledge, impart with you our wisdom, and leave you encouraged and uplifted. We swear to protect you to the best of our abilities, even if we lay down our lives for you. We swear to honor you, obey you, protect and serve you from this day, until our last."

They saluted and stood up and went back to their tables.

"Anyone else who has not yet pledged to your queen, now is your time! This is your second chance! Come forward and pledge your honor and loyalty to her!" Vi'o'lah had stepped forward to offer them all a second chance. No one else came forward and the part went on.

There was dancing and more food, lots of ale and wine and sweets, and by midnight I was ready for bed.

"Apologies to all, I know that there are quite a few of you that I have yet to mingle with, I do hope to be able to do so very soon! However, I am very tired. I have much to discuss before I begin packing and traveling tomorrow! If you will all forgive me, I feel that I must retire to my bedchambers." I smiled, they all laughed and bowed me out of the great hall, and the banquet resumed until the sun came up.

Myself, Vi'k'tur, Vi'o'lah, J'errian'ah, Dy'llian, M'kary'ano and Dru'cyl (along with all three of my hand maids) went to my new bed chambers- the queens' quarters.

"How does it feel?" M'kary'ano asked me as if I was trying on a dress.

"Not as weird as I expected. The redecoration makes it feel more like mine than it did before." I explained. "It kind of reminds me of the bedroom above the inn in Honey River Cove." I smiled.

"Good, I'm glad you like it, I helped design it!" M'kary'ano announced. "Just wanted you to feel at home when you came here." I hugged him and it felt so good that we didn't let go for a few minutes.

"Alright, now, you ladies know how to disguise yourselves in human form, right?" M'kary'ano asked my maids.

"Yes, sir, A'nti'el began teaching us when she took us into her service." Ke'yahn'ah said.

"Good, then you won't mind putting on a bit of a show?" He asked. "Just want to make sure that we don't need to tweak anything before tomorrow." He explained.

They instantly changed into human form. All three kept similar features to their Fae face and body styles, just a bit less skinny, and a bit more cheek.

Ke'yahn'ah had ashy brown hair and blue eyes, not too blue, and not too pale, nothing that would stand out. She had a nice olive color, though she decided to stay a bit lighter than the other two. "I don't get as much sun as they do, as the older sister I have to provide for the family, and that often keeps me indoors." She explained fluidly. Her ears were small and round, and her teeth were a bit crooked, slightly yellow and very human looking. She had a small button nose and few freckles sprinkled across the bridge of her nose.

Ky'wan'ah also had blue eyes, straight brown hair, she was the chubbier one of the three, a bit shorter than her older sister, but cheery looking, she had a nice olive colored tan, a bit darker than her older sister, but still lighter than Ki'ri'ah. She had a big squashy nose, small bright eyes and big ears. She reminded me of the joyful, glass half full kind of kid.

Ki'ri'ah had softer features than her sisters, more olive toned with a quiet, shy demeanor. She had bigger eyes than her sisters but smaller eyes than me, she had a small nose that might be missed upon first glancing her face, freckles littered her cheeks and nose with sun bleached sandy brown hair and yellow highlights.

"Wow, you look great! But your faces don't scream sisters. Ki'ri'ah could be Ke'yahn'ah's sister, but there aren't many similarities in Ke'wan'ah's facial structure." M'kary'ano said.

"Nah, da' I can see it, they look similar enough, leave them alone and don't change it, they have worked long and hard on these disguises, any changes now might well cost us in the long run." I told him.

"I don't understand."

"Well, sir, it's like this, if they forget one morning, that she has a tighter jawline than she has now, or if she changes the shape of her nose or her eyes and she wakes up one morning and forgets that she had changed them, it could be detrimental to your cover story." J'errian'ah explained.

"When we are younger, it is harder for us to shape shift at will. We have to think hard and concentrate on what we want others to see. And over time, after practicing for months on end, we have a particular shape that we can hold onto without thinking too much about it, but to change that on a whim and expect us to hold it without having to concentrate on it, well it's almost impossible. If she slips up and gets overwhelmed in the middle of the day or flustered at something, it could slip and change back to her original human shape… It's dangerous to have them change now." Dy'llian added.

"I understand. Alright, well you all look great! Truly, these are amazing human forms." He turned to me, "Have you been working on your new form to show A'lbi'on?" He asked.

"Yes, I have, and I have finally decided what I want him to see." I shifted into a taller, more mature version of myself, a young lady in every way. I was a vision of beauty and grace, and I looked very much like my mother. I stood tall, straight, relaxed, poised, every bit the princess I was.

"And your cover story for this sudden appearance?"

"Lots and lots of physical therapy, surgery to straighten my bones and my back, rods and pins to hold it all in place."

"Very believable. Well, it sounds like you have everything under control. How are you going to explain your new maids?"

"Oh, they are coming with me from the physician, I needed specialized maids to assist in massages, oils, herbs, herb baths etc ... He's already been informed of this." I said.

"Okay, well off to bed then, we start packing in the morning. You can take anything you want with you, including the bed." Everything that you want to carry with you, pack in the smaller carrying bags, everything else will be packed up and moved to the castle overnight while everyone is sleeping."

"Cool. In that case, can I take the whole room? Cause I like the way this room is designed."

"Why don't we just design your room at the castle to look exactly like this, and have it "ready" in a week? Let your uncle know that you have brought in a contractor to redesign your room" M'kary'ano said.

"Deal." I smiled. "Alright, everyone. Off to bed, we have a busy day tomorrow." I said, Dru'cyl, M'kary'ano, A'nti'el please stay."

"I wanted to discuss you going with me tomorrow, Dru'cyl, I need someone like you in the palace with me." I said, "I don't want to take you away from your duties here though."

"It would be simple for me to go. I have someone here that

pretty much runs things anyways, and if they need anything I can be here and back again in no time."

"Is it something you *want* to do, though?"

"It would be an honor of the highest kind to accompany you in Nah'alba, majesty." He said.

"Okay, just remember, there I'm not queen yet, I'm only a princess, I would be alright with you just calling me "milady", "miss" "Mistress" and the like, while we are there." I told him. "That goes for you three as well," I said to Ke'yahn'ah, Ki'ri'ah and Ky'wan'ah. They nodded and continued getting my hot bath ready.

"That's all then, make the preparations, and be ready to go when it's time to leave, get some good rest tonight, I fear we will all need it." I dismissed them from my room and got into my hot bath.

Chapter Seventeen

I had slept poorly, feverish with nightmares and, as the morning dawned, it met me with an unwillingness to leave my sleep, fitful though it was. I had a bad feeling in the pit of my stomach, not the kind that tells you that your food didn't settle well; the kind that came before bad things happened. I couldn't shake it; even my coronation had been plagued with darkness and I had thought, even then, that it was a bad omen to begin a new reign.

However, Vi'o'lah and Vi'k'tur assured me that the greatest king of all the kings of A'va'lon had met a similar fate during his coronation.

"Mat'eyo, the greatest king A'va'lon has ever seen, had a duel to the death, in the middle of his coronation!" V'k'tur had said.

"And he reigned for nigh on a century, my queen, so do not fret, this is actually a good omen, not a bad one!" Vi'o'lah added.

This bit of history gave me very little assurance; how could bad things be good?? It didn't make sense and leaving my father and my new home didn't help this feeling of dread and anticipation. I couldn't help but think that the worst was yet to come.

Ke'yahn'ah had been prodding me for the last five minutes, if not more. I had hoped that, if I ignored her, that she and this whole foolish notion of leaving would disappear, however, I realized that she was not going to leave me alone until I woke up.

I groaned and rolled over, "Do I have to?"

"'Fraid so, miss. Everyone's been waiting on you for the last hour." She said, sleep deprived as I was, I could feel something wasn't quite right with her.

"What's wrong?" I asked, voice thick with sleep.

"Nothin' miss, no worries, don't worry about me. Time for you to get up." She turned to leave, and I reached out to stop her from leaving.

"Ke'yahn'ah, tell me." I asked.

"It's just, leavin' ya know?" She started, the tears filled her eyes and she blinked them away.

"I know, but yeh'll not be alone, don't forget that." I told her, and a couple seconds later I was snoring again.

"MISS!" she said, I jumped and hit the floor with a muffled thud.

"Right! I'm up!" I said, groaning as I rubbed the back of my head, which had hit the solid wood side table as I fell off the bed.

"It's cold out today, so we kept back a warm cloak and some thick fur tights fer ya." She said, hurrying around the room gathering up last minute things as I got up and pulled on my pants and dress. She brushed my hair and braided it and helped me into my cloak.

"Better wear these today, miss, the weather outside is rainy and wet." She handed me a pair of hard leather boots that had been treated with water resistance resin. I nodded and pulled them on and cinched them tightly against my legs. I didn't want to get up, or move, I yawned. I could go back to sleep just like this. I thought to myself, but Ke'yahn'ah wasn't having it.

"Come, miss, they are all at the gate waiting for us!" She said as she scurried out the door.

At the gate it seemed like the whole kingdom had come to see us off. The small area was very cramped with people. Dru'cyl was speaking with a young Faeish boy who looked upset. The boy wore the Deputy Chief Sentry badge over his heart. He was young, but not as young as his face would indicate.

M'kary'ano was speaking to An'ti'el in a hushed, urgent voice. Though it was painful to look at him that day, it was more painful to look away. I stared hard, committing his every feature to my memory, I didn't want to forget his new face.

Vi'k'tur and Vi'o'lah were striving hard to capture my attention, as I approached them, Vi'k'tur bowed dramatically again, "Majesty!" he said as if he was greatly surprised, I came over to say goodbye to them.

"I do wish we were going with you. I do not like the idea of you going off without us!" He said, head still bowed, right fist over his heart, hair flung down across his body in front of him.

Looks a bit like a white waterfall, doesn't it? I mused, Taem'luck chuckled.

I was in no mood to be kind, but I felt it necessary. "Yes, well, I do wish you were going with us as well." I said, he straightened up and a look of great hope was on his face. "However, I know that you are greatly needed here." I explained, gesturing to An'ti'el and my father, "Someone's gotta keep an eye on him!" I laughed, but the laugh sounded fake even in my ears.

"You do not have to be brave, majesty. Being sad to leave him again is understandable." Vi'o'lah put her arms around me and embraced me in a warm, loving hug. A couple of sobs leaked through my defenses, and my father noticed; at once his arms were replacing Vi'o'lah's.

"Shh, it's alright, I'm not going anywhere! I'll be right here! You can come see me whenever you want!" He held me tight and our journey was prolonged even longer. By the time we said goodbye to everyone, it was nearly mid-day and we had very little time to meet up with Sr'eya at the road by my old home.

"Come, everyone, we need to go." I said brusquely. I led everyone out of A'va'lon without glancing back at all. I was in a bad mood, and the weather in Nah'alba did not help. It was cold, damp and cloudy, not at all the kind of weather I would have chosen to travel in. If it had been up to me, I'd have missed my stupid birthday party all together, however that decision did not lie in my hands. I was miserable, cranky, angry and whenever someone tried to talk to me they got a nasty reply. I didn't mean to, but I couldn't help it. We all walked without speaking, I had set the mood for the whole group.

The rain had made traveling difficult. The forest floor had turned to sludge, frequently causing our feet to get stuck in its thick muddy floor. Our large party made traveling slow enough alone, but with the mud and the rain, it took us longer than anticipated to even get out of the forest.

"Didn't they think to come ahead and check the condition of the woods before sending us traipsing off in the sludge?" Dy'llian muttered angrily.

"Apparently not." I said darkly. "I would have thought that they would have at least given us something to help the journey along! An'tie'el could have transported us directly to Sr'eya, but no! She had to stay there for some unknown reason!" As my mood darkened, so did the sky. Taem'luck was growling at every little thing. Angry, hot tears were making white streaks along my face, washing the mud away, and I wasn't the only one. Everyone had nearly finished crying by the time we reached the end of the forest, however, the relief of having reached solid ground again brought on a fresh wave of tears.

We walked the mile and a half to the road that led to my house and saw Sr'eya standing there waiting anxiously for us.

"Hello!" She called, running to meet us. "I was beginning to get worried about you!" She said hugging her two children. "What's this? Why so glum?!" She asked, noticing our less than happy faces.

"Don't worry about it, Sr'eya. Come I need a hot meal, a hot bath and bed." I grumbled grumpily, but before we could go, Sr'eya had gotten down on one knee.

"Majesty! Forgive my absence from your coronation!" She said, desperately.

"Not now, woman! I am cold, tired, and in a very bad mood." I yelled at her, "Unless you want me to say what is really on my mind, I suggest you not hinder my bath any longer than needed." By this time I'd had enough, I desperately wanted to run all the way back to A'va'lon and be with my father again. However, since that was not an option, I would settle for getting back to the palace with a hot meal and a hot bath and bed. Perhaps things would look better in the morning.

"Majesty, I am sorry, but I feel like this might need to be hashed out now, not left to fester over time." Dru'cyl had come up behind me. I rounded on him and the look in my eyes made him cower slightly for a moment and then he squared up with me. "Majesty, please, trust me on this." He said carefully.

"Fine." I crossed my arms and huffed, "State yer peice, and be quick about it." I commanded.

"Majesty, I am, from the bottom of my heart, so sorry for having missed your coronation! I was on my way when I got nabbed by a band of rogue Faes. They tortured me for information, they wanted me because I was close to you, and thought that they could get something from me." She stopped suddenly, a blank look came over her eyes and in an emotionless voice she said, "Majesty, I offer you my life in service to you, from this day, until my last day." She bowed her head and waited for me to speak again.

As suddenly as the rain began to pour on us again, my bad mood was gone, and inquisition took its place. *Something is not right here.* I thought to Taem'luck.

Yes, did you see that blank look replace her panic and anxiety? He asked. That is definitely not right. Look at J'erri'ahn'ah *and* Dy'llian, *they have that same blank stare as well.*

Yes, I see this. Let me converse with Dru'cyl.

"Dru'cyl, are you capable of telepathic communications?" I asked in an undertone that was barely audible. He nodded his head, *Yes, majesty, I am.*

What do you make of this?

He shook his head, *not good, whatever it is, it seems to be coming from Sr'eya herself.*

You mean that she's the spy?

Not absolutely, no. Could just be that they planted a sleeper bug in her, the one that would be triggered when she began trying to explain to you what happened. One that extends not only through her mind and body, but into J'erri'ahn'ah *and Dy'llian's mind and body as well. Maybe some form of mind control gone wrong?*

Next question, deal with it now, or later?

I'm not sure, majesty. I am uneasy with either option, perhaps you would allow me to scout ahead and see what awaits us at the castle courts before deciding?

Go, and hurry, it's cold and my mood has not improved. He nodded and dissolved into his pearly white mist. Within three heart beats he was back.

"Not good, majesty, better make it here, and quickly too, there's trouble in the lower towns." He said, I nodded.

"Alright, here it is, should we take cover?"

"No, there's no immediate danger, best to just get it over with now."

I nodded and placed my hands on Sr'eya's temples; entering her mind was no easy feat. Inside her mind there were memorie blockers and forgetting spells. I found things as far back as her childhood that had been suppressed.

She may have some ... unfortunate ... side effects to this. Adverse reaction to someone sifting through one's mind can be painful. She's got a lot of memories in here that are suppressed and guarded with maj'ick and some of it, going all the way back to her childhood, has that same blue maj'ick mixed into it. It's weird, there is a whole section of her memories that are saturated in that same strange blue maj'ick. Almost like... No... Can't be.

Majesty? Everything alright? Dru'cyl must have been tuned into me telepathically because he interrupted my train of thought.

Yes, everything is fine, I've found the source of the maj'ick, there are, it seems, multiple sleeper bugs here. I'll just remove all traces of the blue maj'ick from her mind and release her from its grasp.

Be careful, majesty, things may not be as they seem.

I found it! I thought, knowing that the others were listening. I could feel it pulling me in, pulling me closer. Its draw was like gravity itself, heavy and sticky and powerful.

Can you neutralize it?

I don't know, it's powerful, it's already draining my energy, making me weak.

At that moment I felt a surge of power and energy run through me, it was warm and tingly. Thank you. I said gratefully to Taem'luck.

I worked as carefully as I could, the closer to the source I got, the more my energy waned, the more energy I had to pull from Taem'luck and Dru'cyl. I didn't want to remove the blue maj'ick, I just wanted to contain it, and make it harmless to Sr'eya's memories and mind. I decided, in the end, to put it in a big ball at the back of her mind where it wouldn't do any real serious damage, but in doing so I had to tie my mind to her memories, just to temporarily protect them, until I could extract the blue ball of maj'ick and examine it.

"What happened? When did you all get here?" Sr'eya asked suddenly. "What's wrong with her!? Is she okay!?" She asked as she saw me limp in Dru'cyl's arms.

"You had a sleeper bug in you, Sr'eya. She has removed it, but it has taken a lot from her." Dru'cyl stated, his voice full of malice.

"What do you mean, sleeper bug!?" She demanded, deranged and hysterical. I was starting to come around again.

"He means that whatever happened to you, someone placed a sleeper bug in your mind. When you began explaining what had happened to you, it triggered the bug and you, essentially, went to sleep. It caused J'erri'ahn'ah and Dy'llian to "sleep" as well. I had to enter your mind and find the bug, my plan had been to remove it, but I need it, I neutralized it, and later, when we get back to the palace, I will extract it and study it." I explained. Color returned to my face and I looked up at Dru'cyl. When his eyes locked with mine there was a strange flutter in my stomach, like an army of butterflies had moved in. I looked away quickly and he sat me down on my feet.

"Come, now, everyone, I am in desperate need of warmth, a hot bath, a hot meal, and bed!" I stomped my foot grumpily while it tingled with sleep.

As we walked, Sr'eya treated me with fear, she walked as far away fom me as she could. Whenever she would look at me it was like she didn't know who I was. I gave her space, I had probably unlocked a lot of memories that she had suppressed for a long time, and she might be a bit upset at me. What would normally have taken us an hour to travel took us two in the rain and mud. By the time we got to the palace we were soaked through and almost frozen. Every one of us were grumpy and exhausted and in much need of rest and food, but something told me that was the last thing we were going to find beyond the walls.

When we were within eyeshot of the castle walls, the guards dispatched a rider out to meet us and, if possible, dissuade us from coming in at present moment.

"Hello all! At this time, I must ask that you turn around and return from whence you came immediately. We will dispatch messengers when it is safe for you to return." He said, spurring his horse around to ride back to the walls.

"SIR!" I called loudly. "Begging your pardon, but we have traveled all day in the rain and the mud, and I'll be damned if you turn me away now!" I stamped my foot in the puddled road like a spoiled child. "And I think my uncle might have a thing or two to say if you delay my arrival any more than it's already been delayed." I spoke more like a queen now. "I am cold, miserable and hungry! All I want, sir, is to be taken to my rooms and given a hot meal and a hot bath and go to bed! So, you may either go back to the king and explain to him that you turned us away or you may allow us to enter." I said more harshly than I meant to.

"Princess! I apologize! I did not see you!"

"You saw me, and the rest of us, just fine." I told him, "You simply refused to accept that I am who I am until I made a fuss over it. Now, what will it be."

"Well, princess, it's not safe in the lower towns!"

"Why?" I demanded, growing angrier by the moment.

"The lower towns are in chaos, looks like a strange disease is raging through them, making everyone act like cavemen." he shook his head and pressed his index finger and thumb to the bridge of his nose. "It's a nightmare in there right now."

I immediately stood alert, "Take me to where it started, and make sure that someone gets them somewhere dry and warm to wait and something warm to eat." I offered him my arm, which he hesitated in accepting. I gave him an annoyed look and said, "I'm not getting any drier or any less annoyed standing down here."

He swung me up on his horse and we took off towards the walls, "I'll meet you all in a bit! Tay! On me!" I commanded. He playfully loped along beside us as we pushed the horse to the gates at top speed.

"It seems to have started in a tavern in the middle of the lower town, that's where the first case was reported to have stemmed from." The guard said as we entered the opened gates, he stopped just inside to give instruction to the guard, "Send a messenger to the palace and tell the king that the princess has arrived, they will need to send an armed escort to get her home safely. The rest of her party are arriving, put a fire in the command post and get them blankets and warm food immediately. They are NOT to leave the post until the princess makes it back to them."

The guard on the ground saluted his commanding officer, "Right away sir, and where are you two heading?"

"We are going to the old tavern to investigate what's going on, the princess wants to see it."

"Do you need an escort, sir? I have some men I can send

with you."

"No, we've got the mountain wolf, I doubt anyone will bother us with him around." The guard sitting in front of me on the horse nodded his head towards Taem'luck, and we rode off without another word.

"Here it is, Mi'lady." He pulled up in front of a large wooden establishment that looks as if, on a good day, it would be boisterous and bustling with business. However, today it looked rather run down and abandoned.

I got down off the horse and began walking towards the Tavern when a hand grabbed my arm making me jump a bit.

"Princess, I cannot condone you going in there! Whatever this is, it's clearly contagious and if this IS where it started, you could be putting your life in danger!" He said, tightening his grip on my arm as I attempted to wrench free.

"Please, believe me, my life has been in danger since the moment I was born." I said bitterly, my smile was dark and sarcastic, "Besides, how am I supposed to figure this out if I don't go inside?" I finally worked my arm out of his hand and ran to the cavern.

"I'll just stand here and keep guard, princess." he said as Taem'luck growled deeply at him when he attempted to follow me inside.

"That's a good idea, why don't you stand guard out here, and I'll yell if I need anything." I said, trying not to sound patronizing. I shivered and rubbed my hands together, hoping it might be slightly warmer inside, but because it had been empty for several days, it was just as cold, if not more so, as it was outside.

"Alright, I'm going to sit in the middle of the floor and see if I can figure this out, keep an eye out, and don't let anyone disturb me." I told Taem'luck, he came over and curled up around me as I sat down.

I breathed deeply and steadied myself, centered myself with the five elements and then reached out with my mind and opened my eyes.

I saw it clearly, as if it was happening in front of my eyes. A Dark Faey came into the tavern in a dark, hooded cloak, her eyes were an electric blue, and her hands looked as though they had sparks flickering on them. She looked around the tavern, eyes wide with rage, and went to the bar. She demanded a drink, which she did not pay for, and then cast a dark spell, then stumbled out of the tavern and seemed to simply disappear.

I went deep into the maj'ick she cast and found a way to reverse it. I put a reversing spell on it, set to activate at midnight, and added a little bit extra to help us all get away. It seems that everyone, exactly at sundown, will all converge to the middle of the square for precisely one hour, allowing us time to get to the next level of towns and safely back to my uncle. Also allowing us a reprieve to rest and fill our bellies and get warm and dry. I told Taem'luck through our telepathic connection.

"Come, Tay, our work here is done. Let us join the others, and, for the love of all that's holy and sane, get warm and have some food." I said desperate to sit in front of a fire. He and I walked out of the tavern and joined our guard again.

"I was beginning to get worried fer ya, princess! Yer uncle would have flayed me alive if somethin' had happened to yeh!" He said, getting back on his horse, he offered his arm this time, and I wearily accepted it.

"Let's get back, I need to rest now." I said, allowing my exhausted head to lull on his back until we reached the command post.

"Mi'lady" The guard said to me as we navigated our way through the crowded streets. I grunted in reply, "It looks as though the crowd has calmed down some, they aren't so aggressive now."

"Really?" I asked, my voice sounded weak and exhausted.

"Look!" he shouted excitedly, making me jump.

I looked around and he was right, the people were calmer, though now they sort of just stared blankly around at everyone else. "Well, at least they aren't trying to hurt each other or themselves now." I said.

"Well, mi'lady, this is where I leave yeh. Yeh'll be safe enough here until the guard from the palace comes to collect yeh. There'll be food and drink inside and a warm fire and blankets. I can arrange a hot tub of water to you, if yeh'd like?" He offered.

"That's very kind of yeh, but I will wait until I am finished traveling to wash the grime off." I smiled kindly and attempted to dismount, unfortunately I had expended way too much energy on the spell I had to reverse and instead of gracefully sliding off the horse, I fell on my face into the mud.

"Majesty! Are yeh alright?!" Dru'cyl had seen me dismounting and came running towards us, but I fell before he could reach the horse. He picked me up and stood me on my feet, allowing me to lean on him for support.

"On second thought, captain, I think I'll take that hot bath after all." I said, tears brimmed my eyes.

He nodded his head, "Right away, mi'lady!" He hurried off away from us.

Dru'cyl helped me into the command post where the warmth of the fire washed over me and I suddenly realized just how cold I had been. I began to shiver violently and Dru'cyl ordered that I take off all my clothes.

Numb with cold, I fumbled with my clothes, exasperated and exhausted. I gave up quickly.

"Miss, let me help you with that." Ke'yahn'ah and Ki'ri'ah came over and helped, Dru'cyl held a blanket around me to shield me from the view of everyone, and then draped the blanket over my shoulders when I was done. He helped me to the fire and sat me down in a chair where I collapsed gratefully.

When I had eaten my fill of soup, and drank warmed wine, and I had finally stopped shaking and shivering, the guard announced that the hot bath water had been brought in and was ready. I sank into the hot water, and allowed the warmth to soak into my aching, screaming bones. I laid my head back and fell asleep.

I have no idea how long I had been asleep for, but I jumped when a knock sounded at the door.

"Who is it?" I said drowsily.

"Dru'cyl, miss."

"What is it Dru'cyl?" I asked, trying to shake the sleep from my head.

"Sorry to disturb you, miss, but it'll be sundown soon, and I just received word that the castle guards are making their way to us now." He announced, importantly.

"Alright, send in Ki'oyanna and Ki'ri'ah to help me finish up and I'll be right out."

"Right away, miss." He said, I heard his receding footsteps, and a few seconds later Ki'ri'ah and Ki'oyanna ran in to assist me in washing out my hair and drying off.

"Are my dress and pants dry yet?" I asked.

"Yes, miss, they have been hung in here to dry since before you came in." Ky'wahn'ah said.

"Good." I dressed quickly, feeling a bit stiff and still very drained.

I walked more slowly now, incapable of keeping up with the rest of them, we were walking to meet the palace guard through the lower towns.

"I think that we should go ahead and start walking towards the next town, A'lari'jah needs to get back to the castle as soon as possible. I don't think she will make it much longer." Dru'cyl was saying, he was anxiously pacing up and down in front of the doors waiting for the guard to show up, he kept looking at me and then looking out the windows.

"Dru, stop pacing, you're wearing me out. I'll be okay, don't worry." I told him, but my voice was weak and breathy, and did nothing but make his anxiety worse. I drifted in and out of sleep for the next hour, until a loud banging sounded at the door.

Dru'cyl went to the door and demanded, "Who's there!?"

"My name is Ro'thani'el, commander of the palace guards,

I have come to collect the princess A'lari'jah and her traveling party." He said.

My heart warmed at his voice and I told him, "Enter!"

"Ary! What's happened to you!?" He came running over to me and dropped down to his knees.

"Donna fash Thann! I'm alrigh' ... Nothin' a lil' sleep won't fix. Come now, let's get home! I am anxious to be in my own room again!" I said, standing up I walked to the door, Ke'yahn'ah helped me into my cloak and I was ready to go.

"Who's this?" Dru'cyl asked, every word was dripped in suspicion.

"Dru, this is Rohtaniel, my da's closest friend here at court, Thann, this is Dru'cyl, my new bodyguard." I introduced them to each other. They shook hands stiffly, neither trusting the other.

"Thann, he's fae." I said as quietly as I could. "He's alrigh'. Now can we go please?? Plenty of time to get to know each other at home..." I said irritably.

Ro'thani'el nodded and led the way out the door, I allowed everyone else to go ahead of me, so that I could be the last out.

I walked slower than the rest of the party, it was very difficult for me to walk at all, I was struggling to stay conscious. For a time, no one seemed to notice that I was straggling behind, they all were cold and miserable, legs sore, feet hurting bellies hungry again, to notice much else.

"Miss, are yeh alright?" Ke'yahn'ah said loudly, she had happened to look back just as I had stumbled over a cobbled stone that was slightly more raised than the others.

"I'm alright, I just tripped over a raised stone, that's all." I said, my voice sounded better, but I was out of breath.

Dru'cyl slowed down and walked behind me from then on. It felt like it would take us a year to get home, about thirty minutes into our walk, Ro'thani'el announced that as soon as we got to the far side of the next town we would be able to get into the litter and take it the rest of the way to the palace.

"Why didn't you bring it down here?!" J'errian'ah cried

miserably.

"Because of the crowd, we got it as far as we could, but we had to get off our horses and walk the rest of the way. I left half the guard behind to make sure that nothing happened to the litter." He smiled, his voice was full of regret and apology.

J'errian'ah grumbled a bit but we all kept walking, I pulled my cloak in around me and shivered violently.

"Miss," Dru'cyl had come up beside me and offered me his arm.

I looked up at him skeptical, "Dru, you're sweet and all, but I don't think that's really appropriate." I said in a weak attempt to be stubborn.

"Miss, to be frank, a few more steps and I'll be carrying you. At least this way I can extend my warmth and energy to you without having to carry you. Unless you'd like the humiliation of having to be carried back to the palace?" His eyes were teasing, they sparkled when he looked at me and it made my stomach flutter with butterflies.

I accepted his arm, and within a few moments my shivering had stopped, and I was walking better, but I knew that the second he let go, I would be exhausted and out of strength again.

"May I speak freely, miss?" He asked me as we walked up the steps to the next town. I nodded and he continued, "You should not have spent so much of yourself today."

"I know, but what else was I supposed to do? Healing Sr'eya and J'errian'ah and Dy'llian took more than I really thought it would, I underestimated her maj'ick, trust me, that's something I will not do again."

"You have drained yourself too much, you have left yourself weak and susceptible to attack or sickness." He was worried, that was plain to see, but the look in his eyes made it uncomfortable, and I did not understand why.

"I know, I'll be alright once I get back to the palace. I have Ro'thani'el and you and Eir'im'uhs too." I said. "Don't worry so much, I'll be alright." I smiled. I didn't feel like I would be alright, I felt like, at any moment, I would pass out and never wake up again, even with Dru'cyl's warmth and strength surging through me.

"May I say something else, miss?" He asked after a few moments of silence.

I laughed and nodded, "Dru, while we are here you must appear to be my friend, not my loyal subject. While you need to have respect for me, you are free to show emotions and feelings for me. Just don't overdo it, and don't disrespect or humiliate me in public and I'm okay with anything else." I told him, "You're free to speak your mind with me, always."

"I understand, I'll do better at following the customs of this realm." He paused thoughtfully for a few moments, calculating his words carefully before speaking again. "I am concerned about something though, and I would like to share with you my past to help you to better understand what I am about to say." He paused again, this time gauging my face and emotions.

"A long time ago I was married." He paused, thinking, reflecting. "She was the most beautiful creature I had ever seen. I went off to war shortly after we were married, less than a year after, and when I came back, I was different Fae. A different man from the one she had married. I came home distant and almost cold, but she never left me. She was always so patient and so kind with me, she melted my heart all over again, and we had a son. I hadn't been home with her but another year and a half when I got called to arms a second time. I said my goodbyes again and hoped that I came home. The second time I came home was different, I was different again. I came home to two strangers, a young boy of eight years now, and a wife who had to raise him all alone.

She was angry at me for a long time, and I was angry at my king, my country, my realm. Angry at myself, and the world. We spent some time apart for a while, getting reacquainted in a healthier environment so that our son wouldn't suffer our anger.

Over time, we fell in love all over again, remarried and had a happy life for a time. I found some good land in the south where the soil was rich and there was nothing around for miles. The king, Ma'teyo, had promised me anything I wanted under the sun and he'd do it for me for my service a second time. So, I petitioned him for the land and within a fortnight he had the title and deed in my hands and we were building on it. It was a beautiful piece of land; we built a house by the massive red oak tree that grew up on a hill. The land looked out over all the realm; you could see for miles up there." He stopped speaking, his throat had constricted, and he was struggling to keep his calm now.

I placed my hand on his arm and said, "You don't have to..."

He smiled at me, tears in his eyes, he continued, "We were farmers, you see; every harvest we would travel to the town to sell our goods and bring home supplies. One year my wife had gotten sick, very sick, and she couldn't go with me. The morning that I was supposed to leave I woke up with a terrible feeling that something bad was going to happen, but she wouldn't hear of me staying behind. I was going to send our son that year, but she insisted that everything would be alright and for me to go. So, I left my son behind to make sure that she was taken care of and safe. However, I was wrong, and I never should have left home that year. When I came back, one week later, my house was ash and my family had burned alive in a massive fire. My fields were scorched and everything I loved was gone." He finished his story and watched my face as I caught up to him.

"So, I'm confused." I blurted.

"I understand what it's like in all of your situations, Ary. I know what it's like to have lost loved ones in a fire. And I know what it's like to leave them behind after having just found them again."

There was silence between us for a long time before the realization of what he had told me hit.

"You've never told anyone this before, have you?" It was more of a statement than a question

"No, I have never told anyone this before, none aside from the king."

"So, why tell me now?" I asked.

He thought for a long moment, and the replied, "Because I want you to understand that you're not alone in this. That there are people out there who have been through similar situations who understand the pain you are facing now." He looked at me again, his eyes smoldering, and added, "I wanted you to know that, should you ever need, I am here for you, in whatever capacity you should desire."

I blushed, though I did not fully understand why that made me blush, and said, "Thank you, Dru. That means the world to me."

We walked in silence until we got to the litters, "Princess, your litter is at the front of the caravan. Only two may ride with you." Ro'thani'el stated.

I climbed into the litter with Dru'cyl and Ke'yahn'ah at my heels, everyone seemed to be too tired to realize that, should their exhaustion had not prevented it, they would have all been fighting over who would sit with me. The fight scene, that didn't really exist, played out in my head and I laughed out loud and everyone looked at me like I'd lost my mind. In all fairness I probably had.

"Sorry, I was just watching everyone fight for who gets to sit with me." Their brows creased and they looked concerned. "No, it's just that, if everyone wasn't so exhausted, they would have fought for the right to sit with me." After a few moments of paused consideration, Dru'cyl and Ke'yahn'ah laughed as well.

"Aye, that would have been a sight to see." Dru'cyl laughed, and then frowned as a sheen of sweat suddenly broke out across my brow. He came over to sit next to me and brushed my brow. "Yer burning up!" He said, he banged on the wall of the litter and yelled at the driver, "Get us to the palace

NOW!"

"Hey, what's going on?" I heard Ro'than'iel ride up next to the litter and ask Dru'cyl.

"She's burning with fever; she needs a healer!" said Dru'cyl whose voice was on the verge of panic.

"Right, I'll ride ahead and get the court physician on standby, and I'll urge the driver on. Ary, I'll meet you at the castle, be safe!" His horse was running, and we had sped up.

"Dru, 'm alrigh." I slurred. "'m just tired." I said, "Did too much today, spent all my energy. 's alrigh, ma. Donna fash." I said.

"Ary? What did you call me?"

"Ma, I said it's alright, don't worry, I'm okay."

"She's delirious." Dru'cyl shot at Ke'yahn'ah. "Do you have any healing skills at all??" He asked.

"No, I'm sorry, I never was good at healing, that'd be Ki'ri'ah, she's the nature Faey." She said, "I can pop over and trade her places?" Ke'yahn'ah asked, but we were already pulling up to the palace doors.

"No, we are here, maybe she will be alright."

"Come, the physician is waiting in her rooms." Ro'thani'el's voice sounded and pulled me to earth for a moment.

"Thann, tell him 'm alrigh. 'M alrigh." I said, "Put me down." I feebly punched at Dru'cyl, who just flicked my hands away and said nothing.

"Ary, don't be stubborn, you need rest, you've got a high fever." Dru'cyl said it was the first time he'd used my name, my stomach turned to butterflies and my heart did a strange leap.

"Thann, make him stop... make him put me down..." Tears streamed down my eyes, "I can't be seen like this, please, understand, I cannot be seen like this! The Nobles, they already think something is wrong, and if I come in being carried, it'll be war." I demanded. "Please, Dru, Hear me!" I commanded, using a bit of the little energy I had left to compel him.

When he looked at me his face softened and tears were in

his eyes, I reached up and touched his face, "I'm not her, okay? This isn't that. I'm okay, please listen to me. I need to see my uncle before I go to bed. Please." I begged, tears ran down my face, hot angry tears.

"Alright, but yeh'll hold onto my arm and not leave my side until yer safe in yer rooms."

I nodded my consent to his bargain, and he set me gently on my feet. "Lead us to A'lbi'on, Thann." I said, my strength was returning a bit and I felt warm again.

"Use my energy, my strength, at least until we are safely away in your rooms." Dru'cyl's warmth surged through me again, and I felt much better.

"Thank you for understanding." I smiled at him, "Please don't ever forget that I am your queen, and what I say goes, even if you don't think it best. When I need your counsel, I will ask for it, and when you give it, I will heed it. When I do not ask, you may still give, but I do not have to heed. Understand?"

"Yes, mi'lady, forgive me, I forgot my place for a moment." Said Dru'cyl.

"You're fine, nothing to forgive, I understand, but you have to understand that you cannot let feelings get in the way of what needs to be done. If you were in my position and I in yours, tell me if you would be doing anything different?"

"No, mi'lady, I would not. I would do what needs to be done, even if it cost me my life." He replied solmenly.

"Are we good? Are we clear? Or do we need to discuss this more?" I asked, I had stopped and looked him square in the face.

"We are as clear as crystal, mi'lady, I will keep my emotions to myself from now on." Dru'cyl said, a bitter edge to his voice.

A sudden anger rose up in me, my face flushed, and my hands shook. "Do not ever take that tone to me again. Do not ever manipulate me by threatening to withhold things from me, especially your feelings and emotions! I will not have you here if you jump down that road when I speak with you about these things" my voice a deadly whisper now, "If I had wanted you to become an emotionless robot, I would have said, "Dru'cyl, keep your feelings and your emotions to yourself, don't forget who you are and my station. I am your queen, not your friend." I said, still shaking with anger, "Instead, I said, "Please don't forget who I am and what I must do. Do not allow your emotions to alter your judgment or keep me from doing what needs to be done." Meaning do not hinder my business, if you have an opinion, state it, if I do not ask for it, I will, most likely ignore it. But do not emotionally manipulate me again, I will send you packing." I was sheet white at this point, and my fever had come back, I had over-exerted myself again.

He reached out tentatively and pulled me back to his side, "Forgive me for upsetting you, Ary, it was not my intention. I overreacted, and I apologize. Come, let us find your uncle." His face was guarded, even his eyes had gone quiet.

"Dru, I'm sorry. I didn't mean to lose my temper." I said, regretting the way I'd acted.

"You were right to ... it's just ..." He stopped as if his mind trailed off.

"Just what?" I probed, wondering if it was wise to or not.

"It's just that it's easy to forget that you are my queen." He smiled, but his smile was sad this time.

We did not speak again for a long time, I had wounded him, and I had not the words to fix it just then. The silence was not uncomfortable, though it didn't feel quite right, there had never really been a loss of words between us before.

We finally made it to A'lbi'on, he was waiting for us, angry and fuming, "Where the HELL have you been!?" He yelled at me as I entered his study. He was wearing his night gowns and cap; the fire was roaring.

"Dru, take me to the fire and set me in the chair, then wait outside for me." I said simply. He nodded and did as I asked. When he'd gone from the room I rounded on my uncle. "Where the hell have I been?!" I asked, repeating his words. My anger flared again, and this time I let him have a piece of my mind. "WHERE THE HELL HAVE I BEEN!?" I screamed this time; my voice shook the room. "UNCLE CHOOSE YOUR NEXT WORDS VERY, VERY CAREFULLY BECAUSE I PROMISE THIS IS NOT A BATTLE YOU WILL WIN TONIGHT. I HAVE HAD TO FIGHT FOR MY LIFE MORE TODAY THAN I DID THE WHOLE YEAR I HAD BEEN ILL FROM THE FIRE. AND YET, YOU ASK ME WHERE I HAVE BEEN!?" I paused, taking a breath and trying to calm down. My voice was low this time, "I suppose that you have not been to the lower towns in a while then?" It was not a question, "There is rioting and danger in the lower towns, it took me all day to get to the lower towns and then it took me the rest of the day to get here, what should have taken me less than six hours took me more that 13 hours." I said, "Where were you? That is the real question. Where were you while I fought my way through the lower towns? Overexerted myself and fell face first into the muddy road. And you, you were here, cozy and safe in your little palace, while I faced the craziness of the lower town chaos." I paused, breathing heavily, trying to hold onto consciousness, I was gripping the arm of the chair so tightly that my hand was white.

"Child, are you alright!?" A'lbi'on's voice crashed like thunder through the blackness that was trying to take hold of me. He saw, for the first time, that I was not okay.

"No, uncle, I am exhausted, and have been running a fever on and off since we got to the litter."

He was angry again, "Why the hell did you come to see me instead of going to bed!?"

"Because of the words you spoke to me when I entered the room just now, 'where the hell have you been?' remember? That's why. Because I knew that you would be worried and that you would want to see me for a moment. That's why." I said, "And because I missed you and had hoped for a warmer welcome. Perhaps I was foolish to think that, though, I will excuse myself now and go to bed." I stood up and fell to the floor, I cried out as my knees hit and the door slammed open.

Dru'cyl came bursting inside looking as though he was

ready for a fight, but then realized his mistake, bowed low and went back outside.

"Ary, please go to bed before you pass out." A'lbi'on begged. "Call your man back in here and have him take you to bed."

I nodded, "his name's Dru'cyl."

"Dru'cyl, come in at once!" A'lbi'on commanded. Dru'cyl opened the door and bowed deeply to A'lbi'on.

"Yes, my king?"

"Take my niece to her bed, and sit on her if you have to, but make damn sure she does not leave until she is rested."

Dru'cyl bowed his head and scooped me up as the blackness took me and I sank into a dreamless sleep.

Chapter Eighteen

I woke up not knowing where I was or who I was. I tried to sit up, but the whole world went spinning and I was shaking and trembling and shivering all over. "It's cold..." I said through chattering teeth, "So cold... why is it so cold?" I couldn't figure it out, it felt like I was lying in a bed but for the life of me I couldn't understand why it was so cold. I felt like I'd been emerged into a bath of pure ice. "Why is it so cold ... and dark?" I asked, not realizing that I had not opened my eyes yet.

"Try not to move, majesty. You expelled too much energy over the last two days and your body needs rest." It was Dru'cyl who spoke, Dru'cyl who had cleared his throat and who was rustling about the room.

Majesty? Who's that? I don't understand ... Why is he calling me majesty? Who is he?!

Ary, calm yourself, you're safe, you're okay, he's a friend.

Ary ... is that my name?

Yes, your name is A'lari'jah Jayd Riversong McM'kary'ano, you are the queen of A'va'lon, heir to Nah'alba.

The memories returned and I suddenly remembered who and where I was and who was talking to me.

"Dru ... It's so cold." I opened my eyes and suddenly felt like I was falling through the earth; like the earth was nothing but a jelly bowl and I was sinking all the way through it. I could feel the be underneath me and yet I felt like I was falling.

"It's so cold..." I moaned again and tried to roll over. "The world won't stand still, Dru! I'm falling! I can't fall, but I'm falling through the earth!" I cried, tears streaming down my face, "I can't ... I can't move ... What's happening!?"

I felt a cold hand touching my forehead, then Dru'cyl's rough voice said, "Ke'yahn'ah, get Sr'eya, she's burning with fever and delirious!" His voice was calm, commanding and confident. I heard someone playing with water, squeezing out a rag maybe? I didn't know, all I knew was that the world was spinning out of control and I hated this feeling. I felt as if I was falling through all of time and space, like I was falling through the earth itself and into a black hole of never-ending spinning. Dru'cyl put a cold rag on my forehead and I was suddenly convulsing like a child throwing a temper tantrum. I heard someone groaning and moaning and crying and I wished she would stop, it was a pitiful pathetic sound, then I realized that I was making that sound. I felt, who I thought was Dru'cyl, lift me up on my side and clamp my mouth shut and tuck my head into my chest. He was soothing me and stroking my forehead and face with a cold cloth.

"What are you doing!?" Sr'eya demanded. "Get off of her at once!" she sounded as if she was enraged, but from under the water I couldn't really tell.

My eyes were glued open and the world around me was trembling and vibrating and someone was making a terrible choking sound. Oh, how I wished that whomever it was would stop making that terrible noise.

"She's burning with fever, Sr'eya. She didn't even know who she was when she first opened her eyes, she is delirious. I put a cold towel on her head, and she started convulsing." He responded, his calm monotone voice was soothing and helped to calm my stressed-out mind.

"How long has she been doing this for?" asked Sr'eya, her voice softening as she understood the situation.

"Not long, happened about a minute after I sent Key'ahn'ah for you, she needs a cold bath, that's the only hope we have of saving her now."

Sr'eya nodded, from my blurred vision and my muddled mind, she seemed to have gone blank, suddenly unsure of herself, or what to do. Dru'cyl didn't hesitate, he saw her freeze and he acted as quick as Sr'eya normally would have.

"Key'ahn'ah, Ki'ri'ah, draw her a bath with cold water, Ky'wahn'ah go fetch buckets of ice and do it now, we don't have much time, she's convulsing because her fever is too high, and her body and mind cannot cope." I heard a scuffling of feet and dragging of wood on stone, and water being poured.

I stopped convulsing and looked into Dru'cyl's eyes, I saw my eyes echoed back from them and I was terrified. My eyes were wide with shock and fear, there was much I needed to say, much that I had yet to do, and I knew at that moment that I was dying.

"It's ready, Dru'cyl." Ke'yahn'ah announced.

"Good, stand back, she will not like this, but it has to be done." He picked my burning body up and carried me over to the tub, I gasped and screamed and cried and thrashed as the cold water hit my hot skin, but his strong arms held me in the bath firmly. His voice was soothing as he sang a song, a song I had known well once, a song that my father sang to me when I was sick or frightened. I sang along with him and soon my shivering calmed down and I stopped thrashing so badly.

"Dru?" I called, he had walked away from me and I was scared. "Dru?" I called out again, "Dru'cyl?"

"I'm here, majesty, I just stepped out to talk to the guard. What is it? What can I get for you?" He asked, he looked into my eyes again, and I saw the warnings and the look of alarm that was written all over my face. Before he knew what was happening, I was convulsing again, suddenly my lungs were filling with icy water, I couldn't breathe, I couldn't see Dru'cyl's face or hear his voice.

It felt like an eternity had passed before Dru'cyl's strong hands wrapped around my arms and pulled me out of the water. He had me on my side in front of the fire on a blanket in two heart beats.

In that moment there were two things that became clear to me;

The first thing was that Sr'eya was not Sr'eya any longer.

The second thing was that I was dying, within a few short hours I would be dead.

Dru, I need ... I need ... It was very difficult to form thoughts coherent enough for others to understand.

"Save your strength now, you'll be alright, just rest, relax, try to calm your mind." He said out loud.

No ... time ... need Dy'llian and J'errian'ah... now ... no time... will be dead soon if they ... do not come ... quickly.

"I'll send for them, you just rest now, try to conserve your energy." Before he could tell Ke'yahn'ah to go fetch them, there was a knock at the door.

"Ke'yahn'ah open the door and see who it is, but don't let them see her like this." Dru'cyl said, my heart leapt a little at his trying to spare me the embarrassment of other seeing me like this.

"It's Dy'llian and J'errian'ah." Ke'yahn'ah announced immediately.

"Ki'ri'ah, get a thin blanket off the bed and cover her."

Such a saint... I said, my mind becoming clearer as my convulsions came to a stop.

He chuckled and allowed J'erri'ahn'ah and Dy'llian inside.

J'erri'ahn'ah, Dy'llian, we were just about to ... send for you. I said, my mouth was still glued shut.

"We had a bad feeling, and immediately came here." J'erri'ahn'ah said.

Good ... I am dying and it's up to you two to figure it out and correct the problem.

As I finished explaining this another convulsion hit and I was unconscious this time.

I woke up some time later only to find my room full of sad faces.

"Ary! We thought we lost you!" A'lbi'on said

"What do you mean?" I asked, confused.

"Don't you remember, Ary? You were sick." began A'lbi'on.

"Yes, of course I remember." I said.

"Well, that was two weeks ago." Dru'cyl pitched in, A'lbi'on had lost his voice again.

"Two weeks?!" I asked, stunned.

"Yes, miss, two weeks. We all thought that we had lost you." He nodded towards the window of my rooms. It was dark outside, and I could see what looked like the whole kingdom out of my window holding candles. All along my room floor and underneath the window were flowers of all kinds and shapes and sizes.

Dru? Were y'all holding a vigil for me?

Uh... Yeah... Yeah A'lbi'on had to tell them something, the Nobles were getting cold feet on closing the deal, and with your birthday celebrations having to be canceled, they thought that your uncle lied to them. They demanded proof and when that proof was given, they began a vigil for you.

Was it that close?

It means, majesty, that you were in an endless sleep. You were, basically, dead.

Tell me what happened, the last thing I remember was telling J'erri'ahn'ah and Dy'llian that they needed to figure out what was happening to me.

You went into a massive convulsion and when that convulsion had stopped it was like you were not with us anymore, like you had slipped into an eternal sleep. You stopped responding to anything, we pricked your feet and your hands, and you had no response, your mind had been too compromised and no longer registered pain. That was when we knew what had happened, and that was when J'erri'ahn'ah and Dy'llian finally figured out what to do and how to help. We thought that we were too late, even though the day today you didn't have any responses to pain or anything.

Wow. I don't know what to say.

"Ary, love, are you alright?" A'lbi'on asked finally, the silence in the room had been long.

"No... I am not sure how I am supposed to feel right now. It seems as though I was just shy of an early grave..." I shook my head as a silent tear slid down my cheek.

"We wouldn't have done that unless you had stopped breathing. Everyone who knows you, knows that as long as you have a breath in your body, there was hope. Your wolf is in pretty bad shape, though. Seems like since you went down, he's been down. We found him in the gardens, on his side barely breathing. We brought him here, laid him beside you, hoping that the two of you could help each other." A'lbi'on nodded to my right side where Taem'luck laid.

I sat up and leaned over to him, he didn't seem to move, and I feared that he hadn't made it, but as I got close to him, he lifted his head and wagged his tail as he looked at me upside down.

"Tae, you silly boy." I said, tears streaming down my face, I scratched his chin and then leaned back against my pillows putting my hand on my head.

I must have groaned or made some sort of noise because there was a flutter of action and Sr'eya was by my side, hands fluttering around my face and my arms.

"What's wrong? What hurts?" She asked worriedly, she looked more like Sr'eya than she had since the incident at my old house.

"Nothing, I am alright, I just sat up too fast and got lightheaded."

"You need to eat something; it's been far too long since you've had any food." Sr'eya said. "Alright, everyone out! She needs rest." Sr'eya said, shooing everyone out of the room.

"I need J'erri'ahn'ah and Dy'llian and Dru'cyl to stay for a few moments, please." I tried not to demand or command, but when A'lbi'on insisted that he stayed or they didn't I got upset, "Uncle, you *will* leave, and they *will* stay. Thank you." I didn't leave him room to contest, Dru'cyl walked him to the door and waited for him to walk away.

"Thank you, Dru'cyl. Now, to business. Tell me what happened."

"You told us little to nothing before you went under. We

came in just as you were about to send for us, and you told us that you were dying and that it was up to us to figure it out, and we had no idea where to start or what might be causing it. I suppose that we should have pieced it together more quickly than we had, but we didn't, and our mistake nearly cost your life... " J'erri'ahn'ah explained.

"It was weird, Ary, when we got into your head, there was ... well ... nothing... it was like your mind had been wiped blank, like all traces of you were totally gone. However, what we did find... Well ... " he fell silent, his eyes flickered so slightly that I nearly missed it, to Sr'eya. I caught the gist of what he was implying and there was nothing further spoken about this subject.

"I see, and did you two have any issues after? Any side effects? Anything to imply that this was designed to attack anyone who encountered it?"

The silence that followed was worse than any silence that had been previously.

"What? What is it?" I asked, feeling worried and scared.

"It's just ... " Again his eyes flickered to Sr'eya and back to me again.

"Sr'eya, how are you feeling?" I asked.

"I'm alright, a bit tired, but I'm better than I have been." she replied honestly.

"Why don't you go get some sleep, and come back later? I'll have Ke'yahn'ah bring me food in a few minutes." I suggested. "You look worn out." I added.

She thought for a minute and then nodded her head and left the rooms without a fight.

"Now, tell me what's going on."

"Whatever happened started the moment you delved into Sr'eya's mind. We were able to trace it back to that moment, and every moment since that you alone have had contact with I'dhren'ni'el's maj'ick. It looks like it was all a well devised trap for you." Dy'llian said.

"Let's put it this way. I'dhrenn'i'el knew that you wouldn't be able to resist a puzzle. you wouldn't be able to resist saving your friends. And let's face it, Ary, you fancy yourself a hero, like you and you alone can save us all and no one else can help you." J'erri'ahn'ah said, her tone of voice was hurtful.

"What do you mean that I 'fancy myself a hero'?!" I demanded.

"She just means that you think that you're in this alone, that you have to do everything alone and can't ask for help from anyone. It's not a bad thing, it's just a predictable thing. All heroes have this issue, and that's not a bad issue. It's just easy to lay traps for you because of this virtue." Dy'llia jumped in and attempted to soothe my pain; he could feel it rolling off me.

Just then there was a knock on the door, and everyone jumped and went silent and Taem'luck's head jerked up and he growled at the door. Dru'cyl went to answer the door and said, "Come in."

"What are you doing here?" I hear Dru'cyl ask under his breath.

"When she wouldn't respond to my mirror I had to come and see her. What's been going on?" M'kary'ano's voice was like an angel.

"Da?" I asked, craning my head around the bedpost to look at him.

"Ary! What's been going on?!?! I've been trying to contact you and I got worried..." His face looked frightened as he laid eyes on me.

"Well... Da ... I nearly died..." I told him, "J'erri'ahn'ah and Dy'llian and Dru'cyl can catch you up on the details while I eat!" I said and began chowing down the bread and cheese Ke'ahn'ah had brought me.

"Wow, we really need to get someone out there looking for I'dhrenn'i'el! I can't believe this happened! I knew I never should have left your side..." He was angry and worried at the same time.

"Da, you and I both know that would not have been the

right thing to do. You and I both know that you would have ended up in the dungeons or without a head. I cannot believe you are here now! If I wasn't so happy to see you, I'd be very angry with you." I told him, and then the sobs broke free and he was wrapping his arms tightly around me again.

"Mo tinu... it's alright, it's alright." He said rocking me back and forth holding me tight.

"I'm sorry, da' I don't know what came over me. It's been a rough few weeks, I guess." I chuckled weakly.

"You have nothing to apologize for, mo tinu. Nothing at all, you have every right to feel upset, overwhelmed and anything else you might be feeling right now. You're the one who nearly died!"

"Da', you really shouldn't be here..." I said finally.

"I know, but I had to make sure that you were alright. I sent some people out to scout the forest around the castle, and when they saw the vigil they asked someone what was going on and they told him that the princess was sick, so everyone was praying for her recovery. They came straight to me to tell me what was happening, but things were tense, and I could not get away." He said looking at me in the face now, he seemed to be at war with telling me something or not.

"Just tell me, da', what has happened?"

He nodded his head, "A'lbi'on has declared war on us all. A'va'lon is pulling her people back beyond the gates and is sounding her retreat. I came to make sure that you were safe. I am worried, there are rumors spreading that someone close to the king has ma'jick and he's on the warpath, he's raging through Nah'alba forcing everyone from their homes, anyone who is suspected of maj'ick is being killed on site. A'lbi'on isn't playing this time; he's purging the kingdom." There was a fire in my father's eyes that I had never seen before and it scared me.

I shook my head, "Safe or not safe, I must stay where I am, I cannot leave now, or all hell will break loose. It would cause the nations to crumble and the whole world would be at war with Nah'alba. If I disappear the nobles will retreat, and all hope will be lost. No, I must stay, I cannot leave now, I cannot retreat now. Come what may, I was put here for such a time as this. I will endure, and stand steadfast, because that is our Creator's will. We need to prepare in case anything happens to me, a living will, of sorts. Something to ensure that, should my life be in danger or should my life end, my title gets transferred to you to ensure that A'va'lon always has a ruler." I looked at him, serious and somber, and he looked back at me worried and frightened. "There's nothing to be done about it, da', come what may this is where I am meant to be." I squeezed his hand to comfort him.

"Alright," he shook his head, "I'll have A'nti'el draw us up the paperwork and we will get it to you as soon as possible, I'll leave tomorrow night, in the meantime, I'll be here with you." He smiled and leaned back on my bed relaxing.

"Uh ... Da?" I asked

"Yeah?"

"Do you think that wise?"

"Sure, honey, why not?"

"Because you're playing with fire?"

"Nah, the king won't even know I am here. Don't worry, Sr'eya won't even know I am here."

"Um ... How? You're sitting right next to me..." I said, confused.

"I have a little hidden talent; I can make myself invisible to those who I do not want to see me." He winked at me and smiled mischievously.

I rolled my eyes, but smiled. I was delighted to have him there, I laid my head down his chest and closed my eyes to take a nap.

It seems like I had just fallen asleep when someone knocked on the door.

"Speak of the devil and he shall appear." Dru'cyl murmured under his breath, "Good morning, your majesty, won't you come in please?" He was very polite and courteous, but I could hear the bite in his words.

"Good morning Dru'cyl, thank you. Is A'lari'jah up yet?" He asked quietly just in case his knocking hadn't woken me up.

"I'm up, Uncle, please, won't you come in? It's rude to stand in the doorway." I said, yawning and stretching.

"Good morning, Ary, I came to see how you are feeling this morning?" there was something else, something bothering him.

"I don't know yet, I just woke up." I said, teasing him, trying to lighten the mood.

"Yes, I'm sorry about that. The council are actually gathering now and have demanded your presence." He said, "They are not happy, at all, and are demanding my throne be given to you now, instead of waiting for the next year." He looked very disgruntled and very upset. I knew what the stakes were, I knew that we were on the verge of war, I knew what it would mean for my uncle to stay on the throne. I also knew what it would mean for me if I pushed him off the throne before it was his time. I didn't have the heart or the stomach for it. I knew that I needed to keep the world from a massive war, but I also knew that it was not yet my time to rule. The kingdom had not seen the worst of my uncle yet, and I was not meant to stop this from happening.

I nodded my head, calmly, "I will be right there, uncle, I just need to get dressed." I said, dismissing him from my rooms.

"Ary, I know what you're thinking." Dru'cyl said, walking towards me.

"No, you don't."

"You're thinking that this isn't your time, that you shouldn't push him off the throne," he said.

"Okay, so you do know what I'm thinking... So what?"

"I disagree with you." He said, point blank.

"Well, thank you for your opinion, I will take that under consideration."

"No, you won't, but thanks for that." He said, clearly, he

was upset.

"Hey!" I yelled at him as he tried to storm out the door. He turned and looked at me and then remembered who he was speaking to and bowed his head and submitted. "Get yourself right back in this room and let's discuss this! Don't just get all upset and storm out! that never solves anything!"

"Yes, majesty." He came back into the room and closed the door.

"Now, tell me what you are thinking and why."

"Alright, shall I come back when you are dressed?" He asked.

"No, there's no time for that. Either speak now or forever hold your peace." I told him, "When I get done and go in there, it will be too late to change my mind. Now is the time for you to speak up." I told him. I repeated myself a bit, but oh well, I made my point.

"Well, I can't help but wonder if this isn't the Creator clearing a path for you to take the throne. I just keep praying that He shows us a way to avoid this coming war. I know what it feels like, and I know your heart, but I have a feeling that this is your time!" Dru'cyl said, his passion was flaring through.

"Da'?" I asked, waiting for him to speak while Ke'yahn'ah helped me get dressed.

"I disagree with Dru'cyl. Something about this feels like a trap. Something about this feels wrong, off somehow. Ary if you act now, it could be weeks before your coronation and by then, A'lbi'on could have you thrown into jail. I don't think it's wise to make a move now, I think you need to be patient and bide your time." He sounded more levelheaded and reasoning better, his reasons were sounder than Dru'cyl's were.

"Dru'cyl, tell me the advantages of taking the throne now?"

"You can avoid this war; you can act and have A'lbi'on thrown in jail and take the throne by force if he moves against you."

"Dru'cyl, think about what you are saying. Is this any kind

of advice for a fifteen-year-old, inexperienced girl? Is this the kind of advice that you would have given to Veri'si'el? I think not or she would not have kept you around for very long. You need to pull your head out of the clouds and come back to reality man, because what you speak of is treason." M'kary'ano took the words right out of my mouth.

"On top of treason, it goes against everything I am made of, or stand for. I appreciate your desire to stop the coming war, I appreciate what war means for you, but I am unable to do so with a clear conscience, Dru. I'm sorry. " And I was deeply, desperately sorry, because war meant that he would have to be at the front lines of the battle, back to war again, for a third time in his life. I knew how desperately he wanted to avoid this, and it hurt me deeply that I could not prevent that from happening.

"Yes, majesty, I understand. Forgive me, I must take my leave now." He said, his voice was broken and downhearted.

"Dru'cyl," I called, "Don't go far, I need you to be ready to go when I am, you will be at my side during this meeting." I told him; I did not give him a choice in the matter.

"Yes, majesty, I understand. I'll be just outside the door." he said, closing the door behind him.

"Don't feel too bad, Ary, he's had a hard life, and it's understandable that he would panic a bit about the coming war, but there may be something you can do for him, to keep him from having to go to war again." M'kary'ano said.

"What do you mean?" I asked.

"You can retire him as chief sentry and change his title to 'adviser to the queen'."

"Will he go for that, though? As upset as he is now, won't he be even more upset if he can't go with his men when the time comes?" I asked.

"Not if you make him an offer he cannot refuse." M'kary'ano said.

I was confused, "Da', please speak your mind and stop this game, I don't have time for it." I said, exasperated with the guessing game.

M'kary'ano chuckled, "You used to love to play twenty questions, but alright, I mean you will have to make him an offer that he can't refuse, make the deal as sweet as honey and irrefutable, do not play it to pity, or make him feel like you are just doing this for charity or he will never accept it. He cares a great deal about what happens to you, and I think that you and I know what that means. You can either keep him close and take the chance of things going farther, or you can leave things the way they are and let them play out the way they will." M'kary'ano was implying that Dru'cyl was in love with me. I knew exactly what he meant by what he said, and I was shocked and outraged by it, but it also made sense.

"I hear you Da', you have A'nti'el work on papers for it, making it a sweet deal that he can't refuse, and I'll present it to him, whether he accepts or not is up to him, but he deserves the chance to choose. He's seen too much war, and I cannot ask him to fight this one for me unless his whole heart is in it, and that will be exactly how it is presented to him. I will not lie, and I will not cover up the truth, he would know it anyways. He seems to have some connection to me that I don't fully understand, like Tay, he knows what I am thinking and how I am feeling." I said, looking my father in the eyes. "Well?? Are you coming or are you going to lay in my bed all day?" I asked him.

"Oh! Am I invited? I didn't want to step on your toes or anything..." he said, unsure of what he was supposed to do.

"Nah, come one, I need you there, you're the one who will be carrying the message back to A'va'lon, not me and not Dru'cyl, so you might as well be there." I said to him, walking towards the door.

Da' stood up and followed me, his footsteps as silent as the wind on the floor. Dru'cyl was waiting for me outside the door, he was more composed and steadier now than he had been before.

Chapter Nineteen

"Follow me, your highness." A castle guard said as he turned and walked away.

He led me and my silent (invisible) party to the council chambers, outside the doors I looked at him and said, "You may leave us now, thank you."

"Ma'am, not to be rude or anything, but the king asked me to stay."

"I am aware of what the king asked you to do, and I am telling you that I will not go in those doors whilst his spy stands outside of them. I will not have him spying on me nor will I have this meeting misconstrued by anyone." I crossed my arms and planted my feet looking at him in the eyes, he seemed to be trying to stare me down.

"Yes, highness, right away, highness." He leaned back on his heel and circled around and walked down the hallway. "Ro'thani'el! What are you doing here?" I asked.

"I thought you might need some moral support this morning." He smiled, "But it looks like I am just going to be in the way." He noted Dru'cyl standing behind me.

"I could use your assistance, Ro'thani'el, if you wouldn't mind?" I asked

"Anything, name it."

"Will you stand guard at the door? My uncle has already sent one of his spies to listen in, I would appreciate it if you could keep them away from the door. I want to tell my uncle what the meeting was about myself, I don't want it to be misconstrued by his mongrels." I told him, as I said this there came a voice around the corner, "I am *NOT* a mongrel!" I motioned my hand at the sound of the voice as if to say, "point proven" and walked into the council chamber.

"Good morning everyone! How wonderful it is to see you all again!" I greeted the nobles and the counsel men warmly. "This is Dru'cyl, he's my trusted adviser slash bodyguard, I asked him to sit in with us today, I hope you won't mind!" It was not really a matter of if they minded, it was a mere courtesy for them to think that I cared.

"Of course! Welcome, Dru'cyl!" The nobles all greeted him warmly and shook his hand.

"Now, down to business, what seems to be the issue at hand today?" I asked.

"It's your uncle, he's gone totally insane!"

"Yes, that's right! He is hunting the people with maj'ick in his kingdom like he would hunt a deer. No one stands a trial, no one is tried and tested, they are just hunted down and put to death!"

"I see, and what, may I ask, do you think I can do about this?" I asked.

"Well, you support the maj'ick folks of your kingdom, do you not?"

"Yes, I should say that I am most sympathetic towards them." I offered, not wishing to incriminate myself.

"Well, we think that your coronation should be moved up to now, and that it should be you on the throne, not A'lbi'on. A'lbi'on was never supposed to take the throne, it was always supposed to be your beloved mother, G'rai'ce to take the throne. You are the rightful heir! He never was!"

"I hear what you are saying, and I hear what sounds like treason being committed behind my uncle's back. I may be heir to the throne, but nevertheless, my uncle is the king, and until such time as his mind becomes unreliable and can no longer rule, then I will take the throne, before then, I shall not."

"Princess, believe us, we do not mean any disrespect to your uncle. He has been a good king; he has brought the countries back together again. I just think that he has taken things a bit too far."

"Be that as it may, he is my king, and I have sworn him my fealty until my coronation, which is not until my sixteenth birthday. I stand behind my uncle; I support him and advocate for him. Do not ever bring this subject up again, I do not want to hear any talk about this any farther! If he knew what you were discussing, he would accuse you of having been bewitched, then he would torture you, to death, so that he can know the name of the sorcerer you work for. Since there is no bewitching taking place, there is no sorcerer, then he will torture you, to death. I will hear no more of this. Now, if you have another matter to discuss with me, that does not include treason, I am listening carefully." I said, folding my fingers together and placing them upon the table, smiling and waiting patiently for them to process what I said.

Slowly each of them came up for air after I berated them, I knew that was not what they had expected me to do or say. They all wanted to know what had happened to me on the road home, and all I told them was that I overexerted myself and was overly exhausted.

"What made you almost die then?"

"My body was way past the point of exhaustion which left my body open and susceptible to germs, I must have caught a fever that, attached with my already exhausted state, my body couldn't fight off. My mind went into overdrive and I had convulsions and a high fever. There was no way of stopping it, or preventing it, what happened could have happened to anyone in my state of being. There is nothing to worry about, no need to fret. You all need to have more trust in my uncle, he is doing all he can do to support me and do things the way I want them done, he is jumping through hoops and rings of fire for me. You all need to be a bit more relaxed and trusting of him. I know that he did some bad things in the past, but he's not the same person as he used to be. Give him some trust, and let him show you what he's really made of." I tried to reassure them, but it felt fake even to me, I knew that as soon as he got wind of who I really was that he would have me killed, or he would kill me himself. This was not something that I took lightly, and it was hard for me to tell them to trust him. It was hard for me to sit there and not take his throne from him, but this was the best thing for me to do, this would buy me some time, I hoped.

"We hear you, princess. On a different note, your uncle is setting up birthday party arrangements for a late birthday celebration for you, everything is ready, he just has a few last-minute things to finish. We are looking at a banquet later tonight or tomorrow for sure." Everyone was extremely excited about the aspect of having my party.

Good, a shred of normalcy is exactly what we need to get things back on track now. I thought to myself, *I have a lot of fires to put out, and not a lot of time to do it in.*

"Fantastic! All right, well, shall we continue about our day as normal then? I don't know about y'all but I am starving!" I announced, bringing the meeting to an end.

Dru'cyl and I left the room and walked out to the gardens, my invisible dad was trailing along behind us.

"I think you handled that very well, Ary, I am very proud of you." M'kary'ano said to me when we were in the gardens and out of the ear shot of everyone else.

"Thank you, da'! Here comes Ro'thani'el, don't speak." I said through a clenched smile.

"Ro'thani'el! How good it is to see you!" I said, hugging him tightly. He tickled and teased me, and we laughed like old times.

"Ary! You are looking better! How are you feeling?" He asked.

"I am still a bit drained, but I'm doing all right. I'll have to refrain from a few things for a while, but other than that, I'm peachy!" I beamed up at him.

"Okay, so tell me what really happened !!" He said, a gleam in his eyes as he sat down opposite of me and waited eagerly.

"Wait until our breakfast is brought, then I'll explain

everything!" I said.

"Okay, well, I have some news, it's not the greatest, but it's news nonetheless." He said.

"What news, Ro!?" I asked using his nickname that I have not used in years.

"Well, I am due to ship out soon, I'll be going back across the seas to Hesperia on a diplomatic mission. A'lbi'on is sending me to bring negotiations for some specific things to the table and to close them out." He said, his eyes had lost some of their excitement and his attitude had visibly dropped.

"Why?" I asked.

He shrugged, "Don't know, I suppose it's because he trusts me to make this deal go through?" He sounded uncertain, and an unspoken thought crossed his mind loud and clear.

"Or it's because he thought it best to clear out all of those loyal to me, once everyone is out of the way then he can put spies in my midst to cower me to his will." I said thoughtfully. "Nah, Ro'thani'el, yer not going anywhere. I want you here, by my side, end of story. Don't worry, I'll talk to A'lbi'on and I will take care of this." I told him.

"Nah, Ary, you don't need me, you have Dru'cyl now." He said, I swear his face turned a little green as he nodded towards Dru'cyl.

"Hey! No! You donna get to be jealous of him! I have known you all my life, Ro'thani'el! I am not sending you to certain death! I need you here, with me! Dru is only one person, I need a few more, especially after what happened on my journey home!" I told him, fierce in my demand for him to stay.

"She's right, Ro'thani'el, she needs all the people she can get that she can trust." My father's voice nearly blew Ro'thani'el right into the pond we were standing near.

"Ary... I think I'm hearing a ghost..." He said, face as white as snow.

"Nah, that's just Da' he is not supposed to be here, but he came anyway, *he is supposed to be staying silent,* but .... " I shrugged my shoulders, "I guess he thinks he can trust you." I said.

"Oh, gods, we've all gone mad, haven't we?!" He was shaking, and looked at me with his ashen face, "Ary, love, are you all right? You know that your da's gone, right?" He was looking at me like I had lost my mind.

"Da' I think yer gonna have ta show yerself to him... He thinks I've lost it..." I told M'kary'ano, but there was no response. I shrugged, "Oh well, guess that's a no." I said, "Anyways, Da's right, I need people here that I can trust, trouble is brewing, and I need only those who I can trust absolutely close to me." I told him.

"Does that include Sr'eya, then?" M'kary'ano asked me, his disembodied voice startling Ro'thani'el again.

"Da' either show yourself to Ro'thani'el or stop talking.... And yes, and no."

"Explain that?" he said, sounding confused.

"I mean that, while I do not trust her, she will be staying close to me. I might be fooling myself into a false sense of security, but as long as she is here, we can keep an eye on her better than if she wasn't." I explained, Ro'thani'el looked ready to faint. "Da... Stop mucking about, I'm serious."

"Awe, come on Ary, it's fun to muck around. I've been dead for years now, I like watching his face as he hears my disembodied voice." M'kary'ano laughed his deep rich laugh and then appeared so that Ro'thani'el could see him.

"HOLY GODS ALMIGHTY!" Ro'thani'el screamed like someone had set his pants on fire.

"Ro'thani'el! Calm yourself! Please! You will have my uncle out here with half the palace guards! Settle down and I'll explain everything after our breakfast gets here, but you have to calm down." I spoke calmly, slowly, and softly, trying to bring his panic down to earth again.

"Is this a joke?" he asked me. I motioned for my dad to stay quiet.

"No, Ro'thani'el, it's not a joke, it's not fake, and he's not an imposter. It is really him. He is alive. I promise. Look at me, look me in the eyes, I promise." I repeated my promise as he locked eyes with me, I compelled him to calm down and compelled him into a more peaceful state of mind. "Better?" I asked.

"Yes, thank you, are you sure? I mean... " but he stopped as he explored M'kary'ano's face. "It really is you, isn't it?" He asked.

"Yes, Ro'thani'el, it really is me, I'm here, and I'm alive." M'kary'ano said, tears streamed down both men's faces as they stood and took each other in.

"Okay you two, breakfast is heading this way, get a grip." I hissed. Ro'thani'el shook his head and looked at me and started up a friendly conversation.

"While you were away, Eir'im'uhs pined for you so badly. He moped around all day long." We both laughed.

"Where is Eir'im'uhs? Why haven't I seen him yet?" I asked, my brow creasing.

"Ah, well, about that..." Ro'thani'el seemed hesitant to respond, and he could see my anger building at his refusal to answer.

"He is in the neighboring village on an errand for the king. He should be back in a day or two." Ro'thani'el explained.

"I see, so the king really is sending everyone who is close to me away?"

"No, at least not as far as Eir'im'uhs is concerned. There were some... problems ... in the next village over and they were demanding to see you, but since you were ill, Eir'im'uhs volunteered to go in your name. He thought it best, in the moment, that he be the one to go, he felt like he could better represent your wishes than anyone else could."

"Oh, well, what kind of problems?" I asked curious.

"Just some trouble at the orphanage, nothing to worry about." Ro'thani'el reassured me.

"What sort of trouble?" I asked, my curiosity piqued.

"The locals there don't like the orphanage, so whenever something goes wrong, or someone gets sick, they blame it on the orphan kids. They do this every year when the seasons change and the kids get sick, it's usually the kids in the orphanage that get sick first because they are under fed and malnourished and crammed together in a tiny space, one on top of another and extremely understaffed." He explained, his eyes sad and ashamed.

"What is Eir'im'uhs doing about it?" I asked.

"There's nothing to be done, Ary, the only thing that can be done is to try and calm the townspeople down." He said.

I left it alone for the moment, but my mind was running wild with possibilities and ideas to help the kids at the orphanage, but it would take a while for me to gather up my ideas and put them into place, first, I would need to visit the orphanage and see for myself what their conditions are and how many kids reside there.

"Take me to the orphanage tomorrow, Ro'thani'el." I said, not asking.

"I will make the arrangements; how many people are coming with us?"

"I will take Ke'yahn'ah and Ky'wahn'ah, and J'erri'ahn'ah and Dy'llian and Dru'cyl. Dru can ride a horse along with Dy'llian and yourself, the rest can ride in the litter." I offered.

"I will prepare the litter and make sure the kitchen makes enough food for the journey, what time shall we leave?"

"How long does it take to get there?"

"About two hours."

"I would like to leave at first light then." I said, "I would like to spend the entire day there, if not more."

"I see. Shall we take extra food then?" He asked.

"I have all day today, I will be gathering supplies and things to take with us, I will let you know when they are ready, I would like to see the court physician, please have him sent to my rooms. Dru'cyl, I need you to go take a headcount of all the kids in the orphanage. I need to know the conditions of the place, how many boys and how many girls, and tell me what their food and medical supplies look like. I need as many details as you can provide." I told him there was an urgency in my voice that told him what he needed to do.

"I'll walk to the forest and then go from there; I should be there in five minutes."

"Let's get moving, it will probably take me the rest of the day to gather things up and be ready, Ro'thani'el, I'll need you and Dy'llian to help move things from here to the litter or wagon, have the stables bring up a flat wagon to the doors so that you can load all the things I'll be taking with me. Also have them bring one to the kitchen's door. We will need transport and guards to take us from here to there with all our wagons. Also, I need to speak to my uncle and the nobles, have them gather in the throne room, please."

"Which would you like first, ma'am?" He asked, a little overwhelmed by what I was trying to do.

"Right, gather the nobles and my uncle first, then get the wagon for the kitchen and then the other one. I'll work in that order." I told him, he nodded his head and left the gardens. Within a moment, though, he was back.

"When are you going to tell me this story about your da'?" He asked.

"Ah, tonight, when I have collected all that I can collect, meet me in my rooms at dark and we will tell you all about it." I told him with a smile that made my eyes twinkle, he nodded and hurried off to get my uncle and the nobles all gathered up.

"What is your brilliant little mind planning over there?" M'kary'ano asked.

"I am going to take food, blankets, clothes, toys and medical supplies to the orphanage, and I will, every month, make sure that they are more adequately fed and clothed and taken care of. Those poor kids are not to blame for their situation, and if I must, I will bring in people from A'va'lon to take care of the children so that the orphanage has enough caretakers and is more capable of handling the children's needs."

"It is commendable, what you're doing." A voice came

from behind a large bush by the pond. Sr'eya came around the bush and confronted me.

"Sr'reya, what are you doing sneaking around like a snake?" I asked, with brazen confidence.

"I couldn't help but feel like I was being intentionally left out of the loop on somethings, with your secret meetings with J'erri'ahn'ah and Dy'llian and Dru'cyl."

"So, you have taken to spying and sneaking around instead of asking?" I asked, "Since when do you stoop to this level?"

"I did not feel as though you would be honest with me, I did not feel as though you would be straightforward with me." she said, her voice was bitter and scathing.

"Let me ask you a question, Sr'eya. When have you ever known me to beat around the bush or lie?"

She paused for a moment and then answered, "Just because you have not, does not mean you will not."

"Stop avoiding my question, you know full well that I have never lied before, nor have I ever skated around the bush about things." I told her; my anger flaring. I took a deep steadying breath and fought to remain calm and collected while I fought this battle with the woman who I once thought of as a second mother.

"Why don't you just ask me to leave?"

"Who said anything about leaving, Sr'eya? You have yet to ask me what you really want to ask me. You have yet to bring this conversation to an actual point, instead you babble on in circles of non-sense that does not have any real meaning to it. Come now, and tell me, what is it you really want to know?"

"I want to know what secrets you are keeping from me."

My face softened, and my anger ebbed away, "Sr'eya, we are not keeping anything from you, it saddens me to think that you think this." I said kindly.

She laughed a mocking laugh, "Even now you stand there and lie to me. I know what you're up to, I know what you're about, and I'm going to stop you." She said, laughing maniacally.

"Sr'eya, what exactly do you think I am doing?" I asked.

"You are going to poison the king; you are going to take his throne from him before it's your time. Push him off the throne and kill him if he doesn't go willingly." There was a dark glint in her eyes that I had never seen before and for the first time in my life I was frightened of her.

"Sr'eya, I don't know what you have heard or where you heard it from but that is a lie!" My anger seeped through me now, and I felt my father put a hand on my shoulder.

Ary, she's too far gone, there's no point in arguing with her, come, let us leave this place now.

He was right, of course, I knew it, but there was a huge part of me that wanted to stand there and yell at her and hash this out and get it all off my chest. I allowed him to lead me away and out of the gardens.

Ro'thani'el met us just inside the garden's doors, "They are ready for you." He said hurrying away to get the wagons put into place.

I hurried the opposite way to the massive throne room where my uncle and all the nobles had gathered. I had an idea of what I was going to propose but not a precise idea of it. When we arrived at the doors the guards opened them and announced me to all in the room..

"Princess A'lari'jah."

"Hello, everyone, thank you for gathering so quickly for me. It has recently come to my attention that we have a problem that needs to be investigated; a situation in which a solution needs to be thought of." I announced as I walked up to the throne and curtsied to my uncle. My father was invisible behind me and Taem'luck had joined us, he rubbed his head at my thigh nosing at my hand for attention.

"What is this urgent matter, A'lari'jah?" A'lbi'on asked, he was being more formal than he normally was with me.

"The situation is the harsh and crucially overlooked condition of our orphanages." As I said this everyone gasped, and murmurs broke out around the room.

"This is an outrage!" Someone cried, it would have been some of the commoners that were allowed to gather in a public petition to the King.

"Yeah! The orphanages should be razed to the ground! Not spoiled and given MORE!" someone else shouted.

"The orphans don't deserve to live in squander, they don't deserve to be malnourished and starved with inadequate medical supplies, no heat, no real food! It's not their fault that their parents perished or didn't want them! They are children, not demons, and it's time that we changed the way they are treated, the way they are looked at. These children, most of these children, are survivors of parents who have died either due to illness or because of destitution. They are children like myself, or like my cousin, or like your children. Their only crime was that they were born into situations that were outside of their control. These children deserve, at the very least, a place that they are safe and well cared for, a place they can call home, if they aren't going to be taken into families, we need to care for these children and get them proper tools to live on." When I was done, there was a profound silence, the people in the back looked ashamed of themselves, and I continued, rounding on the commoners. "What would happen to your children if something were to happen to you!? What would happen if you passed on and you didn't have anyone who would step up and care for them??? Would you want them in an orphanage being shamed and treated horribly by the same people and children they grew up with!? Or would you want them loved, cherished, and cared for? To have warmth in the winter, and food in their bellies and medical supplies in case they get sick??" I paused, and then said, "Be honest with yourselves and with me right now, which sort of establishment would you prefer them to be in?" I was done, I had shamed them all enough and now I needed to address the nobles and the king, and to do that I needed to calm down.

"My king, my fellow nobles, I put this at your feet, and

humbly beg your help and support in this matter." I rounded on my uncle and looked him straight in the face, "What would have happened to me, without you or Sr'eya to take me in? If I had been fortunate enough to survive, I would have ended up in an orphanage, what then? Would you honestly sit here and tell me that you would be okay with me living in those situations now? I would have died, or worse, I would have been terribly crippled and deformed for the rest of my life!" I could see A'lbi'on's eyes soften and when he talked again his voice was thick with emotion.

"I never thought of it like that before, A'lari'jah." He admitted.

"Think about it now and tell me honestly that you would be okay with the conditions of the orphanage if I was living there."

He thought about it and he shook his head, "I can honestly say that I cannot imagine you living in a place like that."

I waited, let the thoughts sink into each of them as they tried and failed to imagine their children living in places like that. I saw the cringes and shivers as their imaginations put their living children in the orphanages and I knew that I had won.

"What do you need from us, princess?"

"I need clothes, food, medical supplies, blankets, toys, anything and everything you can think of that will make these children's lives more comfortable. The orphanages need workers, caregivers, medical care providers, cooks who know how to cook nutritious meals and how to properly clean and care for the dishes, they need to be cleaned, they need workers to make sure that their wells are properly cleaned and maintained, they need upgrades, and fireplace sweeps, wood in abundance for their fires and they need to have good school books and ..."

"What if we started with the basics, what would they be able to get by with for now, that we could add to later on?" A'lbi'on asked, stopping me from getting too overwhelmed.

"They need heat, healthy food, and clothes. They need clean water and good soaps and towels so they can clean up as often as possible." I said, "They need medical supplies so that they can heal their sickness and for a teacher to teach them how to clean their dishes properly so that they aren't spreading their germs."

"I have a ship in bound that will have a ton of supplies on it, we can deliver that ship of supplies to the orphanages across the island, one by one." One of the nobles chipped in.

"I have a ship incoming as well, due in port in a few days, they are carrying medical supplies and blankets along with materials for clothes."

"I have one carrying food products along with spices and such, we can contribute as well!"

Most of the nobles all agreed to contribute a part of the supplies in their ship to help me take better care of our orphanages. I felt immensely proud of myself as I looked around at all these people, I was on the verge of making a massive impact on our kingdom.

"I'll go and gather up some of the old things laying around here, blankets and spare supplies and food. I will be visiting the orphanage where Eir'im'uhs is currently at. I will spend a few days there if needed. I will be taking with me two of my maids and will leave them at the orphanage, when I leave, to help until the children are better." I told them all, "Thank you for your support and assistance with this, I look forward to this important work in our kingdom to better our orphanages."

I took my leave of the throne room and began gathering up all the old clothes and blankets that were in the hand-me-down boxes that we used when we held a banquet for the women and children of the commoners who did not have anything. I didn't take all of them, but I took enough to clothe twenty girls and twenty boys. I took the rattiest of the clothes, the ones that were the oldest and not the ones that were suited for banquets, but clothes that were best suited for playing and everyday wear. I gathered up linens and towels and medical supplies and then oversaw the kitchen giving supplies and loaded up the various wagons; by sundown we had enough supplies to load up three wagons. Most of this stuff would have to come back with me to be distributed throughout the kingdom to different orphanages around the Island.

"Ary, I am very proud of you!" M'kary'ano told me when we were alone in my bedroom again.

"Thank you, Da'! That means a lot to me. I really expected more push back from the nobles and A'lbi'on too." I told him.

"Nah, you have a natural way with words, when you speak, everyone stops to listen. You are so compelling and moving especially when you are passionate about the situation. It was clear in there that you are deeply passionate about this. You've ignited a fire in the nobles and your uncle, a fire that will be hard to blow out." He said.

"I just hope that, should anything happen to me, people will continue the work I have started with this and keep this going." I said hopefully.

"Don't worry, I am thinking that this is something that will catch on like wildfire." He smiled.

A knock came at the door, I expected it to be supper, but it was not. "Who's there?" I called.

"It's Ro'thani'el."

"Come in please."

"So, about that story?" He asked as soon as the door latched shut.

"As soon as our supper comes, I will explain everything, or rather, we will explain everything. I won't start anything until supper comes, though." I explained. "Before we do that, we need to have a serious conversation about Sr'eya." I told them everything that Sr'eya had said to me in the garden after Ro'thani'el had left, "I don't want her here causing trouble, she is more dangerous to me here than she would be elsewhere." I told them finally.

"I disagree, Ary, here we can keep an eye on her, watch her, see what she is doing at all times." M'kary'ano started to explain.

"Like we kept an eye on her when she snuck up on us in the garden? Or any other time she has been spying on us without us knowing about it?" I asked pointedly. "Face it, Da' we don't have the manpower to keep an eye on her and do everything else that needs to be done around here." I told him.

"What's the worst she can do here?" He asked me, trying to think about this from my point of view.

"She knows who I am, she knows that I have maj'ick, she is close enough to the king that she could tell him, she could tell him that I bewitched her for these many years and that I have brain washed her and only recently has she been able to be free of my control enough to realize what a danger I am to the kingdom..." I explained. "She is dangerous to me here, and if I anger her in just the wrong way, that could be the outcome, all this work that I am doing will be for nothing because A'lbi'on will have me killed right then and there."

"Okay, I see your point." Was all M'kary'ano said to me after that. "This will require a lot of thought before a decision is made." He said.

"I don't think that it will require that much thought, I think that it's simple. We send her to A'va'lon, and in A'va'lon she can be under house arrest with your maj'ick and kept in A'va'lon. It's the only way, da'. It cannot be any other way." I said desperately.

"Dru'cyl, what do you say about this?" M'kary'ano was clearly hoping that Dru'cyl would stand on his side of things.

"I have to agree with A'lari'jah on this one. I have seen her in action acting strange and weird, and there is something wrong. Ever since we came back from A'va'lon, S'reya has been acting weird." He concluded.

"Ro'thani'el?" I asked.

"Am I the tie breaker here?" He asked.

"No, we need your honest opinion before I make the final decision."

"I have to say that I agree with A'lari'jah. We just do

not have the capability of keeping our eyes on Sr'eya and everything else that we need to do. We do not have enough trusted people here to do that. Especially not now that we are all on high alert."

"Alright, she will go back with me then, how are we going to tell her?" M'kary'ano asked.

"I have an idea." I said, "Leave it to me, not to worry." They all nodded and Dru'cyl went to answer the door.

"Supper is served, sir." A serving maid from the kitchens announced as she pushed in a tray with several plates of food on it.

"Thank you so much!" I said as she handed off the tray to Dru'cyl and left the room.

"Now, we will tell you the story." I told Ro'than'iel.

M'kary'ano spent the next hour explaining the story from the night of the fire to the day he and I met up in the woods again, and I took over from there and connected all the dots together, and when we were done, Ro'than'iel's eyes were as wide as a gopher hole.

"That's astonishing! I still am having a tough time believing it all." Ro'thani'el exclaimed.

"We had better all head to bed, we have a big day tomorrow." I said, yawning and stretching.

I woke up some time later to a voice outside my door, Sr'eya and my uncle were talking.

"Sire, there is an important matter that I wish to discuss with you about your niece." Sr'eya said.

"What is it? Is she alright?" he asked urgently.

"Everything is fine, but this is a rather delicate matter, I wonder if we could ..." She trailed off.

"Of course, follow me." A'lbi'on said as their footsteps led away from my rooms.

"Is it just me, or does anyone else think we have a problem?" I asked Ro'thani'el and M'Kary'ano.

"I think we have a problem." They said together.

"Da', you shrink and follow, now! Dru, you get to A'va'lon

and let A'nti'el know."

"Ki'ri'ah, you get ready to go to the next town over and tell your sister's to be ready to move at a moment's notice. If things go south, I'll send you a telepathic message, and you all get to the safety of A'va'lon as fast as possible. No dawdling, no coming back here to collect your things, you get out of Nah'alba as soon as possible."

"Now, we wait and see what M'kar'yano has to say about what they are talking about." I told Ro'thani'el and Ki'ri'ah.

As the night ebbed on, the sky darkened and the stars and the moon seemed to shine brighter tonight than usual, like they were more awake and keeping us company this tense night. The longer we waited, the more antsy we became, the more we paced until, at long last, the sun was coming up over the land in the east, we all drifted into an uneasy sleep, still waiting for M'kary'ano to come back and report what he'd heard.

Epilogue

As the hours passed by and midnight came and went, there had still been no report back from M'karyano about what Sr'eya had wanted to talk to A'lbi'on about. I paced back and forth with Taem'luck for so long that I was beginning to see a path where I was pacing back and forth.

Servants came and went to stoke the fire, or to check in on me and see if I had fallen asleep yet or if I needed anything.

Taem'luck and I were both equally on edge and worried about what could possibly be taking them so long.

"Tae, if he's not back by sunrise, I think I had better send Dru looking for him."

"Nah, I think you'd better send Rothaniel. He won't raise any questions or suspicions walking around the palace and going into odd rooms here and there. Also, he will better be able to come up with a story at the drop of a pen than Drucyl, no offence mate, but you just aren't good at making things up as you go." Taem'luck added to Drucyl who was sitting with his back to the fire. "Anyway I bet M'karyano is just being especially cautious and careful, afterall, if anyone saw him, he'd be put to death immediately; and not because he's your da' back from the dead, but because he's now fully embodied Fae."

"Aye, I reckon Taem'luck here's right, mistress. Yer da' knows 'ow to take care of 'imself. 'E'll be alrigh'. Just .... gotta... trust him." Drucyl said, stuffing his mouth with the latest round of snacks the servants had brought in for us.

"I know you're both probably right, but I have a bad feeling, I just can't put my finger on what that bad feeling is." I told them rubbing the butterflies in my stomach.

As the sun came up there came a soft fluttering at my bedroom doors, and then the faintest of knocks. The door opened a fraction of the way, then closed again, though there was no indicator of what had opened the door.

All of a sudden, out of no where, M'Kary'ano popped into view from his tiny fae form, into his bigger human self.

"Oh, good morning!" He said as cheerful as could be, seemingly none-the-wiser that we'd been up waiting for him all night.

"Um... Da'?" I asked tentatively.

"Yeah, what's up love?" He asked cheerily.

"Don't you have some news to relay?" I asked.

"Nah, what news love?" He asked a mischievous smile playing at his lips.

"Um, da? We sent you to follow Sr'eya and A'lbi'on last night to find out what they were saying in their meeting and find out what Sr'eya is up to."

"Nah, I'm pretty sure I'd remember if my daughter set me on an important task like that." He laughed and touseled my hair as he walked by, helping himself to the breakfast food on the table.

"Da! This is serious!"

"Yeah? So's this food! Man, I'm famished, I feel like I haven't eaten in weeks!"

I furrowed my eyebrows together thinking.... Something was definitely off here, but I couldn't quite put my finger on what it was.

"Da, I'm really sorry about this, but I have to do this." I told him, and then, before he could stop me or ask any questions; I delved into his mind to see what had been done to him.

"Dru, Tae, I'm gonna need anchors. Idhrenniel has been in his mind and put a memory charm on him. I may not be able to recover the memories she took from him, I can at least undo the damage she did when she did the spell so forcefully, bring him back to who he usually is."

A few hours later, I asked "Da? Can you hear me?" As I stared into his blank eyes with tears pouring down my face.

"What have I done? How did things go so wrong?" I asked, sobbing into my hands.

"DA! Don't leave me again! I need you!" I shouted as my heart felt like it was breaking all over again.

"Ary, he's too far gone, there's nothing you can do now. You did all that you could do, the rest is up to him now. He has to want to come back to us. This was not your fault. This was a trap, designed to hurt you, and there's only one person who laid that trap. Ro'tha'ni'el, tell her what you told me."

"Last night, with Sr'eya, there never was a meeting with A'lbi'on, the king had already walked away, several minutes prior to what happened. She imitated the king's voice, and lured M'karya'no into whatever this was. It was Sr'eya, A'lari'jah. She did this to him."

"No, that can't be right, that can't be right, she can't be I'dhrenn'i'el, she can't be. She's the closest thing I have to a mother, and you're telling me that she's this horrible assassin slash rogue Fae, slash this horrible dark fae who would do anything to destroy me?"

"Yes, and no, she's not out to destroy you. She's out to bring darkness into your heart, to break you so badly that the dark consumes you, and then she can create a weapon out of you. Use you like a puppet."

There was absolute silence in the room when Rothaniel had finished speaking. Stunned to the soul, I sat there sobbing, holding my dad's hand, praying that there was some shred of him that had a tiny bit left here to hang on to to want to come back to me, because I didn't know how to do this without him. I needed him right now, and she took him away from me.

"Da, I don't know what to do, what am I supposed to do? Tell me what to do? What am I supposed to do? I don't know what to do. Da, tell me, tell me what to do." I said, hysterically crying over and over and over again. He just sat there, eyes wide open and stared at me like his soul had left his body, but his body didn't know his soul had left. He was just an empty shell now, and I couldn't bare the weight of it all.

"Mistress?" A soft whisper came from somewhere close to my ear, "Mistress?" It said again.

Slowly I blinked my bleary eyes and turned my head towards the sound of the whisper.

"What is it?" I said blearily.

"Mistress, I am going to take your Da to the healers, they will be able to help him." It was Drucyl, sitting on the edge of my bed at my back, his warm hand on my cold arm, his eyes pained as they looked into mine.

"No, he's gonna be okay, he has to be okay, you can't take him, I won't let you." I said and tried to sit up, but he pushed me back down and covered me up under my heavy fur blankets.

"Hush now, I'll be back before sun rise." He brushed my hair out of my face and lightly caressed my face as he did so, and then he was gone.

Made in the USA
Columbia, SC
03 May 2023

15908432R00170